DIRTY WEDDING

CRYSTAL KASWELL

Copyright

This is a work of fiction. Similarities to real people, places, or events are entirely coincidental.

DIRTY WEDDING
First Edition
Copyright © 2021 Crystal Kaswell.
Written by Crystal Kaswell
Cover by Hang Le

Also by Crystal Kaswell

Dirty Rich

Dirty Deal - Blake

Dirty Boss - Nick

Dirty Husband - Shep

Dirty Desires - Ian

Dirty Wedding - Ty

Dirty Secret - Cam

Pierce Family

Broken Beast - Adam

Playboy Prince - Liam - coming soon

Ruthless Rival - Simon - coming soon

Inked Hearts

Tempting - Brendon

Hooking Up - Walker

Pretend You're Mine - Ryan

Hating You, Loving You - Dean

Breaking the Rules - Hunter

Losing It - Wes

Accidental Husband - Griffin

The Baby Bargain - Chase

Inked Love

The Best Friend Bargain - Forest

The First Taste - Holden

The Roomie Rulebook - Oliver

Sinful Serenade

Sing Your Heart Out - Miles

Strum Your Heart Out - Drew

Rock Your Heart Out - Tom

Play Your Heart Out - Pete

Sinful Ever After – series sequel

Just a Taste - Miles's POV

Dangerous Noise

Dangerous Kiss - Ethan

Dangerous Crush – Kit

Dangerous Rock – Joel

Dangerous Fling – Mal

Dangerous Encore - series sequel

Standalones

Broken - Trent & Delilah

Come Undone Trilogy

Come Undone

Come Apart

Come To Me

Sign up for the Crystal Kaswell mailing list

Chapter One

INDIGO

I am not picturing Ty naked.

I am not picturing Ty naked.

I am not, under any circumstance, picturing Ty naked.

"Ms. Simms." A perky assistant greets me with a smile. "It's so wonderful to meet you." She leads me through the wide open office.

Steel fixtures, glass walls, cherry desks.

Everything intense, sleek, expensive. Like him.

"Can I offer you something to drink?" She moves past an empty conference room. "Coffee. Tea. Champagne?"

Champagne?

I haven't spoken to Ty in three years. Why in the world would we share a bottle of champagne?

"Ms. Simms? A drink?"

Right. I need to accept the gesture. As if this is a normal business meeting. And not a *what the fuck does Ty want from me* call. "Tea, thanks."

"Mr. Hunt tells me you prefer Yunnan Hong Cha. Will that be all right?"

He's already told her my tea preference.

He remembers my tea preference.

I swallow the questions that rise in my throat. "Perfect. Thanks."

She stops in front of the office in the northwest corner. "Mr. Hunt will be a few minutes."

I step inside. Ignore the sturdy desk in favor of the soft leather couch.

It's long enough for a mid-afternoon tryst.

If Ty wanted, he could let the curtains down, order me out of my clothes, demand I come on his hands, face, cock.

I won't.

And he won't ask.

But memories still flood my mind.

The rough edge of his voice.

The soft pressure of his lips.

The sweet warmth of his body against mine.

I cross and uncross my legs. Focus on my inhale. My exhale. My confidence.

Sure, I'm in a cheap dress and leaky boots, but he called me. He wants me here in his luxurious, expensive world.

Ty steps into the soft light surrounding the silver doorframe.

Is he an angel here to save me?

Or a devil in a designer suit?

I can never tell with him.

"Indigo." He moves through the door.

God, he's so handsome. Even more so than the last time I saw him.

I'm not sure what it is. Age. Experience. Heartbreak.

Or maybe it's the three years. Maybe I forgot the magnetic attraction between us.

My heart thuds against my chest. My toes curl. My thighs shake.

My body doesn't care about practicalities. It's already lost in memories. His hand on my throat, his voice in my ear, his cock—

"You look gorgeous." His voice is the same. The deep tone. The British accent. The complete lack of insight into his intentions.

"You too."

"Gorgeous?"

I nod, even though it's ridiculous. Ty is incredibly handsome in the most masculine way possible.

Deep eyes, dark skin, body of a soccer All Star. And under his suit, all those tattoos. The pieces of him I can't see.

The pieces of him I want to trace, study, commit to memory.

Or I did. Three years ago.

Now, I don't know. I don't know what he wants. How he feels. If I can trust him.

If I can trust myself around him.

I keep my voice soft. "Is fetching a better fit?"

He almost chuckles. He's at ease. Or he's good at pretending.

It's hard to know with him.

"Sure." He turns to the hallway as his assistant arrives with a tray.

A cup of coffee for him.

A tea set for me.

Both in clean white ceramic.

"Thank you." He waits for her to lay the drinks on his desk.

Then she leaves and he closes the door and we're alone.

My body begs for his. It screams *touch him, taste him, kiss him, fuck him.*

But that's not right. I'm not the one who fucks him.

He's the one who fucks me.

And not anymore.

We spent a summer together. It was a fling. That's all.

He hasn't spent the last three years missing me. Or dreaming of fucking me.

He's not asking me here to fuck me.

But what else could he want with me? I don't fit into his big, beautiful world.

Ty pours. Watches as I bring my lips to the pristine mug.

This is good tea. Expensive, perfectly steeped, fresh. But I can barely taste the notes of caramel and fig.

I'm too nervous.

Too in need of him.

I sit.

He takes the spot next to me. Turns his body toward mine.

The wool of his slacks brushes my bare skin. Only one layer between us. One layer too many.

I close my eyes. Focus on the taste of my tea. Try to stay in control.

"You like it?" Need slips into his voice. It matters to him that I like his offering.

"Yes. Thank you."

"Thank Paloma."

"She isn't here. You'll have to pass on my gratitude."

He nods *of course*. Turns a few more degrees toward me.

Enough my breath catches in my throat.

He smells the same. That earthy soap.

Three years and I recognize it.

Three years and the scent takes me back to his bed.

"You wanted to talk. In person." I try to keep my voice even.

He stares back at me with a perfect poker face.

"I'm here." I fail to find the confidence to sell *aloof badass*. "What do you need?"

4

If this was a normal offer, he'd put it on paper. In an email. Something.

If it's not...

His brother is former Mi6. They co-own an information company. He knows how easy it is to find secrets.

He needs me here for a reason.

But what?

He's rich, handsome, charming.

Then there's the British accent.

Rich, beautiful, powerful women fall at his feet.

What does he want with me?

"I have an offer for you." His eyes meet mine.

I finish my last sip. Suck a breath through my teeth. Force a steady exhale.

I can stare back at him. I can mirror his power and presence.

Sure, he's a billionaire with the contacts to ruin me. And I'm a cocktail waitress in a cheap dress.

And I, uh...

God, he's so handsome.

And I'm so out of my league. "What kind of offer?"

"I need something. And I want you, Indigo."

Okay...

"I want to marry you."

Chapter Two

TY

I ndigo's deep blue eyes fill with surprise.

Her wine lips part.

She stares at me for a moment, then she turns to her mug.

"Would you like more?" I ask. "I'll call Paloma."

"Would I like more tea?"

"Yes."

Her eyes flit to mine. "You want to marry me? And you're asking if I'd like more tea?"

"Yes."

"But…" Her chest heaves with her inhale.

She's torn between her desire to fuck me and her desire to tell me to fuck off.

Who do I think I am, calling her after three years of radio silence, asking her to marry me?

It's ridiculous.

I do realize that.

But it's also the only thing that makes sense.

I stand. Take her cup. Fill it with the tea left in the pot.

Her fingers brush mine as I hand her the mug. She looks up at me as she brings the clean white ceramic to her lips.

Her lipstick marks the cup.

My cock stirs.

This is where we should be. No crowd, no pretenses, no strings.

Her body under mine. Her nails in my back. Her lips on my neck.

"Why?" She swallows a sip. "Why do you want to marry me?"

"Does it matter?"

"Of course," she says.

I have to look away. So I won't give in to my urge to touch her.

This is the best corner office in the building. One window across from the Hudson. The other looking up to Midtown.

The bright blue sky, the dark water, the steel and glass of the city.

She's a New Yorker, through and through. She loves the city. This view must entice her.

But that isn't enough. It's not even a start.

"Why would I marry you, Ty?"

"You're about to lose the apartment."

"How do you know that?" she asks.

"It's easy information to find."

Anger flares in her eyes.

She's proud, strong, stubborn. Money isn't enough.

If she needs to understand why I'm asking her—

I can do that.

"Since Rory left, I've gained a reputation." I sit next to her. "One I can't afford."

"So you need a wife?"

"Yes."

"What about volunteering? Issuing a public statement? Claiming you're a sex addict?"

"How much do you want?" I ask.

"I'm not going to marry you, Ty."

"You need the money," I say.

She shrinks back, hurt. "Even so."

She's too proud. But she needs help. And this isn't a handout.

It's a deal.

"What are you going to do if the bank forecloses?" I ask. "Do you want to smile at rich arseholes all day?"

"That's none of your business."

"Do you want your sister following in your footsteps?"

Her cheeks flame.

I'm pushing her too far, too fast. She's protective of her sister. She doesn't want me intruding.

But this is the best card I can play.

"I have work." She stands. "I have to go." She takes a step toward the door. "Thanks for the tea."

I reach for her. "Please."

She stops. Looks up at me, studying me with those ice-blue eyes.

"I need you."

"You need someone."

"I need you."

Her gaze moves down my arm. To the place where my fingers are wrapped around her wrist.

Fuck. I release her. Take a deep breath. Get control of myself.

It doesn't matter that I want to throw her against the wall and fuck her.

I need to convince her first. "I won't take no for an answer."

She shakes her head as she moves out the door. But she

only makes it halfway to the elevator before she turns back to me.

She doesn't want to marry me.

I understand that.

But she'll do anything for her sister.

And I understand that too.

Chapter Three

INDIGO

My body stays tuned to Ty until I'm on the four train, on my way to Midtown.

I want you to marry me.

It's absurd. Beyond absurd.

Even if there's a certain logic. A Ty kind of logic. His heart is broken. His reputation is in shambles.

Why not marry someone he enjoys fucking? Even if he'll never love her.

I don my headphones. Will Amy Winehouse to erase Ty from my mind.

Her gorgeous, deep, throaty voice fills my ears. Then the jazzy instrumental track kicks in and I'm lost in a world of pain and self-destruction.

The pain of Ty leaving.

The self-destructive impulse to say yes to his proposal.

Or maybe it's my need to say no.

Which is more dangerous: My urge to invite him into my life, even though it killed me last time he walked away? Or my desire to run from a solution to my problems?

Money doesn't buy happiness.

But not having money really fucking sucks. And I know that as well as anyone does.

When the train arrives, I pause the music. The cool air steals my attention. Then it's the noise of the city. Taxis, tourists, businessmen on meetings.

Afternoons in Manhattan are always busy. Especially in midtown.

With two hours until work, I don't have time to go back to Brooklyn for quiet. So I find respite in a coffee shop a few blocks from Rick's.

I order a black tea, find a seat by the window, will the steel and glass of the skyscraper across the street to sort my thoughts.

But my cheap dress shows in the window's reflection.

The shop is too loud.

The tea is oversteeped.

This is nothing compared to Ty's office. Nothing compared to his life.

He always wants the best. Of everything.

I was shocked when I qualified.

Three years ago, I was working at a different fancy cocktail bar. Wearing black boots and tight dresses as I fetched drinks for rich men.

He was a customer. A regular. He was staying nearby for the summer.

He already had all that power and presence and intensity.

Only there was a softness too. A softness he tried to hide.

For a while, that was it. He was friendly. He tipped well. I meant it when I smiled.

I didn't enjoy the job, exactly, but it paid well, and I had time to myself. Time for playing my guitar, writing songs, going to shows.

My life was good. Maybe nothing special, but mine.

Then I ran into him.

I was at The Museum of Sex with a friend. And he was there. Taking in what the States had to offer.

It was beyond embarrassing—this handsome, aloof guy catching me blushing at pornographic pictures. Pictures of bound wrists and ball gags.

But then he made a joke, and I laughed, and I felt at ease.

He offered to buy me a tea.

My friend insisted I go. *He's so handsome. And British too. When are you going to meet another hot British guy?*

I said yes.

We sat at a modern coffee shop, sipping our drinks, trading stories about life in New York City.

Then we had dinner. Went to his apartment. Talked all night.

And that was it. I was smitten.

Our first kiss was something out of a fairy tale.

Fireworks. Actual fireworks.

Then he asked me about the pictures. If they interested me. If they showed something I wanted.

I said yes and we got into specifics.

Did I want to be tied up, gagged, spanked?

Hurt?

Did I want to beg?

I didn't even realize I craved a rough touch until I met Ty.

He read me like a book. Knew exactly what I needed, when I needed it, how and when to push me.

I trusted him in a way I'd never trusted anyone.

With my heart—he understood how it felt to lose a father, to struggle to support his mother, to balance ambition and duty.

With my body—he knew I came when he put his hand

around my throat, knew I wanted to be tied to his bed, knew I craved control.

He was only staying for the summer. And I was, am, nine years his junior. There was no way our lives would ever intertwine.

So we agreed.

Three months together. Then he'd go back to London and I'd stay in New York and we'd part with our *Casablanca* moment.

We'll always have Manhattan.

I believed it. That it was better to love and lose. Not that I loved him.

Maybe I did. I don't know.

Love isn't something I want. It's pain. It's always been pain.

Losing my father.

Losing my mother to grief.

Then to the sickness that claimed her lungs and her life.

I'm not sure if I loved Ty, but I know it broke my heart when he left. Even though I expected it. Even though I wanted it.

And when he met Rory and broke his promise to stay in touch—

That killed me.

I don't know the details. Only that he fell in love with her. That he left me a message, two months later, before his first trip to New York.

I'm coming to the city, but I can't see you. I'm sorry, Indie. I'm seeing someone now. I don't trust myself around you.

Was that a compliment, an insult, an admission?

I don't know.

If he really loved her, why didn't he trust himself?

It's hard to believe I have anything she doesn't.

She's a gorgeous socialite who reeks of class and sophistication.

I'm a broke girl who doesn't even play her guitar anymore.

He must have had a reason. Ty always has a reason.

But I don't know what it is.

And now...

He wants to marry me.

I'm sure he's willing to dig me out of debt, but it was hard enough not falling for him once.

Can I really do it twice?

———

Ty stays in my thoughts all night.

As I fetch martinis, pour brandy, listen to a man complain his wife doesn't understand him.

It's a weeknight. The room clears around eleven. We close at one. I tally my receipts, count my tips, cash out.

Find a note from a customer who ordered a four thousand dollar bottle of whiskey.

His cell, room number, offer for one night with me.

More than I make in three weeks.

Why is he willing to pay a price this high?

I'm attractive enough, but I'm not a knockout.

A novelty, maybe. With my asymmetrical haircut, my visible tattoos, my eyebrow piercing.

In high school, I was the weird artsy girl. Too quiet, too gawky, too lacking T & A.

Tall and thin, sure, but not all that feminine or pretty.

Striking maybe.

But not pretty.

Certainly not men's idea of sexy.

Or maybe I don't know men's idea of sexy. The guys who

make overtures don't seem to mind my slight curves or my angular features.

Some of the offers…

I'm proud, yes, but I'm also human.

Sometimes, I'm tempted.

Sometimes, men offer enough to cover three months of bills.

Sometimes, I really need the money.

I try to talk myself into it.

Sienna is starting college in the fall. Sienna needs to stay out of this world—it's bad enough men gawk when she visits.

If this is what it takes—

I would do it. If one night with a stranger was standing between me and my sister's well-being, I would do it in a heartbeat.

So far—

I get by.

I read the man's offer again. Think of Ty. The feel of his hands on my skin. The bliss of his body meeting mine. The sense of loneliness when he walked away.

I can't. I just can't.

So I toss the guy's number. Don my coat. Take the subway to our stop in Brooklyn.

It's a dozen blocks to our place.

I grab the mail, step inside, lock the door.

The usual collection of ads, bills, notices. Sienna's NYU welcome packet. That friendly reminder tuition is due in August.

Not that I have it. I thought her soccer scholarship would come through, but it didn't.

No, it's either loans or…

Fuck.

I can't do this.

It hurt so badly watching Ty leave once. I can't do it again.

But I can't risk my sister's future either.

There has to be something, some way I can do this without falling apart.

I find my cell and text him.

Chapter Four

TY

There it is, on my cell screen. Four words with all the promise in the world.

Indigo: What are you offering?

A message from late last night.

After work. After hours of rich arseholes staring at her tits.

My stomach twists.

I don't want anyone glaring at her. Making her feel unsafe. Making her feel used.

And I certainly don't want anyone touching her.

It's ridiculous. I've been with other women. Where do I get off, hating the idea of her with another man?

But I do.

And there's no reasoning with the jealously in my veins.

I need her to agree.

Not just for my reputation.

Not just to secure our families' futures.

For me.

My publicist doesn't approve. She has a list of eligible women, women who grew up expecting a political marriage.

Women willing to marry a black man. It ruled out more than she expected, but I wasn't surprised. Manhattan is old money. And old ideals die hard.

Some of the women she picked are beautiful.

Some are charming.

None are Indie.

None of them want to understand me. Or want me to understand them.

Maybe it's ridiculous that our three months together left a mark on my soul, but they did.

If I'm doing this, if I'm committing to a life with someone I'll never love, it's her.

Ty: What do you want?

It's early. I don't expect a response. But she sends one right away.

Indigo: You don't have any of the things I want.

Ty: Try me.

Whatever it is, I can find it.

I can give her anything except my heart.

Chapter Five

INDIGO

All day, I ignore Ty's text.

I research scholarships. I apply for jobs at better bars.

I listen to Dad's old records. The ska ones with enough energy to wake me from my haze.

Then I walk to Sienna's school, hug her hello, listen to her complain she's too old for pickups.

The warm smile on her face, the ease in her shoulders—

It's enough to convince me.

Of course, I'll consider his deal.

Whatever it takes to keep her safe. To keep us together.

Indigo: The mortgage. And Sienna's college. That's non-negotiable.

I slide my cell into the pocket of my jeans, but I'm too slow.

Sienna catches me. Taps my shoulders. "You're talking to a guy."

We're at the counter, waiting for our drinks. There's nowhere to hide. No way to pretend I'm suddenly fascinated by my surroundings. "Where would I meet a guy?"

"At Rick's?" She laughs. "I can't believe they actually call it Rick's. Has the owner even seen *Casablanca*? That place is the opposite of Rick's."

The Rick's Cafe Americano in *Casablanca* is all life and energy and heat. The Rick's in midtown is all quiet and stillness and cold.

I'm not sure the guy who owns Rick's has ever seen *Casablanca*. Whereas we've seen it about a thousand times.

It was Mom's favorite movie. She and dad watched it every month, on their anniversary.

They were like teenagers, celebrating their one-month anniversary.

Then he died and she stopped watching. And all the love in the house turned to grief.

"He thinks he's Bogart." I push past my painful memories. Try to hold on to the good ones. Where *Casablanca* felt like home. Even if it's a home I'll never have again.

"Yeah. Like he's an icon, even though he's a short alcoholic." Sienna shakes her head. Checks the still empty counter for her drink. "Oh my god, this is taking forever!"

My phone buzzes.

Sienna notices. "Are you talking to a girl?"

"No."

"Are you talking to a gender non-binary individual?"

"No."

"So you are talking to a guy?"

"It's not a big deal."

"Mm-hmm." Her eyes flit to my pocket. "Then why don't you reply?"

"I'm talking to you."

"Well, I'm going to get some napkins. So you won't be talking to me for a minute." She moves to the counter with a wink.

I check my cell immediately.

Ty: Done.

Done.

He'll pay my sister's tuition.

And the mortgage.

Done.

Indigo: You don't know how much it is.

Ty: I've already agreed.

Sienna returns with a fistful of napkins. "Who's the guy?"

"No one."

"Uh, yeah, someone." She motions to my lipstick. My long necklace. My low-cut top. "You're dressed up for him."

"I can't dress up for myself?"

"You just happened to dress up for yourself the same day you started texting someone? Please." She drops the napkins on a small table. Adjusts her ponytail. "It's for a guy."

My cell buzzes.

I want to see Ty's text. I want to let my guard down and fall into that perfect summer we spent together.

It's May. Almost three years since we met.

Three years and so much has changed.

Mom got sick. Died. Left me with bills I couldn't pay.

I went from holding up half the world to all of it.

"Indie…" Sienna's voice gets singsong. "Who's the guy?"

My fingers glide over the edges of my cell. I want to see him. To hear his offer. To let him assuage my doubts.

"Oh my god." Her blue eyes light up. "It's him."

"It's who?"

"Mr. London."

How did she guess that?

"It is!" She claps her hands together. "I can't believe it. After three years. I knew it. I knew he'd see the error of his ways. Beg to win you over."

She's not wrong. She's not right either—this is about Ty getting what he wants—but she's not wrong.

Thankfully, the tearista saves me from contemplating the

matter. She calls our order. Black tea, hot. Royal milk tea with boba.

Sienna jumps out of her seat and skips to the counter.

I check my cell while she's distracted.

Ty: Meet me for dinner.

"Is it really Mr. London?" Sienna holds my drink to her chest. "I'm going to keep this until you tell me."

"You're going to stain your sweater."

"Don't care." She sets her boba on the table. Holds my take-out cup with both hands.

She looks adorable, holding my tea hostage. Sienna tries to embrace her inner badass sometimes, but it never works.

Don't get me wrong. She's tough. A soccer player with the strong legs and the constant ponytail to prove it.

But she's got the world's sweetest face. Hazel eyes, button nose, chestnut hair.

All of Mom's coloring. And her resting sweetheart face.

Whereas I look more like Dad.

Pale skin, intense blue eyes, dark hair.

And the resting bitch face.

Though no one says that when it's a guy's face. It's more that he looks tough. In control. Serious.

Not that anyone ever complained. Not when he was alive.

And not now.

That's the one upside to death. All compliments.

"In-di-go..." She says it louder. Loud enough the people in line turn our way. Which only makes Sienna laugh. "Tell me. Please." She taps the lid of my cup. "Your tea is getting cold."

"What if it is him?"

"Then I need every detail."

I shoot her a *really* look.

She nods *hell yes*. "I know you remember that summer.

Because I remember the look you had when you came home." She makes a show of fanning herself.

I seize the moment. Grab my tea. Take a long sip.

Mmm.

Yes, it's mediocre, but it's still warm and strong and full of caffeine.

"It is him," she says. "I knew it."

"I didn't say—"

"Why don't you want to tell me?"

"I don't want you to get your hopes up."

"My hopes that you'll finally get laid?" she asks.

Uh…

"How long has it been?"

"A reasonable amount of time that is none of your business."

"That's too long. You should go. See him. Enjoy that, at least."

"I can't."

She raises a brow. "Why not?"

"Because…"

"Because… you're gay?" she asks.

"No."

"It's okay if you are."

"Do you think I am?"

"Well… you haven't been with anyone in a long time. And you do have an asymmetrical haircut."

I can't help but laugh. "You shouldn't stereotype."

"I know. But you also have an eyebrow piercing."

I double over.

God, I love Sienna. She's so… Sienna. Loud and bold and unapologetically herself.

She's been through as much as I have, but she's still bright and vibrant.

Whereas I can barely stomach picking up my guitar.

"What? It's true. And it's not a bad thing. If you're gay. Or asexual. Though we both know you aren't. You're already blushing."

I am.

"Mr. London… I wish I knew more about him. I picture him as different celebrities. Right now…" She presses her lips together, thinking. "Kit Harington."

I shake my head. "Too pretty."

"Tom Hardy?"

"Closer."

"Jeremy Irons."

"He's like a hundred."

"Maybe that's why you won't tell me."

I shake my head.

"Idris Elba."

She's getting warmer. Too much warmer. I call upon my poker face. Well, my *annoying customer complaining his wife doesn't get him, but I'm such a good listener…* face. "I'm not telling you."

"Why not?"

"Because." It's mine. That world we have together is mine.

She makes a show of pouting. "Okay. Fine. But… why is it you aren't rushing to reply to Mr. London?"

"Because I like him." My shoulders ease. It's a relief, admitting it to myself, but it's terrifying too.

"Isn't that a good thing?" she asks.

Maybe. I miss that feeling. The warmth in my chest, the flutter in my stomach, the lightness in my limbs.

But the ache in my soul that came after… I can't do that again.

"It's different for men. Sex doesn't always mean something to them. And he… It won't mean anything to him."

"How do you know that?"

"He left."

"That's what you both wanted, isn't it?" she asks.

Yes. At the time, it made sense.

He had a life in London. I had a life in New York. I was only a year into school. And it was a struggle. Everything was a struggle.

"Indie?" she asks.

"It seemed like the right thing to do."

"But you missed him." It's not really a question.

So I don't answer.

"He made you come. He made you swoon. You still like him. And now he wants to see you again. Why not?"

"Because it's not the same for him."

"How?"

It's a good question. I don't have an answer. Only excuses about not wanting to get hurt. "He did invite me to dinner."

She claps her hands together. "And by dinner you mean his apartment?"

"Will you be okay on your own?"

"Yes. Definitely." She sucks boba through her straw. "And if you want to stay the night… that's okay too." She winks.

I shake my head. Check my cell again.

Indigo: Dinner. If you'll explain.

Ty: Seven. At the Italian place.

There are a thousand Italian places in New York City, but there's only one he could mean: The place we had our first real date.

Which means there are less than three hours until I'm face-to-face with him.

And everything I like about him.

Chapter Six

TY

I spend fifteen minutes steeling myself, but still, I melt the second she enters.

The Indigo I met three years ago. The same deep blue eyes and sharp features. And the new version of her: hesitant expression, tall boots, short, blunt haircut.

The edgy, asymmetrical look suits her.

And it shows off her neck. Like she's asking for my lips, teeth, hands.

Fuck, I want to touch her. I always want to touch her. Every time I think of her.

Right now—

I need to lay her on this table, roll her knickers to her ankles, spread her thighs.

No negotiations, no terms, no ugly memories.

Her under my control. Groaning my name as she comes on my face.

She stops at the table. Sets her simple black purse on the red cloth. Offers her hand.

I stand. Shake. Motion for her to sit.

She does.

"I ordered a bottle," I say.

"Champagne again?" She raises a brow *celebrating already, how presumptuous*.

Is there humor in it?

Or does she think the worst of me now?

It matters to me. She matters to me.

Sure, I'm not going to fall in love.

And I don't want her falling in love with me.

But I want her comfortable, safe, cared for.

"Red wine," I say. "Unless you no longer adore arrabbiata."

She crosses one leg over the other. "You drink wine now?"

"When in Rome."

"Of course." Her gaze flits to the server as he drops off a bottle. He pours. Nods goodbye. Disappears.

Indigo's eyes find mine. That same deep, dark blue. That same curiosity.

Once upon a time, she wanted everything in my heart.

Now, I don't know.

I don't have a read on her. Or the way my pulse is racing.

It's not just the snug dress. Or the pendant between her perfect tits. Or the flush of her cheeks.

I want to tear off her clothes and I want to ask about her day. Her year. Her life.

She wraps her fingers around the stem. Takes a long sip. Marks the glass with her lipstick.

"You like it?"

She nods. "I don't drink a lot of wine. Mostly whiskey with customers at work."

My skin crawls at the thought of some rich arsehole nagging her to share a shot. "The same place?"

She leans back in her seat. "You don't know?"

"Do you want me to?"

She traces the rim of her glass. "Does it matter what I want?"

Of course. "I went there looking for you."

Her eyes fill with surprise. "When?"

"A month ago. I went every night for a week straight. Eventually, the bartender recognized me. She asked if I was looking for you."

"Were you?"

"It didn't occur to me, but I was. I missed you." The words are awkward on my tongue. They're true. Too true. I have missed her. I shouldn't.

We spent a summer together. Then we parted. And I moved on.

I was engaged, for fuck's sake.

"You missed me?" Doubt spreads over her expression. "Really?"

"You haven't missed me?"

Her eyes move over me slowly. "I wasn't engaged to someone else."

"You've spent the last three years single?"

She picks up her glass. Takes another sip. "I haven't had a lot of time for dating. Though I imagine you already know that." Her throat tightens. Some mix of anger—who do I think I am, knowing her business—and grief.

"I'm sorry about your mother."

"Thank you." Her eyes go to the table. She stares at it, looking for something, not finding it. "I'm sorry your fiancée left."

"Are you?"

Her eyes trace a line across the table, up my deep blue tie, my jaw, lips, nose, eyes.

I let silence fall. Watch her study me. Look for cracks.

Are they there? The last year—

I'm not myself. I'm not the tough, in control, impossible to rattle man I used to be.

I need to get there. To find that person.

The man who is never distracted. Who isn't afraid of loss or vulnerability.

Who isn't afraid of anything.

The server interrupts us. With two plates. Shrimp arrabbiata.

Her favorite.

She shakes her head. Stifles a laugh. "You ordered for me?"

"You don't want it?"

"I do." She picks up her fork. Stabs a piece of penne. "But it's presumptuous."

"You didn't always mind."

"Things change."

They do. And I need to up my game if I'm going to convince her.

She still works that awful job. Laughing at bad jokes, letting men leer at her tits, trading on her youth and beauty.

They offer her cash for sex. They did three years ago. That wouldn't change just because she's cut her hair.

She needs money.

Has she ever said yes?

Some arsehole who sees her as a warm spot for his dick—

Who doesn't deserve her—

The thought makes my stomach turn.

But where do I get off? It's not like I spent the last year fucking women who saw into my soul.

And I have options.

She's broke. At risk of losing her apartment. Of not

paying her sister's tuition. Of working this shitty job until she's too old to play the part of the pretty, young thing.

What then?

I don't like that future for her.

"Fuck." She groans over her pasta. "This is better than I remember."

My chest warms. Her bliss still satisfies me. It still fills me with an intense need to take care of her.

"Still presumptuous." She swallows another bite. "But really fucking good."

My eyes stay on her as she brings another forkful to her lips.

Her eyes close. Her brows soften.

For a moment, she's in that world of satisfaction.

Then her eyes blink open. Find mine.

"Are you going to eat? Or did you invite me here just to watch me?" She traces the stem of her wineglass. "That's kinky. Even for you."

"Even for me?"

She nods.

I take a bite. Let the spicy, tangy sauce overwhelm my taste buds. I haven't had arrabbiata in a long time.

It makes me think of her. And I can't think of her. I couldn't. It fucked with my head.

I chew. Swallow. Sip my wine. "Things change. Like you said."

"Have they?" She tries to keep her voice even, but she doesn't get there. When I don't respond, she continues. "Your tastes. Have they changed?"

Fuck.

I can't answer that.

It's been a long time since I've considered asking a woman to submit.

Right now, sitting across from her, watching her chest rise

and fall with her breath, watching curiosity spread over her eyes—

I need it.

It's undeniable.

"You've racked up a reputation," she says. "But that isn't part of it." Her eyes pass over me slowly. Stop on my tie. "None of your *friends* have mentioned your penchant for rope. Or orders. Or pain."

My cock stirs. Blood rushes south. It's not what I need. I need to stay in control.

"Either you're asking women to sign NDAs, or..." She raises a brow, offering me the floor.

I haven't.

I haven't tried. Not since I broached the idea with Rory. Since she looked at me like I was a monster.

"I haven't asked if they'd enjoy rope. Or orders. Or pain," I say.

Her blush deepens. "And your fiancée?"

"Ex-fiancée."

"Did she share your tastes?"

"What does that matter?"

"I'm curious."

"I'm not asking you to fuck me, Indigo."

"We're going to get married and never have sex?" She picks up her wineglass. Takes a long sip. "Really?"

"I'm not paying for sex."

"You don't want to fuck me?" she asks.

"Of course, I want to fuck you. But that's not why I'm here."

"You're here because of your reputation," she says. "Really? That's all of it?"

"Enough of it."

She stares back at me, not quite believing me.

It's not the whole story, but it's all I can give her right now. "You're here, Indigo."

"I am."

"So give me a number. Tell me what it will take. What, exactly, do you want?"

Chapter Seven

INDIGO

*W**hat will it take?***

What, exactly, do you want?

It's not something I consider often.

Immediate needs take up too much space.

Rent, food, safety.

Sometimes, I have time for tiny pleasures. A warm drink on a cold day. A night dancing after a stressful shift. Watching Sienna score a winning goal after a week of losing.

That's what I want. I want my sister to be okay.

But Ty is already covering her tuition. What else could I possibly desire?

What do I daydream about during subway rides and slow shifts at work?

A week in the Caribbean. A trip to Vegas for Sienna's twenty-first. A rich, handsome customer who wants to erase all my problems.

Ty.

Whispering in my ears, spilling his secrets, promising me forever.

This is it.

He's right here. Not only promising me forever but offering cash for it.

A dream come true.

Except for the tiny matter of it being bullshit.

"What are you asking, exactly?" I fold my hands in my lap. Try to hold his gaze.

His dark eyes are as intense as ever.

He still reads me like a book.

Knows exactly which button to press to make me laugh, groan, scream.

Knows he has the power to destroy me.

"I'd like to get married this summer," he says. "But I'm negotiable. As long as we announce our engagement right away."

"It's May."

"I'm aware."

"You were photographed with another woman two months ago."

"I'm aware of that as well."

"People will think this is a shotgun wedding," I say.

"Not if we sell it." His eyes bore into mine. "They'll believe we reconnected."

So that's why he asked me. Because we have a history. One that suits his story.

It makes sense, logically, but it's missing something. Some other detail I can't see.

I try to find the truth in his expression, but I can't. "We'll sell it?"

"Yes."

"How?"

"Photographs. Dinners. Parties."

"You throw parties?" I ask.

He chuckles. "Not usually."

"But your birthday is next month."

His eyes light up. He's surprised I remembered. Or excited.

I'm not sure.

"And this is for your reputation?" I ask.

He nods.

"So can we tell friends and family the truth?"

"No." The delight drains from his expression. "They need to believe it."

"Even your brother?"

His eyes flit to the table. "He wouldn't approve."

I don't know a lot about Ty's brother, but I know he's obsessed with honesty.

Usually, Ty is the same. This isn't like him.

But maybe I don't know him. It has been three years.

"Your friends?" I ask.

"Everyone," he says.

Okay. Everyone. I guess that's clear enough, but-- "I'm not sure I can lie to Sienna. I don't know if I can agree to that."

"It's a deal breaker?"

"If it is?"

"Will you try?"

I swallow hard. I don't like the idea of deceiving my sister. But she wouldn't approve either. And I don't want to put this on her.

I don't want her to feel responsible.

This is my choice.

Even if it's for her, it's my choice.

"I can try," I say. "But I can't promise results."

He nods. "Fair."

Maybe. "And these photographers, dinners, parties—how will we convince people it's real?"

"We'll look madly in love."

"What if I can't sell it?"

"You can."

And what if the line blurs? If I fall in love with him? "But really, we're…"

"Are you still claiming you won't fuck me?"

My chest warms. "Not for money."

"Friends. Maybe friends who fuck. If that's what you decide."

Fuck. Yes. Now. Please. "Only friends?"

"I don't want to hurt you, Indie. I care about you. I'll always care about you. But love is done with me."

"You want me to convince the world I'm in love with you, even though you'll never love me, but you don't want to hurt me. Really?"

"Yes." He picks up his glass. Takes a long sip of wine. Considers something. "Maybe it's not possible, but it's what I'm asking."

Okay.

It's what he's asking.

And, for some reason he won't disclose, he's asking me.

"For how long?" I ask.

"Forever." He takes another sip. Sets his glass on the table. "Isn't that how long marriage is supposed to last?"

"It's supposed to be two people in love."

His eyes stay on his glass. "How much do you want?"

I shake my head. "Forever isn't happening."

"Ten years."

"Ten years without love?"

He nods. "How much do you want for ten years?"

Ten years as Tyler Hunt's wife. "Can I stay in New York?"

"You'll need to join me in London some of the time."

"And what will I do when you're in London?"

"Whatever you want." His voice stays firm. In control.

Impossible to read. "Finish school. Record an album. Live your life."

"My life? Or the life you decide for me?"

"Your life. I'm asking you because I want you. If I wanted a girl from the Upper West Side... there are plenty."

Other candidates.

He has choices. Of course he has choices.

But he doesn't want those women.

He wants me.

It doesn't make any sense, but maybe it doesn't need to make sense.

He has money. I need money. Right now and in the future.

Money is a tool. It opens doors, it smooths cracks, it fixes things. And I have a lot of things that need fixing.

"What else are you offering?" I ask.

"Besides a scholarship for your sister and the mortgage paid in full?"

I nod.

He holds my gaze. "What do you want?"

I have a few ideas. "I asked a friend who works at a law firm." Okay, she's in law school, but close enough. "There's no standard for prenups. But a man with your net worth... his lawyer would advise him to offer at least a hundred million dollars."

He holds his poker face.

"That sounds fair."

"For ten years?"

"For ten years." My heart thuds against my chest. My limbs lighten. I'm asking too much.

I'm going to lose this opportunity.

I can't lose this opportunity.

I need his money.

And I absolutely, positively can't do this.

He shocks me with his response. "Ten million."

Ten million. Fuck. I stop breathing.

He continues, "and you agree you won't be with anyone else."

I swallow hard. "And you?"

"Neither of us will."

"I'm not taking money for sex."

"I'm not paying you for sex." His voice drops to something dirty and demanding. "When I fuck you, it will be because you want it. Because you're begging me."

Mmm. My body whines. It shares none of my concern. It's ready to slide into his lap right here, right now. "If I don't?"

"Then you won't."

"You'll go ten years without sex? Really?" I don't believe it. And I can't handle it either.

Sure, I haven't exactly spent the last three years getting my rocks off. I'm usually too stressed to even consider dating.

But sometimes, the tension fades, and I feel that want.

Attractive customers.

The single dad at Sienna's school with the gorgeous eyes.

A handsome man at a club.

After a few drinks, with music pouring into my ears—

I almost feel like a normal twenty-two-year-old with time for fun. I forget how tired I am and I let desire overtake me.

But I don't trust the men I meet at clubs.

I take my lust home. Touch myself. Fantasize.

Or remember.

It's always Ty.

Not my high school boyfriend. Not the one who came after.

Ty's hand around my wrists. Ty's lips on my neck. Ty's cock driving into me.

Ten years, by Ty's side without sex—

That's unthinkable.

"If that's what you want, yes." His eyes bore into mine. "But you're not going to convince me you don't want to fuck me." His voice is even. Demanding. "If I asked, you'd go home with me tonight."

"I wouldn't."

He raises a brow, daring me.

"Maybe I want to."

"Maybe?"

"Okay. I want to fuck you. But I want lots of things. I don't take all of them."

He stills. Studying me. Waiting.

The intensity in his gaze makes my body buzz. This side of him, patient and teasing and demanding—

I need it.

I miss it.

Why am I fighting?

Why not agree? Go to his place. Come in his bed.

"If you think I'll fuck you, ask," I say.

"No. I'm going to wait until you're begging for it."

Fuck. "If I don't?"

"You will."

"Are you sure?"

"Yes."

"I haven't even agreed. Should you really tease me?"

"No." He folds his hands. "I'm not being smart." He traces a line down my body with his eyes. "I'm not smart when it comes to you."

"What would be smart?"

He doesn't answer. "Ten years. Ten million dollars. Do we have a deal?"

"I want an out if it's not working," I say.

"I'll pay your sister's scholarship now," he says. "And a signing bonus."

"A signing bonus?"

He nods. "A hundred thousand dollars."

Fuck. Yes.

"With an NDA attached. If this goes public, you have to return the money."

"If I tell Sienna?"

"Do you trust her to keep your secret?"

Usually, that's an easy yes. But when there's a hundred grand on the line, I don't know.

"At the end of the first year, the mortgage. The rest is part of a standard prenup."

"And while we're together?"

"I'm going to take care of my wife," he says. "The details don't matter to me."

"And it's just us? You're not expecting anything?"

"Anything?"

"Children? That won't be..." I'm not sure if I want kids, but I know this. "I'm not raising kids in a loveless marriage."

"Of course." He nods like it's nothing.

Maybe he feels the same way.

We didn't talk much about the future when we met. But he wanted to be a father. Is he really giving that up?

He pushes the topic aside. "You'll have to move in soon."

"What about Sienna?"

"I'm paying the mortgage, aren't I?"

Right. "What if I want her closer?"

"I can find an apartment for her in the building."

That's another few thousand a month. Maybe more.

And he's throwing it in like it's nothing.

"What do you say, Indigo?" He holds out his hand. "Do we have a deal?"

Chapter Eight

INDIGO

"**Y**es." I swallow the objections that rise into my throat. He'll never love me. He'll break my heart.

He's sure I'm going to beg him to bend me over the table and fuck me.

My cheeks warm. Then my chest. Stomach. Thighs.

My body is more than willing.

The image is already in my head.

The red fabric against my cheek, my dress at my waist, Ty's hand on my thigh.

I already want him so badly.

Would it be so bad to beg?

What good is pride compared to satisfaction?

"I'll do it." I force the words from my lips. They're heavy with the weight of that promise.

He offers his hand.

I shake.

"What now?" I pick up my fork. Savor the chewy pasta, fresh tomatoes, spicy sauce. As if this is a normal dinner. As if I didn't just agree to trade ten years of my life for ten million dollars.

"I already have the paperwork. I need to change a few details," he says. "Come to my office tomorrow. We'll sign. My assistant will arrange the rest."

"The rest?"

"A wedding planner. A personal shopper. An image consultant if you'd like one." His eyes flit to my chest. "I'd rather you wear this every fucking day, but the people we need to impress—"

"Tyler Hunt wouldn't marry a woman who shops at ASOS?"

"There are high end dresses on ASOS."

"This isn't—"

"It feels like you're setting me up." His voice drops an octave. "To say I hate the dress and need to do away with it immediately."

My cheeks flush.

"Are you?"

"No."

"You look gorgeous. You know that."

"Do I?" I ask.

His voice is stern. "Don't play dumb with me. It doesn't suit you."

Is that a compliment or an insult?

"You look gorgeous in that dress. I don't give a fuck what it costs."

My sex clenches. My body threatens to take over. I'm losing control. And losing interest in holding onto it. "But your friends do?"

There. I push the words out. Anything to keep me here, in reality.

To keep me from falling to my knees and begging.

I want him, yes. Badly.

I'm not too proud to beg him. But only if I make him work for it. Only if he's as desperate as I am.

His voice softens. "You know this world as well as I do."

"Only as the help."

His shoulders tense. His eyes fill with something I can't place. "I'm sorry if I ever made you feel like that. I didn't grow up in this world. I'll never fit into it. But I do know it from this side. And I know what you'll expect."

Scrutiny. Over my hair, my makeup, my clothes, my education, my family.

At least I have that. One American hero for a father. One grieving widow mother, now with her late husband forever.

One Cinderella story and here's Prince Charming.

"I want you. And I want you to feel like yourself," he says. "Just—"

"The rich version?"

"Yes."

"I suppose it wouldn't look great if your fiancée showed up in a fifty-dollar dress."

"If you mention the dress again, I'm ordering you to take it off."

My thighs press together.

"I know this is going to be difficult. I know I'm asking a lot. But… I want to make it easy for you when I can. If you'd prefer, I'll have someone from my team handle everything. The wedding. Your wardrobe. Your move."

"I want the summer with Sienna. It's my last summer before she goes to school."

His nod is understanding. "There are a lot of details. We don't have to decide all of them today."

"Okay." I finish my last sip of wine. Savor the fruity flavor. The perfect balance of light and dark. Strong enough for the tomato sauce, but not so strong it overpowers the spice.

It's just right.

He always knows what I need.

And I want to be there. In that world. With my thoughts gone and my entire body tuned to him.

Which means I need to go. Before my body takes over. "I… uh, I should get back to her. It's getting late."

It's not getting late, but he doesn't call me on it.

"Your office? Tomorrow?" I ask. "Anytime?"

"Lunch. We'll start working on our story."

Right. Our story.

"And we'll practice."

"Practice?"

"Looking like we're madly in love."

———

I SHAKE GOODBYE, EVEN THOUGH I WANT TO HUG HIM. EVEN though I want to kiss him and touch him and collapse in his arms.

I expect the long subway ride to dull the ache between my legs, but it doesn't.

I'm still buzzing. From his touch, his stare, his promise.

And the thrill of my problems dissolving.

Ten million dollars.

It's unthinkable and it's mine.

Not for a while, but a hundred grand will keep me comfortable for a long time.

And the mortgage paid, Sienna's school covered—

It's everything.

"In-di-go." Sienna pulls the door open. She throws her arms around me. Pulls me inside. (We're both tall, but she's an athlete. She's much stronger than I am.) "You have a lot to explain, young lady."

"Do I?"

She nods *absolutely*. Motions to the kitchen table with a stern *we need to talk* expression.

"It's serious?"

"Very serious." She fills two glasses with water. Brings both to the table. Waits for me to sit.

Okay. Sure. I'll play along. "What is it I need to explain?"

"Look at the time."

I make a show of looking at the microwave clock.

"Indigo Simms! Are you even listening?"

"It's eight thirty."

"Yes."

"Am I home too late, Mom?"

She shakes her head. "Too late? Too early! I Google Mapped the restaurant. Twenty minutes on the subway."

"Okay."

She stands. Slams both hands on the table. The ultimate show of toughness. "How much time does that leave for dinner?"

"Do you have a point?"

"It's not even nine! Unless you spent the last two hours in a limo, canoodling with Mr. London, I demand an explanation."

A laugh escapes my lips. Then another. Another.

"Is this funny?"

Yes. I double over. Press my hand into my stomach. Oh my god. This is perfect... "Sienna..."

"You're supposed to be getting laid."

"I..."

"You... have an explanation, I hope."

"Oh my god."

"No, no, no, don't bring your god into this." She shakes her head with mock outrage. "This is between you and..."

"My god?"

She folds her arms. "Why aren't you enjoying carnal delights right now?"

"Because..."

"Because…"

Oh my god. She's ridiculous. I stand and pull my sister into a hug.

"This is not an explanation."

"You're not getting an explanation." I release her. "My sex life is not your business."

She frowns.

"When did you become so obsessed with sex?"

"Uh… always?"

As soon as she hit puberty, yeah. That is accurate.

"You look all—" she draws a circle around my face. "Needy. Like you wish you went back to his place after dinner. And why did it end so early? Did he get fat?"

"No."

"Oh, so you wouldn't sleep with a fat guy?"

"Don't even."

"Then why?" She raises a brow. "Is he engaged now? Married? Does he want you to be the other woman?"

"I haven't seen him in forever."

"He booty-called. You answered. What gives?"

Is that really all he wants? Ten years to have his way with me? "We…" What can I tell her that isn't a lie? "I'm going to see him again tomorrow."

"Where? His apartment? His office? A bar? Will you have sex in the bathroom?"

"Hmm…" I press my finger to my chin. "Still none of your business."

She pouts. "All right, fine. But we're still going to celebrate." She claps her hands together. "Whiskey?"

"No."

She exaggerates her frown, then lets it fade to a smile. "How about gelato? The place down the street is open until eleven."

And they have a great pistachio. My favorite. "Gelato is perfect."

"Next time, come home after it's already closed, okay?"

I can't help but laugh. It's sweet, how much she wants me to get laid.

Weird. But sweet.

And I...

I want to say yes, but I have no idea what Ty has in store for me.

Chapter Nine

TY

The second I arrive home, I finalize the details.

The contract on the way to the courier.

The wedding planner on retainer.

My assistant ready for the afternoon.

Paloma assures me Indigo is in good hands.

Still, I toss and turn.

I've never slept well. There was always something inside me, this fear I'd wake up to news my father was never coming home.

He was in the military and he was usually deployed.

In some foreign country, in a secret location, doing work he couldn't discuss.

When he was on leave, when he was home, smiling at my mother, taking me and Ian to football games, knocking back pints with friends—

That was the only time I slept well.

Then Ian enlisted and—

I thought I'd never sleep again.

My older brother. The man who raised me when my father wasn't around. The man who always knew what to do.

Who knew how to talk to girls, fix the sink, cook Mum dinner.

I was only twelve when he enlisted.

I wasn't ready to be without him.

I wasn't ready to be the man of the house.

I wasn't ready to pick up slack for my mother when she was tired or overworked or lonely.

She did her best. She's a tough woman. Strong.

But it wore on her too. Her husband and her oldest son were off someplace risking their lives.

She tried to hide her loneliness. She tried to pretend nothing was wrong.

But everything was wrong.

Ian was away. My best friend, my older brother, my mentor—

He wasn't there.

When he and Dad were home, they tried to make up for lost time.

But there was never enough time.

Mom was the one who taught me to shave, knot a tie, talk to a girl I liked.

I was hopeless, honestly.

But it was okay.

I was used to being alone.

Loneliness was comfortable. Like an old pair of pants.

Maybe I wouldn't win an award for best dressed, but I felt like myself.

I didn't have to worry about saying goodbye. Tossing and turning. Swallowing that awful fear I'd lose someone forever.

I focused on school. Work. Football.

My teammates became my friends. I was good at football. I needed to win. I'd never cheat or sacrifice sportsmanship, but I'd practice for hours, memorize plays, run until my legs gave out.

People wanted to be around the star player.

Girls flocked to us.

I learned enough.

How to flirt, how to charm, how to explain what I wanted.

I discovered I had unusual tastes. Some part of me knew —I hadn't seen these things in films or television—but I had no idea how deep they went.

I tried to ignore my desires for a long time. Girls my age weren't all that receptive to being tied up.

In university it was easier. Women wanted to experiment. We'd play for a few weeks or months then part ways. It was never long enough to earn their trust.

It was never long enough to develop a real intimacy.

I didn't give in to what I wanted. Not completely. Not until I met Indigo.

But that was easier. Safer. I didn't want to fall for someone. I didn't need the ache of distance or the pain of parting.

Even when Dad retired and Ian returned to London—

It was too late. The ache was too deep. My heart was too closed.

It was easier, having Dad home, starting a company with Ian.

Work kept me busy. Family dinners erased the loneliness.

Ian and I did well.

We made enough money women saw me as a dollar sign instead of a fun few weeks.

Dad died.

Ian divorced. Moved to the States.

I followed for the summer.

Met Indigo.

I keep thinking about that night.

The bar in midtown. The sunset behind us. Her almost black hair falling down her back.

The drive and determination in her deep blue eyes.

The silky lilt of her voice as she asked what I'd like to drink.

There was something special about her. I knew it the second I saw her.

Then I ran into her, at the fucking Museum of Sex, no less.

And the look she gave me. Bashful, curious, intense—

I knew I needed to have her.

But I had no idea how deep it went.

How much I'd crave her.

How much I'd miss her when I left.

Did I love her? I'm not sure.

The word wasn't in my vocabulary at the time. Until I met Rory and she—

It was easy.

I wasn't afraid of losing her.

I don't know why. Logically, it doesn't make any sense.

She was part of this world—money and manners and propriety.

She understood it in a way I didn't. Helped me navigate it.

She convinced me I could be the kind of man who wanted this life.

Now, I don't know.

But then, I believed it. I believed I could belong in her world of manners and propriety. I believed I could be a gentleman who made love, not a man who fucks like an animal.

For the first time in my life, I didn't feel an ache in my chest, a tension in my shoulders, an empty spot deep inside me.

Then one day, she woke up, and she didn't love me anymore.

I'm not sure how long she went, how many months she spent trying to fall back in love with me, trying to convince herself to stay.

Only the day she left.

The look in her eyes as she pressed the ring into my palm.

I'm sorry, Ty, but I don't love you anymore.

Like it hurt her more than it hurt me. Like she wanted, more than anything, to still love me.

She just couldn't.

And now—

I'm not capable of love. Not anymore.

I won't fall for Indigo.

But I can take care of her.

I can earn her trust.

I can do everything in my power to give her a good life.

Support, orgasms, and ten million dollars.

It's not love, but it's something.

I only hope it's enough.

———

I wake early. Run the loop at Battery Park. Shower. Dress. Walk the five blocks to the office.

It's a cool day. Big grey clouds, soft white light, brisk air.

Spring weather is strange in New York. Some days the sun is blazing. Others, the sky fills with heavy raindrops.

It's a nice day. Temperate. But even in my office I can't get comfortable.

One minute, I'm burning. The next, I'm frozen.

Then Indigo arrives and I'm on fire.

Paloma introduces her. "Mr. Hunt, your fiancée is here." She squeals with pleasure. A love of gossip or an actual desire to see me happy?

I'm not sure.

"Mr. Hunt." Indigo raises a brow. "I remember when I called you that."

She's in a casual outfit today. Short boots, ripped jeans, a tight black top. The same pendant between her perfect tits.

I force my eyes to hers. "Do you miss it?"

"Mr. Hunt, whatever do you mean?"

"You know exactly what I mean."

"Do I?" She raises a brow. Crosses one leg over the other. "Or are you going to have to spell it out for me?"

Fuck. The image fills my head instantly.

Indigo, in my bed, in only her necklace, cooing *Mr. Hunt, what would you like tonight?*

Would you like to fuck me?

"Mr. Hunt? Can I help you? Or should I come back later?" Her voice drops to a teasing tone.

My thoughts stay in the gutter.

Thankfully, Paloma keeps me from giving in to my urges.

She steps inside. Places a tray of drinks on my desk. "I took the liberty of brewing the Yunnan Hong Cha when security informed me of your arrival."

Indigo shoots me a *really* look.

Really. Paloma is Paloma. She's always fast and attentive, but when it's my supposed fiancée, she's hovering.

"Has Mr. Hunt told you about our schedule for the afternoon?" Paloma smiles at Indigo. "I've got space booked at an independent department store. It's perfect for you. Bold and modern in a completely chic way."

All the color drains from Indigo's face. "You're taking me shopping?"

"I'll stay out of your way. I promise." She smiles and skips out of the room.

I close the door. "I'm sorry. She's—"

"Excited."

"Yes."

"She wants to see you happy," Indigo says.

Maybe it's that simple. Maybe I'm not trusting enough. "Did you look over the contract?"

"I did."

"And?"

She pulls a manila folder from her black purse. Sets it on my desk. To the right of her tea. "Signed." She pushes the paper toward me.

I pull out the contract. Find the dotted line. Sign my name.

She does the same with my copy of the contract.

And then it's official.

We're engaged.

Chapter Ten

INDIGO

My fate. On the dotted line. *Indigo Nicole Simms.* On our initial agreement.

A nondisclosure agreement.

A traditional prenup.

Another nondisclosure agreement.

All these little details. I stay in New York, but I come to London when he asks. Six times a year minimum, then I have free rein to refuse.

A reasonable allowance.

A credit card for incidentals.

A deadline for the wedding.

By the end of September.

I can stay with Sienna until then.

After that, I live with him.

Ten years at Tyler Hunt's beck and call.

Then we can renew the contract, part ways, or tear the thing in half and declare our love real.

He taps a few keys and it happens.

My cell buzzes. The screen flashes with an alert from my banking app.

New deposit in Checking.

A hundred thousand dollars.

In my account.

Fuck.

"Indie?" Concern drips into his voice. "Are you all right?"

I slide my cell into my purse. Place my hands in my lap. Attempt to copy his cool demeanor.

The second my eyes meet his, I lose my composure.

There's worry in his dark eyes.

He does care about me.

But I can't dwell on that if I want to survive this without falling for him.

I try to think of something to say. Some way to explain my current state.

I'm terrified.

And over the fucking moon.

There's a hundred grand in my bank account.

It's absurd.

Paloma saves me from articulating my thoughts.

She knocks. Enters with a take-out bag and a smile. Unpacks two salads in big plastic bowls. "I wasn't sure what you like, Indigo, so I ordered a Caesar and a Cobb. If neither of those work—"

"That's great, thank you." I'm not sure I can eat. My stomach is in free fall. My everything is in free fall. Ground, what ground? I'm flying.

She beams and skips out of the room.

Ty motions to the bowls *you first.*

I grab the Caesar. A fork. A tiny packet of pepper. "This isn't what I imagined when you said lunch." The bright green sticker bears the logo of a fast casual restaurant. Ten-dollar salads. Ordinary ingredients. Normal people food. Good for the price, but not the best. Not worthy of Tyler Hunt.

"I thought you'd appreciate the privacy." He taps a button under his desk and the blinds descend.

"I do. Thank you."

The fluorescent lights of the hallway fade. It's just the soft white of the cloudy sky.

It's beautiful. Flattering.

But then Ty always looks handsome in that powerful, untouchable way.

He's wearing a different suit today—a deep navy, not yesterday's black—and a complementary purple tie.

Blue and purple. Indigo.

That must be intentional. But I don't mention it.

I pop open my salad, tear the pepper, stir the dressing.

Ignore the tension in the air.

Already, I want to touch him. I want to climb across the desk, slide into his lap, run my fingers over his tie.

I want to feel his lips on my neck, his hands on my thighs, his cock—

"I know this is strange," he says. "It's strange for me too."

Is it? He seems so calm and in control.

"I want to make it easier if I can."

I'm not sure what he means, exactly. But I have to admit the money helps. Knowing I have that money in my bank account, knowing I have a solution to any problems that arise... it's everything. "I appreciate that."

"I don't want to push you in public." Intention drips into his voice. Only a hint.

But it's enough to make my cheeks flush. "What do you mean?" I ask.

"As soon as you leave, you're my fiancée. People don't know yet, but they will. We're going to spend the week making sure we're seen."

I can do that.

"We need to look like we're madly in love."

Of course. "I understand our ruse."

He nods. "Is there a line you don't want me to cross when we're in public?"

"Are you going to do something out of the ordinary?"

"Let's try this." He stands. Motions for me to follow.

When I do, he moves closer.

"It's been a long time since I kissed you." Ty takes another step toward me. Another. Until he's there. In my space.

I swallow hard. "So we need practice?"

He half-smiles as he slides one hand around my waist. "Yes."

"Should I take offense?"

"If you'd like." His fingers brush the hem of my tank top. "But it's not that you don't know how to kiss."

"Then what?"

"You're nervous." His fingertips skim my lower back. The bare skin between my tank top and jeans. "I am too."

He is?

He doesn't show it.

My thoughts evaporate as he brings his hand to my cheek.

His fingers skim my jawline.

Fuck, that feels good.

I forget our conversation. Lean into his touch.

It's pure reflex. My body responding for me.

He presses his hand into the small of my back. One inch at a time, my body melts into his.

Legs, hips, stomach, chest.

Lips.

A soft brush. A whisper of a kiss.

Then his hand curls around my neck and his lips find mine again.

Those soft lips. The taste of coffee and honey and Ty.

God, he tastes good.

He feels right. He still feels so fucking right.

My hands go to his shoulders. His back. The thick fabric of his suit jacket.

There's too much of it.

I need my hands on his skin.

I need his body against mine.

Now. Here. Everywhere.

My heart thuds as he pulls back.

I stare into his eyes for a split second. They're still dark and deep and intense. Like he needs me more than anything. Like he's going to devour me.

Then he blinks and the room rearranges.

He steps backward, taking my warmth with him. Taking that safe, soft, impossibly dangerous feeling with him.

"Good?" My heart thuds against my chest. I want to kiss him again. I'm terrified to kiss him again.

He nods. "Again?"

"Again," I agree.

This time, he's slower. More careful.

He slips his arm around my waist. Slides his hand into my hair.

He stares at me like he's madly in love with me.

I stare back. Trying to project some kind of affection.

But what does love look like?

I have vague memories of my parents' happiness.

Mom smiling *you're ridiculous* when Dad played *Purple Rain* for the tenth time that week.

The way he wrapped his arms around her as he asked her to dance.

The teasing tone of his voice when she complained takeout was too spicy.

And the devastation that claimed her when he died.

Months in bed. Still. Barely eating.

Barely managing to keep me and Sienna alive.

She never recovered. Not really.

She had most of a decade and she never recovered.

That's love.

The pain of losing someone.

I didn't love my high school boyfriend.

Or the guy I dated my freshman year of college.

He made me feel special. Until I fucked him and he threw me away. Like I was a cheap toy.

Ty didn't throw me away—he was always clear about his intentions—but he left.

He took some part of me with him.

Did I love him?

I don't know.

But I did want him. I do want him.

I know how to sell that.

I close my eyes. Try to soften my thoughts. Try to let my body take over.

My fingers curl into his neck.

God, his skin is so soft. And he smells so good. Earthy shampoo. And Ty.

I rise to my tiptoes.

He pulls my body into his.

His lips find mine. His tongue slips into my mouth. His fingers skim my lower back.

The strip of exposed skin between my tank top and my jeans.

He kisses me like he's claiming me. And I yield completely.

For a few beautiful seconds, the world is perfect.

Only the sweetness of his kiss and the safety of his body against mine.

Desire floods my body.

Every part of me is awake and alive.

Every molecule inside me wants the same thing: Him.
Now. Later. Forever.
"Perfect," he says.
It is.
I barely manage an inhale. I can feel it already.
My heart screaming *love him, love him, love him.*

Chapter Eleven

INDIGO

As promised, Paloma picks me up from Ty's office, helps me into a taxi, takes me to a modern department store.

White tiles and walls, black dividers, blinding yellow lights.

She leads me through rows of attire, assessing my outfit with a careful eye.

I'm not sure what she sees in my black tank top and skinny jeans, but it must be something, because she's brimming with enthusiasm.

"What speaks to you, Indigo?" She runs her fingers over the faux leather of my moto jacket. Studies my long chain necklace, my neat hair, my dramatic makeup.

"What speaks to me?"

"Your outfit. Why did you choose it?"

"It's comfortable."

"I do wish I could wear jeans." She taps her pencil skirt and shakes her head. "My ass looks fantastic, but can I run to catch the subway? Never." Her eyes pass over me again. Stop at my hair. "You're a musician?"

I don't call myself one. Not anymore. I haven't picked up my guitar in ages. I don't even sing along to the radio anymore.

Not since Mom died.

But I still live, eat, breathe music until it hurts and I have to stop.

"I play guitar," I say.

"And sing?"

I nod.

"You write songs?"

"I have."

"Is that what you want to do?"

"I don't know. I haven't had a lot of time for dreams recently." I still write songs sometimes. Lyrics. But they're too messy, too ugly.

No one wants my raw pain.

And I don't want to give it to anyone.

It's mine.

She makes this *mm-hmm* noise that's something between pity and sympathy. "What do you do for fun?"

"What's fun?"

"You're twenty-two."

"And you're so old?"

She smiles at the compliment. She looks around twenty-five, but between her boundless enthusiasm and her maternal demeanor, it's hard to place her age. "Mr. Hunt told me a little about your life."

I swallow hard. I don't like her knowing my business. But I have to get used to it. That comes with the tech mogul fiancé territory.

"I'm sorry," she says. "About your mother. I can't even imagine… if I lost my parents… I'm not sure I'd ever breathe again."

That's a good way of putting it.

"But you must blow off steam sometimes. Or you'd explode."

"I still go to shows. Go dancing."

"And your sister?"

"Yeah." My smile is involuntary. "We watch classic movies. Or reality TV. Or soccer. She plays."

"She's good?"

"Amazing."

"Is that enough? Or do you still feel… pent up?"

Sometimes. But I try not to think about it. And I don't want to talk to her about it.

Paloma seems nice, but she's not my friend. She's Ty's assistant.

"What does that have to do with clothes?" I ask.

"It's called conversation. Are you familiar?" She laughs. "You're a lot like Ty."

"How's that?"

"You don't suffer fools."

That is Ty to a T.

"I'm surprised he puts up with my enthusiasm."

"He needs a little enthusiasm."

She smiles. "He does." She looks me over again. "There's something about you… I can tell you have that in you."

"Enthusiasm?"

She nods. "A well of passion. One you only share with people you trust." She looks to a rack of black dresses. "You don't trust me. That's fine. But I have to imagine… you'll share it with him one day."

Maybe. Or maybe she's projecting.

"In any case, people are going to want to know your story," she says. "What will they say if you keep working at that awful bar?"

"What's wrong with being a waitress?"

"Nothing. But it's not you. And it's not…"

Fitting for someone of my new station. I know. That's in the contract too. I have to quit before my next shift.

"You want more. I can sense that. It's just there. Maybe it's your—"

"Resting bitch face?"

She laughs. "Dramatic features. You're very angular. And your haircut—"

"I like you so far, Paloma, but if you insult my haircut—"

"No." She smiles. "It's perfect for you. But it's not a low-effort style."

"So?"

"You blow dry it straight. You always wear winged eyeliner. Maybe you choose this outfit because it's comfortable, but you choose it intentionally too. Because you want to look a certain way."

"And what is that?"

Her eyes flit to my black boots. My jean-clad hips. My tight tank top. "You want to drive Mr. Hunt crazy."

"That's not really—"

"I organize Mr. Hunt's schedule. I schedule his dinners, send his gifts, cancel his morning appointments when he's indisposed. I'd know if you were seeing each other."

Oh.

"It's none of my business. I'm not going to pry. Even if I wanted to tell someone, the nondisclosure agreement I signed... I'd basically give up my firstborn." She looks me in the eyes. "Are you sleeping together?"

My cheeks flush. "Not now."

"But you have?"

"A few years ago. We spent the summer together."

She nods with recognition. "Of course. The girl from the bar. I've heard that story." She lowers her voice to a whisper. "You know how it is, working with rich men. You stay invisible. They forget you're there. You hear things."

I nod. "I pick up a lot. At the bar."

"Enough to go away for insider trading?"

"If I had the money for it."

She smiles. "You do now." She leads me into one of the mini-stores. "And people will talk. They'll see your ambition. If you don't have a story about what you're after, they'll think you're after his money."

"Is that so bad?"

"You want people calling you a gold digger?"

"Won't they? No matter what?"

Her frown drains the color from her face. "People will wonder why Ty is marrying you. If you stick with the down on your luck waitress story..."

They'll fill in the blanks. I'm marrying him for money. Or maybe because he knocked me up.

But that's worse. The idea that I somehow tricked him. Trapped him.

Which is bullshit—it takes two people to have sex, especially unprotected sex—even if it's hard to get mad at Ty for something that hasn't happened.

That would never happen—

He was adamant about using protection.

Is he still? Is he safe? He's been with a lot of women.

I shouldn't judge, I know, but it's hard not to feel irrelevant.

I've only been with two guys since Ty. One attempt at a boyfriend. And an ex from high school after my mother's funeral.

I thought it would help make me feel something, but instead I felt more alone.

"Ms. Simms? Are you all right?" Paloma pulls a jumpsuit from the rack. It's a long, black thing with a deep v-neck. Sexy. In a boss bitch way. "Have you thought about how you want to present yourself?"

"A rock star," I say. "I want to look like a rock star."

"Perfect." She smiles.

———

I HAVE TO HAND IT TO PALOMA—THE WOMAN KNOWS STYLE. She sends me to the dressing room. Pulls items. Asks me to model them.

I let her adorn me in jeans, blouses, t-shirts. Even a few sundresses.

Soft black fabric with a square neck and a high slit.

Short emerald chiffon.

Stiff white sateen.

Then clothes for dinners. She deems jumpsuits perfect. Formal but rebellious. A *fuck you* to the rich men who expect women to wear dresses at all times.

I change into a fuchsia one-piece with a high neckline and a low back.

Sleek silk.

Expensive enough to cover two weeks of rent.

Is it me? I don't know. I trust Paloma to tell me if it fits into Ty's world, but she doesn't know me. Not really.

I pull out my cell. Snap a pic for Sienna.

She responds right away.

Sienna: OMFG, Indie! Explanation.

Indigo: Am I pulling it off?

Sienna: Mr. London is dressing you. It's a sick fetish of his.

Indigo: Uh-huh.

Sienna: It's a pretty sweet fetish. For you. You can get a lot of free stuff out of it! What's that cost? Oh my god, don't tell me. Not until it's in the closet and we can put it on ThreadUp.

Indigo: Since when do you know about ThreadUp?

Sienna: Since always. Where do you think we live? And yes! You look hot. You just need some dramatic makeup to match. And shoes. But, no offense, Indie, can you walk in heels?

Indigo: I've worn them to work.

Sienna: And sprained your ankle.

Indigo: Only the one time.

She's right, of course. I can barely walk in heels.

But it's not like I'm planning to walk in these clothes.

Or wear them for long. Necessarily.

Indigo: I'll figure it out.

Sienna: Has he seen it?

Indigo: Not yet.

Sienna: You're seeing him again?

Indigo: I am.

Sienna: I want you home at the crack of dawn. Not a second sooner.

Indigo: Maybe I want to make him wait.

Sienna: Carpe Diem, Indie. You might die tomorrow. Would you rather die satisfied or horny?

A laugh spills from my lips. God, I love her so much. She's just... Sienna. Loud and brash and completely sure of what matters in life (soccer, sex, sugary drinks, in that order).

Talking to her, I can imagine Ty is some rich guy I like.

Maybe I can hold on to that. To some hint of normalcy. Something.

I *do* want this to be a surprise. But I want to tease him too.

I turn to the mirror. Hold out my cell.

Try a few angles. *Click, click, click.*

There. This picture is perfect. The slope of my shoulder. The line of the fabric falling to my lower back.

I hit send.

He responds immediately.

Ty: Gorgeous.

My cheeks flush.

I'm glad I'm here, in the privacy of this tiny dressing room, the door blocking out the prying eyes of Ty's assistant.

But then—

I want him here. Stripping me out of my clothes. Running his hands over my body. Issuing dirty demands.

Ty: Are you showing that off tonight? Or something else?

Indigo: It's a surprise.

He isn't asking enough. He isn't as desperate as I am.

I need him desperate.

So I do away with the jumpsuit. Try on the lingerie Paloma pulled for me. Snap a picture of the sheer black lace.

It's only a sliver of my skin. My nose to the top of my breast. The black strap. The hint of lace. The Latin quote on my shoulder.

alis volat propris

She flies by her own wings.

Reversed by the camera's mirror.

There.

I don't think. I send.

My blush deepens. My sex clenches.

I grip my phone tighter.

It buzzes against my fingers, sending desire to every molecule of my body.

Ty: Are you trying to tease me, baby?

The pet name makes my sex clench. I can hear it on his tongue. I can feel his hands on my skin.

Indigo: If I am?

My heart thuds against my chest. I close my eyes and see it.

His tie around my wrists, his lips on my neck, his hand on my ass.

Ty: This is the only warning I'm going to give you, Indie. If you don't want to play this game, stop now. Because once you start, I'm not going to stop until you're screaming my name.

Chapter Twelve

TY

All afternoon, I think of Indigo.

The deep purple-red of her lips. The long curve of her neck. The delicate strap of her lingerie.

Is she wearing it now? Under that thin black tank top?

Matching knickers under her torn jeans.

Or maybe the gorgeous backless number.

Or some dress designed specifically to drive me out of my mind.

Who am I kidding? I'm already out of my mind. This entire plan, this idea—it's crazy.

I can hear my brother's voice in my head. Mocking me the way I've mocked him.

One heartbreak and you're giving up on love? You're tougher than that, Ty.

A year ago, I'd have rolled my eyes. Asked him who the fuck he was to give me advice, since he reacted to his divorce by moving across the Atlantic and putting an expiration date on every one of his arrangements.

Then he met Eve. Fell in love. Started singing the praises of trust and devotion.

It's horribly annoying.

Even if she's perfect for him. Sharp, wounded, smart enough to challenge him.

She's a lot like Indigo. They have the same *don't fuck with me* attitude born and bred in New Yorkers. Only it runs deeper. Enough, it informs their worldview, bleeds into their taste in art and music.

Eve is passionate about words, books, *The Handmaid's Tale* especially. She's something between a fan and a critic. She usually acts more like a thirty-year-old than a nineteen-year-old, but the teen in her breaks free when she discusses her favorite book.

I know her taste. Her life. Her routine.

I know my brother's girlfriend better than I know my fiancée.

But I want to know her.

To fix her favorite breakfast every morning, watch her groan over her tea, listen to her sing along with her favorite album.

Is it still *Back to Black*?

Or has she found something new in the last three years?

I don't know her life. Not enough.

I know she loves spicy food. That she doesn't care for sweets. That she lives and breathes music.

Loves her sister more than anything.

Enough she watches entire football games.

It's not enough. I want more. Every drop of her world.

I want it the way I want to strip her out of her lingerie.

It clouds my judgment. Makes my thoughts hazy.

I finish work. Text Paloma on my way to the restaurant.

Ty: Are you finished?

Paloma: Almost. I'll send her to the bar when she's ready. Feed her well. It's been a long day.

Ty: You think I don't know how to take care of my fiancée?

Paloma: There's something else on your mind. Before food.

A laugh escapes my lips. She's rarely this direct with me. It must be something about Indigo.

No, there is something about Indigo.

I need to protect her. Even though she's tall and tough and strong.

Especially because she's tall and tough and strong.

She's right, of course.

That picture. It's still right there, on my cell, begging for all my attention.

But she hasn't replied yet.

And I fight fair.

Victory is only sweet if it's earned.

I want to win this game. But first, I need her to agree to play.

———

I ARRIVE EARLY. CLAIM A TABLE IN THE CORNER. ONE WITH enough privacy for conversation, but enough visibility someone will see us.

This restaurant isn't my favorite, but the food is good, the drinks are strong, the view is gorgeous.

Even I appreciate the soft glow of sunset.

New York may not be London, but it's beautiful all the same.

I can already see the passion in Indie's eyes, hear her gasp, feel the tremble of excitement—

Fuck, I need my head in the game.

I order a Manhattan. Thank the waitress when she returns.

She smiles, bats her eyelashes, lingers at the table.

Small talk.

Because she wants a better tip? Or because she wants to fuck me?

Usually, I can tell. Right now, I'm too tuned to Indie. I don't give a fuck what this woman wants.

She calls all my attention as she appears at the entrance.

Long legs. Patent leather. A thick silver bracelet on a delicate wrist.

Indigo steps into the restaurant in a short black dress and knee-high boots.

Fuck. All the breath leaves my body at once.

The neckline cuts between her breasts, ending in a sharp v beneath her chest.

How the fuck is that thing staying on?

It needs to be on my floor.

She needs to be in my lap.

The world needs to make sense. And that's the only thing that does.

The waitress turns. Follows my gaze.

Gasps. Or maybe it's a sigh.

I can't tell. I don't care.

My entire universe is Indigo. Her deep blue eyes. Her wine lips. Her long legs.

She spots me. Flashes the world's most dazzling smile as she crosses the room.

"Ty." She sets her purse—some tiny rectangular thing—on the table. "You look gorgeous."

"Gorgeous again?"

She nods *of course*. Looks to the waitress, unsure why the woman is here.

But Indigo is smart. She slips into her role right away.

"A Manhattan." She smiles. "However he's having it." She nods a thank you.

The waitress pouts as she leaves.

I stand. Wrap my arms around Indie. "And here I was going for dapper."

She releases me. Smiles. "You're just too pretty."

"Not compared to you."

She watches the waitress leave. "She was flirting with you."

"Women always flirt with me."

"Should I be jealous?" She reaches for the chair.

I shake my head. Motion to the booth.

She nods *of course*. Sits.

I take the spot next to her. Stay close enough my knee brushes hers. Close enough I feel the heat of her skin. Even through the thick fabric of my slacks.

I slip my hand around her waist. Pull her into a slow kiss.

Her hand goes to my chest. Her fingers dig into my shirt, pressing the soft fabric into my skin.

My head spins. My thoughts cloud.

I need her.

I almost believe I love her.

But I don't. I'm not capable.

She pulls back with a sigh. Looks around the restaurant, suddenly shy.

"It's quiet here," I say. "We can talk about anything."

She nods with understanding. "What would we talk about? If someone was listening?"

It's a fair question. Soon, we'll be dining with friends and colleagues. Attending larger events.

Those don't worry me.

Dinner with her sister, Ian, even my cousin Cam—

They know us. Know what we look like happy.

It matters if they catch us in a lie.

If we lose their trust.

"We've been dating in secret a few months," I say.

"We have?"

I nod. "There must be happy memories."

"Ah, yes." She nods. "I loved that day in April. We were caught in the rain. Went into a coffee shop to get warm. Gave up on drying off to go back to your place and made love."

"Made love?" I raise a brow.

"We went to your place to fuck." Her eyes meet mine. "So you could fuck me."

My balls tighten.

"Is that more appropriate?"

"Truer."

"It never happened."

"It could."

Her eyes flit to my lips, chin, shoulders, thighs. "Is that the reputation you want?"

"A man who satisfies his wife?"

"Is that what people will say?"

No. Of course not.

It doesn't matter what she thinks, what she wants, how badly she craves a rough touch—

People will come to their own conclusions.

When someone like Shep—a CFO from a respected family, who's also the spitting image of Prince Eric—gains a reputation for a rough touch, it's fun gossip.

When it's someone like me—

It's still fun gossip. But instead of *boys will boys,* it's *you know what those people are like; they're animals.*

She's right, but I'm not going to claim I *make love.* That's ridiculous.

"What would you call it?" I ask.

"Who would ask?"

"Your sister?"

"Sienna is obsessed with sex."

"So you'd tell her?"

"Of course not." She brings the glass to her lips. Marks it with her lipstick.

"If a friend asked?"

"Meghan... this girl at the bar, she's the closest thing I have to a good friend. We go dancing after work sometimes. But I wouldn't trust her with this."

"What kind of music?"

"Anything."

"You still love everything?"

"Yes. But you know my favorite."

"Wounded female singer-songwriters?"

"They're all wounded. They have to be," she says. "Or they're pushed into pop music. Women are either spilling their guts or praising partying."

"Are men different?"

"Probably not."

"But they don't move you?"

She smiles. "Are you going to bring up The Kinks again?"

"They're iconic."

"I appreciate it. For what it is." Enthusiasm spreads over her expression.

She still adores music.

Fuck, it does something to me. Something I haven't felt in a long time.

"I have found some new favorites," she says. "I only listen to *Back to Black* twice a day now."

"It always makes me think of you."

"You listen to Amy Winehouse?"

"She's British."

"You don't say?" she teases.

"We're proud of our singers."

"Even when your paparazzi pushed them to destruction?"

"Especially. Who's more loved than Princess Di?"

She stares at me, feigning confusion.

"I know. Before your time."

"You explained it to me." She smiles. "I get it. Kind of."

The waitress interrupts with her drink. "Another?" When I nod, she looks to Indigo. "And are you two dining with us tonight? Or just the drinks?"

Indigo's eyes find mine. She raises a brow. "You haven't ordered yet."

"I didn't want to be presumptuous."

Her lips curl into a sly smile. "We'd love menus when you have a chance. And water. Thanks."

The waitress nods and disappears.

Indigo motions to her drink. "I owe you a sip."

"I still have half of this one."

She nods *so you do*. Wraps her fingers around her drink. Takes a long, slow sip.

"What do you do? When you aren't listening to music?"

"Or dancing with strange men?"

"Do you?"

"Does it make you jealous?" When I don't answer, she smiles. "What a hypocrite."

Yes, but no sense dwelling on that. "What else do you do?"

"Mostly, I hang out with Sienna. She makes me jog. Even during soccer season." She sticks out her tongue in distaste. "But she cooks after. And she's a wiz with pasta."

My lips curl into a smile

Someone is taking care of her.

Someone loves her.

She needs that.

I need her to have that.

"Then, we'll watch TV," she continues. "Sometimes a rerun of something trashy. *90 Day Fiancé* or *America's Next Top Model*. Mostly soccer." She laughs. "It's football, I know. I forget that about you."

"You forget the rest of the world calls it football?"

"That you used to play." She takes another sip. Sighs as she swallows. "Fuck, this is really good."

"Still your favorite?"

"Yes. But I'm still a... what do you call it?"

"Irresistible?"

Her cheeks flush. "Without a refined palate. Bourbon all tastes the same to me. Even the bottles that cost more than your suit."

"You know what you like. No shame in that."

"No." Her eyes flit to my tie. "No shame in that." Intent drips into her voice.

Neither one of us is talking about bourbon.

Both of us are imagining that tie around her wrists.

But she says nothing. Just takes another sip and sets her drink on the table.

"We should go to a game," I say. "The three of us."

"She'd like that. She'll love you. Not that it takes a lot."

"My ego." I press my palm into my side as if I'm mortally wounded.

She smiles. "Your ego is big enough."

"Is it?"

She nods. "You can pull off a lot, Ty. Man who doesn't know he's handsome isn't on the list. One look at you and Sienna would approve."

"I'm hot enough for your sister?"

She laughs. "That is what I said, isn't it?"

"It is."

Her expression stays easy. "It's true. She's eighteen."

"And obsessed with sex?"

"Very. She likes guys if they're attractive. And she already likes you. The idea of you."

"What does she know?"

"I had a fling with a rich guy from London. And now, I'm on a date with him. None of the other details." Her cheeks flush. She's teasing.

I need to tease her back. "Which would you tell her? If she wasn't your sister."

Her gaze flits to my tie. "I wouldn't. I want those details for myself."

Blood rushes south.

"I haven't… I've been with two other guys since you. Neither of them was important to me. Neither one of them took your place."

"My place?"

"Who I think about. When I touch myself." Her fingers brush my thigh. "Do you think of me?"

"Of course." I wrap my fingers around her wrist. Hold her hand where it is, against my thigh.

I can't have her touching me. Not yet.

I'll tell her when she's allowed to touch me.

I tighten my grip. Not hard enough to hurt. Only hard enough she knows I can overpower her. If she wants me to.

Not yet.

After I earn her trust.

The waitress interrupts with our next round. Clears her throat. "I'll come back if you're not ready."

Under the table, I release Indigo's wrist. "I'm ready. Are you?"

She nods *yes*, still in a daze. "I am starving."

I order the seared sea bass. Point to the item she'll like best. A spicy seafood pasta.

She repeats the words. Passes back the menu with a smile. Waits until the waitress is out of earshot.

"I do get jealous." She brings her drink to her lips. Takes a long sip. "Of the other women. Not just now. Before. And when you were with her." She sets her drink on the table.

There have been a lot of women. I was with Rory for a long time.

The women didn't matter, but Rory—

There's nothing I can say to soothe Indigo. Nothing true. I was in love with Rory. I wanted to spend my entire life with her.

I would have done anything to make that happen.

Then she broke my heart. Took it with her.

"You loved her. I know that." Her eyes find mine. "And you'll never love me. I know that too." She pauses. "But this..." Her fingers skim my tie. "You don't do it with your *friends*. With her?"

"I told you—"

"I asked. You didn't answer." She runs her fingers up my tie, over the knot, along my neck. "I told you the truth. That you were the only one. That's all I want from you. The truth."

"The truth?"

"Yes." She nods. "You knew what you were doing when we met. You knew what you wanted."

I did.

"So tell me. Was I the first? The last? Or just another in a long line?" She licks her lips. "Will it mean anything to you"—her fingers skim my thigh—"if I close my eyes and promise to obey? Or will I be another girl you tied to your bed?"

Chapter Thirteen

TY

Fuck. She's winning and she's not even trying.

I sift through the details. There were women before her. And after.

Rory was the only one who mattered.

And I wanted her. I did. I wanted to possess her in every way I could.

She was a good girl from a nice family. Accommodating, sweet, willing to try.

But not interested in anything out of the ordinary.

"There were others before you," I say.

"How many?"

"Does that matter?"

Indie holds my gaze.

"A few. It always interested me, but it scared me too." It still does. The man I became with her. Rough. Brutal. Willing to do anything. "And it scared her."

"Rory?"

I nod. Push aside memories of the fear in her eyes. The tremble of her chest. The shakiness in her voice. "We found a middle ground."

"And that was enough for you?"

"Yes." I thought so. I loved her. And I loved making her come.

So what if she didn't appreciate a rough touch?

I didn't appreciate ballet.

We both made compromises.

That's what grown-ups do.

It was enough. I told myself it was enough. I believed it. Now—

I don't know. Maybe something was missing.

Maybe that's why she left.

"I missed it," I say. "But I was satisfied." The words don't feel true, but that's ridiculous.

I never considered leaving her.

I wasn't going to be that man. The one who traded his wife for a newer, younger, more adventurous model every ten years.

I was committed.

And that mattered more than anything.

Being there. Living up to the promises I made her.

Being what she needed.

Indigo's voice is soft. "And since Rory… have you?"

"No."

"What if I said I wasn't interested?"

"Are you going to lie to me?"

Her cheeks flush. "Hypothetically."

"You wouldn't."

"But what if I did? What if we stayed married forever and I wouldn't fuck you?"

"What are you asking?"

"Well…" She presses her lips together. "Would there be someone else?"

"No. Never."

Her eyes meet mine. "I believe you. You would deny that part of yourself. Even if it killed you."

"I have a hand."

A laugh spills from her lips. "Yes. I've experienced it." She takes a long sip. "I haven't agreed to fuck you, you know."

"Yes, you have."

"I haven't agreed to obey."

"You know what happens when I have to repeat myself."

"I... uh..." She pushes past her blush. "Were you ever tempted? With Rory?"

I shake my head.

"Even though she didn't fill your needs?"

Fuck, how does she state it so plainly?

I can barely admit the idea to myself. And she says it like it's the weather. Like it's obvious to anyone with half a brain.

"I guess... I don't know what that's like. I've never been in love. You were the closest I came," she says. "And that was the most I came. With you."

"You need it rough?"

"I don't know. I haven't trusted anyone else enough to really try."

"But you've enjoyed fucking other men?"

"Will you get jealous if I say yes?"

"Yes."

"It was better with you. If that's what you're asking." Defiance fills her expression. "It was always better with you. But you already knew that."

When we were together three years ago, sure.

But I don't know what she's done.

Who she's fucked.

How hard she's come.

"Did you enjoy it?" I ask.

"Yes," she says. "But not as much as I enjoyed you fucking me."

My veins buzz. She's daring me.

She's pushing every one of my buttons.

"These other guys?" I ask. "What did you want from them?"

"Which ones?"

Fuck. "The last one?"

"An ex… it was one time. Rushed. Not satisfying."

"Before that?"

"I dated a guy for a while. Noah."

"What was he like?"

"Sweet. Funny. Tall."

"Tall?"

She laughs. "Yes."

"He must have been a fascinating man. If tall is his third descriptor."

"You're still jealous." She smiles. "I kind of like it."

I'm too fucking jealous. I want to kill him.

Because he's touched her.

Because he groaned her name.

Because he was capable of loving her.

She smiles. "I should milk this for all it's worth. Since I only have the one ex-boyfriend."

"And these other guys."

She nods. "I didn't think you'd be jealous."

Me either. But here we are.

"I really shouldn't tell you the truth," she says. "But I will. Because… that will make this easier. If we're honest when we're alone."

It might. Or the truth might hurt her. "Is that a promise?"

"What would it be? I'll never lie to you? That seems unreasonable."

It does.

"I'll try. To be honest. And you try. The best you can."

"Even if it hurts?"

Her gaze goes to the table for a moment. She's stays quiet as she considers it. Then she nods. "If it matters."

"If it matters." I hold out my hand.

She shakes. "The boyfriend... it was short. He was sweet. Too sweet. When I asked him to go harder, rougher—he couldn't do it. And that was the end."

"You broke up right there?" The image flits through my head immediately.

Indigo in her apartment, in a tiny twin bed, in black lingerie. Some clean-cut All-American guy kissing her as he slips his hand between her legs.

Jumping backward as she asks him to spank her or slap her or tie her up. Dressing. Leaving.

"No," she says. "But we didn't recover. He looked at me differently."

"Like there was something wrong with you?"

She nods. "Is that what it was like? With Rory?"

No. It was worse. The fear in her voice. The disgust in her eyes. Like I was a monster. "It scared her."

"Right. You said that." She taps her glass. "These *are* going to my head."

"You should eat something."

"We already ordered."

I don't care. I'm overwhelmed with the urge to take care of her. Wrap my arms around her. Carry her into my bed. Keep her safe.

She presses on. "You could have found someone who shared your interests. A professional, even. *"*

"I invited you here, didn't I?"

Her eyes brighten. "Is that it? Why you want me?"

"Part of it." I haven't admitted that, even to myself, but it's true.

I've had that craving for a long time. And no way to feed it.

She holds my gaze until the waitress drops off our food.

I finish my last sip. "I do like you. I enjoy your company."

"My company?" She raises a brow as she picks up her fork. "I can imagine."

"I hope you do."

She half-smiles. "I like you too." She swirls a strand of pasta on her fork. Brings it to her lips. "Whatever that means."

I'm not sure what it means. If it means anything.

It's been a long time since I've liked a woman. Since I've considered liking a woman.

And now it's Indie. The woman I'm going to marry.

We're committed to ten years together and we're only at *I like you*.

But that's all I can offer her. It's not fair to ask for more.

Or promise more.

Only this.

———

I PUSH THE CONVERSATION TO SAFER TOPICS. HER SISTER. Her hatred of jogging. Her love of Carole King.

She groans over her pasta. Accepts bites of my seared fish and sautéed spinach. Teases me about ordering something so healthy.

"Always in control." She finishes her last sip. "Always restrained." Her eyes pass over me slowly. "Until you aren't."

My balls tighten.

She's daring me. She knows better.

So I tease her back as we order tea and dessert.

Indie doesn't like sweets, not really, but she still groans over the rich chocolate torte.

She takes tiny bites between sips of her hand rolled black tea from China.

The best. For her.

Always.

When we finish, I pay, make a show of helping Indigo to her feet, walking her to the door, all the way to the car I have reserved.

"A limo." Her eyes meet mine. She moves a half-step closer. "Is that really what you think would impress me?"

"No." I wrap my arm around her. Hold her close. So she won't stumble. "But I have to do something to make sure you get home safely."

"You don't think I can handle it?"

"I know you can." I open the door for her. "But this way I can offer to ride with you."

"Oh."

"Is that what you want?"

Her chest heaves.

"Do you want to go home alone?" My eyes fix on hers. "Or do you want me to come with you?"

Chapter Fourteen

INDIGO

Do *you want me to come with you?*

What a question.

Of course. I want him to come with me. I want him to press me against this limo, peel my panties to my ankles, fuck me right here, on the street, in front of everyone.

I don't care about the consequences or the risks or the practicalities.

Only the satisfaction of his body over mine.

But what was it he said?

Once he starts, he won't stop. It's true for both of us.

My body is already begging me to relent. It doesn't care that he's going to break my heart. That it's hard enough kissing him in public without falling for him.

After three drinks, my inhibitions are fuzzy.

The voice in my head, the one that's supposed to say *do the smart thing, protect your heart, keep it far, far away from Tyler Hunt*—

It's a whisper. Nothing compared to my body screaming *yes, now, more.*

I want him. So badly. And I'm tired of saying no to what I want.

"Yes." My fingers dig into his jacket. "I do."

He presses his palm into my lower back, pulling my body into his.

His eyes close. His lips find mine.

He tastes like bourbon and chocolate and Ty. And, fuck, I need that.

I need him.

I pull back with a sigh.

He stares back at me. "You remember what I said?"

He won't fuck me until I beg him.

At the moment, I'm ready to drop to my knees. Plead, grovel, promise the moon. It doesn't matter. As long as his body joins mine.

Does that mean he wins?

Those are his rules. I have my own.

I win if he fucks me.

"I remember," I say.

He helps me inside.

It's the first time I've been in a limo.

It's smaller than I expected, but bigger and grander too.

A long bench runs into a short one. Soft carpet covers the floor. A moonroof—or is it a sunroof—closed, but clear enough it lets in the soft blue light of the sky.

That perfect New York City blue.

Ty slides next to me. The space is too small for him—he's at least six two and his build is athletic. His head nearly hits the roof. His legs bend too high.

Somehow, he manages to look imposing rather than awkward. Or maybe that's just Ty.

God, he's so sexy. My body remembers the feel of his hands, the taste of his lips, the pressure of his cock against my walls.

I want it. All of it. Whatever he'll give me.

"The lights?" Ty taps a switch next to the door.

"Don't." I motion to the sunroof. "I like it like this."

"The light of the city."

I nod.

He follows my gaze. The car starts. The edges of skyscrapers blur together. All blue and yellow and grey steel. "You always loved the view in my flat."

Of course. And I want to see it again.

But he didn't invite me to his apartment. And I'm afraid to ask.

I'm not ready to be there, in his space, in his life. To see if he lives in the same apartment or someplace grander. To see if the room is filled with touches of his ex-fiancée or completely barren. To see if he's made a separate room for me or if he expects me to sleep in his bed.

"The partition blocks sound. But if you want more privacy." He motions to a stereo system.

I nod.

He taps the screen a few times. The area fills with a familiar electronic sound.

Depeche Mode.

The album I picked out the first time he fucked me.

He remembers.

My chest warms. My stomach flutters. My head fills with ideas. Ideas I can't afford.

This isn't love. This is sex.

That's all.

I suck a breath through my teeth. Turn toward him. So my knee brushes the outside of his thigh. "It's been a long time for me."

He nods with understanding.

"What was it you said three years ago? That you'd ruin me for other men."

His eyes go wide. He forgot. Or didn't think I remembered.

"You were right." I arch my back, pushing my chest forward. My breasts strain against the stiff fabric of my dress. This isn't a neckline designed for movement. More for him pulling the straps off my shoulders. "No one else compares. No one ever will."

He studies me, all softness and curiosity, then he swallows and the softness disappears. He changes into that other version of Ty.

The one only I know.

The one I imagine when I stroke myself to orgasm.

"Take off your knickers." His voice shifts too. Still steady and in control. But dripping with equal parts need and demand.

I press my knees together, lift my hips, slide my panties off my feet.

"The dress too." His voice stays that steady, in control tone. "Now."

"Help me." I turn so my back is to him.

His fingers skim the zipper, then he pulls it down, all the way to the small of my back.

He traces its line back up my spine. Then down again. Even more softly. So softly I can barely feel his touch.

Fuck, that feels good. Too good.

He's being gentle with me.

Too gentle.

I can't take that. I can't take the romantic implications.

I need rough to keep my head straight.

I need him to take control.

How can I give him more control?

Everything in my life is dictated by someone else. The mortgage my parents signed. The aid colleges offer. The dress code at work.

But that's different.

I don't ask assholes from the bank to control me.

I don't give them permission.

With Ty—

I do.

Ty traces the line again. Only harder. Harder. Until there's no tenderness.

Only promise.

"You remember your safe word?" he asks.

My breath catches in my throat. "Will I need it?"

"You'll always need it."

Because it's sensible to be ready to stop? Or because he's going to push me constantly? I'm not sure.

"Indigo." His voice is impatient. "Do you remember?"

Of course I remember. "Azure," I whisper.

In response, he hooks his fingers around the strap of my dress and pushes it off my shoulder.

The right. Then the left.

My breasts spill from the fabric. His hands find them immediately. He pulls me into his lap, so my back is against his chest, my ass against his cock.

He's hard. I can feel him through his slacks. It wakes something inside me. Some primal sense I've forgotten.

I need him. I need him so badly.

"Ty," I breathe. "Please."

He brings his lips to my neck. Places a tender kiss there.

It's soft, so soft I can barely feel it.

Then harder.

The hint of his teeth.

"Your hair is shorter now." His teeth scrape my neck. "Do I need to worry about bruises?"

Does he need to what? I try to find the thread of my thoughts, but they're unspooled. I'm a puddle of desire.

My neck. Bruises. Should he worry about leaving a mark?

No. I don't want to worry about anything. Only about obeying his commands.

"I have makeup," I say.

"Is it enough? You bruise easily."

"You remember that?"

"I remember everything."

It's too sweet. Too much. Too close to *I love you.* "Send me a scarf, then. I'll figure it out."

He scrapes his teeth against my neck again. Softly. "I've wanted to do this since I saw you." He brushes my hair behind my ear. Traces the line it leaves against my chin. "Your haircut drives me out of my mind." He bites me again, a little harder. "Like you're offering your neck to me."

"Ty…"

He slips his hand around my neck. Cups my chin. Holds me in place as he scrapes his teeth against my flesh. "You want me to bite you, baby?"

"Yes."

"Yes, sir."

My sex clenches. We didn't do that before, but now it's the only thing I want. "Yes, sir."

He does. Softly to start. Then harder. Harder.

Hard enough I groan.

My eyes flutter closed. My head falls to the side, into his hand.

He has me.

I trust him.

It terrifies me and thrills me in equal measure. I'm in his lap, halfway out of my clothes, groaning as he runs his teeth over my skin, and the only thing I want is more.

He tugs the other strap off my shoulder. Pushes the dress to my waist.

I lift my hips to help him. Then it's gone. A heap on the floor. And I'm in his lap, naked except for my boots, my bare skin against the soft fabric of his suit.

He holds my body against his. Shifts his hips just enough, I feel his cock against my ass.

"Please." It falls off my lips. "Please, Ty. Please fuck me."

"Not tonight." He wraps his hand around my wrist. Brings my palm to the back of the bench seat. Just outside his torso. "This stays here. Understand?"

I nod.

He does the same thing with my other hand. Then his lips find my neck. Soft kisses. Then harder. The scrape of his teeth.

This sharp burst of pain. Only enough I feel it. Only enough it mixes with the anticipation flooding my body. Only enough I need him more.

"Please." I don't know what I'm asking. Only that I want it.

He bites me as he brings his hands to my chest. He cups my breasts with his palms. Groans as he runs his thumbs over my nipples. "Fucking beautiful."

I let my eyes fall closed again. Let my body flood with that perfect mix of pain, pleasure, need, anticipation.

He toys with me. Soft circles, hard zigzags, the barely there pressure of his index finger.

I gasp as he runs his digit over my nipple. "Fuck. Ty." I reach for something. Find his suit jacket.

Instantly, his hand is on my wrist. "Do I have to bind you? So you behave?"

Fuck. My sex clenches. "Yes."

"Bad girl." He rolls my nipple through his thumb and forefinger. It's hard enough it hurts.

But that only winds me tighter.

He releases me to undo the knot of his tie. He pulls my

arms over my head. Loops the tie around my wrists. Attaches it to the headrest.

It's not the world's best binding. It's not tight enough to really stop me, but it's enough to remind me I'm under his control.

He tests the knot. When I groan, he purrs, "Good girl."

My sex clenches. It's wrong. How much I crave this compliment meant for a child or a pet. But I can't bring myself to care. Not right now.

Again, Ty holds my body against his. Brings his lips to my neck. Kisses a line to my shoulder.

Then back up to my jaw.

He turns my head enough his mouth finds mine. I part my lips to make way for his tongue.

He kisses me hard, swirling his tongue around mine, claiming me as his.

Right now, I am.

After this, I don't know. But right now, I'm exactly where I'm supposed to be.

He scrapes his teeth against my lower lip. Then he releases me. Kisses a line over my jaw, down my neck, along my shoulder.

He presses his palm into my pelvis, so I feel his cock against my ass.

"Please," I groan. I need that. Need him. Now.

He responds by pressing harder.

I rock my hips, grinding my ass against his flesh. All that fabric between us, but still, he feels so fucking good.

He groans into my neck. "Do you want to come?"

"Yes."

"Yes?"

"Yes, sir."

"Then stop trying to tease me. I'm not fucking you tonight, Indigo." His fingers skim my thigh. "Understand?"

I nod.

"Now, baby, do you want to come on my hand?"

"Yes, sir."

"Say it."

"Please, sir." My chest heaves with my inhale. "Please make me come."

He murmurs a *yes* into my neck. Keeps one hand on my thigh. Brings the other to my breast. Toys with me, soft brushes of his thumb against my nipple.

He's still hard against me. And I still want that so fucking badly.

But I need this.

I need his hands on my body.

I close my eyes. Utter another 'please'." Let my head fall to one side.

He runs his finger over my inner thigh. A soft line.

Closer. Closer. Closer.

There.

His index finger brushes my clit. The middle, ring, pinkie, thumb.

I spread my legs a little wider.

He rakes his teeth against my neck. "Open your eyes."

I do. The soft blue light floods my senses.

"Watch."

My eyes go to our reflection. Of course. The limo has mirrored walls.

Our reflection is distorted, but still, I can see me splayed out for him. Me, naked, except for my boots. Him in that navy suit.

His hand between my legs.

My wrists bound by his tie.

I almost come on the spot. It's not the first time I've caught our reflection—his apartment was all mirrors and windows—but it's the first time he's asked me to watch.

The first time I've felt so completely at his mercy.

Before, we were two people who wanted satisfaction. He was rich, and I was broke, yes, but there wasn't any expectation.

Now, we've made promises. Signed on the dotted line.

Now, if I defy him, he might use his power to crush me.

The knot inside me tightens.

He's barely touching me, and I'm already so close. So desperately near the edge.

He knows me, knows how to toy with me.

But I know him too.

"Please." Through the mirror, I make eye contact. "Please, sir, make me come."

His pupils dilate. His grip around my throat tightens. Enough I gasp.

Then his first two fingers are on my clit and I can only groan.

Fuck.

He doesn't tease. Doesn't toy. Doesn't explore me the way he once did.

He finds the spot where I need him and draws slow circles on my tender flesh.

Again and again.

Winding me tighter and tighter.

It's too much. My eyes close. I remind myself to open them. Watch him draw those slow circles. Watch him scrape his teeth against my neck.

Watch him hold me in place. By the throat. The most vulnerable part of my body, completely at his mercy.

And it feels so fucking good.

A groan falls from my lips. Then another.

He rubs me harder.

Harder.

There.

"Ty," I breathe his name. "Fuck."

Those same slow circles. Again and again.

Then he sinks his teeth into my neck and I go over the edge. The tension in my core unspools, sending pleasure to my fingers and toes.

Bliss overwhelms me. My world goes white. Then it's that perfect, soft blue. The New York City night sky. Warm and pure and perfect.

Ty rubs me through my orgasm. Then he releases me. Undoes the binding on my wrists. Helps me into my dress.

Not the panties. He leaves those on the floor.

I return to my senses slowly. The music is still going. The car isn't moving.

We're in front of my apartment.

How long have we been here? When did we stop?

I don't know. I don't care.

I'm still buzzing.

"This is you." He picks up my purse. Pulls the door open. "Should I walk you up?" He raises a brow. *Or will there be too many questions?*

I'm not sure. But I'm barely coherent. I'm not ready to explain this to my sister. Not the truth. And not a lie. "Next time."

"No." He presses his lips to mine. "Next time, you're coming home with me."

Chapter Fifteen

INDIGO

Sienna shakes her head as I step inside. She points to the clock. "Not even midnight."

"Thank you for the concern." It's true. It's not quite tomorrow, but it's late, and—"It's a school night. Go to bed."

She pouts.

"I know, I know. I'm not Mom. You don't have to do what I say."

She frowns in that teenage way of hers. *How did you know what I was going to say?*

"You're right. You don't. But I don't have to tell you about my date with Mr. London either."

"I saw the limo. And the jumpsuit." She stands, picks up her cell, turns the screen to mine. It's there, the bright pink jumpsuit on the designer's website, along with the four-figure price tag. "He's really rich, huh?"

"Yeah."

"Put a ring on it, okay."

"There's more to life than money."

"Yeah. Soccer and hot sex. And you obviously have the latter covered."

My cheeks flush.

"You two fucked. I knew it!" She giggles and she crosses the room. "I'm proud of you."

"Oh my god."

"It was good, yeah?" She releases me. Takes in my expression with a smile. "Yeah. It was."

"Bed. Now."

"Is that what you said to him?"

"Now."

"Or maybe it's what he said to you?"

Fuck. My blush deepens.

It must be obvious, because her face lights up. She claps. Mouths *nailed it* as she fist-pumps. "I'm proud of you, kid. Keep on… coming."

I try to adopt a maternal stance, but I don't have it in me.

I want to tell her. I want to feel like her older sister and not her mother.

Like before Dad died and I had to take over most of that role.

Before Mom died and I had to take over all of it.

"I will go to bed." Sienna takes another step backward. "But you should know one thing, Indie."

"That you love me?"

"Yeah. And you're already starting to bruise." She winks, turns on her heel, moves to her bedroom. She calls, "good night, sleep tight, don't let the rich guys bite," from her closed door.

This time, I let my blush win. Let the alcohol dissolve my inhibitions. Let my head fill with beautiful mental images of me and Ty.

Tonight.

Three years ago.

All the possibilities of the future.

It might be hell, falling in love with him, trying to unlock the safe around his heart.

But the sex…

That part is heaven.

———

FOR THE FIRST TIME IN FOREVER, I SLEEP SOUNDLY. No nightmares of Sienna moving to Florida for a full ride. No dreams of overdue electric bills.

Only the hardness of Ty's body, the warmth of his skin, the smell of his cologne.

I wake at peace. Comfortable.

Surprised by gifts in the living room.

Sienna brought them in before she went to school. There's a note from her.

I didn't peek. This time.

Love you.

- Sienna

P.S. You owe me extra details for my self-control.

My lips curl into a smile. Sienna is Sienna. And this is thrilling.

My head fills with ideas. My body buzzes. I shake as I finish my morning routine. I don't make breakfast. I go straight to the white gift boxes.

Three of them. With sleek purple bows and a matching card.

Enjoy your morning. This should help.

I'll pick you up tonight. Eight o'clock.

Wear this.

- Ty

It smells like his cologne. Did he spritz the paper? Or am I that attuned to the smell of his skin?

Tonight.

He's picking me up tonight.

I get more tonight.

It's too far away. I need him now. I need his hands on my skin and his lips on my lips.

I need him groaning my name as he comes.

Will he give me that tonight?

I don't know. I never know what he's going to do. Only that he'll figure out what I want and give it to me.

This is the start.

I peel open the largest box. Find a fancy electric kettle, a ceramic tea set, a bag of the Yunnan Hong Cha I sipped in his office.

He's taking care of me.

It makes my stomach flutter.

It makes my thighs shake.

Is this love or lust or something else entirely? I need it to stay carnal. I need this to be about how much he wants to fuck me.

He's not falling in love with me.

I need to understand that.

I unwrap the next box.

Lingerie. A sheer bodysuit. Soft black mesh with a plunging neckline and a low back.

It's incredibly sexy.

I need to wear it now.

I need to tease him now.

I set up the kettle—we have one already, but Ty's is so much better—move to my room, strip, don the lingerie.

My eyes go to the mirror against the closet door. This is the master bedroom. It was Mom's. Sienna and I shared a room. Now that Mom is gone—

The room is big, by Brooklyn standards. And the mirrored closet wall is its most impressive feature.

Usually, it mocks me. Reminds me I'm trading self-respect for an extra hundred dollars in tips a night.

Right now—

My breath catches in my throat. I don't look gawky or flat. I look like a lingerie model. And knowing Ty sent this, knowing he's picturing me in it—

Fuck.

I pull out my cell. Turn toward the light. Snap a picture. Then another. Another.

There.

I stop on a photo. My reflection, from my nose to my waist. Clearly me. The Latin quote on my shoulder in full view.

My breasts visible through the sheer material.

It's dangerous to send it. But I trust Ty not to share it. And, well—

If he wants to destroy me, he has far easier ways.

There.

I send the picture. No context. Just mesh and bare skin.

The kettle steams. I move into the kitchen, fix the tea, start breakfast. Eggs and toast with plenty of sriracha. I'm an okay cook—Sienna is much better—but I know my eggs. And, really, everything is good covered in hot sauce.

Sunny side-up, scooped onto buttered toast. I bring my plate to the table. Pick up the third box. It's small. The size of two fists.

A sex toy maybe.

More tea.

Some other surprise.

I undo the neat bow. Open the box.

Concealer.

The heavy-duty kind. For covering tattoos, scars, bruises. In two shades, both close to my skin tone.

He sent me concealer. Because I bruise easily. Because he wants to bruise me.

My neck *is* covered in hickeys.

The other implications make my sex clench.

Rope burns on my ankles. Palm marks on my ass. Bruises on my wrist.

Is that what he's promising? Or is he following up on last night's concern?

I'm not sure.

It's sweet, in an illicit way, him sending me concealer.

And Sienna didn't open it. But what if she had?

I don't want her knowing this.

I don't want her to know how I like it.

And I don't want her to jump to conclusions about Ty. I know my sister. She'll think *kinky sex* before she thinks domestic violence.

But it's still none of her fucking business.

My cell ringing interrupts me. Fuck. I sent him that picture. Now—

I jump into my room. Answer my phone. "Hello."

"Are you teasing me, baby?" His voice is low and demanding.

My thighs shake. "What do you mean, Mr. Hunt?"

"Do you know what you're doing?"

"Yes."

"Are you sure?"

No. Not at all. "Yes."

"Good."

My sex clenches.

"Are you alone?" he asks.

"Am I alone?"

"It's not a trick question."

Right. He's asking if I'm alone because he wants more pictures. Or he wants to hear me come.

Something in that ballpark.

Something really fucking tantalizing.

"I'm home," I say. "Just me."

"You're hesitating."

"It's nothing."

"It's something."

Okay. "The gifts. They're sweet."

"Sweet?"

"I like them. But I, uh... next time, not where Sienna could find them. I wouldn't want her to get the wrong idea."

"Oh." The playfulness drops from his voice.

"I'm sorry, Ty."

"Don't be. Practicalities are important."

"I know you wouldn't—"

"You don't," he says. "It's been three years. You don't know if you can trust me."

"I do."

"Completely?"

No. Of course not. There are too many strings. This is too complicated.

And I'm too slow to answer.

He knows I'm saying no. It's in his sigh. "It's smart that you don't."

"I just—"

"You don't have to justify yourself to me, Indigo. Your safety is more important than my feelings."

"It's not that I think you might—"

"It is. And it's fair."

But that's not true. I don't think Ty would hurt me. Not physically. Not the way he means.

He's careful with my body.

But my heart?

This plan—me, living by his side, accepting his gifts and

his tenderness and his fuck, without falling for him—ends in heartbreak.

Either he can't see it or he doesn't care.

And that means I can't trust him completely.

"No," I say. "It's not. I don't think that about you. I need you to know that."

"You don't have to justify your apprehension."

Maybe, but—"Most guys aren't this careful. I… I need you to know that I see it. That I appreciate that you take your time with me."

"Indie, you don't—"

"Yes, I do." I suck a breath through my teeth. "I appreciate your care. Your patience. Your tenderness and your roughness." But I don't want him to know how it makes my stomach flutter.

That's mine and mine alone.

"I need you to know that," I say it again.

He's quiet for a moment. Then he says, "Thank you," in a tone I can't place.

Okay.

Thank you.

I guess it's an acknowledgment.

I can't bring myself to say *you're welcome*, so I let the silence fall.

I let the sounds of the city fill the space. A passing car. A conversation on the sidewalk. A honking horn.

Then Ty's voice flowing from my speaker. "There's a picture. I was going to tell you tonight." His voice is that same impossible-to-read tone. "From the restaurant. It's blurry. *I* can't tell it's you and I know you were there. All I see is black fabric and light skin."

"Oh."

"I barely recognize your dress. But then all I know about your dress is that I want it on my floor." Playfulness drops into his voice. Just barely, but it does.

The tension in my shoulders eases. This is... complicated. But we can figure it out.

"My cousin Cam saw the image," Ty says. "He's asking about it. About you."

"Oh."

"He wants to have dinner Saturday."

"Yeah. Sure."

"I had a photographer reserved for tonight, but with the picture going live... I figured you'd want time to explain to Sienna."

He's canceling for tonight.

Because he's upset?

Or because it's convenient?

"Sure, uh, we can do that," I say. "Dinner Saturday."

"You'll meet Cam," he says.

"Just him?" I ask.

"You can invite Sienna, but he's a flirt."

"She is too."

"Exactly."

Oh. Right. I don't need to watch his cousin flirt with my eighteen-year-old sister.

"We'll be live soon," he says. "People will know."

"People?"

"Everyone. Ian will want to meet you."

"He's already met me."

"What is it you say? As the help?"

"But he knows. Doesn't he?" I ask.

"He knows I had a fling with a girl I met at a museum. Not that it was you."

"Oh." It doesn't fit the image I have of Ty. Or of Ty and his brother.

"He'll like you."

"Because I'm hot?"

"Because he'll believe you make me happy." His voice is matter-of-fact.

But I still feel the pain in it.

Ty not believing he'll ever be happy with anyone. Desperate to convince the entire world, and his closest confidants, that he's capable of loving someone.

Desperate to convince himself maybe.

"Okay," I say. "Saturday. We can figure out the rest of the details then."

"I'll pick you up at eight," he says. "Wear the lingerie under your clothes."

Intent drips back into his voice. Not enough to convince me he's past our conversation, that he's okay, that he thinks only of my orgasm.

But enough to make my pulse race and my toes curl.

Saturday at eight.

Saturday we take the steps to go official.

But what about after that?

Is he going to drop me here?

Or take me to his bed, like he promised?

Chapter Sixteen

INDIGO

I have the entire day to myself.

Normally, I'd have work at four. Sienna already has afternoon plans.

There's no one else I want to see. No one I want to call.

I'm used to time alone—I work nights—but it's been a long time since I've had an entire day to myself, much less the mental space to use that time.

I don't have to worry about rent. Or dinner. Or Sienna's future.

Sure, I have a lot to figure out. But I have the space to do it now.

It's strange. New. Like I just dropped a heavy backpack.

My shoulders still ache, but they feel lighter too.

Easy.

Free of a burden.

There *is* a hundred thousand dollars in my checking account.

I can do anything. Whatever I want.

But what the fuck do I want?

———

AFTER A LONG MORNING AT A NEW SPOT—A PLACE WITH TEN-dollar pots of tea and delicate raspberry scones—I return to my empty apartment.

Find my guitar in the closet.

I close my eyes. Press my fingers to the strings.

They feel like home.

That home I can never have again.

I play a scale. Slowly. Then faster.

My fingers warm up.

Then I start a song. One I wrote a million years ago.

I make it through four chords, then I break.

I can't do it. It's too painful.

It opens that hole in my heart. All those memories of Dad teaching me to play. Of Mom gushing over a song.

Those days after he died, sitting in the living room all night, trying to make sense of my thoughts as I scribbled messy lyrics.

There's too much.

I can't take it. Not now.

Soon.

I'll go back to it soon. But not yet. Not when I have to guard my heart so closely.

———

SATURDAY MORNING, SIENNA AND I GRAB BRUNCH AT OUR normal spot.

We walk to her favorite coffee place in the Village (she's picky for a girl who drinks anything sweet), admire the purple NYU flags that dot the neighborhood, talk about anything except everything changing.

She starts school in August.

And I marry Ty. Move into his place.

Start my life.

I wait until we're home, until I'm dressed, until Ty's already sent a message that he's on his way (not that he needs the message. He's always a few minutes early, no matter the occasion).

I perfect my winged liner. Curl my eyelashes. Apply another coat of mascara.

There. I slip into my black ankle boots and move into the main room.

Sienna's on the couch, watching a reality show about people who only have three months to decide if they want to get married or never see each other again. She turns to me and drops her jaw. "Holy shit, Indie."

"Too much?"

"Only if you're meeting his parents." She studies the snug dress. The deep plunge, the sleek black fabric, the short hem. "Are you?"

"No." Would I know if I was? "Just him."

"Don't you work Saturdays?"

"I quit."

"You didn't mention that until now?"

I shrug like it's no big deal.

She raises a brow. "I guess… it's good. That you have your own secrets now. And it really sucks there. Even if Meghan slips me drinks." Her nose scrunches. "You knew, huh?"

"Suspected." Meghan is always making sure the other girls are doing well. Of course, she's slipping Sienna drinks.

"I wouldn't like you working there either if I was him. But is he uh… making up the difference?"

"Don't worry about it."

She shoots me a *get real* look. "Listen, I'm all about this *Pretty Woman* thing you have going with Mr. London. And I'm glad you have secrets worth keeping. But I'm not a kid. If something is up, you can tell me."

Maybe. I promised I'd try to keep this secret, but I can tell her some of the truth.

"'Cause if you're fucking him for money, that's okay with me. Respect to you, for deciding what you do with your body. Especially because you finally look satisfied."

Oh my god. I can't help but laugh.

"I know guys have offered. At Rick's. But you've never… you've never agreed, right?"

I've considered it. I almost said yes a few times. Especially right after Mom died. When bills were tight and I was exhausted. But I always found a way. A different way. "Never."

"It's okay if you want to say yes. But do it for you and your love of fancy tea. I can take care of myself," she says. "I have math."

"You have math?"

"Yeah, no offense Indie, but that's a real skill. I mean, charming rich guys is a real skill too. But music… it's not very marketable."

"Thanks for believing in me."

"I do. You're this close to putting a ring on it."

That is true.

"And I'm okay. Without your help. Hell, if this thing doesn't work out with Mr. London, and you can't find another rich guy, I'll be the one helping pay your bills."

"You think marrying a rich guy is my best bet?"

"In the entire history of civilization, marrying a rich guy has been the best bet for most women, most of the time."

"Perceptive."

"And you're tall and thin. Guys like that."

"You really know how to schmooze. Has anyone told you that?"

"He likes you," she says. "Let him buy things for you."

"I appreciate your advice on relationships."

My phone buzzes. Ty. He's here.

And my sister thinks he's here to offer me a few grand for one night. Which, really, wouldn't be so bad. If it was Ty.

Maybe better than this.

Or maybe a million times worse.

My phone buzzes again. Not a text this time. A call.

"Is he coming up?" she asks.

"Hey," I answer the call. "I uh, I'm talking to Sienna. I'll be a minute."

"Of course."

"Actually... Do you think you can meet her now?"

"You want me to meet her tonight?"

"Yeah? Could you? Please."

Chapter Seventeen

TY

I take a deep breath. Inhale the warm air.

It's past sunset—the sky is that soft shade of blue Indigo loves—but it's as hot as it was this afternoon. The mix of humidity, concrete, and steel trap the heat.

New York City blue. New York City weather.

Two things Indigo loves.

She always says this blue only exists here, but how does she know?

She hasn't traveled much. A few trips upstate to visit family. One to Florida. To go to Disney World (she hated it, Sienna loved it).

Two vacations in the Caribbean. Before her father died.

She doesn't remember much. Only the warm water and the soft sand.

Despite her New York City style, I can see Indie at the beach.

Spread out on a lounge chair in a black bikini, listening to music as she stares at the waves, beckoning me to a private cabana.

Would she have liked the resort Rory picked for our honeymoon?

It's not her—too much propriety—but we wouldn't spend enough time outside our room for it to matter.

I don't know what she wants now. If she wants to go to Hawaii or Paris or upstate New York.

Only that I want to spend the week making her come.

With Rory, it was different. She picked the resort because her mother recommended it, because it was a place for the rich to avoid the hoi polloi.

She dismissed her family's snobbery, but she was never comfortable outside that world.

She didn't understand what it was like to suddenly have everything.

Indie does.

She didn't let her guard down the way Indie does.

Those are the reasons why I called her, but how big were they, compared to how much I want to fuck her?

I can't deny it when I'm with her. I can't deny how much I want to pin her to the wall, bind her wrists, bend her over my lap and spank her.

She doesn't trust me yet.

It's fair.

Smart.

Practical.

But it still stops me in my tracks. It still amplifies that voice in my head.

What kind of monster wants to hurt the woman he loves?

"Ty?" Indigo asks. "Hey. Is that you?"

She's standing in front of her door, a vision in her short black dress and dramatic makeup

Her eyes light up as she spots me. "You look gorgeous."

"Gorgeous again?"

She nods *yes*. Takes a half-step toward me.

I meet her. Wrap my arms around her waist. Pull her into a slow, deep kiss.

She rocks her hips against mine. Parts her lips to make way for my tongue.

I kiss her hard. Like I'm claiming her.

She kisses back with everything she has. Sighs as she releases me. "Do you really need to come in and meet Sienna?"

"You invited me."

"And we really need to see your cousin?"

"I can tell him to fuck off."

"Would you?"

"Are you going to ask?"

She looks up at me, desire in her blue eyes. "No, I, uh... I really want you to meet her."

I want to meet her too. I want to know her life and this is a huge part of it.

"But, first, I, uh... I wanted to say something. About our call."

"You were clear."

"Maybe. But I want to look at you when I say it." Her fingers curl around my neck. "I want to get there. Where we trust each other completely. I know it will take time, but I do want to get there."

That's the only thing I want. "Me too."

"And I will be honest with you. Even if it hurts. I promise." She presses her lips to mine. "But, uh, that's the last I'll say of my desire to—"

"Feel my hand around your throat."

Her cheeks flush. "Because Sienna... she's uh, god, she's going to have a field day with you." She smiles. "You have a little." She runs her thumb over my lower lip. "You're wearing my lipstick."

"Does it suit me?"

"It does. You look good in wine." She smiles. "And Sienna will love that we're making out in the hallway."

"Really?"

She nods. "I told you. She's obsessed with sex. And she's going to ask so many questions, so—"

"Do you really doubt my restraint?"

Her blush deepens. "No. I just want you prepared."

My shoulders fall. My jaw softens.

She doesn't think I'm a monster.

She wants this as much as I do.

More even.

"She's easily distracted. So bring up soccer. She's really into that one player," she says.

"The one player?"

"His thighs. She goes on about the soccer player's thighs." Her eyes flit to my legs. "You do have great legs."

"She's the one who wants to talk about sex?"

She mimes zipping her lips. Motions to the door *are you ready?*

My chest gets light. My limbs too.

I'm nervous. I didn't expect to be nervous.

How hard is it to charm a teenage girl who loves football and handsome men?

But this isn't an intern desperate for my approval. Or a waitress looking for a tip. Or even a woman seeking a connection with a man.

It's Indigo's sister.

The most important person in her life. The only person she loves.

I know Indigo. If her sister asks her to end this—

I'm not going to win that battle. I don't want to fight that battle.

I need to impress her, now. To convince her my intentions are good.

They are.

I'm committed to Indie.

That's better than something as mercurial as love. I won't leave if my feelings change. I won't wake up one day and decide I can do better.

I won't abandon her.

"Ty?" Indigo's voice softens. "Are you ready?"

I nod.

She offers her hand. When I take it, she sucks in a heavy inhale. Opens the door slowly. "Sienna, this is Ty." She moves aside.

I step through the doorframe.

A tall teenage girl in a grey jumper stares at me. Her jaw drops. Her light eyes go wide.

She has Indigo's strong nose, and her long frame, but the rest of her features are softer. Light hair, hazel eyes, casual attire.

"Holy fuck, Indigo." She's obvious about checking me out. "I thought he got fat."

"Oh my god." Indigo shakes her head. "Sorry, she—"

"He's so hot." She presses her lips together. "I mean, uh, that's right. I'm Sienna." She holds out her hand. "Is Ty short for something? Or is it some kinky nickname?"

Indigo laughs.

"Right. Yeah. She asked me to be on my best behavior. And not make everything about sex. But come on…" Sienna looks to her sister. "She hasn't gotten any in forever and suddenly she's walking around with a satisfied look and hickeys? I'm not an idiot."

"It's nice to meet you, Sienna." I offer my hand.

"Has that been—" Sienna motions to Indigo's short skirt.

"Oh my god." Indigo hides behind her palm.

I chuckle. "Not yet, no."

Sienna moves forward to shake. "But later?"

"If I'm lucky."

"Okay, this has been a good talk," Indigo says. "Now we're going to leave and—"

"Uh, I don't think so." Sienna looks to her sister. "I haven't met one of your boyfriends since Noah. And, honestly, he was hot, but a zero. You know the type, right, Ty?"

"I'm not sure I do," I say.

Sienna shoots me an incredulous look, but she still explains. "Nice. Family oriented. All right on paper, but just... dull. They didn't have anything in common either. But I guess I don't know what the two of you have in common besides—" She makes an *o* with one hand. Pushes two fingers through it.

"Sienna!" Indigo turns bright red. "Please don't discuss my sex life."

"But you do have one now. A sex life?" She looks to me. "Do I have to get you drunk first? Or will you tell me all my sister's secret desires if I ask?"

"You can try. If you think that will work," I say.

"I'll consider that." She gives me a slow once-over. Looks to her sister. "I'm not supposed to comment on your appearance."

"No?" I ask.

She nods *yeah*. "It's rude. To congratulate my sister for having a hot boyfriend in front of him."

"You are objectifying me," I say.

"Sure, but, come on. You've never told a guy congrats on the hot girlfriend?" She raises a brow, the exact same way Indigo does. "Really?"

"Not in front of her," I say.

"But you have." She looks to Indigo. "See. This is how guys act. Why can't we act that way?"

"What do you want to say?" I ask. "Maybe *congratulations,*

Indie, your boyfriend has a fantastic arse?"

Sienna nods. "Seems reasonable, yeah."

"And if I went to my brother and said, *Eve's tits look fantastic in that dress. You're a lucky man?"* I ask.

Sienna makes that *hmm* noise. Her forehead scrunches as she thinks.

Indigo shoots me an *I'm sorry she's ridiculous* look.

"Maybe… it does sound kind of bad like that," Sienna says. "But I wasn't specific. I didn't say, 'good job, Indie, your boyfriend has abs. I hope you lick them.'"

"Would you?" I ask.

She laughs. "Maybe. If we were at the beach or something. Or… you play soccer, right?"

"I do," I say.

"Aren't you a little old for that?" she asks.

My laugh is loud. Honest. "You New Yorkers are so blunt. It's charming."

"We're assholes. But it saves time, getting to the point. Life would be easier if everyone got to the point. Don't you think?" she asks.

It's a good question. Insightful.

Brutal honesty would make life easier, yes.

But it would be painful too.

And most people aren't honest enough with themselves to be honest with someone else.

I promised Indigo I'd try to be honest with her, even if it hurt. And I will. I am.

But it's not as easy as it sounds.

Sienna moves on from her philosophical inquiry. "It's Tyler Hunt, right? I'll look it up when you guys leave."

"I'm thirty." I move to Indigo. Wrap my arm around her waist. "I was in a league in London. Now, I play the occasional game at the park. It's casual. With friends."

"Are you good?" Sienna asks.

"Not as good as I was in university," I say.

"You played then?" Sienna looks from her sister to me. "And I'm totally keeping you guys from having dirty sex, huh? I can go. It's still early. And I have finals next week, so…"

"We're leaving." Indigo looks up at me, equal parts embarrassment and approval in her blue eyes. "Or do you want to talk about soccer for a while? I can… I'm going to fix my lipstick, actually. I'll just be a minute." She mouths *okay*?

I nod *okay*. Kiss her softly. Release her.

Sienna watches her sister move to her bedroom. "We're not really going to talk about soccer, are we?"

No. Of course not.

"You seem honest, Ty, but I've had enough experience with men to know better." She lowers her voice to a whisper. "Indie doesn't talk about you much. She doesn't talk about what happened three years ago. When she does, she insists it was for the best that you left. That it was the only thing that made sense. I know it was your agreement, but it broke her heart."

It did?

"The entire semester after… she wasn't herself. And by the time she was, Mom… she's done a lot. Stepping up to take care of me. And she's lost a lot. She needs someone who will stick around, who will take care of her."

"I'd like to."

She stares into my eyes, assessing my words. "I believe you. That you think that. But this… she's different than she was three years ago. But I see the same things. That same giddiness. Don't hurt her again."

"I don't want to."

"Did you want to the first time?"

No. Of course not. "You don't forgive me?"

"Of course not. But it's not mine to forgive." Her voice

rises. "I don't care if you have the world at your fingertips, Ty. I don't care if you can crush me like that—" She snaps. "If you hurt her, I'll ruin you. Even if takes years. Even if it takes everything I have."

She looks to the bedroom as Indigo rises. Moves toward the door.

Sienna turns back to me. Holds out her hand. "Understand?"

"I appreciate your loyalty." I shake.

She smiles *good*, releases me, turns back to her sister. "So, really, forward, huh? Do you drag people running too? I think Indigo might kill me if I take her on another run. Though, honestly, she's so slow, it's not even exercise."

"Talking about me?" Indigo crosses the room. She gives her sister a hug. Whispers something in her ear.

Sienna laughs. "Of course. I asked for the exact inches."

Indigo turns bright red. She releases her sister. "We'll get dinner. The three of us. After your finals."

"Why don't you come with us?" I ask. "Tonight."

Indigo shoots me a *really* look.

"If that's okay with you, Indie," I say.

"Ooh, impromptu invite." Sienna laughs. "That doesn't seem like your style, Ty."

"I know when I meet someone I'd like to get to know."

She smiles *ah, two can play that game*. "I haven't eaten."

"It's late," Indie says.

"Just dinner," I say. "Then we'll go for drinks. The two of us. Somewhere private."

Her eyes flare with desire.

"That was not as sly as you think it was." Sienna laughs. "But, yeah, please?" She presses her hands together. "I'll even put on a dress."

"How much will your cousin flirt with her?" Indie asks.

"There's a hot cousin!" Sienna fist pumps. "Yes. I'm coming."

"Did I say he was hot?" I ask.

"Hmm… yeah, he might be ugly. I'd introduce ugly family members first too," she says. "Even so." She turns to her sister. "If you'd rather I not c-block you, that's okay."

Indie smiles. "No. It's okay." She turns to me. "Does she have time to get dressed?"

"Fifteen minutes," I say.

Sienna nods *hell yes*. "Why don't you guys, uh, go wait in the limo. I'll meet you there." She winks.

Indigo shoots her sister a look. "You don't need help?"

"Please." She hugs her sister. Whispers something in her ear. Then she winks at me. Disappears into her room.

Indie squeezes my hand. "She likes you."

"Does she?"

"I can tell." She leads me out the door. Down the stairs. "Is your cousin hot?"

"He does well with women."

"Are you related to anyone who isn't hot?"

I shake my head.

She smiles. "I had a feeling." She stops on the sidewalk. Turns to me. Pulls me into a tight kiss. "Fifteen minutes isn't enough time."

"Are you sure about that?"

Chapter Eighteen

INDIGO

Maybe it is enough time.

Fifteen minutes.

That's ten minutes longer than I take when I'm alone.

And I've certainly had fucks that finished faster.

Never with Ty.

But if I climbed into his lap and begged him to fuck me now—

Maybe.

He helps me into the limo.

I cross my legs.

My phone buzzes against my thigh.

Sienna.

Ty chuckles. "Is she really texting you?"

"Yes."

Sienna: OMFG HE IS SO HOT.

Indigo: Get dressed.

Sienna: I'm multi-tasking.

Indigo: What are you wearing?

Sienna: Save that for him.

Indigo: You know you can't walk in heels.
Sienna: I have strong ankles.

A laugh spills from my lips. "She wants to gossip about you now. Since she'll have to wait until later."

"What does she want to know?" he asks.

"I think she's working up to cock size."

He chuckles. "You can tell her."

My cheeks flush. "I don't think so."

He moves closer. So his knee brushes the outside of my leg. The rough wool of his slacks against my bare thigh. "What's her number? I'll text her."

"Really?" I ask.

He nods. "I'll answer her questions."

"No details."

He raises a brow.

"About sex."

"You don't want your sister to know you're wearing my lingerie under your dress?"

Fuck. I shake my head.

"Or that I'm not going to fuck you until you're begging."

And I'm going to beg. We both know that.

He's teasing me.

But I can tease him too. "No. I don't want her to know I've been fucking myself thinking about the taste of your cock."

His pupils dilate.

"Thinking about sneaking to a secluded part of the restaurant, dropping to my knees, sucking you off." I tap my cell screen so it's showing her number. Hold it out to him.

Desire spills over his expression, but he stays strong. Holds his poker face. "You want the risk of getting caught?"

"I think about it."

He copies the number into his phone. Taps a text.

My cell buzzes instantly.

Sienna: Your boyfriend just texted me.

Indigo: I know. I'm right here.

Sienna: And you'll be mad if I ask him for details?

Indigo: I'm going to ask you not to.

Sienna: Boring!

Indigo: Is that a no?

Sienna: No, I'll be a good sister. If you give me one detail. Something juicy.

Juicy.

What am I okay with her knowing?

Sienna: I just looked up his net worth and holy fuck! You are going to put a ring on it, right?

He chuckles as his cell buzzes.

Oh god. "What did she say?"

"Nothing important." He slips his phone into his pocket. Brings his hand to my cheek.

I look up into his eyes. "You keep daring me to beg you like it means you win somehow."

"Do I?"

I nod. "But that isn't how I feel." I press my hand to his thigh. "If I go like this..." I drag my fingertips up his thigh.

He grabs my wrist.

My sex clenches. "If I say, Ty, please... Please fuck me. Come in my mouth. Bend me over this bench and fuck me until I'm screaming. Please, sir, I'll take whatever you're willing to give."

He brings my hand to his hardening cock.

Fuck. I might be pushing him too far, but I don't care. I need this. "It makes me wet."

Something changes in his posture. Some reserve of his falls away. "Why do you think I ask you to beg?"

"Because you think it means you win some game we're playing."

"I do." He motions for me to rise. When I do, he pulls me

into his lap. Slips his hand under my dress. Presses his palm against my sex. "We both win."

"What if you beg?"

"I won't beg."

"What if you do?"

"I won't." He pulls me into a deep kiss as he rubs me over the lingerie.

I kiss him back.

He rubs me harder, pressing the lace against my clit. It's softer than his hand, but somehow harder too.

I'm already wound so tight. I'm sure I'm going to come right here, right now.

"Ty…"

His lips find my neck. A soft kiss. Then the scrape.

"Do we have time?"

"No." He keeps his hand where it is. Draws another slow circle around my clit. Scrapes his teeth against my neck.

Daring me.

Always daring me.

And this is it—

I tell him to stop or I beg him to finish.

Does it matter that I have time? Sienna will wait.

My phone buzzes against the seat.

Fuck. "Why did you invite her?"

"Are you asking me to stop?"

I should. That's the smart thing. The reasonable thing.

But I don't want to be reasonable.

"No," I whisper.

"Good girl." He slips his fingers under my lingerie.

My body catches flame.

Yes.

Hell yes.

Every yes.

I'm already wound so tight. I'm already so desperately in need of him.

A few more circles and I'm on the edge.

So, so, fucking close.

Then his teeth scrape my neck and I'm there.

I groan his name as I come on his hand.

He works me through my orgasm. Adjusts my dress. Straightens.

Brings his hands to his lips. Sucks the taste of me from his fingers.

"I have something for you." He taps his cell screen a few times. Shows something to me. A recent STD test.

It's a promise.

And I want everything in it. Now.

I don't care that Sienna's arrival is imminent. I don't care that I'm meeting his family.

I only care about satisfaction.

I'm worse than my sister.

Than any guy.

"Are you safe?" he asks.

I nod. "I have a test. From my last yearly."

"Are you on birth control?"

"No," I say. "But I can be."

"Is that what you want?"

"If it means you'll come inside me." My nails curl into my palms. "I've never done that before." I know he has, with his ex-fiancée, so I don't ask. "Will you?"

He nods. "After."

"Next weekend?"

He chuckles. "What are you going to do?"

"For birth control?"

"Yes." His posture changes. Not serious, exactly, but matter-of-fact. No longer toying with my desire. "You don't want to have children with me."

"I just meant—"

"I know what you meant. I'm not offended."

I'm not sure I believe him.

"Even if you felt differently, if we agreed to different terms—" he swallows hard. "I'd want to wait."

Right. That's reasonable. And I'm not going to linger on the subtext in his sentence. That he would still have children with me if I felt differently.

That it's still what he wants.

I'm drowning in hormones.

I'm not thinking straight.

"Indie?" he asks. "It's your body. Your choice. But I'm not going to have unprotected sex with you if you aren't on birth control."

Right.

"That's my choice."

"I'm a little—"

"Distracted by the thought of my cock?"

"Yeah. Kind of. But, uh, an IUD maybe. Since it will just be us. And they work for a long time. And—"

"You tried taking the pill in college, but it made you sick."

"Yeah." Fuck, having sex without a condom. That's… I want it so much. "Will you come in my mouth now?"

"Right now?" He chuckles, still at ease. Not tense from the mention of pregnancy, birth control, children.

Not at all like my conversations with other men.

They're terrified of broaching the topic. Even the sweet ones start whining about condoms after a few months.

I haven't trusted anyone else with this.

But with Ty—

God, I want to do this with Ty.

"Tonight," I say.

"Maybe."

"Maybe?"

He shifts, back to toying with me. "I said maybe. Don't make me repeat myself."

Fuck.

My phone buzzes against the seat.

Then there's a knock on the limo door.

Sienna.

Shit.

"Do I need to give you guys a few more minutes?" she says. "I can meet you at the restaurant. But I'm not standing in these shoes. And you're paying for my car, Ty."

He smiles. "Should we tell her?"

"No." I pick up my cell. Slide it into my pocket.

He scoots aside. Taps something to the driver.

Sienna enters. Shoots us a *yeah, I know what you were doing look.* "God, Indie, you really wear that sex glow."

I turn bright red.

He laughs.

"But seriously, Ty, that was fast," she says. "Have some class next time."

Chapter Nineteen

INDIGO

During the twenty-minute drive, Ty and Sienna work through every soccer player I know, and a dozen others.

She shakes her head, gesturing wildly as she discusses why a player is the best or the worst.

He listens carefully, replies with a few well-chosen words.

Both of them refuse to budge from their positions.

They're not walking on eggshells. They're not holding back. They're just... friendly. Like they've known each other for ages.

I marvel over their rapport. And how grown-up Sienna looks in her cream dress. It's a simple fit-and-flare style, but between her gold heels and her chignon—I can't believe she knows another hairstyle—she looks elegant.

Still sweet and innocent, but not like a little girl.

She's starting college in three months.

I have to let her go in three months.

Everything changes in three months.

I can handle that.

I can totally handle that.

"HOLY SHIT." SIENNA'S FINGERS DIG INTO MY FOREARM AS she stops in her tracks. "Is that your cousin?" She motions to a table in the middle of the restaurant.

It's the only table occupied by a single person.

Or a person who looks like Ty.

But that isn't why Sienna's asking.

It's because this guy is also the hottest guy in the restaurant.

Granted, the competition isn't stiff. There are about a dozen guys here, and most of them are older. But there is a cute hipster bartender. And one of the rich men has a handsome boy toy on his arm.

The other tables are a mix. Two well-dressed couples having dinner. Three men talking business. An older man with a woman young enough to be his granddaughter.

And a handsome black man in a charcoal suit, in the middle of the restaurant.

"Why do you ask?" Ty teases her.

His cousin—Cam, I guess—spots Ty and nods hello.

Sienna squeezes my arm harder. Grabs Ty's. "Are you serious right now?"

"How can you tell if he's hot?" Ty asks. "He's wearing a three-piece suit."

"How can I tell you're hot? Please." She releases his hand to swat the air. "I always know." She looks at Ty. "Besides, hotness is more than shoulders and abs."

"This is the first I'm hearing of this theory," I say.

"There's the face and ass too," she says.

A laugh spills from my lips.

Ty's too. He shoots me a look that's pure *ah, our silly old friend, we know her so well. She's always like this.*

It warms me everywhere.

"There is a personality component," Sienna says. "There's this guy at my school. All the girls think he's hot. He's very physically attractive, but he's dumber than a door-knob. Not hot."

Sienna doesn't wait for us. She moves inside. Goes straight to the table.

"That is your cousin?" I ask.

He chuckles. "What gave it away?"

"I know you aren't really asking, but he has the same posture as you."

"The same posture?"

"Yeah. You sit like you know you have command of the room."

He presses his palm into my lower back. "Tell Cam you noticed that. He'll love it."

"What is he like? I thought you'd give me a few pointers, but..."

The whole trust thing kind of killed the mood. Are we past it? I don't know.

Trust is easy to destroy. Building it takes time. And we—

We need more time.

His shoulders tense, but he doesn't mention our awkward conversation. "He's a flirt, but for the sport of it."

"He doesn't sleep around?"

"He doesn't tell me if he does."

"You're too old to be cool," I say.

"Am I?"

My gaze goes to Sienna and Cam. They are flirting. Already.

"He's a good guy. Friendly. British."

"What does that mean?"

"Good poker face. Good at saying *bugger off* in a way that sounds like *nice to meet you*. A football player."

"Oh no," I say.

He laughs. "Give me a minute. I have to wash up."

Oh. Right. "I, uh, I should fix my makeup."

He leads me down a hallway. To the restrooms.

They're gorgeous, of course. Marble counters, porcelain fixtures, soft lighting.

I pee. Wash my hands. Fix my lipstick.

This is nothing. Dinner with Ty's cousin. While Sienna flirts shamelessly.

While my heart begs me to drop every one of my inhibitions and fall head over feet.

No problem. Really.

I meet Ty in the hallway. Follow him into the restaurant. "Should I be worried? About your cousin believing us?"

"He isn't naturally suspicious. Not compared to Ian. But this is sudden."

"We have to sell it."

Ty nods and leads me to the table. He motions to Sienna then his cousin. "Sienna, Cam. Cam, Sienna."

"We did that," she says. "But I know you have to throw your weight around."

His smile is easier than Ty's. More troublemaking too. "You must be Indigo." He stands. Shakes with a firm grip.

"I must," I say.

"Not Ty's usual type," he says.

"He has a type?" I ask.

"Wasn't Ty whoring it up for the last year?" Sienna says this casually, as if it's not at all loaded. "Sleeping with anyone with a pulse?"

Cam laughs. "How did that work out for him?"

"Uh, hello, do you see my sister?" Sienna nods *duh*. "She's a total babe. In a boss bitch way."

"Is that considered a compliment?" he asks.

"Obviously." Sienna looks to me for backup. "I mean, that haircut doesn't say sweet and approachable."

"Thank you, Sienna," I say.

Cam laughs. "I'm not sure she agrees." He looks to me. "What do you think, Indigo? Do you want to be a babe in a boss bitch way?"

"We're getting hung up on minor details. The point is, she's hot," Sienna says.

Cam nods *true*.

"And smart. And caring. And tall. Look how tall she is," Sienna says.

"She's such a sweet talker," I say.

Cam and Ty chuckle.

"You're tall, too, aren't you?" Cam asks.

"Only five eight. She's five eleven." Sienna looks to us. "See. Tall. Hot. Smart. It's obviously working out well for Ty."

Ty pulls me closer. "I'm a lucky man."

"Yeah. Very lucky. Indigo has many suitors," Sienna says.

"My wing woman," I say.

Cam's dark eyes flit from Ty to me, then back to Ty. "You didn't warn me you needed a wingman. You know Ian's better at that."

"Not everyone can share the spotlight." Ty pulls out my chair. Motions for me to sit.

I do.

The guys follow.

Sienna looks at them carefully. She's across from me. Next to Cam.

Way too close to this very attractive man who's much too old for her. How old is he? I know he's younger than Ty, but that's about all I know.

Troublemaking grin.

British accent.

Strong shoulders.

And a soccer player—

He meets all of her criteria and then some.

But then I'm not here to defend my sister. I'm here to convince Ty's cousin we're madly in love.

Sienna is an adult.

I can handle that.

I can handle her flirting with Ty's very attractive, very rich, very athletic cousin who is a decade her senior.

It doesn't bother me.

And if I let on that it bothers me, she'll do it more.

So, uh, ultimate chill. Yes.

A server interrupts with a bottle of wine for the table.

Sienna shoots me a *please*.

I shoot her a *no way*. "Could we get waters?"

She holds the *please* like a lovesick puppy dog.

God, I want to say yes. I want to be her sister.

So I nod. Mouth *one*.

She shoots me a thumbs-up. Smiles wide as the server fills our glasses.

"I've seen that exchange before," Cam says. "You're not twenty-one?"

"Maybe," Sienna says. "Only if that won't get in the way of our future tryst."

"We have a future tryst?" he asks.

"Oh yeah. Look at how much it bothers them." She motions to me and Ty. "They're about to burst, right?"

He looks to me. Then to Ty. "A little."

"It's too easy, honestly." She holds up her wineglass with a giddy smile. "I love you, Indie. I'll even stop flirting with Cam if you ask."

"I hope you don't," he says.

I bite my tongue.

Ty notices. Chuckles. "You're worse than Ian."

"I am not." I fold my arms. "How am I worse?"

"More over-protective," he says.

"Ian won't let on that he's over-protective," Cam says. "He wanted to be Ty's cool older brother. The guy who gave him his first pint and taught him the importance of cunnilingus."

Sienna fixes on him. "Go on."

"What's there to say? A gentleman always makes sure his partner is ready," Cam says. "It's good manners."

"Are you a gentleman?" Sienna asks.

"No, but I have manners." Cam winks at me. "Your boyfriend taught me that one."

"The importance of cunnilingus?" My cheeks flush.

"The line. About not being a gentleman," Cam says.

"Do you not appreciate the importance of... performing?" Sienna looks to Ty. "Really, Ty, first the quickie, now this."

"Do you, Ty?" Cam holds up his glass of wine. "That would be the first I've heard of a lack of generosity on his part. But you can never be sure."

"Ty has a reputation for being generous?" Sienna taps his glass. "Should we toast to it?"

"To making a woman come? Absolutely." He taps his glass against hers.

Before Ty or I can react, they take their first sips.

Ty leans in to whisper, "I like the toast."

My blush deepens. I look to my sister. His cousin. "To true love."

"That's a downgrade." Sienna pouts, but she toasts anyway. "But I guess you two already covered sex."

"How do you know?" Cam asks.

"In the limo. I didn't see anything, but they had this look when I got to the car. Like their parents had walked in on them."

"It's horrifying when it happens," Cam says. "But I

imagine you'd stand there and offer technique advice, Sienna."

She laughs. "I wouldn't watch."

He raises a brow.

"Okay, maybe for a minute. Just to make sure Ty is treating her right. But I don't want to see my sister have sex." She looks to me. "No offense, Indie."

"Thank god," I say.

She turns to Cam. "Would you watch your siblings?"

"No," he says.

"Ty?" she asks.

"Not on purpose," Cam says. "Once. When he was in university. Our families were on holiday. And he brought a girl back to the house we'd rented."

"Go on…" she says.

"Fuck." Ty chuckles. "Don't tell her that."

"It highlights your generous spirit." He turns to Sienna. "I slept in that day. And when I came out of my bedroom, Ty was on the couch with this girl. He was dressed. She was naked."

"Oh?" Sienna raises a brow.

"And her legs were around his head." Cam chuckles. "It was the first time I saw a woman come. I couldn't look away."

Ty actually blushes.

God, it's so sexy.

I want to jump him right here.

And tell his cousin to stop offering Sienna sex stories. But he's just like her. He's doing it to push Ty's buttons.

Are we really this predictable?

"Did that really happen?" Sienna asks.

"What do you think?" Cam motions to Ty. "Does his expression sell it?"

"Ty seems honest." She studies Ty's expression. Turns back to Cam. "You... not as much."

"To perceptive women." Cam holds up his glass to toast again.

She taps her glass against his. "You're a proud liar?"

"What is it you call it here? A tall tale. It's not true, but it speaks to a great truth," he says.

She laughs. "So you didn't walk in on Ty performing on a woman?"

"I did. But at a party. And I left the room instantly," he says.

"So what's the greater truth?" she asks. "Ty's generous spirit and sexual talents?"

"Exactly," he says.

"Yeah, I think I got that already." She motions to me. "My sister hasn't gotten laid in a long time. It's pretty obvious that she's suddenly satisfied."

"But what if it's just that it's been so long?" he asks.

"And not his skill?" Sienna looks to Ty. "Are you going to take this lying down?"

"I'm secure in my abilities," Ty says.

"What a cop-out," Sienna says.

"You need to try harder than that to bait him," Cam says. "He grew up with me."

"Hmm... what do you suggest?" she asks.

"Aren't you her wing woman?" Cam stage whispers.

Sienna nods.

"Something about how he could never make her come four times in one night then," Cam says.

Sienna laughs. "Could you, Ty?"

He shrugs, effortlessly aloof.

Sienna looks to me. Catches me blushing. "I think he's done it before."

"He still has to prove he can do it again," Cam says.

Ty leans in to whisper, "Should I?"

Even though they know what he's saying—they must—I nod.

Yes. Of course.

I'll take whatever he has to give.

Chapter Twenty

TY

Sienna is just like her sister. Good at pushing buttons.

She flirts with Cam at every opportunity. Teases Indie about sex just enough to make her blush. Shoots me *I know you think this is cute, but I didn't forget about ruining you if you hurt my sister* looks every fifteen minutes.

Cam steps into his role as wingman. It comes naturally to the troublemaking athlete. He's like Sienna that way.

Loves getting a rise out of people.

If I didn't know better, I'd be horrified by their flirting. Cam's much too old for Sienna. And Indie will do anything to protect her sister.

But I know Cam. He won't fuck her.

Even so, I bite my tongue as they flirt. I don't like it. I want to protect Sienna too. But if they know they're riling me, they'll push even harder.

And then they'll forget why they're flirting and end up fucking.

So I toast to sex tips and promises of future orgasms. I shift the conversation to football players as we order dinner.

I order the same spicy seafood pasta Indie does. It's

perfect with the rich red wine. Fresh pasta, tangy tomatoes, perfectly cooked shrimp, the bite of roasted red peppers.

More wine.

Sambuca dessert. Anise flavored liquor. Sharp, sweet, unique.

Indie giggles as she finishes her glass. She's tipsy, happy, at ease.

But Sienna—

She's on her second limoncello.

"You're giving your age away by ordering the sweet stuff," Cam stage whispers.

"I like dessert," she says. "I can get with that whole when-in-Rome thing Ty was going on about. Here we are, eating fine Italian food, enjoying the after-dinner liqueur tradition."

"But..." Cam raises a brow.

"It's not dessert."

"But more will fill your craving?" His voice is flirty.

"Well... maybe." She smiles. "Or maybe I need something else."

I shoot him a *don't*.

Which only makes him smile. "I hate to say it, but it's getting late. Should I escort you home, Miss Simms? To give our friends some alone time?"

Sienna's eyes light up. "Good idea."

"Over my dead body." Indie clears her throat. "I mean, that's a very generous offer. Thank you, Cam."

"But over your dead body?" He laughs. "You think I'd make a pass at your sister?"

"No. I know she'll make a pass at you," Indie says. She gives her sister a look I can't place.

Sienna nods. "Or... we can ride home together. You can drop me off. And have your way with Ty after I go to bed."

Cam chuckles. "You just realized you failed your wing woman duties?"

154

She nods. "It's a deep shame to be the excuse."

"Stop at one next time." Indie stands. Motions for Sienna to follow. "Come on. Bathroom. Then we'll go."

"Oh, wow, are we actually doing that? Girls going to the bathroom together for a pow-wow." She laughs. "I love it." Sienna stands. Nods a good night to me. Blows Cam a kiss. "Until we return."

"Until then." He catches the kiss. Presses it to his heart.

Indie laughs, but she still leads Sienna to the bathroom with quick steps. They giggle as they walk.

Happy.

Comfortable.

Like the four of us are old friends.

Like this is real.

Cam finishes his glass of wine. "Is there any point in offering to pay?"

I shake my head.

He chuckles. "You'll have to let me one day."

"If Ian ever lets me pay for him," I say.

Cam watches the girls disappear in the hallway. "I don't think you're getting lucky tonight."

A laugh escapes my lips. "Do you think I'd invite you if that was my plan?"

He smiles. "Is it hard being surrounded by men more handsome than you?"

"Painful."

He looks to me. "She's funny. Like you."

"Like me?" I ask.

He nods. "Serious on the surface. Waiting to be drawn out."

"The opposite of you?"

"Of course. This nonsense is an act to hide the pain in my soul." His voice is teasing, but there's a truth to it.

We both know the playboy act is a put on.

"She's striking," he says. "But not pretty the way Rory was. She's sharp. Angular."

"Are you complimenting her or insulting her?" I ask.

"Which would upset you more?" he asks.

"If you implied you were going to fuck her."

He chuckles. "I would if it wasn't so ridiculous. She doesn't have eyes for anyone else. I can tell."

That's true.

"She's not like Rory," he says.

That could mean a lot of things. "How's that?"

"She's not dating you for the cache then bailing when she realizes what it means."

"Rory wasn't—"

"It's your life. You'd know better."

"I was with her for two years."

"And you loved her, I know. But I won't pretend I liked you together," he says. "She didn't want to be a part of your world, Ty. She wanted you to be a part of hers."

She did, but that was what I wanted too. I wanted to fit into this perfect image.

"Gorgeous though. I can't blame you for staying."

"Yes, that was it. Her tits. Two years because I liked her tits."

He chuckles. "You wouldn't be the first man to stay for nice tits."

That is the sad truth of our gender. "We're all ruled by our cocks."

He raises his glass. "I'll toast to that."

I chuckle as I raise my wineglass.

"Are you two compatible there?" He takes a sip.

"You're just like her sister."

"Sienna?" He smiles just to rile me. "She's cute. Don't you think?"

"Adorable." I try to hide the *don't even think about it* in my voice, but I fail.

He laughs *you're too easy*. "And funny too."

"She's eighteen," I say.

"So?"

"Don't."

He chuckles, easy. "You could distract me by answering my question."

"Yes. I enjoy fucking my girlfriend."

"Does she share your taste?"

"Why do I tell you shite?"

He motions to the bottle of wine on the table.

"Fuck off."

"You fuck off. You think I don't know why you invited me out?"

"Why?" I ask.

"I'm your practice run," he says. "Before you introduce your girlfriend to Ian."

"You are not."

"I'm used to it. Everyone knows you idolize him." He looks to the hallway. "And this is big. He was relieved when Rory ended things."

"He's got issues with marriage."

"He's a fucked-up mess."

"Strong words from you," I say.

He shrugs *true*. "But it was more than that. It was because she wasn't right for you. And everyone knew that too."

"Everyone knew?"

"Yes. But Ian thought he was blinded by his marriage. He didn't realize he was seeing straight."

"Ah, it's not that you're an arsehole for telling me you hate my fiancée. It's that he was blinded."

He nods. "Sometimes the truth hurts. You're the one who taught me that, Ty."

"Thank god you're repaying the favor."

Cam chuckles. "I'm glad I did. Now you know I'm being honest when I tell you I like her."

That's a fair point. And I do strive for full disclosure. But I also realize it's fucking difficult.

"And I can tell she's good for you. Even if you were photographed with another woman two months ago."

"We already knew each other," I say. "Three years ago—"

"The girl from The Museum of Sex." His eyes fill with epiphany. "The one who fucked up your head. So you couldn't enjoy normal anymore. Of course. All the better."

"You really are an arsehole. You know that?"

He raises his glass again. When I toast, he continues. "Good for you, Ty. Thinking with your cock. Making men everywhere proud."

The girls reappear at the table.

"Hey." Indie bites her lip. "I'm going to take her home."

"I can get myself home," Sienna says. "Or Cam could help."

"Nope." She squeezes my hand. Pulls me into a quick kiss. "Call me in the morning. You can make good on your promise tomorrow."

"Oh my god, we all know that means sex!" Sienna laughs. "Just go do it now. Stop pretending like you're sly." She motions for me to come with her. "Come on, Ty. Ride home with us. Then take Indie back to your place. We all know you want to."

Cam raises a brow. "I'm not seeing a flaw in this plan."

"Tomorrow." I kiss Indie goodbye again.

Sienna pouts, but she still follows her sister out of the restaurant.

Cam shoots me a curious look. "You're cruel, teasing her like that."

"She likes when I'm cruel."

"Fuck. I hope you hold on to her. You're never going to find someone who suits you better."

———

AFTER I PAY, CAM INSISTS ON TAKING ME OUT FOR ANOTHER drink.

He wants to go dancing. To meet other women. To tease me about finally being monogamous.

I should say yes. Go somewhere he can't interrogate me. But I don't.

I go to a quiet bar around the corner. Let him buy the first round.

Then a second.

Tell him too much about Indie and how I want her and how fucked up I felt with Rory. How fucked I still feel because of the way she looked at me.

He toasts to it, of course. *We're all fucked up, Ty. As long as she's satisfied, what else matters?*

I hold on to that thought as we part.

As I head home.

Text Indie.

Ty: Is Sienna okay?

Indigo: Drunk, but okay. She fell asleep during our second episode of 90 Day Fiancée.

Ty: How do you watch that show?

Indigo: It's very dramatic.

Ty: It's ridiculous.

Indigo: So are you.

Ty: I'm not sure that has any relevance.

Indigo: It's fun watching with her. I can't explain it. Making fun of something, but loving it anyway. It feels right.

Ty: I'm glad you have her.

Indigo: Thanks.

Ty: Even if you kill my cousin to protect her.

Indigo: You won't try to stop me?

Ty: I wanted him aware of your lethal power. He knows the risks.

Indigo: Do you think he would?

Ty: Honestly, I don't know. He's like Sienna. Pushes buttons for the fun of it.

Indigo: You do that too. With me.

Ty: And you don't?

Indigo: That's what you're doing now. Teasing me. Or is this a booty call?

Ty: Would you leave your drunk sister alone?

Indigo: Of course not.

Ty: Do you think I don't know you enough to know that?

Indigo: Maybe you're inviting yourself here.

Ty: No. I like making you wait.

Indigo: So you will? Tomorrow?

Ty: I'll do what?

Indigo: Come in my mouth.

Fuck. I'm too pissed to stay in control.

I want to go over there. Order her onto her knees. Tug at her hair as she wraps her lips around my cock.

I want to throw her on the bed. Climb between her legs. Lick her until she's screaming my name.

Ty: Maybe.

Indigo: Okay. Fine. I'll just think about it tonight.

Ty: You'll think about it?

Indigo: When I fuck myself.

My balls tighten.

Ty: Are you thinking of it now?

Indigo: Yes.

Ty: Show me.

Indigo: Show you?

Ty: Send me a picture. Of your face.

Indigo: My face?

Ty: I wouldn't mind if it includes your tits. But I'm not after that.

Indigo: What are you after?

Ty: The need in your expression.

Indigo: I'm not sure if I should be flattered or offended.

Ty: I love your tits.

Indigo: Okay. You saved it.

Ty: You're pissed too?

Indigo: A little.

My phone buzzes with a picture message.

Indigo, lying on her dark purple sheets, hair falling over her blue eyes, lips parting with a sigh.

Then another.

From her head to her belly button.

Wearing only her necklace.

Fuck, she looks gorgeous draped in those dark sheets.

I need to be there watching pleasure spill over her expression.

Ty: Do it now.

Indigo: Do what now, sir?

Ty: Fuck yourself.

Indigo: If you promise.

Ty: This isn't a negotiation. Do it now. Or you won't get what you want.

Indigo: Right now?

Ty: Yes.

Indigo: Does that mean I'll get what I want if I do it?

It does. And she knows it.

She knows how to play me too fucking well.

Ty: Don't make me ask again.

Indigo: Yes, sir.

My cock whines.

The line goes quiet for a few minutes. Then my cell buzzes with a message.

Indigo: Not as good as the real thing. At least, not what I remember. Good night, Ty.

Ty: Good night.

She's too good at this.

All night, she's all I think about.

The part of her wine lips. The flush of her cheeks. The sound of her laugh.

Tomorrow night isn't soon enough.

I need to find a reserve of patience somehow.

I'm the one who makes her wait.

Not the other way around.

No matter how well she pushes my buttons.

Chapter Twenty-One

INDIGO

All morning, Sienna alternates between asking me to turn down the sun and asking me to turn down my music.

I tease her by raising the volume on the music. But I keep the playlist to albums she enjoys.

Okay, albums she doesn't hate. Lorde, Fiona Apple, Amy Winehouse.

She threatens to destroy my computer if I play *Back to Black* one more time, but we both know she won't. I play it twice a day, most days, and she always taps along to *Tears Dry on Their Own*.

Besides, I need to make her hangover painful. So she thinks twice before drinking heavily again.

I meant to cut her off at one drink, but maybe this is better. She overdid it in a safe place, with me watching over her. And now she's feeling an agony that will encourage future moderation.

She starts school soon.

She lives her own life soon.

I stop seeing her every day soon.

I'm proud of her. I want her to soar. I want her to stay the strong, independent woman she is—

But, fuck, I'm going to miss her so badly.

So I savor every one of her complaints. And I drag her for an afternoon coffee. And I even give her a few details about Ty.

Nothing important. Nothing that needs to stay mine.

Only enough to tune all my thoughts to him.

His text is on my cell. He's picking me up at eight. He's not asking, really. But I know I can say no.

I know he'll respect it.

But there isn't a single part of me that wants to deny him.

————

I DON ANOTHER BODYSUIT.

A short black dress. Heeled leather sandals. Wine lipstick.

There. I look good. Like me.

The sex goddess version of me.

Sienna is still hung over on the couch, but she manages to get up for long enough to tell me I look hot. And demand I show up no sooner than dawn.

I promise to do my best. Then I meet Ty downstairs, in front of another rented limo.

He helps me into the car. Shoots me a look that dares me to ask for more.

But I don't. Not yet.

"You look gorgeous," he says.

"You too."

He smiles. "Exactly what I'm going for."

"I know."

"I rebooked the photographer," he says. "He'll be fast. Half an hour. Then we'll have the balcony to ourselves."

"Just us?"

He nods. "There's a private booth."

"Oh."

"It's not, what do you say here, it's not the Pentagon, but it should be secluded."

My sex clenches. "You did promise."

"No, I didn't."

Fuck, he didn't. He never does.

He's always teasing me.

Pushing me.

Daring me to ask for more.

"Will you?" I ask.

His eyes meet mine. "Will I what?" He holds my gaze with patience. Waiting for me to expand.

He knows it's harder now that I'm sober.

But I…

I can get past that.

"Will you come in my mouth?" My chest heaves with my inhale. "Please."

His pupils dilate. "Maybe."

"Maybe?"

"Do you really want to make me repeat myself?"

———

HE EXPLAINS THE LAYOUT OF THE BALCONY, THE DETAILS OF the photographs we're taking, the idea behind the plan.

But I absorb none of it.

My thoughts are in the gutter.

I barely notice when we step out of the limo to flashing lights. When a short man follows us into the building. Up the elevator. Onto the balcony.

We're supposed to look in love.

Maybe we do. I don't know.

I only know that I want to touch Ty.

So I get close. And I kiss him like I'll never get enough.

When he kisses back like I'm the only thing he needs, I believe it.

Maybe I don't have his heart.

But I have his body.

And that's something.

It's a lot.

It's the only thing in my head, until Ty leaves to walk the photographer out.

Then my surroundings hit me.

Fuck.

This place is gorgeous.

The restaurant is one big open room, with windows that span from the floor to the very high ceilings.

The diners can't see us. Here. Not in the semi-private booth in the corner. Not really.

It has a high back and sheer curtains.

Secluded and exposed at the same time.

Ty is daring me again.

Why is he so good at daring me?

I move into the booth. Check the space.

A low couch, more suited for drinks than dinner.

Drinks.

Or sex.

It's about the size of my room, with a soft floor, a low table, flickering candles.

Beautiful.

But too far from the view.

I can only see one sliver of skyline. Blue against fluorescent yellow and steel. The big silver moon.

God, it's beautiful. Especially in the dark. There's something about the city at night. This power and peace.

It takes my breath away.

I must stare for a while, because I'm still sitting, my eyes on the view, when Ty returns, a Manhattan in each hand.

He moves into the booth. Sits next to me.

"Thanks." I pick up my drink. Take a sip. Let the familiar taste of bourbon and vermouth flood my senses. "You always order a Manhattan."

He raises a brow.

"Part of your… when in Rome credo?"

"Usually, I drink it straight."

"But…"

"I like tasting your lips." He gives me a slow once-over. It's pure desire.

Fuck. I'm not ready to answer his dare. Not yet. I stand. Motion to the open space. *After you.*

He follows me onto the balcony.

All the way to the railing.

I take a long sip. Let the bourbon warm my lips and dissolve my inhibitions.

If I know Ty, this is expensive bourbon. And it's good. The perfect mix of sweet, rich, spicy.

Ty watches me study the city. "Twenty-two years and you're still in love."

"I'll never get tired of it." How could I? There's something about the soft yellow against the deep blue sky. All these buildings, offices, homes, people, and they're all awake and alive.

Is there anything better than the city at night?

If there is, I haven't seen it.

Admiration slips into his voice. "That's one of the things I love about you."

Love. That's a loaded word. I try to ignore it. "Thank you."

We stand there in silence, the word hanging in the air.

Slowly, we finish our drinks.

Ty takes my empty glass. Looks to the restaurant. Then the booth.

"Are you hungry?" he asks.

"No."

"You are."

"This first. Please."

He half-smiles. "I should make you wait."

"Maybe." I rest my hand on his chest. Dig my fingers into the soft fabric of his shirt. "But you're not that cruel."

"Yes, I am." He leans in to press his lips to mine. "But I'm feeling generous." He places the cups on an empty table. "So, Indie. Tell me what you want. Right now."

"What I want?"

"Anything. Tell me and I'll decide if I'm going to give it to you."

Chapter Twenty-Two

TY

Her eyes fix on mine.

Her cheeks flush.

She's shy, but she's eager too.

"You know what I want," she says. "You always do."

Yes, but I still need her to say it. "Tell me."

"What I said. Yesterday."

"What's that?" I run my thumb over her lower lip.

"Ty—"

"Say it."

"I want you to fuck my mouth." She raises her voice. "Please."

"Please?"

"Please, sir."

Fuck. My balls tighten. I want her. I want her every way I can have her. And this—

I study her. The intensity in her eyes. The part of her lips. The heave of her chest.

She's here. And she's tuned to me.

It's what I want.

The only thing I want.

"I won't go easy on you," I say.

Her pupils dilate. "I wouldn't want you to, sir."

Fuck. "Sit down. Wait for me."

She moves into the booth.

I need to make her wait. And I need to get ahold of myself.

I slip into the restaurant. To the bathroom. Piss. Clean up. Inhale deep breaths.

She trusts me.

But not completely.

I need to be careful with her.

I need to earn all her trust.

I move through the restaurant, onto the balcony, to the booth.

Indigo is sitting in the middle of the red couch, her knees pressed together, her lips in a pout.

"Stand up." I move closer. So the sheer curtains are behind me.

She rises.

"Someone might see." I motion to the balcony behind us. "The waitress might get curious." I motion to the building across the street. "Someone working late might get a show."

Her eyes brighten.

"Is that what you want, baby?" I take another step toward her. "You want someone to see me fuck your pretty mouth?"

"Yes."

It fills my head—the two of us in some crowded club, Indigo on her knees, her lips wrapped around my cock. "You want someone to see how well you suck cock?"

"Yes, sir." She takes a half-step toward me. "If it's you. And it won't cause lasting consequences. Then yes, I want someone to see." Her eyes meet mine. "I want someone to watch you have your way with me."

My cock whines.

I take a deep breath. Try to straighten my thoughts. She's ready to fall into this. She's on the edge.

Indigo is begging to suck me off. Why the fuck am I hesitating?

I exhale. Let my voice drop. "Come here."

She brings her hands to my waist.

I pull her into a slow, deep kiss.

She's soft. Pliable. Her lips part for my tongue. Her fingers dig into the fabric of my shirt. Her body melts into mine.

I scrape my teeth against her bottom lip.

She groans against my mouth. Digs harder. Melts further.

I release her.

She stays in place, her hand curled around my side, her eyes on mine.

Again, I catch her lower lip with my thumb. This time, I slip my digit into her mouth.

Her eyes close. Her lips curl around me. She sucks hard.

There's no fear in her expression. No hesitation. No concern.

She's there. Lost in this.

"Good girl," I purr.

She groans against my thumb.

I pull my hand away.

She sighs. Looks up at me. Ready.

"Take off your dress." I let my voice drop to something dirty and demanding.

She nods. Reaches for the zipper at her side. Looks me in the eyes as she pulls it all the way down, presses the sleek black fabric off her hips.

Moonlight falls over her pale skin, her dark hair, her blue eyes. She takes a step toward me, into that perfect blue light.

Fuck, she's gorgeous. The perfect mix of long, lean curves and sharp lines.

Wine lips and sheer mesh.

"Fucking beautiful," I say.

She lights up. Turns on her heels. Shows off her perfect arse.

My balls tighten. I need that fabric gone. I need to pin her to the couch, bind her wrists behind her back, fuck her from behind.

To order her to groan my name as she comes on my cock.

It overwhelms me—

How much I want to take her.

How much I want her under my control. Bending to my will.

She turns to me, her entire body shaking with anticipation.

She needs this.

And I need to give her what she wants.

I let the last hint of softness fade from my voice. "On your knees."

She nearly falls onto the mat.

"Beg me." I cup the back of her head with my hand.

"Please, sir." Her voice firms. "Please fuck my mouth."

Fuck. I dig my fingers into the back of her head. "Unzip me."

She brings her hand to my trousers. For a second, she cups me over the fabric.

My eyes threaten to close. It feels too fucking good, the pressure of her palm, the warmth, the need.

Then her hand goes to my zipper. She pulls it down. Gasps as my cock springs free. "Can I?" She holds her hand a centimeter from my cock. "Please?"

"Please?"

"Please, may I touch you, sir?"

I nod.

She wraps her fingers around my cock. Explores me with her soft hand. She runs her thumb around my tip. Slides her hand to my base.

"Keep it there."

She hasn't done this in a long time. I need to ease her into it.

She wraps her hand around me. Looks up at me, asking for permission.

Again, I nod.

She takes me into her mouth.

Pleasure floods my senses. She's soft and warm and wet. And it's Indigo.

Her hand on my skin, her on her knees, her wine lips around my cock.

I give her a moment to explore me. Then I push my palm into the back of her head.

"If it's too much." I take her free hand. Place it on my belt. A signal to stop. Since she can't exactly use a safe word. "I'm in control now, baby, understand?"

She groans a yes against my flesh.

Fuck. I keep my hand on the back of her head. Hold her in place as I push into her slowly.

Until her lips are at her hand.

Then I pull back, do it again.

Again.

She feels like heaven, but this isn't enough. This isn't what either of us likes and we both know that.

I test her one more time, then I pull back. "Can you stay in place with your hands behind your back?"

She tries it. Shakes her head.

"Hands at your sides then."

She nods.

"Sit up."

She does.

"I'm not going easy on you because it's been a while." I knot my hand in her hair. "I'm going to fuck your pretty mouth until you can't take it anymore."

She yelps as I tug at her hair. "Yes, sir."

"Is that what you want, baby?"

"Yes, sir." Her tongue slides over her lips. "I want to taste you. I want to swallow every drop."

Fuck. She still knows how to play me. She's still good at this fucking game. Better because she doesn't realize she's playing it. "Lips around your teeth."

She does.

"Good girl."

Her blush deepens.

"Come here." I don't wait for her response. I pull her onto my cock. Drive into her mouth.

Then I do it again.

Again.

I keep one hand on her head, holding her in place as I fuck her mouth. I bring the other to her shoulders, collarbone, chest.

My thumb brushes her breast. I rub her over her lingerie, pressing the mesh into her tender skin.

She groans against my cock.

I toy with her as I drive into her.

Again and again.

Until she's groaning so hard I can't stand it.

Fuck, that feels good.

For a moment, my eyes close. My other senses take over. The sound of her moan, the softness of her mouth, the rough mesh against her nipple.

Then I look down at her. Take in the perfect image of Indigo Simms, on her knees, groaning against my cock.

I tug at her hair.

My body takes over. Harder. Faster. Deeper.

She gags against my cock, but she takes me.

Again and again, I drive into her as I dip my hand under her lingerie, draw circles around her nipple.

Again and again.

Until I'm there.

Pleasure overwhelms my senses. Every part of me tunes to every part of her.

The world is a beautiful, perfect place where everything makes sense.

And everything feels so fucking good.

I rock through my orgasm, spilling every drop in her pretty mouth.

She takes me. Takes it. Pulls back to swallow. Wipes her lips with her hand.

Looks up at me like she wants only one thing: More.

And I only want one thing.

I want to give her more.

Chapter Twenty-Three

INDIGO

W e order dinner.

It's torture.

Everything is delicious, from the peppery arugula salad to the fresh sea bass, but I don't want food.

I want him.

Will I ever have enough of him?

Ty can make me come, yes. He will make me come.

And, fuck, the thought of his body over mine, his cock inside me, his lips on my neck—

I need it so badly.

Forever.

There's no way I'll ever have enough.

I try to steer my thoughts to the table. To his dark eyes, his soft lips, his deep voice. The story he's telling. About some trip he took with Ian. Some place he wants to take me.

How he wants to fuck me there.

It's not just me. He's distracted too. He's thinking it too. He wants this too.

We finish. He signs the check. I try to collect myself in

the bathroom, but the second I reapply my lipstick, I fall into memories of Ty.

The taste of his skin. The feel of his rough touch. The bliss of his orgasm.

I can still taste him. I've never craved that with anyone else. Only him.

With Ty—

I want everything. I'm going to want everything forever.

I meet him by the elevator. Take his hand. "Do you think someone saw?"

"No." His eyes find mine. "Are you relieved? Or disappointed?"

"Both." My cheeks flush. I've never admitted it, even to myself, but it's true. I want someone to watch. "It's... what was it you said? Practicalities are important."

He nods. "And someone catching you sucking cock in public—"

My blush deepens.

"—money can't solve everything."

"Would you?"

He leads me into the elevator. Pushes the button for the ground floor. "Would I?"

"Invite someone to watch?"

The silver doors slide together. "Do you have someone in mind?"

"If I did?"

"I'd be jealous." He pulls me closer. "Do you?"

"No."

"Is it something you think about?" He wraps his arms around me. Presses his lips to my neck. "When you fuck yourself?"

"Sometimes."

"Tell me."

"I..."

He slides his hand over my hip. My other thigh. The hem of my dress. "Like this? Coming in an elevator?" He slips his hand under my dress. "Security watching?"

"Ty…"

"Yeah, baby?" His fingers skim my inner thigh. The edge of my bodysuit. The sheer mesh.

Fuck. My eyes close. My inhibitions fall aside. Alcohol dissolved them. Or maybe he did. I'm not sure.

"Is this what you want?" He runs his finger over the mesh, rubbing the fabric against my clit. "To come with some anonymous stranger watching?"

"Would you?"

He responds by rubbing me harder.

My head falls to one side.

His teeth find my neck. He bites me. Softly.

Then harder.

Hard enough he sends pangs of desire to my core.

The elevator dings. The doors slide open. But he stays exactly where he is. Rubbing me over my lingerie. Dragging his teeth over my neck.

"I won't share you." He nips at my ear. "I have my own limits."

"I know. I don't want… I don't want anyone else touching me."

"What is it? What exactly do you think about when you fuck yourself?"

"I…" Fuck. His hand is still on my clit. I can't think of other fantasies. Of anything but this beautiful moment, right here, right now.

A door opens. Footsteps move closer.

Instantly, he releases me. Rights his posture. Adopts a poker face.

He leads me out of the elevator. Past a middle-aged couple in formal wear. The old money type.

The woman shoots us a look. Like she knows we were about to fuck in the elevator. Or maybe like she wishes she were about to fuck in the elevator.

I can't tell.

We pass. Ty leads us outside.

Then we're on the sidewalk, crisp night air around us.

Inside the building, the couple steps into the elevator. The silver doors slide together. And they're gone.

Judging us silently.

Or engaging in their own elevator make-out session.

That's what will happen if we stay married. He'll stay devoted to making me come.

It's a tempting offer.

A lifetime of good food, financial security, mind-blowing sex.

And all I do is give up love.

———

It's the same limo, but it feels different. Like it's ours.

We sit the same way, on the bench parallel to the car door, legs pressed together, eyes on the mirrored wall.

The reflection. My wine lips. The color smeared on his. The hickeys on my neck. From last time.

Or maybe this time.

"Indigo?" Ty runs his thumb over my skin.

It feels so fucking good. Too fucking good. "Who?"

He smiles.

It's rare for him. A real smile. And this is so real and broad and beautiful.

I want it so badly.

"I'm a little distracted." I make eye contact through the mirror. "Someone is keeping me on edge."

"Someone cruel."

"Very."

His smile widens. "I meant what I said."

"I'd think… that covers begging." My breath catches in my throat.

"For now."

Fuck.

He turns toward me. Looks me in the eyes. "What do you think about? When you fuck yourself?"

My cheeks flush.

"You're shy now, baby?"

"A little."

He brings his hand to my cheek. Runs his thumb over my temple.

It's more sweet than carnal, but it warms me all the same.

"I'd hate to send you home alone," he says.

"Would you?"

He nods.

"That doesn't seem fair. I tell you everything. You tell me nothing."

"You want a deal?"

I nod.

"A fantasy for a fantasy?"

"We keep trading until someone says uncle?"

His eyes flit to my lips, breasts, thighs. "If you go first."

I can do that. And I want to. I want to tell him. To drive *him* crazy. "I do think about you. Coming to my apartment. Surprising me," I say. "I'm wearing some slick silk robe. You knock. I answer. You don't say anything. You enter. Pin me to the wall, pull my robe aside, toy with my breast. Kiss me. Touch me. Fuck me."

"I could."

"Sienna would be home."

"When she's not."

My sex clenches. The image threatens to consume my brain. I fight to hold on to some hint of sense. "It won't be my apartment for much longer."

"No. But it is now."

"Maybe." For a moment, I see it. Me in a long purple robe, him in a black suit, pinning me to the wall, sucking on my nipple as he drives into me. I can feel the pressure of his hand. Smell his soap. Taste his skin.

Fuck.

I take a breath. Force myself to look him in the eyes. "Your turn."

"Any fantasy? Or one of you?"

"Do you think about other people?" I bite my tongue. "No. Don't answer that. I'm sure you do… That you think of her."

His smile disappears.

"But I don't want to hear it. I just… I want to hear if it's me. Or if it's no one in particular."

"I do think of you."

"When was the last time?"

"Last night."

Of course. I was teasing him last night. And he was teasing back. "Before that?"

"I thought about taking you home, ordering you to do away with your dress. To sit on my lap and fuck yourself for my viewing pleasure."

"And?"

"Then I threw you on the bed, on your stomach, and I fucked you until you were groaning my name."

Again, desire floods my senses. "What else?"

"That isn't enough?"

"Is it?" I place my hand on his thigh. Just above his knee. "Or do you need it harder? Rougher?"

"It's your turn."

It is. "If you asked, I'd take control. Climb into your lap and fuck you. I'd still like it. I don't need it rough to come. But I want it." It's strange, admitting it out loud. Admitting I'm going after my desire for the first time in forever.

Admitting I'm out of my fucking mind.

Did I really say yes for the money?

I need the cash, sure, but there *are* other ways of making money.

It's him. The feel of his presence, his touch, his kiss.

His fuck.

I force myself to look him in the eyes. "I want you in control. I want you pinning me to the bed, binding my wrists, ordering me to take your cock like a good girl." My chest flushes, but I press on. "I think about that. The way your hand felt around my throat. The rough edge to your voice when you purred, '*Come for me, baby.*'"

His eyes stay glued to mine.

"For a long time, I tried not to think about you. Tried not to think about that. But I always go back to it. I always think of you when I fuck myself."

"You remember?"

"Remember. Or fantasize about more. Harder. Rougher. Riskier."

His pupils dilate. "Someone watching?"

"Sometimes."

"Watching us?"

"Watching us." I take a deep breath. "When I saw that picture of you at Paradise."

"That wasn't—"

"It was."

He tries to hold a poker face, but his eyes betray him. We both know it. Some paparazzi caught Ty's fuck of the night getting him off under the table.

"I was angry. You fell in love with Rory. I understood

that, even if I hated it. But she left, and you came here, and still, you didn't call. And you were with some girl you barely knew... I was angry. And jealous. And I couldn't stop thinking about it. Imagining it was us. At some crowded bar. Dancing to throbbing electronic music. Then finding a quiet spot on the balcony where we have just enough privacy..."

"We could."

"Could we?"

His eyes bore into mine. "I could pull strings. Minimize potential consequences."

I nod.

"But that isn't what you want." His fingers skim my thigh. Higher, higher, higher. "You want the danger." Closer, closer, closer. "The thrill." He presses his palm against my sex. Over the mesh. But still so, so close to where I need him. "The risk of getting caught."

I swallow hard.

"Tell me." He brings his other hand to my cheek. Tilts me so we're eye to eye. "Do you want the risk, baby? Do you want the entire world to see how well you take my cock?"

Fuck. "It's a fantasy."

"But you do."

"I do. But the... practicalities."

"Fuck the practicalities."

"Ty—"

"We're going to my place. The practicalities don't matter. Not now."

Later.

"Now... I want to know exactly what you want. Every dirty fantasy. And I want to fill them all."

My sex clenches. "It's your turn."

"It is." He rubs his palm over me, pressing the soft fabric against my clit.

184

The friction is divine. So different than his hand. Softer and rougher at the same time.

Pleasure floods my senses. But still, my body whines for his touch. I need the fabric gone. Need everything else erased.

The rest of this is complicated.

But sex?

That makes perfect sense.

"But I'd rather show you." He pulls his hand away, right as the car stops. "If you're ready to play."

I swallow hard.

"Are you?"

Chapter Twenty-Four

INDIGO

A m I ready to play?

It's a good question. Simple and enormously complex.

It's one thing to invite him to fuck me.

But to cede control? To let go completely?

Ty waits for my answer. As he helps me out of the limo, guides me into his apartment building, past a knowing security guard, into the elevator.

This tiny space that's all ours.

The shiny silver walls. The turned key. The illuminated Penthouse button.

At a glance, we look like a normal couple on our way home. He's in his suit, no hair out of place, no visible tattoos, no sign of the aggressive, rough lover I know.

And I'm leaning against the wall, my leather jacket covering my cocktail dress, my lipstick smudged, my hair a little messy.

The normal wear of a night out.

No sign I was on my knees, begging for his cock.

No sign I'm wound so tight I'm going to break.

No sign I'm about to offer him every ounce of control.

I want to. I do.

But I'm not sure I can handle it.

The elevator door slides open. Ty presses his palm into my back. Leads me down a short hallway. Unlocks the door.

"After you." His voice is soft. Gentle.

He knows I'm nervous.

He's waiting for me.

Or maybe his accent is masking his intentions. Maybe I don't have a fucking clue who Tyler Hunt is or what he wants.

He's offering me ten million dollars for ten years of marriage.

He's paying me to marry him.

I believe him. I believe his reputation is tarnished—I've read the gossip blogs too. I believe this is the easiest fix.

I believe he's sure love is done with him.

But he chose me.

I'd like to think it's because of my strength, my wit, my discretion even.

But it's not. It's this.

Ten years because he wants to fuck me.

I suck a breath through my teeth. Step inside.

He follows. Closes the door. Locks it behind us. "A drink?"

I nod.

He moves to the kitchen. It's on the right side of the massive living room slash dining room slash den.

Fuck, it's huge. Gorgeous.

A thousand square feet, easily. Hardwood. Floor-to-ceiling windows. A glass coffee table in front of a sleek leather couch.

A corner view. Southwest. The Hudson, a deep, almost

black-blue, reflecting the crescent moon and the yellow light of the city.

And there. A sliding glass door to the balcony.

I don't wait or ask or speak. I move across the room, through the door, onto the wraparound balcony.

Great food is one thing. Fancy clothes are another.

But living someplace like this?

Money buys so much.

My knees knock. I reach for the railing. Steady myself.

We're up high, forty stories maybe, and the air is clear and warm.

"You'd prefer a view of the city?" Ty's voice flows into my ears.

"This is beautiful." I turn to him. "Perfect."

He holds out my drink. Another Manhattan.

My fingers brush his as I take it. "Thanks." It's such a small, simple touch, but it warms me all the same.

He slips his hand around my waist, motions *follow me*.

When I do, he leads me around the corner, up a small set of stone stairs, to a rooftop terrace.

It's simple. A small couch with weather-proof fabric, a side table, a few potted plants.

A three-sixty view of Manhattan.

I nearly drop my drink. "Ty... holy shit."

He watches me stare. "You like it?"

"Do I like it?"

He nods.

"Of course." I turn, do my own three-sixty, stop at him. "It's perfect. It's... you... I... do you own this?"

"Yes."

"Since..."

"A year now. Give or take."

I turn toward the Empire State Building. The lights are

purple today. Is it NYU graduation already? Or are they purple just because? "So it was after…"

He follows my gaze. "What do people call it? Retail therapy?"

"Most people buy clothes. Makeup."

"Bondage gear?"

I blush. "Probably." I turn to him. "Really? You bought a breakup apartment? What's wrong with a haircut?"

"How much shorter could I go?"

"You could shave your head."

He raises a brow *really?*

I nod *really*. Move closer. Run my fingers over his neck. Around the back of his head.

His eyes flutter closed as he leans into my touch.

It's not our usual dynamic. It's soft, romantic, sweet.

Me, tending to him.

Not—

I don't even know how to describe it.

"Or dye it red," I say.

His eyelids flutter open. His soulful browns fill with intensity. Affection. Or need. Or demand.

Or all three.

"I like it this way." He slips his arm around my waist. Holds my body against his. "But you're right. I could have."

"I cut mine after Mom…"

"It suits you."

I motion to the terrace. "It suits you."

"Thanks."

"You too." My gaze shifts to the balcony beneath us. "Maybe next time, I'll be able to afford the apartment."

His posture stiffens. He releases me. Turns toward the water. "One day."

He's pulling away.

He doesn't want to talk about it. This ending? Or the financial nature of our arrangement?

Or the fact he bought this apartment because his fiancée dumped him?

I'm not ready for the answer.

I'm barely ready to be in his space.

"Have you spent a lot of time here?" I motion to the stairs. Move down to the first level.

He follows me into the quiet, clean room. "I was fifty-fifty for a while. Then we launched a new division. It made sense to be here." He pulls the sliding door closed. Clicks the lock.

It's silly. A lock on the door to the balcony. How could anyone access the terrace?

But that's Ty.

Always guarded.

"You were here, half the time, for the last year?" I cross to the couch.

"Yes," he says.

"And full time for the last few months."

"You want to ask me something."

I swallow a sip of my drink. Will it to make this less complicated. It doesn't. "Why didn't you call?"

"What?"

"My mom died and you didn't call. You must have known. You knew and you didn't call or send flowers or see how I was."

"I did."

"What?" I swallow hard. "You did?"

He nods. "I sent flowers. I wanted to do more. But I didn't trust myself to see you. And I wouldn't be that man."

"Did you really think you'd fuck me?"

"I wasn't willing to risk it."

He was worried he'd cheat on his fiancée.

I don't know if I want to slap him or congratulate him on the restraint.

"And after that? After your fiancée left?" I ask.

"You won't like my answer."

"Try me."

His eyes meet mine. "I wanted to fuck you."

"What are we doing now?"

"We're getting married."

"So you could only fuck me if I'd marry you?" That makes no sense.

"I can't fuck you then let you go."

"What if I call this off now?"

"I haven't fucked you yet."

"Technically."

"It's different," he says. "Don't pretend it isn't."

It is. And it's not just that he hasn't been inside me.

He hasn't been rough yet. Not the way he can be.

Not enough to scare me.

"So you'll only fuck me if I agree to ten years without other men?" I ask.

"You already agreed. Are you changing your mind?"

"No."

"But you're angry I didn't call."

I nod.

"It was selfish," he says. "I knew if I saw you, I'd fuck you. And that would be it. I'd need you to be mine."

"Even though you'll never love me?"

"Yes."

Either he spends his life fucking me.

Or he ignores me.

It almost makes sense. From a certain angle.

But not one where he'll never fall in love with me. Ty is possessive, sure, but he's not that possessive.

No one is that possessive.

He wouldn't claim me just to fuck me. Would he?

Am I really so crazy that I'm okay with that?

"You're right. I could have called. I could have made sure you were okay. I'm sorry." He runs his thumb over the space between my thumb and forefinger. "You deserved better."

It's so strange on his tongue. *I'm sorry*. It's new, any man apologizing, but especially Ty. He gets things right the first time. "Thank you."

"If you want to leave—"

"No."

"Good." His grip around my wrist tightens.

He pulls me into a kiss. It's hard. Fast. Hungry.

And under that, tender.

Like he's desperate to give something of himself to me.

Whatever it is, I want to take it.

My lips part. His tongue slips into my mouth. Dances with mine.

There's no other way to explain it.

He kisses me like he's claiming me.

Maybe he is.

Here—

He can have me here.

No, *I* can give myself to him here. I have just as much power as he does.

He loosens his grip, then tightens it again. Not enough to hurt. Or restrict blood. Only enough I know he's in control.

He brings my hand to his cock. I cup him over his slacks. There's too much fabric. I need him. Now.

For a moment, I press my palm against him. Soft fabric against hard flesh. The warmth and pressure of him against me.

I kiss him harder.

He releases my wrist. Brings both of his hands to my zipper.

There. In one quick motion, he tugs it down my back.

He retraces the line with his fingertips. A light pressure. Soft. Gentle, even.

He lingers there, in this soft, sweet, tender moment.

Then he shoves the dress off my shoulders. Pulls my body against his. Wraps his hand around my throat.

Fuck.

Desire floods my senses.

He shifts his hips, so his cock grinds against my ass. There's all this fabric in the way—his slacks, my lingerie—but the friction still sets me on fire.

I need him.

All of him.

Any way I can have him.

Every way I can have him.

It consumes me. My need for every inch of his flesh.

He holds me in place as he slips his hand between my legs. He rubs me over the lingerie, pressing the mesh into my clit.

Fuck. It's softer and rougher at once.

More and less at once.

I need his hand.

I need his hand on me.

Now.

Still, he holds me in place as he rubs me. Again and again. In slow, perfect circles.

A groan falls from my lips.

His grip around my throat tightens.

Fuck. I almost come from the pressure. From knowing I'm completely at his mercy.

Why do I need to be at his mercy?

I don't know.

I don't care.

I don't care about anything but following his demands.

He'll give me what I need.

He'll give me everything I need.

He rubs me again and again. That sheer mesh, impossibly thin, but still far too thick.

This perfect friction. Rough. Intense.

Too much.

Not enough.

My eyes close.

The tension in my sex winds. Tighter, tighter, tighter.

Almost—

He slows—

Draws these impossibly light circles against my clit again and again.

Pushing me closer and closer—

Almost—

There—

He slips his hand beneath the lingerie. His index finger against my clit. That soft, perfect pressure.

One perfect circle.

Winding that tension inside me tighter and tighter—

So much. Too much to take.

Then I go over the edge.

I groan his name as I come.

The spool unwinds. My sex pulses with my orgasm. Bliss spills through my pelvis, stomach, thighs.

He rubs me through my orgasm. Then he releases me. Brings his hands to my hips. "Bend over the couch."

"Here?"

"Here."

I place my hands on the arm, lowering my torso, rocking my sex against his crotch.

"All the way."

"Yes, sir."

His breath catches. It drives him crazy too.

And it winds me tighter, knowing it drives him as crazy as it drives me.

I bring my hands to the cushion. Drape my body over the arm.

"Good girl," he purrs.

I nearly come from the compliment.

It's too fucking hot. I'm at his mercy. I can barely move. I can't do anything but take him.

He pushes the bodysuit aside. Slips two fingers inside me. Hard and deep.

Enough it hurts.

A gasp falls from my lips.

He does it again. Harder.

Like he's daring me to ask him to stop.

To drop my safe word.

To beg for mercy.

But I don't want mercy.

He drives his fingers into me again.

"Fuck," I breathe.

Then he pulls back. Does it again.

Again.

Then three fingers. "You're mine. Understand?"

"Yes, sir."

"This is mine." He pulls back, pushes his fingers inside me again. "As soft or rough as I want."

I nod into the couch.

"Do you know how I want it, baby?"

"Rough."

"Good girl."

Fuck.

He pulls his hand from my cunt. Brings his fingers to his lips. Licks the taste of me off them.

Then he takes something from his pocket.

A condom.

My heart thuds against my chest.

Every molecule of my body tunes to him. I need this. I need him inside me. I need it so fucking badly.

He undoes his zipper. Rolls the condom over his cock. Moves closer. Closer.

In one swift motion, he drives into me.

Fuck.

Pressure floods my senses.

And that overwhelming feeling of wholeness. Like I'm finally complete. Like I'm finally exactly where I need to be.

It's hard. Rough. Enough it hurts.

But that only winds me tighter.

Ty hooks his hand around my thigh. He holds me in place as he fucks me.

There's no other way to describe it.

Hard, fast, intense.

Too much to take.

And not enough.

My eyes close.

My body tunes to him. The feel of his nails on my skin. The tug of rubber. The pressure of his cock inside me.

The heavy breaths.

The low grunt.

The slap of my thighs against the soft leather.

He drives into me again and again.

Winding me tighter and tighter.

Closer and closer—

Then his thumb is on my clit. He rubs me with fast, rough strokes.

I come fast this time. The tension inside me winds to a fever pitch. With his next thrust, everything unravels. My sex pulses.

It's too hard. Too much. So much I'm sure I'm going to push him out of my body.

But I only pull him closer.

Deeper.

He brings his hand to my back. Pins me to the couch as he drives into me.

His breath speeds.

Then his thrusts.

He fucks me hard and fast. Then he's there, groaning my name as he comes, working through his orgasm, claiming me completely.

When he's finished, he pulls back. Takes care of the condom.

Returns to me, still sprawled over the couch, still panting and sweating and completely soaked in bliss.

Then he helps me up and he kisses me.

And, for a perfect second, I'm a woman kissing the man who knows exactly what she needs.

Nothing more.

Nothing less.

———

HE SHIFTS INTO THAT OTHER VERSION OF HIMSELF. THE gentle caretaker.

He helps me into the bath.

He doesn't join me. He sits there, his sleeves rolled to his elbows, soft and sweet as he helps me soap, shampoo, rinse, dress.

He has clothes here. My clothes. Ones I picked out with Paloma. And extras.

Her picks, I think. She has a certain flair for the dramatic. This midnight blue silk pajama short set—

It's completely her.

And this bedroom, with its bare walls and its Egyptian cotton sheets—

It's pure Ty.

A side he tries to ignore. The scared boy who's afraid of losing everything. Who's already lost far too much.

He lays me on the bed and pulls the sheets to my shoulders.

Then he leans down and kisses me good night.

Like he means it.

Like he wants more than sex.

Like he really does want to spend the rest of his life taking care of me.

Chapter Twenty-Five

TY

Except for the black dress on the hardwood floor, and the cocktail glasses on the coffee table, the room is the same as it was this morning.

Same soft leather.

Same clear glass.

Same Hudson River.

And the impression of Indigo changing everything.

Changing me.

I close my eyes and taste her lips, smell her shampoo, feel her soft body.

I feel her yielding, hear her begging, see that look of surrender—

I clear the cups. Hang her attire.

Undress. Shower. Don pajamas.

She's in my bed, sleeping soundly.

She looks right there, her dark hair blending into the black sheets, her body soft and still, her expression serene.

She looks right in my bed, in my space, in my life.

It shouldn't be a revelation. I asked the woman to marry me. Of course she's going to be in my life.

But this—
This lightness in my chest—
This warmth filling my entire body—
It's familiar.
The warm, soft, sweet danger that ends in pain.
I can't fall in love with her. It's out of the question.
But still, I climb into bed next to her.
Still, I pull her body to mine.
Still, I hold her close as I fall asleep.

Chapter Twenty-Six

INDIGO

The sun streams through the windows, casting morning light over the black sheets and hardwood floors.

I close my eyes. Turn to the pillow. Soft, cool cotton. And it smells like Ty. His soap, his shampoo, his sweat—

Some perfect mix that's entirely him.

I roll onto my back. Stretch my arms over my head. Soak in the warmth of the sun.

Did I dream it?

Or was he really here last night?

Did I really feel like he loved me?

No, not loved. He isn't going to love me. But there must be some word that works. Something between the painful stab of *care* and the sweet promise of *love*.

I rise. Move to the bathroom, the one here, in the master.

It's already set up for me.

Purple toiletries. Toothbrush, razor, comb, towel set.

Dark purple. My purple.

Did he pick them out for me? Or was it Paloma, taking

care of everything? Ink purple is straight out of her playbook.

Maybe that's his life. Maybe he lets the help run his household. But it's hard to imagine Ty ceding that much control.

He picked this out.

He made space for me.

He really is ready to commit to a lifetime with me, even though he'll never love me.

It's strange, but it makes sense in a Ty kind of way.

I brush my teeth, wash my face, comb through my messy locks as I move into the main room.

Fuck, this place is just as gorgeous in the day. The sun bounces off the river, casting a soft glow over the leather and hardwood.

Ty isn't here. And it's quiet.

According to my cell, it's early. And Sienna is proud of me for staying out all night. She's taking a victory run in my honor.

I can't help but smile. Some of this is hopelessly complicated. But helping my sister find a better life—

That's pure, unadulterated good.

I tap a coy reply. Move into the kitchen.

It's incredibly neat, of course. A French press and coffee grinder against the wall. Next to an electric kettle. And in the sleek cabinet above them—

Jackpot.

Some dark roast coffee and a neat row of tea tins. A Japanese green tea, a spicy chai blend, and the black tea I loved at his office. Yunnan Hong Cha.

I set the water to two hundred degrees. Find a teaspoon. Scoop leaves into a sleek white mug.

While the water heats, I check the apartment for signs of him. The room at the end of the hall is an office.

It's exactly what I expect of Ty. A modern sit to stand desk adorned only with a computer. No decorations, no touches of home, no photos of family. Work. Ergonomic work, sure, but only work and the view.

If it was my office, the view would be enough. The Hudson on one side. Uptown on the other. Beauty everywhere I look.

But it's hard to imagine Ty sitting at his desk, staring at the river or the Empire State Building.

No, more likely he lowers the fancy, almost invisible blinds so the light doesn't cast a glare on his computer.

There's another room, similar to his bedroom, but clearly designed for someone else. The purple sheets and black desk are a dead giveaway.

Then there's the guitar in the corner.

The model I have at home. The one I told him about three years ago.

Plus a very expensive stereo and a bookshelf stocked with old favorites.

This is supposed to be my room.

Maybe that's for the best. The feeling of his arms around me, his chest rising against my back—

I'm still craving it.

I can't sleep next to him for ten years without falling in love with him.

I move toward the stereo. Connect my cell.

Play *Back to Black*.

Amy's throaty vocals fill the space. I close my eyes, soak in the warmth of the sun, the coolness of the air-conditioning, the sweet sound of the music.

It feels like home.

Already, it feels like home.

That's scarier than anything. But it's a nice place to spend the next ten years. Big room, gorgeous view, walk-in closet.

The hangers are filled with my clothes. Finds from my trip with Paloma and a dresser packed with Ty's picks.

Lingerie.

Handcuffs.

Harnesses.

My thighs shake as I run my fingers over the soft leather. Two delicate cuffs joined on a thin metal chain.

Ready to attach to the wall, desk, bed, harness.

There's more in the next drawer. A riding crop. A paddle. A sleek vibrator, new, in a velvet box.

Did he buy all this in the last week?

The lingerie is my size. Everything. From the sexy yet practical black nylon bra to the sheer.

"Your water's ready." His voice interrupts me. He's standing there, in the doorframe, in running shorts and one of those sweat-wicking tanks, bathed in soft light.

"You're quiet."

"Your music's loud."

"Too loud?"

"No. I like it." He stands there, all tall and broad and sexy.

He's handsome in his suit, but this—

Sweat dripping off his strong shoulders, down his muscular thighs, over his tattooed arms—

Fuck.

What if I throw this harness on the bed? Ask him to go right now?

Will he get naked with me?

I want him naked. I want to touch every inch of his skin. Feel every ridge of his muscles. Trace every tattoo.

There's something new on his chest. And another, on his arm, above the geometric rose he shares with his brother.

"Would you like me to fix your tea?" he asks.

"You were on a run?"

He nods. "I can invite you next time."

"Please no."

He chuckles. "Your sister then. If she moves into the building."

If. That's a lot for him. An if, not a when. That's practically a promise to compromise. "She's fast."

"So am I."

Probably. Really, Sienna only invites me out of some mix of pity and sisterly duty. She says I need to exercise. Then she does a few laps with me, lets me walk the rest, breaks into a gazelle-like run. "She would like that. She likes you."

"Because I'm hot?"

"Mostly." I can't help but smile. "She texted her congratulations."

"Oh?"

"On getting laid."

He smiles. "Did you tell her?"

I shake my head. "She assumed. Since I didn't come home."

"My ego."

"Yes, your ego must be horribly wounded by me not telling my sister you rocked my world." I hold up a pair of leather handcuffs. "You'll only buy a single harness next time."

"You don't like it?" His voice is a challenge. A dare even.

I take it. "Isn't it obvious?"

"Yes." He releases the doorframe. "You can wear one next time."

Next time. I want that already.

I want to be here, in this gorgeous apartment, fucking him all day.

And I want to run back home, to claim everything in my life as *mine* for as long as I can.

There's a beep in the kitchen. The kettle.

"I'll make breakfast." He moves into the hallway

I sit with the lingerie. This symbol of my new life. Gorgeous, expensive, lush, erotic.

The perfect place for a beautiful, tended-to toy.

Part of me wants that. Part of me craves it.

Being Ty's toy. His plaything, to bend or break or fuck until he's done with me.

I'm already imagining scenarios. The two of us at his office. Him ordering me out of my dress. Binding my hands with these cuffs. Attaching them to the harness around my waist.

Bending me over his lap and spanking me.

Fucking me with his fingers.

Throwing me over his desk and driving into me.

I'm already wet. That's all it takes. The thought of him.

I want that. This. Even though it's completely fucked up.

But what about when we're not alone, in our apartment, giving into our dirty desires?

What about when we're out in the world?

We're still two people who want to fuck each other.

But we're not madly in love. Not like we're pretending.

Are we friends? Fuck buddies?

Two people who understand each other?

I don't know.

I don't know what he wants when we're dressed.

But I want to find out.

I want to know him. All of him. As much as I can.

I'm not sure if that's love, but it's close. Dangerously close.

Close enough, I'm sure he's going to break my heart.

Chapter Twenty-Seven

INDIGO

I linger for a few songs, then I follow the smell of coffee into the kitchen.

The scent brings me back to mornings with my dad.

He was a firefighter. He worked for days at a time.

He told me his job was safe, but a part of me worried I'd wake and he'd be gone.

When I woke to the smell of coffee, I knew he was home. I knew he was safe.

I knew he'd take me to the park, tell me stories, teach me guitar.

We'd sit there, in the den, practicing scales until I was exhausted. Then he'd play his favorite albums. Even the ones he promised Mom he wouldn't show me.

He had everything—old standards, British punk, ska, eighties pop, singer-songwriters. I still remember the first time he forgot to mute the stereo during *You Oughta Know*.

I asked him what it meant to fuck someone.

I was old enough to have an idea of sex, but he still sat me down and talked to me about what it really meant. Told me it was this beautiful thing I'd experience one day. That I should never be ashamed of what I wanted, so long as I was with someone I trusted.

What would he say about my arrangement with Ty?

Would he be terrified I want someone who hurts me? Or proud I'm able to embrace my desires?

I wouldn't tell him. I won't even tell Sienna.

But I wish I could tell someone. I wish someone was proud of me. For something.

The way Dad was when I learned a new riff or wrote a new song or came home with an A on a test.

I wish someone would say *good work, Indie. You survived the last two years with style and grace. You kept it together.*

I know how hard that was.

I'm proud of you.

Even if you had to put away your passion. Even if you've run from your talent. Even if you aren't ready to face your pain.

"You still take them sunny side up?" Ty sets a perfect white mug of tea on the dining table.

"Yes. Thanks." I wrap my fingers around the mug. Bring it to my lips. Inhale the warm, familiar smell. The mix of fine tea and fancy coffee. Then just the strong black tea.

Mmm. Fig and caramel.

Warmth and strength.

"Do you want help?" I take another sip. "Or are you horrified by the thought of me messing up your perfect space?"

"I want you here," he says.

"I mean—"

"I know what you mean." He sets a pot on the stove. Turns a burner on high. "I lost half my deposit over your lipstick stains."

"Really?"

"And the scuffed hardwood."

"Oh." My chest flushes at the memory. Him fucking me so hard his bed scraped the floor.

"I could have argued normal wear and tear." He half-smiles. "But a few thousand dollars was a small price to pay for the bragging rights."

For him, yeah. "It's an accomplishment."

He nods *I know.* "I like finding pieces of you. The eye shadow on a counter. The lipstick on a collar. The smell of your shampoo in my shower. It feels like I have something of you."

"You thought about me?"

"Of course."

"But you were... with her."

"It's not as if she thought she was my first." His laugh is soft. "I'm turning thirty-one next month."

"Old man."

"Who can lap you."

My lips curl into a smile. Fuck, this feels so good. So... normal.

I sit. Sip my tea. Watch him crack eggs into the pan, slip bread in the toaster, pull hot sauce from the pantry.

He cooks the way he does everything: with precision and grace.

This could be our life. Our morning routine. Only —"Don't you have work today?"

"Yes."

"It's past work time."

"Is it really?" His voice is teasing. "I didn't realize."

"You're taking off?"

He nods.

I smile. He's taking the day off. For me.

Because he wants to fuck me, probably.

But it's not like I want something else.

"Oh. Good." I take another sip. "What will we do with our time?"

"You're not good at coy."

A laugh spills from my lips. "You can't fuck me all day."

"Is that a dare?"

"If it is?"

"Is it?" He shoots me a look that begs me to say yes.

But I don't.

I do want to fuck him all day. But I want this too. This normal morning together.

Ty fixing breakfast.

He's a good cook. From taking care of his mom, I guess.

I did the same, but I'm terrible. Sienna's the one who can cook.

I watch him work. He showered and dressed while I was in my room. He's in jeans and a white t-shirt.

Normal clothes.

Well, a suit is normal in the financial district. Anywhere in New York, really. We dress to impress here.

This is the Ty I get on weekends and vacations.

The Ty who's mine and mine alone.

Is there a part of him that's all mine? Besides the part that fucks me?

If that's all I get—

It's not nothing.

It's a lot.

But—

"Do you think of her?" I ask. "When you're with me?"

"Not the way you mean."

"What do you think I mean?"

"I don't think about fucking her."

I swallow hard. "But other things?"

"I was with her for two years. I have a lot of memories."

Right. That's fair. But it doesn't soothe the knot in my stomach. "That's all? Memories?"

"What are you getting at?"

"You don't talk about her."

"There's nothing to say."

Maybe. "But you did think of me. When you were fucking her?"

"I was committed."

"But you did."

"Yes." His expression darkens. "When we were first trying things my way. Then after. When I realized she'd never want that."

"You imagined me?"

"I'm not proud of it."

I don't know if I want to slap him or mount him. I thought of him sometimes. By myself. With Noah. "But you were going to commit to her, even though she didn't have the same tastes? Even though you had to imagine me?"

His eyes meet mine. "I thought I could find a compromise."

"Did you?"

"No. But I told myself it didn't matter."

"And it did?"

He nods. "No one can be everything."

"Maybe."

"You think about someone else watching us," he says.

My cheeks flush.

"Joining?"

"Sometimes."

"It's not going to happen. I'm never going to share you."

"I know."

"But you're still satisfied?"

"So far."

He chuckles. "You're daring me."

"Answering honestly."

"And if you weren't satisfied? If you needed that and I wouldn't give it to you?"

"That's different. It's one thing. One very specific scenario."

"But the same idea."

I nod.

"Would you leave because I won't give you something you want?"

"No. But it wouldn't happen. You'd find a way to give it to me."

He shakes his head.

"You would. You might not invite someone to watch. You might not share me. But you'd find a way to fill that need. The mirror. A semi-public place. A video."

His pupils dilate.

"You're thinking about it now. Are you really going to argue otherwise?"

"No."

"It's different."

"Yes," he admits. "But I told myself it wasn't. I told myself a lot of things… maybe she saw it. Maybe she realized I'd never be satisfied. I don't know."

"And that was when you thought of me?" I ask. "When what you two were doing wasn't… enough?"

"Not every time."

"So sometimes it was enough?"

"I am capable," he says. "Of soft. Gentle. Loving. Sometimes, it's even what I want."

"Really?"

"Do you need me to demonstrate?" The dare slips back into his voice.

My blush deepens. "If it's what you want right now."

"No."

"What do you want?"

"I want you to eat your breakfast."

"After that."

"Is that an invitation?"

"If it is?"

"Is it?" His voice drops to that demanding tone.

I press my thighs together. Is it? I don't know. I want him. But can I handle fucking him and leaving?

Can I come without falling harder?

No. That's a lost cause. If he's going to break my heart either way, I may as well enjoy the process.

"Yes." My chest heaves with my inhale.

"After breakfast."

I must pout, because he laughs. Smiles the world's most dazzling smile.

Fuck, he's so handsome. And his joy—

It's rare, but it's so fucking beautiful. I want to bottle it, hold it close, drink it when I'm feeling down.

"But you have to promise you won't think of her when we're together. Ever," I say.

"I'd never think of someone else."

"But with her—"

"I won't. Not with you. And you won't think of anyone else when you're with me."

Fuck. My entire body is already buzzing. What the hell is wrong with me, wanting him to tell me what I'm allowed to think? "Okay."

"I'm jealous. Just considering it."

"Me thinking of someone else?"

"Yes." He offers me the hot sauce. "I can't promise you many firsts, Indie. But this—I don't let go with anyone else. I wouldn't buy anyone else a drawer of harnesses. I wouldn't trust anyone else."

I take the hot sauce. Draw circles on my eggs. It's fancy sriracha, the kind without preservatives or artificial colors.

The same, but different, more expensive.

The eggs are fresh in a way mine aren't.

I fail to stifle a sigh of pleasure.

His posture changes immediately. He shifts into that other Ty. The one attuned to every single one of my wants.

For a moment he studies me. Then he returns to normal.

And we're two people making conversation over breakfast.

Talking like friends.

Or maybe like lovers. I'm not sure anymore.

I need to fuck him. Now. But I know Ty. Even if I strip naked and climb under the table, he'll hold to his edict—

After breakfast.

And he's still on his first piece of toast.

I swallow another bite of eggs. Try to push my thoughts out of the gutter. Reach for some focus that isn't how much I want him inside me. "What would you do? If you went into work?"

"It's not that interesting."

"I don't believe you." I take another bite. Swallow. Focus on the intensity in his eyes. "That you would do anything that bores you."

"Not that interesting to you."

"Try me."

He lets out a small laugh. "I research, run numbers, negotiate. Ian does most of the digging. I do all of the practical and most of the negotiating."

Negotiating. I can see that. "Is that your favorite part of your job?"

"Yes."

"Why?"

216

His eyes meet mine. "What was your favorite part of working at that awful bar?"

"The tips."

"That doesn't count," he says.

"The way men wanted something from me."

"Men everywhere want you."

"Maybe." My cheeks flush. "But this was different. They were trying to win me over. I hated men staring at me like I was a piece of meat. I hated having to laugh at their jokes. Or listen to them complain their wives didn't understand them. But there was a power in it too. And I liked that power."

His eyes fix on mine. "Is that why you like me?"

"I don't have any power over you."

"Do you really believe that?"

No. "Not exactly." But he is the one with more power here. He's richer than god. I'm no longer a broke cocktail waitress, but my net worth is still half a dozen zeroes short of his.

"You don't realize it." His voice is soft. "How much you could sway me if you wanted. How easy it would be for you to have the upper hand." He half-smiles. "You're not a good negotiator. I could teach you."

"Now that I've signed your contract?"

His laugh is soft. "Are you unsatisfied with the terms?"

The no love thing, yes. But that's not what he means. That's not something we can negotiate.

He'll fall in love with me or he won't.

No amount of money can change that.

"I would have agreed for a lot less," I say. "Maybe just the mortgage and Sienna's scholarship."

"I would have offered more."

"So we both lose?"

"We both win. It's fair."

"Then why should I take negotiation tips from you?"

He chuckles. "I'm not smart when it comes to you."

"Thinking with your cock?"

"Yes."

"Oh." My blush deepens.

"It's not usually an issue. At work. Even if I'm dealing with a gorgeous woman, or a woman I want to fuck."

"New York is full of gorgeous women."

"But there's only one Indigo Simms."

Do I mean that much to him? It's hard to believe.

But he did offer me ten million dollars.

And we do understand each other. We do have something special. Even if it isn't love.

He continues, "Negotiation is an exchange of power. It's never clear to all sides exactly how much anyone has. Even if everything is in the open. Say, I'm investing in a company. One with a set valuation. Other investors bought in at six million dollars. I have the opportunity to buy twenty percent. It should be easy math. Twenty percent of six million. One point two."

"You buy at one point two or you don't?"

"In theory. But what if the owner needs the money now? What if she can't risk a no? What if the company is the only one that will do?"

He's talking about us.

"No one can say what that's worth," he says. "No one can say who has the upper hand. And there's always the human factor. Something a person cares about more than money."

"And you exploit it?"

He dips the corner of his toast in egg yolk. No hot sauce. Just the perfect square half piece of toast and yolk. "I use leverage to get what I want."

"And us… this is an exchange of power."

"Yes. But I don't take it. You give it to me."

My breath catches in my throat.

"You're waiting. Because I asked you to wait. Because *I* say when I'll fuck you." His posture shifts. Into that other Ty. The ruthless man who gets exactly what he wants. "And you're waiting because you want to wait. You want to be under my control."

"Yes."

"Now?" His voice isn't a dare. It's an honest question.

And it's up to me to answer.

Am I ready to be completely under his control?

Chapter Twenty-Eight

INDIGO

"Yes," I breathe. "Now. Please."

He watches me for a moment, then he nods with understanding.

His posture shifts.

That other Ty.

The one who revels in every ounce of his power.

His voice drops. "Come here."

I move around the table.

He turns his chair so he's facing me. Then he beckons me with his first two fingers.

I move closer.

His hands go to my hips. He pulls me into his lap, so I'm straddling him, my legs around his thighs, my feet on the floor.

He brings one hand to my cheek. Pulls me into a slow, deep kiss.

Soft for a moment.

Then hard.

His hand trails down my neck. Slowly, he traces the neckline of my pajama top.

Slowly, he undoes the first button.

The second.

The third.

The last.

The sides fall open, revealing my breasts, leaving me topless in his lap.

He kisses his way down my neck. Over my chest.

His lips brush my nipple. Softly.

Then harder.

The scrape of his teeth.

"Fuck." I bring my hand to his chest. Tug at his shirt.

He bites me again. Harder. Hard enough it hurts.

"Ty—"

Again.

I hook my arm around his neck. Let my nails find his skin.

Again.

My hips rock against his. He's hard beneath me. So close to where he's supposed to be. Only this stupid fabric between us.

Again.

"Fuck."

Then harder—

Harder—

He's pushing me.

Daring me.

Daring me to ask him to stop.

But I don't want him to stop. I want that sweet, perfect pain.

He scrapes his teeth against me again.

And again.

Harder.

Harder.

The brush of his teeth sends a pang to my sex. The

perfect mix of pain and pleasure. It hurts. But that only winds me tighter.

It only makes me achier.

He winds me tighter again and again.

Harder and harder.

Until it *is* too much.

I close my eyes. Try to take it. To focus on the feeling of his cock against my sex. His legs between my thighs. His hands against my waist.

Again.

Again.

Fuck—

"Azure."

He stops immediately. Looks up at me. Studies my expression. Waits.

I suck a breath through my teeth. "I still—"

"I know."

"But you—"

"Should I check in? Red, yellow, green?"

"No."

"Are you sure?"

"Yes."

He holds my gaze for a long moment, then he pulls me into a slow, deep kiss.

Again, he drags his lips down my neck. Over my collar-bone. My breasts.

He bites softly.

Then harder.

Harder.

Until I let out a groan that's agony as much as it's ecstasy.

Then he stays there.

He toys with me with that same perfect pressure, sending pangs of pain and pleasure to every inch of my skin.

My entire body tunes to him.

The softness of his lips. The sharpness of his teeth.

His cock, hard, between my legs.

My hips rock of their own accord.

He groans against my flesh. But still, he toys with me. Mercilessly slowly, again and again.

Until I'm sure I can't take anymore.

And, still, he toys.

"Please." I rock against him. "Please, fuck me." Again. "Please, sir."

His nails dig into my skin.

It drives him crazy too.

But still, he's patient. He pulls back. Looks into my eyes. "Stand."

I do.

He tugs my pajama bottoms off my hips. Then my black panties.

I'm standing in his kitchen, naked, next to our used breakfast plates. A perfectly normal breakfast and now he's ordering me out of my clothes.

It's absurd.

It's absurd how much I like it.

Want it.

Crave it.

"You're beautiful, baby. Have I told you that?" His hand curls around my hip.

"Yes."

"I haven't said it enough." His fingers dig into the flesh of my ass.

He looks me up and down slowly, waiting, reveling in every ounce of his power.

He doesn't need a suit or a limo or a fancy restaurant. He has it. No matter what he wears or where he goes, Ty knows exactly how to play me.

He keeps one hand on my hip. Slips the other between my legs.

His palm brushes my cunt. "You're wet."

"You're hard."

"Do you think that will make me relent?"

"No."

"Smart girl." He teases me with two fingers. Then he pulls back. Brings them to his lips. "That's one of the things I like about you."

"Thank you."

His eyes find mine. "You're going to come on my face."

My breath catches.

"Do you want it here? Or in the bed?"

"Will you fuck me after?"

"Maybe."

Fuck. "Please."

"I said maybe. Don't make me say it again."

"Yes, sir."

"Here? Or the bed?"

"Here."

"Sit." He places his hand on the table. "And spread your legs."

I turn. Slide onto the table.

"Fuck." His breath catches in his throat. "Beautiful." He rises. Pushes his chair aside. Places his body between my thighs.

I hook my legs around him reflexively.

He brings his hands to my thighs. Holds them in place.

He kisses me. Though I'm not sure I can call it a kiss. His lips are against mine, yes. His tongue is in my mouth, yes.

But it's not a kiss.

It's a command.

And all I want to do is obey.

I reach for his shirt. Pull it over his head.

He releases me. Lowers me onto my back.

Drops to his knees between my legs.

He's kneeling in front of me, but still, he has all the power.

Still, all I want to do is give him more.

I let my eyes close.

His fingers curl into my thighs. Then it's the heels of his hands. He pushes harder, until my thighs are digging into the table.

Until I ache.

Until I know I'm his.

Then he brings his lips to my inner thigh. One soft kiss, then his mouth is on me.

His lips against my clit.

His tongue against my folds.

He licks me up and down, slowly tasting every inch of me.

I hook my legs over his shoulders. Reach for something to steady myself. Get only the edge of the table.

He brings his tongue to my clit.

Soft flicks.

Then hard ones.

Back and forth.

Up and down.

There—

Exactly the spot I need.

"Fuck, Ty." My heels dig into his back.

He shoves my thighs against the table. Hard. Enough it hurts.

Enough I'm completely at his mercy.

Enough my sex aches.

Then it's the scrape of his nails against my skin. That perfect, sharp burst of pain.

He does it again. That same sharp scrape as he licks me

exactly where I need him.

Again and again.

The knot inside me winds tighter and tighter.

Until it's too much to take. The pain and pleasure and control.

With the next brush of his tongue, I come.

My sex pulses. Pleasure spills through every inch of my body. All the way to my fingers and toes.

He works me through my orgasm. Then he stands. Pulls something from his back pocket.

A condom.

"Stay." He looks down at me as he undoes the button of his jeans. Pushes them off his hips.

Fuck, it's the first time I've seen this much of him in the light of day.

Those broad shoulders, the strong chest, the tattoo snaking around his ribs. That one is new. And there's something on his hip.

And he's—

Fuck.

He rolls the condom over his cock.

Brings his hands to my thighs. He holds me in place as he drives into me.

Fuck.

That feeling of his cock inside me—

I'm whole, I'm complete, I'm home.

Ty lifts my legs, holds them against his chest.

I'm not bound, not really, but I'm still at his mercy. I can barely move. Only to grab the table or rock my hips.

The table shakes as he fucks me.

My head hits the wood. My back. My ass.

Still, he holds me in place as he drives into me again and again.

He stretches my walls with every thrust.

It's intense.

Hard.

Rough.

Deep.

My eyes close. My head falls to one side.

He winds me tighter with every intense thrust.

Again and again.

So, so close.

His nails scrape my calves. Softly.

Then harder.

It's almost enough.

I'm almost—

"Touch yourself." His voice is all rough edges.

My eyes blink open. Meet his.

Fuck, the look on his face—completely in control, completely wild.

I slip my hand between my legs.

He holds me there, watching as I rub my clit.

Fuck. I'm almost there. I'm going to—"Please, Ty."

His nails scrape my skin.

"Please, sir. Please fuck me."

He stays in place for a moment, looking down at me, watching with rapt attention as I bring myself closer and closer.

Almost—

Almost—

Without warning, he drives into me.

I come instantly, my cunt pulsing against his cock, pulling him closer, deeper.

It pushes him over the edge.

He digs his nails into my thighs, groaning my name as he comes.

He thrusts through his orgasm, then he lowers my legs.

He leaves me panting on the table as he does away with the condom.

Then he helps me up. Brings me to the shower—the one in his bedroom—and runs the water warm.

He gets in with me.

Stays there, in that perfect space, the two of us naked and spent and utterly without defenses.

Chapter Twenty-Nine

TY

After we wash and dress, we watch a movie on the couch. *Sabrina*. One of her favorites.

She lingers through lunch and another cup of tea.

Then she leaves to meet her sister at school and walk her home.

It's sweet. How much she cares. How willing she is to do anything for her Sienna.

Indigo insists on taking the subway. I insist on walking her to the station. Kissing her goodbye on the quiet concrete street.

The Financial District is bustling—it's almost rush hour—but I don't feel the need to hustle.

I don't care that I'm underdressed.

That I'm supposed to be at work.

Only that she's leaving.

I head home, but the apartment is different without her. Wrong somehow.

I give her time. I work out in the gym downstairs. Fix dinner. Watch an old thriller.

My contact sends the proofs. Our photos on a gossip blog, going live at midnight.

I warn her.

Ask her to meet me at the office.

Tell her what to wear under her dress.

But not what I'm going to do with her. I save that thought for myself. It warms the space until it's too hot to bear.

Until I have to strip to nothing.

Think of her.

Resist the urge to fuck myself.

It's more fun, reveling in the sweet torture of anticipation.

All night.

As I get ready for work. Head to the office.

Find my brother waiting for me.

With the paper turned to Page Six and a look on his face that screams *you really expect me to believe this bollocks*.

Chapter Thirty

TY

Ian is standing in the lobby, in a sleek black suit and fuchsia tie, the picture of calm composure.

He motions to a take-out cup on the counter. Cold brew. Black. Decked in a sleeve from the shop around the corner.

My favorite.

It can't be that bad. If he's bringing coffee and not the too sweet, too creamy English Breakfast our mother prefers.

It can't be that good either. The milky tea is a peace offering. A promise of mercy. Even when the recipient won't admit he needs it.

Five years ago, he divorced. I brought him milky English Breakfast every day.

After he fled the scene, moved to the States, returned only for quarterly meetings—

I brought him a cup every time.

He had to see his ex-wife. A cup of tea was the least I could do to ease that pain.

Laura took a portion of the company in the divorce. And

when she finally sold him the rest, offered to sever the last tie between them—

Maybe it doesn't mean anything. Sure, he prefers his cuppa without milk or sugar, but he still drinks tea most of the time.

"You look exhausted." He lifts his take-out cup. Smiles with satisfaction.

And he's wearing his fuchsia tie. The one that complements his girlfriend's teal hair.

It's a badge of honor for him. *I'm in love and I make my woman come.*

I'd hate it if I didn't love him so much.

If it wasn't so obvious they're madly in love.

As it is—

"You look smug." I take the cold brew. Motion to my office.

He nods *of course*. Follows.

The office is full, but it's quiet. This early, everyone is waiting for their first cup of coffee to kick in.

Most people ignore us. A few look twice. Ian's presence is rare enough to draw attention.

I let him into the office. Lock the door. Sip the cold brew.

It's good. Rich, strong, dark. A coolness I need.

I want to tell him to fuck off and mind his own business.

And I want to thank him for looking out for me.

I want to beg him to stay in one place. So I know where to find him. So my nightmares end.

It's ridiculous. He's been a civilian for nearly ten years. But my amygdala doesn't listen to reason.

"You're welcome." He motions to the take-out cup in my hand. Moves past me, to the leather couch.

He sits, sets the newspaper on the cushion next to his, and he waits.

Like he has all the time in the world.

"Thank you," I say. "If that's all..." I motion to the door. "I have a full day."

"I imagine."

"Don't."

He chuckles. "I'm not sure I have a choice." He pulls out his cell. Brandishes a popular gossip site. And the photo on it.

Indigo and I at the restaurant, kissing like we're madly in love, the secluded booth behind us.

"I know what I'd do after. You..."

"Is this a who's more depraved contest?"

"Hard to play with someone who doesn't want to partici-pate." He slips his cell into his pocket. Settles into the couch. Sips his take-out tea.

He's giving me shit.

But that's his job. Even if we're both in our thirties now.

Is that all this is, some brotherly ribbing?

I try to find concern in his eyes. Or suspicion.

There's nothing. Or I'm not good at reading him.

"How's Eve?" I ask.

"Good." He smiles. "Sleeping."

"You wore her out?"

"Of course." His smile widens. "But I know you hate bragging."

"Is it that difficult, keeping news of your girlfriend's orgasms to yourself?"

"It is." He takes another sip. "Thank you for acknowl-edging that."

"Anytime."

Again, he chuckles. "You're tense for a man who spent the weekend with his new paramour."

"How do you know that?"

"You just told me."

Fuck. I know better than to fall for such an obvious ploy.

"You *are* tense."

"Surprised." I reach for a better response.

He makes that *hmm* noise.

"Yes?"

"You went out with Cam last week."

"And?"

"You didn't think he'd relay the news?"

I shrug as if I didn't consider it.

"You're hiding something."

"You're too suspicious."

"Probably." He studies my expression. "You're still hiding something." His gaze flits to the pictures in the paper. "These are... careful."

"Yes."

"Like you chose them."

"Maybe people are tired of labeling me a playboy."

"Maybe." He stares at me, waiting for me to expand. "I guess this is how you felt after I moved to New York."

"How is that?"

"You knew I was lying to myself, chasing something I didn't really want."

"You were," I say.

"And so were you. Or maybe you are. You've never been a—"

"Slut?"

He chuckles. "It doesn't suit you."

"I appreciate the feedback."

Again, he chuckles. "I'm not here to cross-examine you, Ty."

"Aren't you?"

"I'm not trying."

I raise a brow.

He shrugs with apology. "Old habits die hard."

"Once a spy, always a spy?"

He nods. Even though we both know he was never really a spy. Not the way people imagine it.

He wasn't James Bond, running around tropical locations, sleeping with dangerous women. (Well, not for long.)

He was the man in the office, directing the field agent, searching for information the modern way—

On the computer.

But maybe that isn't what he means. Ian's never been a paragon of trust—that's what made him a good candidate for MI6—but since he discovered his ex-wife cheating, he's been completely without trust.

I'm not exactly blameless there.

I suspected she was fucking someone else and I said nothing.

Even when she confessed to me, drunk one night, I said nothing. I thought it was best to let her be the one to tell him.

I believed her when she promised she'd tell him soon.

But she didn't.

For one month.

Two.

Six.

Even when she served him with divorce papers—

He put it together. He's not an idiot. Some part of him knew. But he managed to ignore it.

It's ridiculous how good people are at lying to themselves. Even people who swear they live and die by honesty.

"I'll admit," he says, "I asked your assistant if you were seeing someone. She invoked her NDA, of course, but the way she giggled—"

"She has a crush on you."

"It wasn't that kind of giggle."

"You're an expert?"

"On when a woman wants me? Yes."

"It must be painful, being so irresistible."

"It is. Thank you for acknowledging it."

My laugh eases the tension in my jaw. This isn't about Laura. He isn't here to berate me for keeping her secret.

He doesn't know I kept her secret.

That guilt is mine and mine alone.

His inability to trust, his need to run from intimacy—

Maybe I'm not completely responsible, but I certainly didn't help things.

I clear my throat. Take another sip of cold brew. Try to forget his ex-wife's name.

Ian is happy now.

He's in love.

He trusts his girlfriend.

That mistake I made, keeping his ex-wife's confidence—

I thought it was for the best. That it would hurt him the least. It wasn't all selfish.

Was it?

My brother places his hand on the armrest. He gives me a chance to confess, tease him, brag about making Indigo come.

When I don't, he continues, "If you want me to go, I will. I'll tell Mum you're fine. I'll tell Eve you're fucking interns in the break room—"

"Don't."

"You care what she thinks of you?"

"She's good company."

His girlfriend is passionate, witty, intelligent. She can discuss classic literature or punk rock for hours.

And she knows.

I told her I kept his ex-wife's secret.

I thought it would help her understand why Ian can't trust anyone. Why he'd ask more than was fair.

It did. It must have. She's still here.

But—

I push it aside. Try to tease him back. "She's smart. Too smart for you."

"Undoubtedly," he says. "But she doesn't like me for my intellect."

My laugh eases the tension in my shoulders. Maybe he's only here to say hello. Maybe this isn't an inquisition.

He doesn't need to know. It will only hurt him more.

Even so—

Ian won't approve of my arrangement with Indigo. And if he finds out I withheld any part of the truth—

No matter how badly I want to tell him, I can't.

"What did she say about the pictures?" I ask.

"It's nine o'clock. It's her summer. I doubt she's seen them."

"When she does?"

"You saw her three weeks ago."

And when Ian was in the bathroom, she told me casual didn't suit me. She supported whatever I wanted. But I looked exhausted. Worn. Like I was tired of running in circles.

She's right. Of course.

She *is* a smart woman.

Don't get me wrong. I don't approve. She's nineteen now; she was eighteen when he offered her half a million dollars for her virginity.

It's all very complicated. He fell in love with her via her online journal. He didn't know how old she was until he was smitten.

He had no intentions of meeting her. Of doing anything except reading her anonymous posts. But when he found out someone else was trying to buy her, he stepped in.

I don't approve, but it's hard to blame him.

If I found out someone was trying to pay Indigo for sex—

I'm not sure I'd step in and outbid the man the way Ian did, but I'd do something to stop him.

"Mum is worried about you," he says. "But I'm sure she's told you that."

I nod. "She still believes I'm a gentleman."

"You are. In your way." Ian looks to the crowded office. He stands. Moves closer. "You were honest with all your conquests."

"Conquests?"

"What do you call them?"

"Partners."

He chuckles *if you say so*. "Tell me to fuck off if you'd like, Ty. Tell me you're keeping this to yourself. If not, well… you know I love details."

"Fuck off."

Again, he chuckles. "You like her."

"Of course."

"No. You *like* her."

"I wouldn't fuck someone I don't like."

He shakes his head *I don't think so*. "Maybe you liked some of your… partners. But not most of them. I know the look you have when you fuck someone you like."

"How do you know that?"

"Am I wrong?"

Not exactly. I did enjoy the company of plenty of women. But I wasn't proud of myself after. That changed things. "Yes, I like her."

"Is it serious?"

"It is."

"And you didn't tell me. Arsehole."

I flip him off.

Which only makes him laugh. "How serious?"

"Serious."

"Cam likes her."

"Cam likes everyone."

"Cam hates everyone." Ian chuckles.

"Her sister plays football."

"He mentioned a cute sister," Ian says. "I imagine he wanted to convince you he has eyes on her."

He might. I can't tell with him. "Does he?"

"Who can tell with Cam?" He lowers his voice. "I realize you were fucking someone else two months ago."

"And?"

Ian nods *whatever you want to tell yourself.* "That's an abrupt change."

"You're one to talk."

He nods *true.* "What's her name?"

"Indigo."

"Indigo…"

"Indigo, I don't want you spying on her."

He chuckles. "If I promise I'll be on my best behavior?"

"So you'll only spy on her a little?"

He chuckles in that *you've got me* way. "What is she like?"

"Strong." My eyes go to my watch. She's supposed to arrive soon. Paloma is taking her to a few venues. They book early in New York.

"Strong?"

"Yes, strong."

He nods with understanding. "What does she like? Besides your bed?"

"Fucking in places that aren't my bed."

He smiles in a way I rarely see. With brotherly pride.

The way he did when I told him I'd lost my virginity.

Ian turns to the hallway. Watches Paloma skip to the door.

She knocks. "Mr. Hunt. Ms. Simms is on her way up. Should I prepare her tea?"

"Yes, thanks," I call back.

Ian smiles. "Indigo Simms. Why is that familiar?"

"I wouldn't dare contemplate your mind."

Something spreads over his face. Some realization.

I try to distract him with a few questions about my division, but he stays half-here, half-digging his memory.

Then she steps into the hallway and his eyes light up.

"The girl from the bar," he says. "Of course."

"There's no 'of course.'"

He shakes his head. "Who wanted it rough so badly it fucked with your head."

"Fuck off."

"You haven't—"

"Don't say anything to her."

"When have I said anything?"

Indigo moves through the hallway. She notices Ian. Nods hello. Enters without knocking.

His eyes light up as he studies her. He doesn't just recognize her name. He recognizes her.

And every fucking thing I told him about her.

How I fucked her.

How I wanted to fuck her.

The holiday I got too pissed and went off about how I couldn't stop thinking about fucking her.

Even though I was with Rory.

Even though I was satisfied.

Even though I'd never be that man that left because of sex.

"Hey." She nods hello to me. Turns to Ian. "We've met. I'm not sure you remember—"

"Indigo Simms. Of course. Ty couldn't stop talking about you." Ian offers his hand. "It's nice to see you again."

"You too." She looks to me for an explanation.

I try to sell my nonchalance.

"I've heard a lot about you," she says.

"All terrible?" he asks.

"Of course. But your girlfriend—I think she's Ty's favorite thing about New York," she says.

"Before you?" he asks.

"I'm almost jealous when he talks about her hair." Indigo motions to her blunt, asymmetrical cut. "It's threatening."

He smiles. "She'll want to meet you."

"That means he wants to make out in front of you," I say.

"With your consent, of course." He winks at her.

She laughs. "I'm more of an exhibitionist, but thanks."

He shoots me a look.

I shoot him a *don't*.

"If only you met me a few years ago, I would have invited myself," he says. "Ty would deck me, of course. But I'd still offer."

Her laugh gets louder. "And I'd find out later you orchestrated the whole thing so he could defend my honor?"

"It's my duty as his older brother." Ian turns to me. "Friday? Eight o' clock?"

I nod. "If it works for you, Indie."

"Sure," she says. "If you don't mind watching me and Ty make out."

"Is that a dare?" he asks.

She nods.

He holds out his hand to shake. "You're on."

He nods goodbye. Leaves.

She looks back at him. Watches him pretend he's not watching us.

Then she turns to me. Closes the distance between us.

She places one hand on my chest. The other on my waist.

Her eyes close.

Her lips find mine.

She kisses me like I'm the only thing she needs.

For a moment, I believe it.

For a moment, she convinces me we're marrying because we're madly in love.

Chapter Thirty-One

TY

Paloma interrupts with a knock and a take-out tea. "Yunnan Hong Cha." She smiles at Indie. "Ready to go?"

"I probably should." Indie looks at me. "Or I'll be too tempted to stay."

"Mr. Hunt has a busy day. We don't want to distract him." Paloma shoots me a *keep it in your pants* look.

Indie nods to my assistant. She turns to me. Pulls me into another slow, deep kiss. "Of course." She winks and follows Paloma out of the office.

A few minutes later, my phone buzzes with a new message.

A picture. The lingerie I asked her to wear. Sheer black knickers curving around her hip.

Peeking out of her black jeans.

The jeans she's wearing today.

Indigo: I don't want you too distracted.

Ty: You don't?

Indigo: If you had to spend the entire morning wondering if I followed your instructions… I'm sure that would take up a lot of space in your mind.

    Ty: Are you baiting me, baby?

    Indigo: No, sir. I'm just letting you know I followed orders.

My balls tighten.

She's too good at pushing my buttons.

    Ty: All of them?

    Indigo: Of course.

    Ty: Show me.

    Indigo: I'm in the car with your assistant.

    Ty: And?

    Indigo: Do you want me to flash her?

    Ty: She's signed an NDA.

    Indigo: Yes. She told me it's airtight.

    Ty: And?

    Indigo: I'm not even supposed to think about someone else watching.

Fuck.

    Indigo: Unless that's what you want, sir.

    Ty: The second you have privacy.

    Indigo: Of course.

She sends another picture. One from her apartment. The mirror in front of her bed. The same black fabric stretched over her hips and arse.

Now she's daring me. To ask her to strip in front of my assistant.

Or some other New York elite.

If she thinks I'm backing down—

She knows better.

FOR HALF AN HOUR, I WORK. MY MIND IS SPLIT—HALF ON Indie, half on finding information—but I can't exactly complain about the circumstance.

Finally, my phone buzzes with a text.

The strap of her bra. All the way to the start of the cup. Her crop top pulled aside.

She's against a clean white wall, but I can't place the other details.

Indigo: Is this to your satisfaction, sir?

Ty: You know what happens when you dare me.

Indigo: Are you going to keep asking me that?

Ty: Should I tell you to take off your knickers right now?

Indigo: It depends what you'll say after.

My mobile buzzes with a picture message. Another from this morning. Indigo, from her nose to her toes, sheer black lingerie barely covering her tits and arse.

In her bedroom.

Ready for the day—her lips painted Bordeaux, her hair in a neat line.

Then another picture.

Her and Paloma in a rooftop garden. Under a white lattice.

She's standing there, in black jeans and a matching top, in the position for the bride.

She's not turned to Paloma. She's looking at the camera.

And she's certainly not dressed in typical wedding attire—

But it still steals my breath.

Sends an entirely different set of mental images through my mind. Indigo in some gorgeous white dress, staring into my eyes like she's madly in love with me.

Taking my hand. Smiling as we dance under the stars.

Laughing as we feed each other cake.

Then the entire thing shifts. And it's Rory.

And I need out of this fucking office.

I ignore the buzz of my cell. Leave the office. Lock the door.

Take the elevator to the street.

Walk the half a dozen blocks to Battery Park.

It's warm today. Too warm for a three-piece suit.

Still, I move toward the water. Watch the sun bounce off the tiny waves.

Once I've caught my breath, I pull out my cell.

Indigo: Not how I imagined picking out my wedding venue.

Ty: What did you imagine?

Indigo: I haven't. Not really. I never wanted to get married.

Ty: Even when you were young?

Indigo: I am young.

Ty: When you were a girl.

Indigo: I went to a cousin's wedding in a hotel ballroom. It was very Jersey. You might know the type of place, with all your travel. It had that hotel ballroom look. Dated. Stuffy. With these over-the-top tablecloths and decorations trying to hide it as a place for business.

Ty: Are you close with your cousin?

Indigo: I see her at Christmas.

Ty: They're still married?

Indigo: With two kids.

Ty: Are they happy?

Indigo: I don't know. She wanted to be an actress. But when she got pregnant, she stopped trying. Maybe she gave up. Maybe she realized she wanted something else.

Ty: And you?

Indigo: And I?

Ty: You always wanted to be a musician.

Indigo: Yes.

Ty: Do you still play?

Indigo: Not often. Not since my mother died. It hurts too much.

My heart breaks for her. When we met three years ago, she loved two things more than anything else: family and music.

I hate that she's lost so much.

Ty: Have you tried recently?

Indigo: No. I've been busy.

Ty: Not anymore.

Indigo: Actually, my fiancé is sending me all around the city to look at wedding venues. I'm booked all week.

Ty: I can pick one if you'd prefer.

Indigo: No. I'll pick the venue. And the dress. You can arrange everything else.

Ty: Done.

Indigo: Done? You've already hired a hair stylist and makeup artist?

Ty: We haven't set a date yet.

We'll have to see what's available at the venue she chooses. They all have open spots this fall. And most have last-minute cancellations.

But something tells me Indigo is going to want to wait until the very end of September.

Indigo: We haven't announced our engagement yet.

Ty: We will. Friday.

Indigo: Dinner with your brother?

Ty: Yes.

Indigo: Do you have a ring?

Ty: I'm having something made for you.

Indigo: You know my size?

Ty: I know everything.

Someone bumps into me. A teenager taking a picture of her friend. They're in trendy clothes—those ridiculous Mom jeans and the Fjallraven backpacks everyone wears in Europe —but they hold themselves like tourists.

It's sweet, the way they're looking at the Financial District like it's this big, beautiful mystery they want to solve.

Maybe they're not tourists. That's how Indie looks at New York. Like she can't believe she's lucky enough to live in this big, beautiful city.

"Sorry." The teenage girl looks at me and blushes. "Do you work here?"

"Yes," I say.

"Do you know how to get to the bull statue?" Her blush deepens. "My friend wants to grab the balls."

"You won't be the first." I give her instructions.

She thanks me and runs off to her friends. Whispers something.

About the hot old guy in a suit? Or something else?

I don't often concern myself with the opinions of high school girls. Only Indigo's sister. And she's not a high school girl for much longer.

My cell buzzes again.

Indigo: I want you to propose.

Ty: What happened in my office a few weeks ago?

Indigo: With a ring.

Ty: On my knees?

Indigo: Only the one.

Ty: And you on your knees after?

Indigo: Maybe. If that's what you want, sir.

I take another deep breath. Try to find a sense of calm.

My thoughts refuse to sort. There's too much shit going through my head. All the possibilities of a life with Indigo.

The life I used to imagine.

The paths I can no longer walk.

Indigo: You bring up sex when you don't want to talk about something.

Ty: Did I ask you to call me sir?

Indigo: Yes. You asked if I'd be on my knees after. Were you referring to the two of us attending yoga class?

Ty: That's a new way to celebrate an engagement.

Indigo: If you don't want to discuss this, that's fine. We're already in the cab, on our way to the next venue. Paloma can help. She's probably trying to read this text. She hates being left out.

Ty: She's paid to deal with it.

Indigo: She's still spying.

My assistant won't say anything to anyone. But Indigo doesn't want her knowing this.

I don't want her knowing this.

It's ours. Only ours.

Ty: I want to tell Ian Friday.

Indigo: That gives you three days to propose.

Ty: Did you have anything in mind?

Indigo: Besides you on one knee, with a ring?

Ty: Yes.

Indigo: I want you to surprise me.

Ty: During my three-day time limit?

Indigo: Are you not up for the challenge?

Ty: You know better than to dare me.

Indigo: I know exactly what happens when I dare you, Ty. That's why I dare you.

She's bringing it back to sex this time. I can't exactly complain, but I need a clear head. Especially if I'm going to ask her to submit.

Right now, I don't have it.

I slide my phone into my pocket. Walk to my favorite coffee shop. Order a cold brew. Return to work.

The air-conditioning cools me. The propriety, the people looking at me like they expect something of me—

It's enough to straighten my thoughts.

Mostly.

I wait until I'm alone in my office to check my cell.

She's at the next venue. A grand hotel ballroom. Old money and elite. Too stuffy for her. But Paloma insisted on offering Indie a range of options.

Indigo: I want to tell Sienna. We can tell your brother first. But I want to tell her next.

Ty: She'll probably tell you to go celebrate by fucking my brains out.

Indigo: Probably.

Ty: How do you tell teenagers things? Instagram?

Indigo: I think it's Tik-Tok these days. But she'll only notice if there's a soccer ball in the frame.

Ty: I can write it on a football. Ask her to play.

Indigo: Maybe write it on your chest and take off your shirt.

Ty: Has she told you more about how I'm hot?

Indigo: She's asked for specifics.

Ty: Specifics?

Indigo: You know the specifics.

Ty: I'm not sure I do.

Indigo: What you like. How long you last. How well you fill out your boxers.

Ty: I don't wear boxers.

Indigo: She doesn't know that.

Ty: Did you tell her?

Indigo: That you go commando? Of course not. It's enough she's asking about the size of your cock. I always thought it was only men who are obsessed, but she has a lot of questions.

Ty: Really?

Indigo: I think she wants me to break out a ruler.

Ty: What did you tell her?

Indigo: That it's none of her business.

Ty: Indie.

Indigo: Your ego?

Ty: My ego is fine.

Indigo: You're just worried about her getting the correct information?

Ty: She'll keep asking. If you don't tell her something.

Indigo: I know.

Ty: You like her asking?

Indigo: You like your brother asking about me?

Ty: Maybe he didn't.

Indigo: Of course he did. I saw the way he looked at me. Like he'd heard a very explicit, very dirty story.

Ty: He may have.

Indigo: Oh?

Ty: I'm not so tight-lipped when I'm pissed.

Indigo: I need to get you drunk?

Ty: And take advantage of me?

Indigo: No. I'll be good. Keep my hands to myself.

Ty: Oh?

She's quiet for a few minutes.

Then my phone buzzes with a text from Paloma. Telling me to lay off the flirting so she can do her job.

Indigo: Paloma is insisting I put my phone away. She thinks I'm too distracted…

Ty: Tell her we're talking about the proposal.

Indigo: Doesn't she think we're engaged?

Ty: People get engaged without formal proposals all the time.

Indigo: Maybe.

Ty: I didn't think you'd want one.

Indigo: Me either. But I do.

Ty: Why?

Indigo: I want that moment. Of looking into your eyes, wanting to say yes to spending my life with you.

Would she say yes now? If there weren't any strings? If we were two people who wanted each other?

I can't ask. Not right now. Not when my heart is breaking for her loss.

If she says no—

I might call this off, right here, right now.

And I can't.

I need her.

Ty: And the wild sex after?

Indigo: Maybe it will be in the middle of wild sex. Knowing you.

Ty: Don't tempt me.

Indigo: What do you mean, sir?

It's an offer.

No, it's a request. She wants me to tease her. To answer her dare.

My body whines. It's not confused about what it wants.

Her. Any way.

Every way.

My head is a mess. My heart is a lost cause.

But this—

This is crystal clear.

I make her wait a few minutes, then I reply.

Ty: Take off your knickers.

Indigo: Now?

Ty: Where are you?

She sends a picture. Another rooftop bar. More sleek than the first. Perfect for her.

Ty: Go to the bathroom. Take off your knickers. Show me.

Indigo: If it's not a single stall?

Ty: Find a private spot. You're smart. Figure it out.

Indigo: Paloma will ask questions.

Ty: Do you care?

I give her time to reply.

A few minutes.

She sends a picture. The jut of her bare hip, her jeans pulled aside, her knickers MIA.

I don't wait for her response.

I call her.

She answers on the first ring. "Ty." Her voice is breathy. Heavy.

"Where are you?"

"The bridal suite."

Fuck. So much for clearing my head. "Show me."

"Give me a minute." She pulls the phone away. Fumbles. Sends a picture of the small, white room.

It's perfect. A white vanity. A floor-to-ceiling mirror. A leather fainting chair.

Then a mirror selfie. She's still in her clothes. Except for the knickers around her finger.

"Is that enough detail, sir?" Her voice drops. Into that perfect mix of dare and obedience.

"Take off your top."

She fumbles for a moment. "Done."

"The bra."

"Paloma will—"

"Let me worry about her."

"But, sir—"

"But, what?"

"I just… know you're concerned about your reputation."

"She won't say anything."

"The rest of the staff?"

"I'll handle it," I say. "Don't ask again."

"Are you sure?"

"Positive."

She murmurs an agreement.

"Take off the bra and show me."

"Ty—"

"You're going to come for me now. Or you're not going to come at all."

"At all?"

"Until I decide you've earned back the right."

"Fuck." Her breath hitches. "Ty—"

"It's your choice, Indigo. Which is it? Are you going to come for me? Or are you going to disobey me?"

Chapter Thirty-Two

TY

S he teases me back.

Makes me wait.

The minute feels like an eternity. I need her. I need her groan, her bliss, her submission.

Now.

My body whines.

It's impatient.

But I've been waiting a long time for this. For her.

I have plenty of practice enduring impatience.

My phone buzzes with a picture message. Indigo, from her nose to her hips.

The sharp line of her dark hair.

The pout of her wine lips.

The silver pendant hanging between her perfect tits.

The soft curve of her chest, waist, hip.

The waistband of her jeans.

Fuck.

"Ty?" Her voice is soft. Breaking character. She's nervous.

"Yes."

"I'll have to be fast."

"You'll go as fast or slow as I tell you to."

Her breath catches.

"Understand?"

"Yes, sir."

"Put the phone on speaker."

"And hold it?"

"Put it on the vanity. Stand next to it. Your back against the wall."

"Yes." There's movement on her end, then the feedback that comes with speaker phone. "Done."

"How do you feel?"

"Exposed."

"What else?" I ask.

"Dirty."

"Do you like it?"

"Yes," she breathes.

"Do you like knowing someone is outside the door, wondering what you're doing?"

"Yes."

"Unbutton your jeans."

She tugs the zipper. "Done."

"Are you wet?"

"Very."

"You like teasing me."

"Yes, sir."

"Do you think you can do that without consequences?"

"No, sir."

She wants the consequences. I need to give her a chance. To disobey me and meet punishment for it.

My balls tighten at the thought of Indigo bent over my lap, gasping as I bring my hand to her arse.

As I drive my fingers into her, throw her against my desk, fuck her until she's screaming.

God dammit. I may have patience, but my body doesn't. I'm too hard. Too ready.

This is not the fucking place.

And I don't fucking care.

I lower the blinds. Press my back into the glass wall.

"Push your jeans to your thighs," I say. "Then keep them there, so they're binding you."

Her breath hitches as she does what she's told.

"Show me."

"Yes." The cell brushes the desk. Her breath gets closer. More shallow.

My phone fills with the image. Indie's reflection.

Her gorgeous blue eyes, her soft wine lips, her sweet curves on display for me, all the way to the jeans binding her thighs.

What the fuck did I do to get so lucky?

"Beautiful," I say.

Her breath flows through the speakers.

"Look at yourself in the mirror."

"Okay." Nerves slip into her voice.

The situation? Or some insecurity?

It defies explanation. How could she think she's anything less than perfect?

But I know better than to push her. Not now, when I'm unable to show her how much I want her.

"Watch your face," I say. "The way your expression changes as you get closer."

"Watch myself come?" she asks.

"Is that a problem?"

"No, sir. Just… different."

"Try. Look yourself in the eyes. Then touch yourself."

"How?"

"How do you normally fuck yourself?"

"My fingers against my clit. The index."

"Which hand?"

"My right."

I want to demand she show me, but there isn't time. And I can't pull her from the moment again. "Touch yourself."

"Like I'm alone?"

"Like I'm watching."

"Yes, sir." Her breath slows for a moment.

Then it speeds.

Grows louder.

She gets closer. Closer.

Lets out a soft moan.

Then a louder one.

"Fuck," she breathes. "Ty... I can't... I can't keep watching. It's too much."

"Try."

"But—"

"Try. Or I hang up right now." I keep my voice firm. It's what she needs right now. She needs the rules, the structure, the release from her thoughts.

"Yes."

"Yes?"

"Yes, sir." Her voice fades. She's already slipping into that perfect world of pure bliss.

Her breath catches.

Again.

And again.

Her groan flows into my ears.

It's music. The best I've ever heard.

Then her groans run together, and she's the only thing in my universe. The sharp breaths, the low grunts, the expression of utter bliss.

Her groans run together as she comes.

There's a soft thud.

Her grabbing for something. Or slamming her back into the wall.

I can see her. Here. On my couch, legs spread, eyes on me. One hand between her legs. The other digging into the leather.

Or bent over my desk. Her head turned. Her hands bound behind her back. Her fingers curling into her palms as she comes.

She slows for a minute. Then her breath speeds. Her groans grow louder.

She comes quickly.

In thirty seconds. A minute maybe.

Her orgasm steals every second of my attention.

For a moment, the world makes perfect sense.

I know exactly what I'm doing.

I know exactly what she wants.

And exactly how to give it to her.

"Fuck." She catches her breath. "Was that... Are you..."

"Fucking beautiful."

"Yeah?" There's a blush in her voice.

"Yes."

"Are you... Will you go now?"

"No."

"If I beg?" she asks.

"No," I say.

"Are you hard?"

"Very."

"So you're just... going to stay that way?" she asks.

"Yes."

"Can I help you with that? Later?"

"Later?"

"Thursday. I have an appointment later. For the IUD."

Fuck.

"Some people say it hurts for a few days. But—"

"Do you want me to come with you?"

"With me?"

"To your appointment?"

"No. I've got it. Thanks though."

"Of course."

She lets out a shallow breath. "I, uh, I forgot what I was saying."

My chest warms. I wore her out. It *is* an accomplishment. "You want to fuck me Thursday."

"I want to fuck you right now. But, uh, Thursday seems smart. You can come over. Or I can. Sienna is studying at the library all week."

"Let me know after your appointment," I say. "How you're feeling."

"You're going to ask me to wait if it hurts."

"Do you want to have to wait an extra few days?"

"No."

"Then let me know. Please."

"Okay." Her voice returns to normal. "It's a real skill, making being caring sound like a cruel order."

"Thank you."

"You're welcome."

"Come over after work. In the harness."

"Oh."

"Any of them. Nothing else under your clothes. Or I'll have to punish you."

Her breath catches.

"I won't tease. Or warn you. Understand?"

"I do."

I'm giving her the chance to disobey me.

It's up to her to take it.

Chapter Thirty-Three

TY

All afternoon, I think of Indigo.

I consider texting Sienna to ask for an update. Offering her depraved details in exchange for intel on Indie's condition.

But I know better.

No matter how badly I want to know everything about her, I have to trust her to tell me.

I'm halfway through a run when she texts.

Indigo: Done. Painful. But done.

Ty: I can come over. Fix dinner.

Take care of her.

Indigo: No. If you come over, I'm going to fuck you. And I'm supposed to wait twenty-four hours.

Ty: You doubt my self-control?

Indigo: No. But I don't want to experience it.

Ty: Are you alone?

Indigo: I would say I like where this is going, but I have a feeling I won't.

Ty: Is your sister around to fix dinner?

Indigo: Studying with a friend.

Ty: I'll send something.

Indigo: You're going to send me dinner?

Ty: It's that. Or I come over. Your choice.

Indigo: You come over and you don't fuck me.

Ty: Yes.

Indigo: Can I suck you off?

Ty: No.

Indigo: No?

Ty: Is there something unclear about no?

Indigo: I've never known men to turn down blow jobs.

Ty: You won't distract me by making me jealous.

She will. Easily. But maybe she doesn't realize that.

Indigo: That isn't what I meant.

Ty: No? You didn't want me to think about some other man coming in your mouth?

Indigo: I've never let someone else come in my mouth.

My balls tighten.

She is trying to win this game. Just not the way I guessed.

Indigo: If I want it, and you enjoy it, why not?

Ty: Because I want to come inside you the next time I touch you.

Indigo: Tease.

Ty: I warned you.

Indigo: I won't convince you, will I?

Ty: You can try.

She's quiet for a few minutes, then she replies.

Indigo: Fine. Send dinner. Just dinner.

I ring Paloma with instructions. The Italian restaurant. Her favorite dish. The wine we shared.

Ty: It will be forty-five minutes.

Indigo: Is Thursday really a day and a half away?

Ty: It is.

Indigo: Are you sure? Can we just cancel Wednesday?

Ty: No.

Indigo: Will you fuck yourself?

Ty: Right now?
Indigo: Right now.
Ty: What did I just say?
Indigo: You're not touching me.
She's right on a technicality.
Ty: I want to come inside you the next time I come.
Indigo: Oh.
Ty: You're going to have to wait.

———

SHE TEXTS A THANKS FOR THE FOOD.

And an update on her condition Wednesday morning. She feels fine. Like she could come over tonight.

But she knows better than to ask.

I think of her all day. As I arrange everything for our date. As I toss and turn all night.

I give up on sleep just before sunrise.

The deep blue of the sky fades to a softer shade.

The sun rises. Streaks the sky red. Orange. Yellow.

The soft light of dawn.

Then the bright blue of mid-morning.

Another hot day.

And the messy thoughts in my head—

Indigo standing at the altar next to Paloma.

Then next to her sister, in some gorgeous ivory gown, looking into my eyes like I'm all she's ever wanted.

Studying the ring on her left hand.

Whispering *I love you.*

Then my thoughts shift and it's Rory and I don't know what's up or down.

I run. Shower. Fix breakfast.

Find the handcuffs for tonight.

The image fills my head—her hands on the wall, her ass in the air, her legs trembling as she awaits punishment.

Instantly, my messy thoughts straighten.

What the fuck does it matter what happened with my ex-fiancée?

Whether or not I'm capable of love?

Why waste time on anything else?

I let the thought consume my morning. Then I arrange everything for tonight.

I wait until I can't stand it anymore.

Then I give her a chance to change her mind.

Ty: My flat. Six o'clock. Nothing but the harness under your clothes. Or I'll have to punish you.

Chapter Thirty-Four

INDIGO

I t's still there. On my cell.

Ty's offer.

I could call it a lot of things:

A dare.

A promise.

A warning.

But we both know the truth.

I want him to punish me.

He wants to punish me.

Because he takes a sadistic pleasure in it. Or because he wants me under his control. Or because he promised to give me what I need.

I don't know.

I don't care.

My entire body is buzzing. Since he first teased me, I've been buzzing.

Through wedding venues, pasta dinners, too many episodes of *90 Day Fiancée*.

Except for the hour I was at the gynecologist and the few hours of cramps after, I've been buzzing with desire.

A being of pure desire.

Today's trek through wedding venues—one grand, one quaint—didn't help.

We have possible dates. In July. August. September.

That's our deadline.

Three months.

Three months until I'm a Mrs.

It's crazy. Crazier still, I'm getting used to the idea.

Looking forward to it.

I don't want to lie to my sister or Ty's family, but this isn't a lie.

We are committed.

And the thought of standing at the altar in some bold backless dress, kissing him like the ship is going down?

There's a part of me that wants it.

The real thing.

A real proposal, a real engagement, a real wedding.

Him really falling in love with me.

I can't have that.

But my sister walking me down the aisle, smiling with pride, standing up to embarrass me with a toast about Ty's sexual prowess—

I can have that.

The night of dancing in his arms.

The week in Fiji or Paris or Maui or Naples.

A room in his big, beautiful apartment.

Space in his big, beautiful life.

And all that time to deal with my pain and find my passion.

I've seen what happens to the idle rich working at Rick's.

Either I face this or I hide behind a drug problem or a bottle a day or a blade on my wrist.

Some means of self-destruction. One will find me.

I know better. I've been close before. Keeping Sienna safe was the only thing that kept me sane.

Now that she's an adult, with her own big, beautiful future—

I swallow hard. This is a problem for later. Tomorrow. Next week. Next year.

Or maybe it's exactly what I need right now.

Ty has a pretext for punishing me, but there's some reason I want it. Something beyond an intense desire to submit.

Is this why I'm craving pain and punishment?

I've been a bad girl, running from my pain, my gift, my passion.

I'm sorry.

I don't deserve mercy.

It's true.

It's ridiculous, but it is true.

I read his message again.

Ty: My flat. Six o'clock. Nothing but the harness under your clothes. Or I'll have to punish you.

My fingers slide over my cell screen. It's too slick. I'm too nervous.

I'm really doing this.

Intentionally disobeying him.

Asking him to punish me.

I'm out of my fucking mind.

I'm risking everything for sex.

I'm marrying him for sex.

Sure, there were other factors, but let's face it, I said yes because I want to fuck him.

And now I'm here, outside his fancy apartment building, ten minutes to six, waiting.

The Financial District is bustling. It's rush hour. Of course it is.

Men and women in suits run to catch their trains, chat on the street, grab dinner from a street vendor.

In an hour, this place will be a ghost town.

Even now, it's slowing. But it's still alert and alive and vibrant. Everything I love about the city.

Even the day traders and bankers who do nothing to earn their fortunes. The assholes who decided to raise the rate on our mortgage.

But then I'm not here to complain about the ills of capitalism.

I'm about to marry a billionaire. I'm about to join the one percent.

And I—

My cell buzzes. Slips from my hands. I bend just in time to catch it.

A text from Sienna. Teasing me about staying out late.

She knows not to wait up.

Does she know what I'm doing here?

What the fuck would she say if I told her?

Something supportive, probably. Supportive and horny.

She'd look at me differently. If only in a *damn, Indie, I didn't know you had it in you* way.

And she'd look at Ty differently too.

Like he's some depraved pervert. Which is a compliment, coming from her.

But maybe like he's a monster too. I don't know.

I'm over-thinking things. It doesn't matter what Sienna thinks of my desires. It's none of her fucking business.

And this—

My cell buzzes again.

Ty.

Ty: You're late.

I am. It's six on the dot.

Extra disobedience. Unplanned.

I can apologize, admit I'm nervous, ask for mercy.

He might give it to me.

But I don't want mercy.

I don't want a single scrap of mercy.

I swallow hard. Slide my cell into my jeans. Ask myself what the fuck I'm doing one more time. For good measure.

You're thinking with your cunt, Indigo.

Sienna isn't the only one acting like a guy.

This is what men do. They think with their dicks.

I am.

And I don't care.

I slip into the building. Nod to the security guard. He recognizes me. Waves me through.

I slip into the shiny silver elevator. Slide my key into the lock.

Ty lives in the penthouse. You need a key to access the elevator. Even though it opens in a separate room.

That's security.

Safety from everything outside the apartment.

Not from him. Or how badly I want him. Or how much power I'm willing to give him.

Deep breath.

Slow exhale.

The shiny silver doors close. I stare at my reflection, trying to project confidence.

I'm wearing a thong under my jeans.

A bra under my top.

No harness.

And I'm late.

I'm not following any of his instructions.

I'm not giving him a choice.

My fingers curl around the metal safety bar. What if I'm wrong? If this isn't what he wants?

This is the one place we make sense. If I'm not reading

him right, if I'm pushing too far, asking for too much, asking for things he doesn't want—

If I can't handle the things he does want—

The elevator dings.

My heart thuds against my chest. It's not role playing. It's not the scene.

I am scared.

Of his reaction.

Of losing him.

Losing this.

The shiny silver doors slide open.

My shoes tap the floor. Simple black wedges. Not the cheap ones I bought for work. A designer brand Paloma selected.

More expensive than the rest of my outfit.

More expensive than anything I bought before this.

The tap echoes around the narrow hallway. The dozen steps feel like a thousand.

My heartbeat echoes between my ears.

Thump-thump.

Thump-thump.

Thump-thump.

There. I stop at his door.

This is it. My last chance to back out.

I search my head for some bit of sense. Enough to convince me to turn around, walk into the elevator, take the subway back to my apartment.

But I'm out of sense.

My body is too tuned to this.

It's been so long since I've really given it what it wants. I can't stop now.

I knock.

Ty makes me wait. Ten seconds. Twenty. Thirty.

A minute.

Two.

Finally, he opens the door.

He's standing there, tall and proud and strong.

An angel in the soft blue light.

A devil in a designer suit.

A madman or a monster, maybe.

My monster.

"You're late." His voice is sharp. Curt.

"I know."

His eyes meet mine. He pauses. Gives me a chance to explain, expand, ask for mercy.

I don't.

He continues. "Come in. Close the door behind you."

I step inside. Push the door closed.

The slam echoes around the wide, open room.

It's the same apartment as last time.

The same soft leather couch. The same sliding glass door. The same hard dining table.

The same hallway leading to his bedroom.

He moves into the kitchen. Fills two glasses with water. Brings one to me.

My fingers brush his as I take it.

My body catches fire. That's how turned on I am.

That's how badly I need him.

I might come just from the sound of his voice.

I'm not sure that's possible, but right now, it feels like it.

"Drink," he says.

"Water?"

"Yes. You're going to need your stamina."

Fuck. I take a long sip. Then another. Another.

He watches me finish the glass. Takes it. Places both—my empty one, his half-drank one—on the kitchen counter.

"Do you know why you're here?" he asks.

"We're engaged."

"Yes." He chuckles, breaking character. "Why you're here tonight?"

"So you can fuck me."

"So I can have my way with you," he corrects.

My body whines. This has to end with him fucking me. I need him inside me. In a way I've never needed anything.

He must know that.

He closes the distance between us, wraps his arm around my waist, pulls me into a soft, slow kiss.

"It might be tender." His fingertips trace the waistband of my jeans. His other hand goes to my hair. He pulls me into a hard, fast kiss, and releases me with a sigh. "It might be rough." He brings his palm to my ass. Pulls me closer. So I can feel his hard-on. "It might be nothing."

"But—"

"You're mine. To use however I see fit."

Fuck.

"Go to the bedroom. Now."

"If I don't?"

"I won't fuck you." His voice is hard. Rough.

He means that.

Whatever else happens here, he means that.

"Which bedroom?" I ask.

"Ours."

"Ours?"

"You know which bedroom I mean, Indigo." His voice drops an octave. "Go. Now. Or I'm not going to fuck you."

Our bedroom.

It steals every ounce of my attention.

He thinks of it as ours.

God, I want something that's ours.

Even if it's our place to fuck. Especially because it's our place to fuck.

This is where we make sense.

Perfect sense.

I turn. Move down the hall.

His bedroom door is open.

Floor clear, walls bare, sheets tucked.

The exact same, except for the leather handcuffs on the bed.

My breath leaves my body. I try to hold on to some amount of conscious thought.

This is—

I'm daring him to punish me. I don't know what it will look like.

I don't even care.

He knows what I want.

He'll give me what I want.

I try to take deep breaths. I try to keep my feet glued to the ground.

His footsteps move closer.

Closer.

He steps into the room. Takes off his suit jacket. Lays it on the dresser.

Then the tie.

He lays it on top of his jacket.

His gaze flits to the mirror. The closet wall. Like so many closet walls.

Like mine.

Not just a place to check an outfit.

A way to watch.

He turns to me. Takes another step toward me, so there are five feet between us.

It's five feet too many, but I know better than to test him.

"Did you follow my instructions?" He stares into my eyes. Waiting. Offering me the next move.

This is it.

It's already in motion, but this is really it.

The match that sets this whole place ablaze.

"No." I push the words from my lips.

"No?" He moves closer. Until there's a foot between us.

"No," I say it again. Firmer. Surer.

"Would you like to elaborate?" He steps toward me.

I back up.

Again, he moves closer.

Again, I back up.

Again.

Until I hit the bed. Until I have to look at him. "No."

His pupils dilate. His posture shifts. The last bits of softness fade.

He pushes me onto the bed.

Hard.

Like he means it.

The mattress is soft enough to take the impact. Still, I bounce, land on it again.

He pins me, his knee against my thigh. "Don't move."

"Or?"

His breath catches. He likes this game as much as I do. He wants to push back. "You have no idea how brutal I can be."

I shake my head.

"Don't move," he says it again. Firmer. Harder.

I watch as he rolls his sleeves to his elbows. The left. Then the right.

Light falls over his strong arms. Casts highlights over his dark skin. His tattoos.

The geometric rose.

The ouroboros.

The Latin quote.

vincit qui se vincit

He conquers who conquers himself.

Is there anything more Ty than that?

He releases his leg. Shoots me a look that dares me to defy him. But still, I stay in place as he moves to the dresser, gathers his tie, tosses it on the bed.

"Sit up," he orders.

I do.

He sits next to me.

His hand goes to my cheek. He pulls me into a hard, fast kiss.

His teeth scrape my bottom lip.

His other hand finds my thigh.

He presses his palm against me. Over my jeans.

Fuck. The hint of pressure is enough to wind the knot inside me. I'm already so close, so on edge.

"Ty," I groan as I pull back.

He responds by rubbing me over my jeans. Harder. Harder.

Hard enough it hurts.

It winds me so quickly.

Tighter and tighter and—

He pulls his hand away.

I nearly buckle from the release. "Please."

"No."

Somehow, I wind tighter.

He stills. Looks me up and down, savoring every inch of my skin, from the tip of my head to the toes of my shoes, then back up.

He brings his hand to my hip. Over my jeans. Along the waist band. To the hem of my top.

Under it.

His fingers trace the line of my bra.

My eyes fall closed.

He cups my breasts over my bra. Runs his thumbs against my nipples, pressing the sheer fabric into my tender skin.

It's too much friction.

And not enough.

I need his bare hands.

"Please," I groan.

"No." His voice is rough. Hard. Harder than I've ever heard it.

He runs his thumbs over me again and again.

Until I need him so badly, I might scream.

Then he pulls back, does away with my top, leaves me sitting on the bed in jeans and a black bra.

He stares at the sheer fabric with equal parts admiration and anger.

Then, without warning, he pulls me into his lap.

My stomach against his thighs, my head on the sheets, my ass in the air.

Spanking position.

He presses one hand into my back, pushing my stomach against his thighs and pelvis.

Against his hard cock.

"Ty—"

He does it again. "You want me to fuck you."

I murmur an agreement.

"Here." He runs his fingers over my jeans, pressing the fabric against my cunt.

I nod into the bed.

"Here." He drags his hand along the seam, until his fingers are at my ass.

It's not a question. I say, "yes," anyway.

"Here." He slips his thumb between my lips.

I suck on his digit. It's not enough. I need more of him. All of him.

"You want me to fuck you." He pulls his thumb back.

A sigh falls from my lips.

"But you test me."

"Yes."

"You do this to me—" He presses his palm against my back, pushing my stomach against his hard-on again. "Then you dare me to leave you without satisfaction."

"Yes."

"Do you know what that does to me?"

"No."

"How crazy it drives me?"

I shake my head.

He undoes the button of my jeans. Rolls them over my hips.

My ass.

To my thighs.

He keeps them there, binding my legs together.

"Do you have any idea how rough I can be?"

"No."

Smack.

Without warning, he brings his hand down against my ass.

A hard spanking.

Then another.

Another.

"Bad girl." He purrs it with equal parts approval and scolding.

Then he spanks me again.

Again.

My eyes close.

My body goes into overdrive.

I feel only pain and pleasure and the intense need to take whatever he'll give.

He spanks me again.

Again.

Again.

Again.

"This is ten." He brings his hand to my ass again. "Do you need ten more? Or have you learned your lesson?"

"I'm not sure what you mean, sir."

Smack.

He hits harder this time. Hard enough I gasp.

But he doesn't stop. He doesn't check in. He doesn't tease.

His palm comes down against my ass again and again.

Until it hurts more than it pleases.

But that hurt is so fucking good.

He stops.

Was that ten? I don't know.

His hand goes to my wrist. Then the soft leather of the cuff.

He secures my left wrist.

The right.

He pulls my hands behind my back. Binds them with a short chain.

He pushes my thong to my thighs.

Pushes my jeans and my panties off my feet.

Then his hand is on my ankle. And he's binding my legs with his tie.

He straightens.

Presses his hand into my back, holding my stomach against his hard cock, daring me to ask for more.

Daring me to plead for mercy.

Smack.

He hits me again.

The other cheek this time.

Again and again.

Until I can only feel the sting of pain.

Then his hand is on my sex. A soft touch.

The rough push of his fingers inside me.

"You're wet," he growls.

"Yes."

"You like defying me."

"Yes."

"You want to be punished."

"Yes," I breathe.

"You won't earn what you want that way."

"What is that, sir?"

He presses his hand into my back again, pressing my stomach into his cock.

Fuck. No. Anything but that. "Please."

"Please?"

"Please, fuck me. Please, sir."

He drives his fingers into me again. "Why?"

"Why?" What does he mean, why?

"Yes." He drives his fingers into me again and again. "Why should I reward your disobedience?"

I try to find some reply, but the pressure of his hand overwhelms me.

He stretches me deeper.

Again and again.

Pushes me closer and closer.

His thumb finds my clit.

Three circles and I come.

I groan his name as pleasure spills through my torso. My world goes white. Only the blinding, beautiful light of bliss and the sharp, perfect sting of pain.

"Please." It's the only thing I have.

"Do you think you're in charge here?"

"No, sir."

"Do you think I'll give in because you beg?" he asks.

"No, sir."

"Then why do you keep asking?"

"Because it's all I can do."

A groan falls from his lips. Again, he brings his hand down on my ass. "I don't have mercy."

"I know."

"Remember that next time."

"Yes," I breathe.

He spanks me again. Hard enough my entire body stings.

Then he tugs at the chain holding my wrists.

He stands, pulling me up with him.

For a second, his eyes go to the mirror. Mine follow.

I'm naked, except for the sheer black bra, the cuffs on my wrists, the binding at my ankles.

And he's behind me, in his suit, one hand on my wrists.

Completely in control.

He brings his hand to my throat.

A groan falls from my lips. "Ty, please. Please. You know what that does to me."

His grip tightens.

"Please."

Through the mirror, his eyes meet mine.

He holds me in place for a long moment.

Then he pushes me onto the bed.

I turn my head, but still, my cheek hits the sheets. The mattress dulls the impact, but not enough.

It hurts.

In a way that makes my sex clench.

How can I need to come again so quickly?

How can I be satisfied and in need at the same time?

How can I want it rougher than this?

I'm so empty, so painfully aware of how much I need him to fill me.

And I have no idea if he's going to keep me here waiting forever or fuck me right now or something in between.

Some beautiful, horrible torture like watching him fuck himself.

He presses one hand into my hip, pinning me to the bed.

He's behind me. Right behind me. His cock against my sex. Only his slacks between us.

His bed is exactly the right height.

Like he planned it.

Of course, he planned it.

He keeps me there, on the edge, waiting.

Finally, he unbuttons his slacks.

He looks me in the eyes, through the mirror, as he drives into me.

No condom.

Nothing between us.

Just his flesh against mine.

It feels so fucking good. Like he's mine. Like we're one.

Like every cheesy metaphor in every single pop song.

My body stretches to take him.

I need it.

Even though it hurts.

More because it hurts.

"You're mine." He keeps me pinned. "I'll decide what you need."

"Yes," I breathe.

"I'll do whatever the fuck I want with you."

Mmm. It winds me so fucking tight.

I can't believe I have more, but I do.

He keeps me pinned to the bed as he drives into me again and again.

He pushes me closer with every steady, deep thrust.

Again.

Again.

Again.

Then he tugs at the chain binding my wrists and he pushes me over the edge.

I groan his name as I come.

My sex pulses. My senses flood with pleasure. That beautiful, pure white light of bliss.

And that sweet sense of submission.

Knowing I'm his.

Knowing I'm bound.

Knowing he can hurt me.

Overpower me.

Destroy me.

I love it and I don't care how wrong it is.

My toes dig into the floor.

My fingers dig into my palms.

Then he's there, growling as he comes inside me, thrusting through his orgasm.

His cock pulses as he comes.

It's fucking perfection.

It's everything.

When he's finished, he pulls back. Does away with his clothes. The rest of mine.

Then he's on the bed. Undoing my bindings.

Wrapping his arms around me.

Holding me like he'll never let go.

Chapter Thirty-Five

INDIGO

He runs his fingers through my hair as I catch my breath.

That other Ty. The soft, gentle caretaker.

He murmurs something about shifting back to reality. Asks if I'm okay.

I only manage to nod.

Okay doesn't cover it.

I'm fucking fantastic.

After I come down, I move into the master bathroom.

Door closed. Space to myself.

New purple robe hanging outside the shower.

Exactly like the one in my fantasy. Exactly how I described it.

After I clean up and towel dry, I slip into the robe. Soak in the feeling of the space.

Our space.

Does he see this as ours too?

Between the massive shower, the bare white wall, the hard countertop, the wide mirror—

There are plenty of places to fuck me. Plenty of ways for him to tease me or wind me tight.

Our space to fuck.

I run a comb through my hair. Reapply my lipstick. Wipe my sweat-smudged eyeliner.

It's not enough. I still look just-fucked. This isn't a hairstyle that stands up to sex.

But I like seeing satisfaction in my reflection.

Does it drive him crazy too? Seeing what he did to my hair, lips, wrists, neck?

No hickies today.

He was careful today.

Or maybe it didn't fit the scene. I don't know.

I don't care. I only care about getting more.

Can I really ask for harder, rougher, more brutal?

I take a deep breath. Move into the bedroom.

My clothes are neatly arranged. Wedges at the foot of the bed.

The rest folded.

Jeans.

Top.

Bra.

A ring box on top of my black thong.

Ty steps into the bedroom. "I thought you'd want to add it to your outfit."

He's in his slacks and shirt. His tie is still on the bed. His jacket is still on the dresser. His sleeves are still rolled to his elbows.

A side of him only I get.

He crosses the room to me. Picks up the ring box.

Drops to one knee.

"Indigo Simms, will you marry me?" He peels the lid back.

The ring is beautiful. Bold. Intense. Me.

"Ty..." My heart catches in my throat. My mouth gets sticky.

He's there, on one knee, looking up at me like I have his heart in my hands.

Like he'll die if I don't agree to spend the rest of my life with him.

He's not pretending.

Maybe he doesn't love me. Maybe he'll never love me.

But he needs me.

And that's something. It's so close to everything.

"I'm wearing a robe." The words fall off my lips.

He smiles. "I know."

"Am I supposed to tell people you surprised me after you fucked me senseless?"

"How else could I be sure you'd say yes?"

A laugh falls from my lips.

It's so beautiful and perfect, him on one knee, surrounded by the soft blue light of dusk, looking up at me like I'm the only thing he needs.

I am.

Here.

Maybe not anywhere else, but here.

"Yes," I whisper. "Of course."

He slides the ring onto my finger.

Rises.

Wraps his arms around me.

My hands go to his neck. I can feel it. The pressure of the ring between us. Metal against our skin.

This time, he's gentle as he lays me on the bed.

Undoes the sash of my robe.

Slips between my legs and licks me until I come.

———

AFTER I SLIP INTO MY WEDGES AND A DEEP PURPLE DRESS, I take pictures of the ring.

Normal pictures. With my cell. Like we're a normal couple, excited to post news on social media.

He poses with me for a dozen selfies.

Then he takes a few of me, in front of the window, so we have natural light.

It's so normal. Asking my fiancé to take pictures of me.

He knows photos better than Noah. He's good at cell pics for a guy, but he's still a guy.

I have to tell him how to hold the phone, how to cheat the camera, how to find the light.

It's so strange, being the one to explain something to him, seeing him take instructions.

Looking at a photo of the two of us smiling at my ring clad hand.

"You could send it to your sister," he says.

"Should I?"

"She's your sister."

I want to tell her. I want to tell her now. But—"She's studying for finals."

"It's okay if you want it to be yours for a while."

Is that it? That I want it to be mine?

Or am I afraid of what she'll say?

I don't have to lie to her. Not really.

She might ask questions when I tell her *he proposed after he fucked me*, but they'll be questions about sex.

"Tuesday," I say. "After her last final."

"Does that mean I get you here until Tuesday?"

"What are you offering?"

He smiles. "Don't tempt me to delay dinner any further."

"Don't tempt me to tempt you."

He wraps his arms around me and pulls me into a soft kiss.

My lips part.

His tongue slips into my mouth.

My body melts into his.

Yes. I can stay here until Tuesday. I can stay here forever.

I pull back with a sigh. "The weekend maybe. I need her to get used to the idea of me not being around."

"Indie, I hate to break it to you, but she's dying to get you out of her hair."

"She is?"

He nods. Grabs my coat. Leads me out of the apartment. "She's an eighteen-year-old girl who always has her older sister keeping her in line."

That's true.

"She wants to invite a boy into her room, drink cheap liquor, play music too loud."

"You're not encouraging me to stay."

"You'll have to let her go soon."

"I know." I press my lips together. "I just don't know how."

————

WE HAVE DINNER AT A QUIET RESTAURANT.

No photographers to capture our moment.

No paparazzi.

No one looking at us, really. No more than the usual.

He teases me that it's because I turn heads.

Maybe it's true.

Maybe it's us.

I don't know. Or care. I just want to stare into his eyes and trade stories about family all night.

It's perfect.

And it's mine.

We go back to his place. Fuck against the wall. Fall asleep in his bed.

Our bed.

I get home after Sienna's already left for school.

There's a note for me on the table.

Good work getting laid! I'll be at the library until ten, so feel free to bring your festivities home.

Love you.

Hate AP Gov.

- Sienna

I hold the note to my chest. I love her so much. I need, so badly, for her to be okay.

And she is.

She's smart and bold and funny and strong.

She's on her way to a great future.

She doesn't need me anymore. Not the same way she did when we were kids. When we lost Mom to grief, and I had to pick up the pieces.

When I had to get the groceries, cook our dinners, make sure she studied and made it to school on time and had enough so she could play soccer.

That was her way out. A scholarship.

If Ty hadn't stepped in—

She might have dropped out of NYU. Asked a school that gave her a full ride to reconsider, even though she'd missed the deadline.

Moved to Florida or California or Boston.

Maybe that's better for her.

But it's not better for me.

I tape her note to the fridge, go to my bedroom, pick up my guitar.

I have to take off the ring. It's too heavy. I'm too out of practice.

But when I close my eyes, and press my fingers to the strings, I slip back into scales.

Chord progressions.

Songs.

I don't sing. I'm not there yet.

But I manage this.

For a few songs, everything crashes into me. My dad laughing as he turned down *You Oughta Know*.

Smiling as he asked my mom to dance.

The two of them in the living room, dancing to Marvin Gaye, giggling like teenagers.

The three of us—me, Sienna, mom—at my cousin's wedding. Mom bursting into tears when their wedding song played.

As Time Goes By.

The song from *Casablanca*.

We couldn't watch it after he died.

I put my guitar down. Fix a cup of tea. Put on the classic film.

It still feels like home. Like a home that will never be the same.

Maybe that's life. Growing up. Leaving my parents' home. Finding my own.

But it hurts.

It really fucking hurts.

So I keep my engagement ring in my drawer.

And I don't tell Sienna anything when she gets home.

Because she has finals. Because I can't distract her.

Because I can't say goodbye to the home we've made yet.

Chapter Thirty-Six

TY

All day, I think about Indigo.

The sound of her groan, the taste of her lips, the feel of her nails against my back.

The sweet sight of her smile lighting up her deep blue eyes.

That is real.

I do want to marry her. So what if my motives aren't entirely romantic?

I repeat the mantra again and again as I head to dinner.

This is real enough.

I want her.

I care about her.

I need her.

Tonight, I'm forgetting the other details. They're gone.

We're two people who want each other.

It's that simple.

My shoulders relax as I move into the restaurant. It's a familiar space. One of Ian's favorites. Because of the fantastic gin selection and the strong drinks.

Today, I need one.

I stop at the bar. Order a bourbon, neat. Take in the restaurant.

They're already here.

Ian, in a black suit and a fuchsia tie.

Eve, in a low-cut black dress and combat boots, teal hair in a neat line at her shoulders, makeup dark and dramatic.

They're sitting side by side, laughing over drinks.

Gin and tonics no doubt.

That's another reason he likes the restaurant. The Fever Tree selection. And his understanding with management.

They'll serve his girlfriend without asking for her ID.

Necessary, what with her being nineteen and drinking age being twenty-one in the States.

It's ridiculous—why can someone go to war before they can drink—but that's the US.

I pay the bartender. Turn toward them.

There's a half-wall separating us. They can see me, but they're not looking. They're too caught up in each other.

"She's going to be jealous." Ian runs his fingers along his girlfriend's chin. "You're intimidating."

"Uh-huh." She laughs.

"You underestimate yourself." He traces the tattoo on her right arm, the quote from *The Handmaid's Tale*.

He's obsessed with the thing.

It was all he knew about her for a long time. That she had teal hair and a quote from *The Handmaid's Tale* permanently marking her body.

He's obsessed with both.

"It's my intellect?" She leans into his touch.

He nods, curves his hand around her neck, pulls her into a sweet kiss.

It's pure affection.

I expect my eyes to roll. But I don't have a single hint of irritation in my body.

No, there's something else in my stomach.

Envy.

Not because I want her.

Or because I don't want her stealing his attention.

Because they make it look easy.

I know it hasn't been easy. I heard enough of his side. And hers even.

But right now, the way they're staring into each other's eyes, flirting over their drinks—

They're the picture of love.

Of this passionate, beautiful love.

They're crazy about each other. And they're comfortable. In the way you can only be when you let your guard down.

Let someone know you.

Love you.

The real you.

It tugs at the stitches in my heart. Not because I had it.

Because I didn't.

I loved Rory. And she loved me. But I never really let my guard down.

I was so busy trying to fit into her perfect world.

Trying to convince myself I wanted the same things she did.

"Do you think he'll bring up Rory?" she asks.

"What would he say?"

"I don't know. Sometimes... I can tell you're thinking about your ex-wife. Not her, exactly, but—"

"My inability to trust."

"You're getting there."

"My three a.m. phone calls don't drive you mad?"

"Only if I'm too tired to—" she lowers her voice to a whisper.

I can't hear, but judging from her blush, it's something about sex.

He whispers. Teases her back. Makes her blush deepen.

It's dirty and adorable at the same time.

Again, my stomach pangs with envy.

They make it look so easy.

Can it really be that easy?

She pulls back enough to finish her drink. "Do you think it was the same for him?"

"With Rory?"

She nods.

"She wasn't fucking someone else."

"Does it have to be about sex?"

"Have you ever met a man?"

She laughs. "No. This is the first time. I'm Eve."

"Ian."

They actually shake. "Tell me more. About being a man."

He leans in to whisper.

Again, she blushes. "You're obsessed."

"Of course."

She smiles in a way that screams *I love you*. "Do you think that makes it easier for him?"

"I don't know. In some ways, maybe. It's easier to trust again. Harder, not having something to blame."

"Not knowing what happened."

"You never really know. Even when I sat there and listened to Laura explain what happened. Why she felt alone. Why she cheated. She broke it down, step by step. I thought it would be easier if I understood, but it wasn't."

"Did you understand?"

"Intellectually, sure. But how could I ever really understand?"

"You don't talk about it," she says.

"You've read all my thoughts on the matter."

She pulls him into a tight embrace. "You were a mess."

"I'm still a mess."

She shakes her head.

He nods.

They kiss.

Then they're whispering in each other's ears, lost in something that's entirely theirs.

I'm intruding. I should look away.

But I can't.

It's too astounding, seeing my brother in love again.

Seeing him trust again.

Seeing him happy.

He *was* a mess. Miserable. Angry. Ready to destroy anything and everything that reminded him of his marriage falling apart. Including himself.

And now he's smiling. Talking about his ex-wife in a calm, understanding voice.

Talking about me, yes, but still talking as if he's past it.

He's not the same fucked-up mess.

He's okay.

More than okay.

Over the fucking moon.

"Is it really just men that always make it about sex?" She laughs.

"I am the only one you've met, so you'll have to take my word for it."

"Do you really think Ty—"

"He's not as straitlaced as he seems."

"He doesn't seem straitlaced," she says.

"Exactly."

"Oh." Her green eyes light up. Her cheeks flush. "Really?"

He nods *really*.

"Details?"

"I shouldn't."

"Details he'd want me to know?"

"He'd tell you them."

She presses her hands together in a pleading expression.

He whispers some other dirty comment in her ear.

Not one of my secrets. That is one place I can trust Ian.

He doesn't share secrets.

I finish my drink. Leave it there.

Move into the restaurant.

Eve spots me first. She blushes the second she sees me. Then she waves, trying to cover her *fuck, I'm busted* expression.

"Hey, Ty!" She stands. Greets me with a hug. "You look great."

"He knows we were talking about him," Ian says.

She laughs. "All good things, I promise."

"Asking about my sex life?" I release her.

"It's been forever," she says. "I have to wonder."

"Three weeks is forever?" I ask.

She nods. Takes her seat. "When you live five blocks away? Yes. I have to wonder how you're spending all that time."

"He's not going to tell you unless you get him drunk." Ian stands. Hugs me hello. "How much did you hear?"

"Enough," I say.

"Eavesdropping arsehole."

"I learned from the best."

He smiles with pride. That brotherly pride I so rarely see.

It warms me everywhere.

Erases every ugly feeling in my gut.

He motions for me to sit. When I do, he hails the server. "Bourbon?"

"Manhattan."

Ian smiles. "Of course."

"What, of course?" Eve asks.

"That summer, it was all you drank," Ian says. "I thought it was his when-in-Rome bollocks."

"Manhattans in Manhattan?" Eve looks to me. "That's not what he means."

"White Claw in Long Island," I say.

She laughs. "What do we drink in Manhattan?"

"Craft cocktails that sound like aromatherapy," I say.

Her laugh gets louder. "Oh my god, it's true."

"There's a lot of lavender," Ian nods.

"You like the lavender," she says.

"It pairs well with gin. I'm a sensible man." He waits for the server to arrive. Orders another round. "And one for your girlfriend?"

I nod.

He passes it on. Waits for the server to leave. "Are you going to tell us anything?"

"What would I tell you?" I ask.

"What you two have been doing," Eve says.

"They're fucking." Ian raises a brow, daring me to expand. When I don't, he continues. "What else would they be doing? Playing Scrabble."

"You picked Scrabble on purpose," she says.

"Of course." He traces the lines of her tattoo.

Of course. In the book, the commander invites the protagonist to his office for a secret tryst. She thinks he wants sex, but he wants to play Scrabble.

In a world where women aren't allowed to read, it seems kinkier than any sex.

It's the perfect thing to say. Ian knows his girlfriend well.

They're perfect together.

"Ty's girlfriend won't like me if I go on about Margaret Atwood all night." Eve turns to me. "Or will she? Is she my new best friend?"

"Ty is a snob," Ian says. "It would suit him."

I'm not sure if she's read *The Handmaid's Tale* or not. It's a classic. It's possible. But Indie is more of a film viewer than a reader. "She's a musician."

Eve's eyes light up. "Really? What does she play?"

"And does she like Green Day?" he teases her.

"Guitar," I say. "She writes songs."

"Is she good?" Eve asks.

"Amazing," I say.

"And you two… is it true? That you had a fling a few years ago?" she asks.

"We did," I say.

"They fucked all summer," he says. "It was all he did."

Eve smiles. "Was it serious back then?"

"No," I say. "It was only supposed to be that summer." That was the only reason I could let go. Ask for what I wanted. Offer her what she wanted.

Because I didn't think I'd have to face her again.

Because I didn't think I'd have to face myself.

"But…" Eve motions for me to continue.

So I do. I tell her one version of the story. How I missed Indigo after we parted. How I thought of our time together.

Thought of how I'd fucked her.

Sometimes, even when I was with Rory. Because we didn't want the same things.

And I know Eve knows that.

I've been pissed around her enough times, I've told her.

I tell her how I thought of Indigo even though I was committed.

And how I found her when I came back to New York. I didn't mean to fall for her, but I did.

That's close enough to true.

Or maybe entirely true.

I'm not sure.

Eve hangs on every word. Until movement at the entrance grabs her attention.

Indigo steps into the restaurant in a deep navy jumpsuit.

Her hair in a neat line.

Her blue eyes lined in charcoal.

Her lips Bordeaux.

She looks dramatic, bold, sexy as fuck.

And like her.

The version of her dressing up to impress my family.

As if this is a normal dinner.

And we're really in love.

.

Chapter Thirty-Seven

TY

"**A**lways nice to see you, Ian." Indigo extends her hand.

My brother shakes. "Sweet of you to lie."

She laughs. "How would you know?"

"You two had to put on clothes for this," he says.

She blushes. "It is a shame. True." She turns to his girlfriend. "You must be Eve. I've heard a lot about you."

Eve stands. "About my hair?"

"Mostly." Indigo smiles. "It's fierce."

"Yours too." Eve offers a hug.

Indigo accepts.

It's strange, watching my brother's girlfriend hug my fiancée.

A ghost of a possibility.

I met Rory after his divorce. After he gave up on love. He tried to support me, but he couldn't hide his doubt.

I wanted his approval so badly.

As much as when I was a kid.

It killed me that I couldn't have it.

And now—

I still crave his pride. He was practically my father.

Now that our father is gone, he's all I have.

"She won't admit it," Ian says. "But she was jealous."

"I was not." Eve rests her hand on his forearm. "Okay, maybe a little."

"I was too," Indigo says.

"Can there only be one woman with fantastic hair at a time?" Ian asks.

"No, but it becomes your thing," Indigo says. "Suddenly, someone else has your thing. Then what do you have? It's a little threatening."

"A little," Eve says. "But women support women. Even when it comes to upstaging their hair."

Indigo smiles. It's relaxed. Easy.

They like her already. She can tell, but she isn't looking at them.

She's staring at me.

"Hey." She moves around the table. Wraps her arms around my waist. Looks into my eyes. "You look gorgeous."

"Gorgeous again?" I ask.

She nods. "Always." Her hand slips beneath my suit jacket. Her fingers curl into my side, pressing the fabric of my shirt into my skin.

I bring my hand to the back of her head. Pull her into a soft, slow kiss.

A proper kiss for greeting a fiancée.

Then her lips part and I forget about proper.

I forget we're in an exclusive restaurant in front of my brother and his girlfriend.

I kiss her like we're alone, in our flat, about to fuck on the couch.

She melts into me, kissing back like she's desperate to be claimed.

Her left hand goes to my chest.

Eve lets out a gasp.

Then Ian.

"Holy shit," Eve says. "That's a huge rock."

Ian says, "Congratulations."

But when I pull away and turn to my brother, I find doubt in his eyes.

It brings me back to that moment, when I told him I was going to propose to Rory. When I showed him our mother's ring. Explained the plan.

It was simple. Classic. What she would like. During dinner at her favorite restaurant.

Ian tried to encourage me. He tried to congratulate me.

No, he did.

But his heart wasn't in it.

He didn't believe in it.

Now—

His eyes are filled with the same doubt. But, somehow, it's different.

It must be. He's still cagey about the subject of marriage, but he believes in love now.

He wants to spend the rest of his life with her.

I tell myself that's all it is. That he's doubting himself, his intentions, his desires for the future.

But I don't believe it.

"That's one way to drop news." Ian's chuckle wipes the apprehension from his eyes.

"Oh. Right." Indigo turns to them. Holds up her left hand. "Is this what you do in the situation? Show off the ring?"

"Usually, but I'm not sure you have the right audience," Ian says.

"It's beautiful," Eve answers diplomatically. With no mention of her hatred of the diamond industry. "It suits you." She turns to Ian. "Should we order champagne?"

He nods. "Now or after dinner?"

"I'm starving." Indigo squeezes my hand then takes her seat. "After dinner."

I sit next to her.

The two of us across from my brother and his girlfriend. A normal family dinner. A normal double date.

"So, um, how did it happen?" Eve glances at her menu. Nods as Ian points to an entrée.

He usually orders for her.

He tries to take care of her.

But not in front of other people. Not usually.

"Well, uh." Indigo blushes. "It was right after we—"

The server interrupts with our next round. "Are you ready to order?"

I nod. Order for her.

Ian notices. He shoots me a look, but I'm not sure what it means.

It could be a playful *you're stepping on my turf.*

Or it could be an accusatory *you're so full of shite, Ty. You think you're fooling me with this?*

I'm not usually this nervous.

But this is the only place our ruse really matters. The rest of the world will believe we're in love when they see photos of our wedding.

Ian knows me.

Ian cares.

He cares if I'm happy. If I'm full of shit. If I'm lying to him.

"It was after you fucked?" he offers.

Indigo blushes. "Yes. I was cleaning up in the shower. I stepped out. My clothes were arranged on the bed. And the ring box was on top of it."

"Had he made the bed?" Eve asks.

She laughs. "How did you know?"

"Ian's the same way. Makes the bed every day," Eve says. "I thought it was his military training."

"It was," Ian says. "And our father's."

"He checked every day when we were kids," I say. "When he was home."

Under the table, she offers her hand.

I take it. "And she said yes, because I'd just made her come."

Indigo flames red. "I said yes because I want to spend the rest of my life with you."

"But it didn't hurt," I say.

"I don't see how it could fail." Eve smiles.

"He's always been the smart one," Ian says.

Indigo turns to me. "I didn't say I wanted to spend any of that time dressed."

They laugh.

I pull her into a sweet kiss.

Her hand goes to the back of my head. She holds my mouth against hers, kissing me like my lips are oxygen.

Real or pretend?

Right now, I don't care.

I need her.

That's real.

That's as real as anything.

After we break for air, I turn to my brother and his girlfriend.

She holds up her drink to toast. "To the rest of your life together."

Ian follows. "To happily ever after."

Indigo picks up her drink. I do the same.

We tap glasses in the middle of the table.

"Now," Eve settles into her seat, "tell me how it happened. How you met again. Tell me everything."

"Everything covers a lot," Indigo says.

"Only the dirty parts then," Ian offers.

"Don't think I won't," Indigo says.

He raises a brow, daring her.

"That is why you agreed, isn't it?" I ask. "To see me after three years. It was because you wanted to fuck me."

"That's why you called." She looks into my eyes. It's honest. Asking for honesty in return. "Isn't it?"

"I wanted to know you were okay," I say.

"And you wanted to fuck me," she says.

"And I wanted to fuck you."

She smiles. "Me too." She taps her glass against mine. Turns to my family. "Does that cover it?"

They trade a *holy shit* look.

But Eve still transitions seamlessly. She asks Indigo about her life. Her interests. Her family.

They get on like a house on fire.

They're both devoted to their younger sisters.

They both know the pain of serving drinks to pissed arseholes.

They trade tips on the best tattoo artists in the city. And the best venues.

Then they're talking about music. First, what they both love. Then what they don't. The state of music today. Some pop star with wild hair.

They talk all through dinner. Until Eve excuses herself to use the restroom. And like in an old movie, Indigo does the same.

It leaves me and my brother alone.

He looks around the restaurant. Looks at me. "It is fast."

"I know."

"Is she pregnant?"

"She had three drinks."

"I have to ask."

"You don't have to," I say. "You could exercise a little self-control."

"I could?" He chuckles. "I didn't realize." He lowers his voice. "Are you happy?"

"I am."

"And you're sure?"

I nod.

"Then I'm happy for you, Ty. You deserve it."

My chest warms. "Thank you."

"Is it just about the sex?" His voice gets playful.

"Of course. I have to close the deal before she gets tired of me," I say.

He smiles, but there's a sadness to it.

Like he thinks I mean it.

Maybe I do.

That is why I called.

That is why she came.

That is why she's here.

Sex and money.

There are worse reasons to marry.

Still, I can't shake the look in his eyes.

The concerned brother. Worried, not because he doesn't believe me, but because he does.

Chapter Thirty-Eight

TY

After chocolate cake and champagne, we walk Eve and Ian home—their place is only a few blocks away. Then we head toward my flat.

"Warn me next time we're walking." Indigo slips her clutch into the front pocket of my suit jacket.

"Don't New Yorkers walk everywhere?"

"Usually." She taps the pointy toe of her heels against the toe of my dress shoes. "But these aren't walking shoes."

"We're in the Financial District."

"And?"

"I see women in these shoes every day."

"If you wanted a woman who walks in designer heels, you should have proposed to one of them." She smiles, teasing, tipsy. Or maybe all the way to pissed.

"I'll carry you."

"How?" She slides her hand around my waist. Motions toward the quiet street.

I walk with her. "In my arms. Like a bride over the threshold."

"For ten blocks?"

"You don't think I can?"

"It's a long way," she says.

"Would you prefer a piggyback ride?"

A laugh falls from her lips. "You wouldn't."

"I would."

She shakes her head *no way*.

I nod *yes way*.

"Really?"

"Really."

"Okay." She stops. Turns to me. "Let's go."

"You want a piggyback ride?"

"Mm-hmm." She smiles. "As long as it won't wear you out."

"Excuse me?"

"I wouldn't want you to be too tired to fuck me properly."

"Is that a dare?"

She shrugs, playing coy.

"You push my buttons on purpose."

"You like when I push your buttons on purpose." She presses her hand to my chest. "You're an old man. You might have back issues."

"I'm an old man?"

She nods.

"I will throw you over my shoulder."

"Like a caveman?" Her eyes light up.

"Yes. But not here."

She pouts.

"Come on." I turn my back to her. Bend enough to give her a lift. "Hands here." I tap my shoulder.

"Okay." She slides her arms around my chest.

I slip my arms between her thighs. "On three."

"One, two, three—" She squeals as I rise. "Oh my god."

"You didn't think I would?"

"I have to stay like this for ten blocks?"

"Or admit you were full of shite."

"I was not." Her fingers dig into my shirt. "But I'm worried about my shoes."

"What about them?"

"If they fall off. They're expensive. The seven-hundred-dollar price tag is probably nothing to you, but I don't like to waste."

"You don't like them?"

"I like them."

"You don't like owning something so expensive?"

"It's a little excessive."

"Maybe you want to lose them," I say.

"No." Her fingers curl into my chest. "I'd spend all night thinking about how it would normally take me three shifts to pay for them."

"You don't have to wear seven-hundred-dollar shoes."

"Don't I?"

"Wear whatever fucking shoes you like. If Paloma is pushing too hard, I'll tell her to fuck off."

"You'll call her into your office and say 'Paloma, fuck off with the expensive shoes.'"

"How about I call you into my office. Tell you to take off everything but your expensive shoes."

"Can we do that now?"

"No."

A whine slips into her voice. "Why not?"

"You're pissed."

"So? Look." She raises her legs. Flexes her ankles. "I'm keeping the shoes on."

"So you can wear them when I fuck you?"

"*When* you fuck me?"

"When doesn't mean tonight."

She sighs. "You're mean."

"Mean?"

"Yeah, mean. Teasing me with what I want then holding it out of reach."

I can't help but laugh. "I've never heard you use the word mean."

"Kinky makes it sound good."

"It's not?"

She clears her throat.

"You like mean."

"That doesn't change the facts." She rests her head against mine. "But I... this is kinda nice."

It is. It's strange, giving my fiancée a piggyback ride, on a dark street, too close to midnight, but it feels good, taking care of her. It's everything.

"And dinner. That was... I really liked it. Getting to know your family."

"They liked you."

"I'm not sure. Did you see the look Eve gave me when I said I loved Billie Eilish?"

"I don't have a clue who that is."

She laughs. "She's the one doing the Bond film."

"The voluptuous blonde?"

"No. The teenager with green roots. Is that why she doesn't like her? Jealous of her hair?"

"Are you?"

She runs her fingers over my hair. "No. I don't really like it. Eve's hair is way better. Better than mine too."

"Why don't you dye yours teal?"

"Really?" she asks. "You'd approve?"

"I'm not going to tell you what to do with your hair."

"What if I want to cut it off?"

"I'll miss tugging at it as I come in your mouth."

She lets out a soft groan. "Ty..."

"Yes?"

"You're trying to distract me."

"What is it you say? No, I'm answering honestly."

"Do you believe me when I say that?"

"You are. And you're trying to push my buttons."

She squeezes me with her thighs. "Does it work?"

"You know it does."

She lets out a victory squeal. "I might dye it. Maybe. Dark blue. Or dark purple."

"Blue-black?"

"Indigo with indigo hair." She laughs. "That wouldn't be obnoxious."

"It would suit you."

"Would it finally be cooler than Eve's?"

"I can't say I think about whether or not your hair is cool," I say.

"I'm okay losing sometimes. She even matches it to her shoelaces. Did you notice that?" she asks.

"And complements Ian's tie."

She lets out a soft gasp. "It did."

"They always do that."

"What about in the middle of summer? Doesn't she wear sandals?"

"Sometimes."

"And he always wears a tie?"

"Baby, do you really want to talk about my brother's wardrobe?"

She nods into my shoulder. "I like that you know them. That you know them together. They seem happy."

"They are."

"You don't approve?"

"Why do you say that?"

"The tone of your voice."

"I didn't," I say. "When I first heard."

"That he was dating a teenager?"

"Yes."

"There's more."

"Yes."

She waits for me to expand.

I don't.

"You're not going to tell me."

"Ask Ian. He'll tell you if he wants you to know."

"Siding with your brother." She tugs at my shirt. "Mean."

"You'd side with me over Sienna?"

"No." Her voice softens. "I admire the loyalty. I know I have that too."

Loyalty. I've never thought of it that way, but she's right.

"I think you're loyal to a fault, actually. I remember our summer. You told me you were here to help your brother after his divorce."

"I was."

"You came for an entire summer."

"I spent most of it fucking you."

"Yeah, and even though you wanted to keep fucking me, you brushed off my questions about him. About what happened."

I never thought about it. It was a reflex.

"And then later… you wouldn't see me when you came to New York."

That wasn't fair to her. But she's right. I did it out of loyalty to Rory. Because I didn't trust myself with Indigo.

It wasn't that I thought I'd fuck her exactly.

I have enough self-control to keep my trousers zipped.

It was more that I knew, deep down, she'd wake up the part of me I was trying to deny.

If I saw her, I'd remember the thrill of tying her to my bed, ordering her onto her knees, bending her over the table.

"It made me angry," she said. "But it's kind of sweet. Really sweet, actually. Would you do that for me?"

"Do what for you?"

"Not see her? If you went to London?"

"If you asked."

Her thighs tense.

"But I wouldn't have to. I trust myself around her."

"But you don't trust yourself around me? You didn't?"

"Yes."

"Why?"

"You know why." I stop at a light. Wait for the car across the street.

Indie taps my chest. "We're almost there."

"And?"

"Down."

"Is that an order?"

"Pretty please."

"You really think adding *pretty* is going to help your case?"

"No. But I don't want to be too tired to fuck you properly."

I let her down.

She straightens. Takes my hand. "Will you tell me why?"

"You know why."

"Will you tell me anyway?" She runs her thumb over the space between my thumb and forefinger. "Please?"

"I shouldn't reward your begging."

"You should. You like it."

I do.

"If you reward me, I'll do it more. That's basic psychology." She presses her hands together. Mouths *pretty please*.

"That side of myself that comes out when I'm with you. I tried to keep it in a box for a long time. I tried to tell myself it wasn't there. That I didn't want those things. But I did. And I knew if I saw you, I'd realize that. I knew, if I saw you, I'd be desperate to fuck you."

"Were you?"

"Yes. But I was still trying to bury those desires."

"Are you now?"

It's a good question. She's only asking because alcohol has dissolved her inhibitions.

Mine are weak.

But they're still there.

I promised I'd be honest with her. If it mattered. Even if it hurt her.

That means being honest with myself.

"I can't," I say. "Not when I'm around you. It's impossible."

Her eyes meet mine.

"Other times... but not when I'm around you."

"I know what you mean." She stops in front of my building. "Last time, I stood out here for twenty minutes. I was scared. Of pushing you. Losing you. Of how much I wanted it."

Fuck, she's doing it again. Pushing every one of my buttons without even trying.

"Even now, it scares me. How much I want it again. How much I want more." Her tongue slides over her lips. "When you said I had no idea how brutal you can be, did you mean that? Or was it part of the scene?"

"I meant it."

Her chest heaves with her inhale. "What if I want to find out?"

"Do you?"

She nods.

"What exactly?"

"Whatever you meant." She runs her fingers over my tie. "Whatever you want to do with me."

Chapter Thirty-Nine

TY

Whatever *you want to do with me.*
My thoughts scatter.
My judgment disappears.

Indigo is standing next to me, in front of my flat—our flat—asking for the things I've pushed deepest.

Asking me to look inside her, find the things she's pushed deepest.

The things she can barely admit she wants.

"Let's talk upstairs," I say.

She looks to the security guard inside. Nods. Follows me into the building.

He compliments her outfit. Asks about our plans for the weekend.

She thanks him. Winks as she says we'll stay busy somehow.

Then she follows me into the elevator.

It's too small. There isn't enough room for all the things I want to do to her.

Her hand brushes mine. "He can't hear, can he?" She motions to the camera in the ceiling.

"No."

"But he could watch?"

"Yes."

"If I asked…"

"Not here. You'd be too embarrassed to look at him tomorrow."

Her laugh is soft. "Probably."

"Probably?"

She nods.

"Should we go downstairs. Tell him what we're going to do?"

"He knows that we're going to have sex."

"Are we?"

Her teeth sink into her lips. "Are you going to say I'm too drunk again?"

"What makes you think I'll say something else?"

She traces the neckline of her jumpsuit. Stops at her breast. Pulls the stiff fabric aside just enough to reveal the leather harness crisscrossing her torso.

Just enough to show me she's not wearing a bra.

Blood rushes to my cock.

"You can say it," she says. "You can always say no too. That doesn't mean I have to make it easy for you."

"You're baiting me."

"By wearing only a harness under my outfit?"

Fuck. "Nothing else?"

"I took off my underwear in the bathroom." She laughs. "That's not making me sound less drunk, is it?"

The elevator stops at our floor. I press my palm into her lower back. Lead her into the hallway.

Her fingers curl into my shoulders as I unlock the door.

She's impatient.

And defiant.

Partly, because she's pissed.

It's not a good idea to do this with her drunk. Especially when she's asking me to push her limits.

"Sit." I motion to the couch.

She steps into the house. Slips out of her shoes. Bends to pick them up. "Just in case."

I pour two glasses of water. Bring both to the couch.

She takes one. Drinks with greedy sips. "Thanks."

"Drink all of it." I take a long sip. Set my glass on the coffee table. Stay on my feet.

She looks up at me with need in her deep blue eyes. "What did you mean? When you said it?"

I swallow hard. "That I could hurt you."

"How?"

"With my belt. A riding crop. A whip."

Her pupils dilate.

"My hands."

"Like last time?"

"Harder. Rougher."

"Do you want to?"

"Yes."

I expect her to recoil, to look at me with disgust, but she doesn't.

She flames red with desire. Sucks in a shallow breath. Forces an exhale.

"What exactly?" she asks. "What exactly do you want?"

"Everything."

"That's not a real answer."

She's right.

I know what she's asking.

And I owe her the truth. "I think about the sound you make when I bite you. When it gets too hard, and you're not sure you can take more. I think about how I can push you past that. So you can take more pain. More control. More force."

"You want to bite me?"

"I do bite you."

"So what?"

"I want to surprise you. Hurt you. Throw you against the wall, rip off your panties, fuck you even though you're asking me not to."

"You want me to say no?"

"Yes."

"Oh." Her eyes go wide. With surprise. "You think about that? Forcing me?"

"With your permission." I suck in a shallow breath. How can I ask her for this? How can I ask her to admit she wants it?

How can I do anything else?

I push my exhale through my teeth. "Is that what you want?"

"Maybe. I don't know." Her chest heaves with her inhale. "I... I like the idea." She stands. Brings her hand to my wrist. "I can't really show you easily in this outfit, but I... Can I take it off?"

"I'm not going to play right now, Indie. Not until you're sober. Not with something like this."

"I understand." She turns her back to me. Motions to the zipper. "Does that mean you won't fuck me?"

"Not necessarily."

Her breath catches. "How do you want to fuck me, right now?"

Twenty minutes ago, I wanted something soft and sweet. I wanted to feel every inch of her bare skin against every inch of mine.

Now that she's asking me to find her deepest desires—

My cock is trying to take over.

"I want to throw you over the couch, bind you with my belt, fuck you until you're begging for mercy."

She lets out a soft groan.

"But I won't."

"If I say please?"

"No. Not until you're sober."

"But maybe soft? Or slow?"

"Maybe." I bring my fingers to her zipper. Run it down her back. Trace her spine back up. I press my lips to the back of her neck. "I want to feel like you're mine."

"I am."

I push the sleeves off her shoulders. Down her arms. All the way to her waist.

I bend to roll her jumpsuit to her ankles.

She's wearing only the leather harness.

A line of fabric between her breasts and around her rib cage. A tiny hook at the place where the lines meet.

One in front.

One in back.

She waits until I'm standing behind her to kick the jumpsuit aside. Then she turns back to me. Wraps her fingers around my wrist. Looks up at me. "May I, sir?"

"Yes."

She takes my hand. Slips it between her legs. So I can feel how wet she is.

"Indie—"

"I know what I'm asking." Her eyelids flutter closed for a moment. Then they blink open. Find mine. "I know this is what ruined your engagement. Even if you can't admit it to yourself."

"I—"

"Maybe it was more complicated than that. Maybe there were other things. But I know… you couldn't accept this part of yourself. And you tried to tell yourself it wasn't there. You tried to stay with a nice girl who wanted nice things."

"I loved her."

"But it still destroyed you." She swallows hard. "I know, asking for this—I might be the one pushing you too far."

"Indie—"

"But I have to." She releases my wrist. "I'm not a nice girl. I don't want nice things. And I don't want a nice man. Not here."

I bring my hand to her hip.

"Please, Ty. It doesn't have to be now. If you'll only do this when I'm sober... that's fair. And I accept those terms." She smiles. "But warn me before I drink next time."

A laugh spills from my lips. "You'd have stayed sober?"

"Maybe. I was nervous to meet your brother. He's your idol."

How does she make these things I can barely admit sound so fucking obvious?

"You're the only one who gets this part of me. Whatever else happens between us, you're the only one who understands." She places her palm on my chest. Digs her fingers into the fabric of my shirt. "You're the only one I trust."

"You trust me with your body?"

"Yes."

"Completely?"

"Completely."

My head swims. It's everything I want. Maybe the only thing I want.

"Please. It doesn't have to be right now, but please, I'll give you that part of me. Let me have that part of you. All of it."

"Indie—"

"Is that a yes?" Her eyes meet mine. "Will you do it? Will you promise to tell me the things you want? Even when they scare you?"

Chapter Forty

TY

"Yes." It's heavy in my chest, but it floats the second it hits the air.

"Everything?" Her eyes stay glued to mine. "Always."

"I'll try."

She holds out her hand. "Me too."

"Will it always take half a bottle of bourbon?"

She smiles. "Only sometimes."

I meet her. Shake.

It's a simple touch. Nothing compared to unzipping her jumpsuit. But it still fans the fire.

I need to touch her.

I need to fuck her.

I need to be the center of her universe.

"Tomorrow," I say. "We'll do the scene tomorrow."

She pouts.

"Would you rather we not do it?"

"You wouldn't."

"Try me."

Her eyes fill with fire. Defiance. Need.

The exact combination that makes my cock stir. "Tomorrow. Understand?"

She nods.

"Good girl."

Her lips part with a sigh. Her chest heaves with her inhale.

It's her favorite pet name. The one that makes her pant the fastest.

It's cruel to drop it if I'm not going to fuck her. But she was right. I am mean.

And this is the best kind of torture.

"I'm not going to warn you," I say.

"You'll surprise me."

"Yes."

Her flush deepens. "Overpower me?"

"If I tell you, it's not a surprise."

"Yes, but I… I want to know what you expect from me."

"To use your safe word if it's too much."

"That's all?"

No. It's much more complicated, but it's my job to worry about that. "I might gag you."

"Oh."

"If I do, and it's too much, hum. Pick something now. So I'll know to recognize it."

"Hum. Okay." She presses her lips together. Looks off in the distance. Drifting into the Indigo I haven't seen in years —the one lost in song.

She hums a single tone.

Shapes it into the melody of *When Doves Cry*.

It's bizarre, my fiancée in the middle of the living room, in only a harness, humming Prince.

Bizarre and perfect.

"Is there anything else I need to know?" She places her hand on my chest.

"No." There's plenty she wants to know, but she needs the surprise.

"Are we done… preparing."

"Are you going to ask me to fuck you?"

"Maybe." Her lips curl into a shy smile. "Will it help? If I get on my knees and beg?"

"No."

"Maybe I should do it anyway."

"Maybe."

She stares back at me, daring me to expand. When I don't, she drops to her knees and presses her palms together. "Please, Ty, please fuck me."

My body whines. It's without reservations. "Why?"

"Because I'm your fiancée. And you're the kind of man who will satisfy his wife."

Wife. It steals my thoughts.

My head is a fucked-up mess.

This is the only thing that makes sense.

The only place where we make sense.

Marrying for convenience and fantastic sex. Those are better reasons than most.

"Please." She runs her fingertips over my belt. "If you won't fuck me, then let me suck you off."

"Did that work last time?"

"No. But I wasn't here. To do this." She hooks two fingers in my belt loop. "It might work better with the demonstration."

Fuck, she's adorable. It's wrong how adorable she is asking to suck my cock.

I offer her my hand.

She looks up at me with incredulity in her eyes.

"Trust me."

"Trust you?"

"Have I ever let you down here?"

"No. Not here."

"So trust me," I say.

She takes my hand.

I pull her to her feet. Then I wrap my arms around her waist. Lift her.

She squeals as I throw her over my shoulder. "Ty." She laughs. "You're crazy."

"I am." I carry her to the bedroom. Lay her on the bed.

She looks up at me with a hazy smile as I attach the under-the-bed restraints to the hook between her breasts.

Then I pry her legs apart, and her smile fades into a groan.

She wants roughness. Maybe I should give it to her. Even if she's had far too much to drink.

But I want this.

I climb between her legs. Bring my mouth to her cunt. Work her until she's groaning my name.

Until she comes on my face.

I pin her thighs to the bed, holding her in place as I work her through her orgasm.

Then another.

Her legs go slack. Her entire body releases.

She sinks into the bed. Looks up at me with those same hazy eyes. Satisfied, yet still in need.

She's so fucking beautiful like this.

I strip out of my suit. Place my body over hers.

She groans as I fill her with steady thrusts.

I'm in control. She's bound. But it's not rough or hard or fast.

It's every molecule of her body against every molecule of mine.

As soft and sweet as I ever get.

The contrast she needs for tomorrow.
The closeness I need right now.
Not quite love.
But as close as I'll ever get.

———

In the morning, we dress. I fix breakfast and tea. Insist
we take a walk.

It's a beautiful day. Warm and bright, with enough breeze
the air is cool.

But I'm still burning up.

I watch her closely, waiting for her to forget our plan.

Waiting for her to lose herself in the moment, so I can
surprise her.

She smiles as she marvels at the deep blue water. I won't
do it here. She knows that. Knows she can relax.

So I wait until we're home.

I tell her I need to take a call.

She looks at me incredulously, but when I check on her
ten minutes later, she's standing in front of the stereo, lost in
Amy Winehouse's throaty vocals.

She closes her eyes.

And then she sings. Softly at first.

Then louder, loud enough the melody makes it into my
ears. Melts my heart.

Her voice is beautiful. And it's dripping with pain.

Everything she's lost.

Everything she's giving up.

She finishes the song. Blinks her eyes open. Looks around
surprised, like she's expecting someone to catch her.

When she doesn't, she drifts into the next song.

I wait until she's lost in the music.

Then I move as quietly as I can.

Down the hall.

Into the room.

To her.

She's distracted. She doesn't realize I'm here until my hands are around her wrists.

Chapter Forty-One

TY

"Ty." She gasps as I pull her wrists behind her back.

I don't soften the way I normally do. I tighten my grip. Enough I'm hurting her.

She lets out a low grunt.

"You think you're safe here?" I dig my nails into her forearm.

"No," she breathes.

"Smart girl." I loop my belt around her wrists.

She gasps as I pull it tight.

"Do you want me to hurt you?"

She mutters a curse.

"I asked you a question." I pull her backward. Until her body is pressed against mine. "Do you want me to hurt you?"

"No," she breathes.

"Then why are you playing with fire? Walking around in this." I trace the hem.

She gasps as I slip my hand under the dress.

"Asking for it." I press my palm against her cunt. Over her knickers.

She's already soaked.

From the restraint or the force or the rough edge to my voice, I'm not sure.

This is her chance to say no, to fight back, to make me force her.

I've been rough, yes. I've ordered her to obey me. But it's always been willingly.

What she wants.

In the moment and in the scene.

This is what she wants too, but it's different. There's a layer of roleplay.

It's dangerous. For both of us.

Physically. Practically. Emotionally.

Indigo lets out a soft groan. "Asking for it?" She's already drifting off. Into that perfect place where she lets go.

This is it. Her last chance to change her mind, deny her fantasy, reject the scene.

She can safe out at any point, but this is the fucking line.

We can't uncross it.

She's still against me, breathing hard, flushed and waiting.

Wet.

It is what she wants.

And I will give her what she wants.

I slip my fingers under her knickers.

She groans as I slide two fingers inside her.

She's soaked. There's no resistance. Only the soft, sweetness of her cunt.

I let my voice drop to a threatening tone. "Tempting me with this skirt. Asking me to follow you home. Make you take it. Aren't you?"

"No." She crosses the line.

I drive my fingers into her.

She groans.

I hook my fingers around the belt. Push her onto her knees.

She lands with a thud. "Fuck."

"Does that hurt, princess?"

She says nothing.

"I asked you a question. Does that hurt?"

"Yes."

"You think you're too good for hurt?"

"No."

"You think you're too good for me. In your fancy dress and your designer shoes." I knot my hand in her hair. "Girls like you are too good for men like me."

Her chest heaves with her inhale. "Please."

"Please?"

"Yes. Please. I'm a nice girl. I like nice things." Her voice is soft. Eager. "I like nice men."

The exact opposite of what she said last night.

She's daring me.

Asking me to push her further.

Harder.

Fuck. I'm the one in over my head here.

I tug at her hair until she groans. The groan I know. The one that's equal parts pain and pleasure. The one that's asking for more of both.

"A nice girl gets wet when a stranger binds her wrists?" I ask.

Her chest heaves. "Please. I like nice men. Please."

"Did some nice man buy your fancy clothes?"

"Yes."

"You want to see him again?"

She sucks in a shallow breath.

I push her dress off her shoulders.

The right. Then the left.

It falls over her chest, revealing her breasts, collecting at her waist.

I hold her head against my cock as I bring my hand to her breast. Roll her nipple between my thumb and forefinger.

She lets out a soft groan.

"You don't sound like a nice girl."

She shakes her head.

"You don't like nice things." I pinch her nipple until she gasps. "You don't fool me, pretending." I release her.

She falls back onto her legs.

I move around her. In front of her.

Indigo looks up at me, that same fire and need in her deep blue eyes.

She needs this.

I need to give it to her.

No matter how badly it scares me.

"I don't think you like nice men." I undo the button of my jeans. "But if you do want to see your nice man again, you'll do exactly as I say. Understand?"

"Yes." Her flush deepens. She watches with wide eyes as I unzip my jeans. Wrap my hand around my cock.

I bring one hand to the back of her head to hold her in place. "Open your mouth."

She does.

"And take my cock like a good girl." I push into her mouth.

Hard enough she grunts against my cock.

Fuck. She feels too good.

For a second, my body threatens to take over. To forget everything she wants. To use her for its satisfaction.

That is what she wants.

But I'm greedy. I want more.

I knot my hand in her hair, then I pull back and drive into her.

Softly at first.

To get her used to it.

Then harder.

Harder.

Until she gags.

I give her a second to catch her breath, then I fuck her pretty mouth.

She relaxes her throat. Presses her tongue flat against my base.

Groans as she takes me again and again.

I tug at her hair, pulling her mouth off me.

She licks her lips. Looks up at me with those proud, defiant eyes.

"Groaning as you take it hard and rough." I bring my hand to her cheek. Run my thumb over her lips. "That's how you like it, isn't it? Because you're not a nice girl. And you don't like nice things." I give her another chance to change course. Say yes. Drop her safe word.

She doesn't. She shakes her head. "No."

"Nice girls don't lie about what they want." I move behind her. "You want me to fuck you."

She shakes her head.

"That's too bad. You're going to take it anyway." I drop to the ground behind her. Push her onto the floor face first.

Her forehead hits the ground. Hard enough to hurt. But not hard enough to leave a mark.

I bring my hand to her cunt. She's still soaked.

I run my finger over her clit.

She groans. Close.

Already close.

I push her knickers aside. Then I push her thighs apart with my knees. And I lower my body onto hers.

"Fuck." She turns to the right. Looks back at me, pleading with her gorgeous blue eyes. "Please."

"Please?" I press my palm into her shoulder. "Please what?"

"Please." She says it again. Only softer.

I'm not sure what she's asking. If I'm pushing her too far. Or not enough.

I study her expression. The flush of her cheeks, the heave of her chest, the softness of her brow.

"You think you can beg for mercy, princess?" I ask. "I don't have mercy."

Her pupils dilate.

"We both know why you're begging. For this."

I push into her. Just enough to tease her.

She groans as my cock brushes her cunt.

"Begging me to fuck you. Because you're not a nice girl. And you don't like nice men. Do you?"

"No."

"Then why are you panting, princess?"

She sucks a breath through her teeth.

"You like men like me. Men who will hurt you."

She shakes her head into the floor.

"No? Then I'll have to show you."

She gasps as I drive into her.

No softness this time. No warm up.

I fuck her hard and fast.

Her eyes close.

Her lips part.

Her expression gets soft. Hazy.

That space she needs to be. Where she lets go of everything except my commands.

She isn't asking herself if this is too much. If I'm pushing too far. If I'm crossing some line I can't uncross.

She's there.

Lost in how much she wants it.

Fuck.

My last inhibition falls away.

I forget about the fucking line.

I pin her to the ground, digging my nails into her shoulder as I fuck her.

Her expression softens.

Her groans run together.

Her cunt tightens around me.

She's almost there.

Then I slip my hand between her legs. Run my thumb over her clit. "Come on my cock like a good girl."

She mutters a curse under her breath.

Then she's there.

She groans into the air as she comes.

I work her through her orgasm, then I give her one moment of relief, and I bring my thumb back to her clit.

Those perfect circles she needs.

She comes fast this time.

Hard enough her groan is pain as much as it's pleasure.

Her cunt pulses around me. Pulls me over the edge.

I bring my lips to her neck, groaning into her skin as I come, working until I've spilled every fucking drop.

When I'm finished, I pull back. Undo her bindings. Fix my clothes.

Then hers.

Then I pull her into my lap, stroking her hair as she drifts back to reality.

When she's lucid enough, I help her to her feet, carry her into the bedroom.

I hold her until her breathing returns to normal. Then I run a bath. Help her into it. Soap her skin. Wash her hair.

She looks up at me with hazy eyes.

Nervous.

Shy.

"Will you join me?" she asks.

This time, I nod. Undress. Slip into the small space with her.

Hold her like I'll never let her go.

Chapter Forty-Two

INDIGO

I stay there, in his arms, for hours.

Quiet. Still. Completely content.

He holds me close, runs his fingers through my hair, strokes my cheek.

Then he helps me dress, makes sure I eat.

I spend the night in his apartment, in our apartment, in his arms. Wake up to a quiet space and the smell of coffee.

It still feels safe. Like home. A new home that's completely ours.

When I meet Sienna at school, I tell her we're engaged.

She squeals *way to go putting a ring on it*, offers to shop for dresses with me, asks if Cam is coming to our engagement party.

Shifts to talking about soccer.

My sister.

Not at all interested in the finer points of weddings.

Even so, she stops by my room before she goes to sleep and insists I bring her when I try on dresses.

"Honestly, Indie. You're so hopeless with style. The whole tall and thin thing is completely wasted on you."

Chapter Forty-Three

INDIGO

"This is not boss bitch." Sienna studies a lace sheath. "It's pretty, but it's not you."

"Pretty isn't me?"

"Don't act offended. You know you're not pretty."

"I do?"

She shoots me a *please* look and takes a long sip of her iced latte. "What do you usually call it? Artsy girl?"

"Usually."

"I can say that instead of boss bitch. If you'd feel better."

I can't help but laugh. "I'll take boss babe. I want the babe in there."

Sienna takes another sip. "Is that what you want to say with your dress? Boss babe."

"I think so."

"Then you should." She holds up a pretty princess gown. "It's your wedding. God, I can't believe it's your wedding."

"I know." It's official today. I picked a venue. We set a date.

We announce it at our engagement party next week, but I've already told Sienna. He's already told his family.

Eleven weeks from tomorrow.

In eleven weeks, I marry Ty.

It's fucking crazy.

"No offense, Indie, but why are you marrying him?" Sienna asks.

"Which part of that am I supposed to not take offense to?"

"All of it."

A laugh falls from my lips. My sister, master of tact. "What do you want me to say?"

"The truth."

There's a right answer here. *Because I love him.*

Do I love him?

I'm not sure. I don't know what that means. But I know what Sienna wants to hear. "The sex."

She laughs. "Really?"

"Really." That's the truth. The money is a factor. A big factor. But I said yes because I want to fuck him. I stuck around because I want to fuck him. I'm still here because I want to fuck him.

She hangs the dress. Drops to her knees to study the tulle skirt. "Is it that good?"

"Yes."

"Details?"

"In your dreams."

"Please." She tries to press her palms together, but her iced latte is in the way. "You owe me a detail. At least one."

"He gives me what I want."

"That's a generalization, not a detail."

What am I willing to tell her?

Nothing.

I don't want to share this with her. With anyone.

"He's..." I bite my lip. "We want the same things."

"Which are..."

342

"None of your business."

She stares at me, waiting for me to break. When I don't, she adopts her game face.

It's Sienna's attempt at boss bitch. And she does look like she's ready for action. But she still looks sweet.

"You both like it rough?" she asks.

"No comment."

"Just admit it."

"Maybe."

"Yes-be."

"Okay. Yes. We both like it rough."

"What kind of rough?" Her eyes light up. "Does he tie you up? Spank you? Call you names?"

"That was one. That's all you get."

She makes a show of pouting. Picks up my iced tea. Moves to the podium in the middle of the room.

This place is as low-key as bridal boutiques get, but it's still decked in powder blue and white lace.

Better than pink and white lace, but still awfully traditional.

Paloma picked it, of course. Because the owner will leave us alone until we need help.

And because it has a selection of gowns that will make me look like a rock star.

"You're holding my tea hostage?" I ask.

"Yep."

"It's not that good." I sit next to her. "I won't tell you."

"What if I get you drunk?"

"Try it if you think it will work."

"That's exactly what he said."

I laugh. "He's smart."

"Well, yeah. If he's marrying you, he's obviously smart."

"Thanks."

"Is it really the sex?" She sips her latte. Shakes my iced

tea *don't you want it.* "I mean, I get it. He's handsome. Rich. Good in bed. And a soccer player. You have to nail that down before it's too late."

"Too late?"

"He's a guy."

"Which means…"

"They get bored. That's what people say." She finishes her last sip. Glares at her empty cup. "And he was sleeping with a lot of women before you two reconnected."

"He was."

"Are you worried he'll miss that?"

"No." I never worry about that.

"Because other women can't give him the things he wants?"

"Because he's loyal."

"And what I said."

"Sure. And what you said."

She squeals as she crosses her legs. She's in her usual tomboy attire—denim shorts, grey tank top, hair in a pony-tail—but she still blends into the girly bridal boutique. "Hot, rich, good in bed, soccer player. I approve."

"I appreciate that."

"And given that you two already set a date… we should pick a dress."

"So you can get more coffee?"

"Yeah." She stands. Moves to the second rack. The dresses Paloma pulled just for me. "And it's my duty as your sister to help."

"Is it?"

She nods. "And I… I kind of want to see you in a gown."

"Really?"

"I know. It's weird." She runs her fingers over a silk sheath. "I feel a sudden desire to wear pink." She blushes, embarrassed at embracing any kind of girlishness. "Just try the dress, okay?"

"That one?"

She nods *this one*.

"Okay. Sure." I stand. Move next to my sister.

"And this one too." She pulls another dress, one with a plunging neckline. "And this." And a third. The most feminine dress Paloma pulled.

A chiffon number fit for a goddess.

I pull her into a tight hug, then I gather the gowns, move into the dressing stall.

The owner knocks. Helps me into the first dress and a pair of silver heels.

I take a deep breath and move into the main room.

"Oh my god." Sienna wipes a tear. "Indie..." She wipes her eyes with the back of her hand. Tries to adopt her game face. "You look so bridal."

She moves away from the podium. Watches as I climb the steps. Turn to the mirror.

She's right.

Bright white chiffon with a deep scoop neck, a long skirt, a high thigh slit.

My makeup is a little simple and my hair is a little messy, but, still, I look like a bride.

I blink back a tear.

"You like it?" Sienna's voice is soft. Gentle. Completely unlike her. "I like it. It's sexy. And almost casual. But I want to see the other ones too."

"I do."

"You're ready to get married." She laughs. Looks to the accessories. "Do you think you'll wear a veil?"

"Too old-fashioned."

"A tiara?"

"No. Like this." My eyes go to my reflection. The blunt

line of my hair. The silver shadow highlighting my eyes. The wine lipstick. "Do you think it's enough?"

"It's not quite boss babe, but it's pretty."

"And I'm not pretty?"

She waves *don't pretend like you're offended.* "You're striking. You need more drama. Try the others." She helps me off the podium.

I return to the dressing room. Let the owner help me out of this gown. Into the next.

Ivory silk. Strapless. Straight neckline. Tight bodice. Mermaid skirt.

It's hard walking in the snug skirt, but I manage to make it to the podium.

Sienna looks up at me. "It's nice."

"Nice? That's a word in your vocabulary?"

"I know." She presses her lips together. "But nice feels right. Pretty. Simple. Nice."

She's right. It's a beautiful dress, but it's just nice.

And I don't want nice.

Not in my fiancé, not in my fuck, and not in my things.

I can accept that.

Can Ty?

"Try the next one," Sienna says. "It has the low neckline. It will go over better with your fiancé."

"Is that how we're deciding?"

"You're the one saying you're marrying him for sex."

It's true.

And we make sense there.

It's everything else that's complicated.

I push aside thoughts of love as I change into the next gown, move into the main room, climb the podium.

It hits me the second I catch my reflection.

This is it.

The dress.

I'm marrying Ty in this dress.

"Oh my god." Sienna squeezes my hand. "That's it."

"I think it is."

"Oh my god." She wipes her eyes with her free hand. "Indie… you look… so hot for someone so flat."

A laugh spills from my lips.

"Is that the secret to plunging necklines?" She squeezes my hand. "It must be. You really own them."

"Thanks."

"You look…"

"Not pretty?"

"Better than pretty." She releases my hand. "Stunning."

The gown is perfect. Ivory chiffon with thick straps, a sharp, plunging v, a low back, a flowing skirt.

"Like an angel here to kick ass."

She's right. The dress is equal parts sexy, dramatic, and ethereal.

And I can see it. The skirt blowing in the wind.

Ty standing in front of me. Sliding a ring on my finger. Pulling me into a tight kiss.

"It's perfect," I whisper.

She nods. "You want this one?"

"Yeah. I think so."

"And the other one, for the party?"

"If there's time."

"I'll ask." She moves to the owner. Relays the message.

I stare at my reflection the entire time.

This is it.

The dress I wear when I marry Ty.

Right now, it's obvious.

I want it all. Everything.

Can I have everything?

God, I really want to have everything.

Chapter Forty-Four

INDIGO

I make it official.

Order the dress.

Buy Sienna lunch to celebrate.

Text Ty the news.

He replies with a promise to take care of everything else. He knows I'm busy with Sienna's graduation.

All I need to do is show up at our engagement party.

So I let her finals take over my week.

I savor my time with my sister.

I fix breakfast in the mornings, meet Ty at his office for lunch, walk Sienna home. Help her study all night.

I fill the free time in my day with movies and music.

Scales. And songs. No lyrics. I can't sing yet. But I can play. By myself, with no one to see everything wash over me, I can play.

And I do. When I'm not with my sister or my fiancé, it's all I do.

She aces her finals.

We celebrate with gelato, reality TV, trips to her favorite coffee shops around the city.

Before I know it, it's the day of her graduation. She's in a purple robe. I'm in a matching sundress. We're walking to her school.

And Ty is there with me at the ceremony.

He holds my hand as I watch my sister walk across the stage, accept her diploma, send an *oh god, I hope she's not crying* look in my general direction.

It doesn't help.

I cry like a baby.

Then I embarrass her with stories at lunch—just the three of us—and let her go off with her friends. To a party.

Ty walks me home. "We have a few hours of the apartment to ourselves."

We do.

"And you have the robe I sent to your place."

"Yes," I say.

"I didn't ask a question." He laughs.

"Yes, you did." My cheeks flush. It's hot today, but I don't mind the extra fire. "Can we do it like before?"

"Later." He pulls me into a tight kiss. "Your walls are too thin."

Even though it's a fair point, I pout.

"Would you rather I say never?"

"That's a bluff."

He smiles. "Then call it."

I don't. "Give me ten minutes to shower. Then surprise me."

He nods. Kisses me one more time.

He waits as I shower, forget the complications surrounding us, don my robe.

Then he comes through the open door, pins me to the wall, fucks me.

Exactly like my fantasy.

Exactly what I want.

Exactly what I want and I still want more.

No matter how satisfied I am, I want more.

No matter how much I want, I trust him to give me more.

———

HE STAYS ALL EVENING. MAKES DINNER. WATCHES *Casablanca* with me. Agrees to sleep over.

When we go to my room, he stares with wide eyes. Studies the posters (all female solo musicians) and magazine tear outs on my walls. The messy lyrics I scribbled on notebook paper.

The guitar in the corner.

"You've been playing?" he asks.

"How can you tell?"

"A sense." He wraps his arms around my waist. Presses his lips to my neck. "A lot?"

"A lot."

"Will you play for me?"

"Right now?"

He nods into my shoulder.

My stomach flutters. Playing by myself is one thing. For Ty?

That's terrifying.

"Please," he says. "I want to hear you play."

Please.

It's so unfamiliar on his lips.

It makes me buzz in an entirely different way.

It's not just that I want to satisfy him, though I do.

It's knowing he craves this enough he'll say please.

"Say it again." I turn to him. Run my fingers over his jaw.

His smile is soft. Nervous. "Please. I want to hear you play."

"Okay." I can do this. I'm terrified, but I'm not letting that fear win. "Give me a minute. I have to tune my guitar."

He nods. Moves into the living room.

I take a deep breath. Close my eyes. Call all my confidence.

My hands are shaking.

My heart is pounding.

But I can do this.

I will do this.

Somehow, I pick up my guitar. Somehow, I press my fingers to the frets.

Play a scale.

A few chords.

An easy song my dad taught me.

Bit by bit, I slip into the music. Into that perfect place where I'm an extension of the instrument. Where I'm not thinking.

I just am.

I finish the song.

Start one of mine.

The first line.

The first note.

The chorus.

The verse.

A song about losing my father.

Then another. One about Ty. Not that I admitted it.

I always told myself it was about loneliness. How hard it was juggling school and work. How impossible it was to find someone who understood me.

But it was about him.

About the need he'd found in me. The need he'd filled. The hole he left when he returned to London.

It was about how I was in love with him.

I've been in love with him for the last three years.

But I haven't admitted it to myself until right now.

When I finish, I blink my eyes open.

He's there. In the doorframe, staring at me with rapt attention.

Is that love? I don't know.

Maybe not.

But it's something. It's a lot.

And I want it. All of it. Everything he's willing to give.

He waits until I set my guitar down. Then he moves across the room. Wraps his arms around me.

I kiss him like I'm saying *I love you*.

He kisses back like he's claiming me.

It's not *I love you too*, but it's close.

It's really fucking close.

Chapter Forty-Five

TY

Even with the window open and the fan on high, the flat is stuffy.

I wake sweaty, sticky, desperate to stay in bed.

I want to be here, in this place that's hers, in this world that's hers.

But it's a weekday. And I can't afford to skip work again.

So I slip to the bathroom. Shower. Dress.

Find Sienna in the living room.

She taps her fingers against her arm. "You spent the night?"

"Am I in trouble?"

She yawns as she stretches her arms over her head. "Did you make her come?"

"What do you think?"

"I think that's a lame non-answer."

I chuckle. "I don't think she'd want me to tell you."

"Ding, ding, ding. Lame non-answer two."

"It's not that easy to bait me."

"Or you're actually a selfish lover and you don't want to admit it."

I can't help but chuckle. She's so much Indie, but she's so different too. "Maybe."

She presses on. "How many times did you make her come?"

"Do you really think I'm going to tell you?"

She nods *yeah, probably not.* "You making breakfast or..." She motions to the kitchen. "Indie is a terrible cook."

"So I hear."

"She hasn't subjected you to her creations?"

"I like cooking."

"Hmmm. Another in the pro column."

I raise a brow.

"Reasons to marry you. Rich, hot, athletic, good in bed, and a good cook. Well, a cook. I guess I'll be the judge of good."

"Is that the order?" I ask.

"No." She waves *yeah, right.* "Good in bed, hot, athletic."

"Fuck the rest?"

She nods *pretty much.* "Why are you marrying her? Are you going to tell me it's not about sex?"

"No." I check the fridge. There's enough to make breakfast. I grab eggs, butter, bread. "You take them sunny side up too?"

She makes that *hmm* noise that means yes.

I motion for her to sit.

She shakes her head. "You drink coffee, right?"

"I do."

"I'll make some. It's way too early. Where are you going, anyway?"

"Where do you think I'm going in a suit?" I roll my sleeves to my elbows.

Sienna shoots me that same *please* look. "You could be going anywhere. You always wear a suit. Like you're making a point or something."

"What's the point?"

"That you're rich and hot. We get it. You don't have to keep selling it."

My laugh is louder this time. "What would I sell if I wore jeans?"

She fills the electric kettle. Sets it to *French Press*. "That you're hot and down to earth, I guess."

"And I'm not?"

She makes that *so-so* motion. Rises to her tiptoes to reach for the coffee on a high shelf.

I grab it. Hand it to her.

"Tall. Tall people are the worst," she says.

"You're not exactly short."

"Yeah, but Indie has like three inches on me. And you…" She looks up at me. "You're ridiculous."

"I'm ridiculous?"

"Yeah. Save some height for the rest of us."

"How would I give you some?"

She makes that *hmm* face. "Okay. Keep your height. But you still haven't answered my question."

"Which question."

"Why do you want to marry her?"

"Sex. Of course."

"Do you love her?"

It catches me off guard. It's not the kind of thing I imagine Sienna considering. Love seems far outside her area of interests.

"I want to spend my life with her," I say. "I want to take care of her."

She scoops grinds into the French Press. "She needs that."

"I know."

"And I'll kill you if you hurt her."

"I appreciate that."

She fills the carafe with steaming water. "But… I think you'll do a good job. And it's okay with me. That she's marrying you. That she's moving on with her life."

"You should tell her that."

"I will," she says. "But I want you to know too. I trust you, Ty. I trust you to take care of her. Don't fuck that up. Promise you won't fuck that up."

It's not a promise I can make her, but I do it anyway. "I promise."

———

SIENNA SLIPS TO HER USUAL TEASING SELF. TALKS ABOUT football and her lust for my cousin. Even when I tell her she's overselling it, she asks what he's doing, where he is, if he's attending our engagement party this weekend.

She squeals when I tell her yes.

I can't tell how much is a put-on and how much is real, but I know better than to argue. So I ask her to promise she'll take care of Indie on all matters of prepping for the party.

Not the practical—Paloma's already booked hair, makeup, alterations—but the emotional.

I want Sienna there with her before we face the world.

I leave when she says *Yes, of course, don't be stupid. Do you really think I need you to tell me to be there for my sister?*

Arrive at work with a text from Indie.

Indigo: You should have stayed.

And a picture. Her in bed, covered only in her soft sheets, lips parting with a sigh.

Ty: I have work.

Indigo: You should have woken me then.

Ty: Your sister would have heard.

Indigo: I can be quiet.

Ty: I don't want you quiet.

She teases back with another picture.

The same only the sheets are at her waist.

Indigo: Tonight then. At your place. You have thick walls.

I do.

And I want to fuck her.

I want to give her everything she craves.

But not yet.

I need to make her wait.

Ty: Friday.

Indigo: You want me to wait until the night before the party?

Ty: Yes.

I want to have her close that night. To feel that she's mine before I go and announce it to the world.

Indigo: Will you do the scene?

Ty: Maybe.

Indigo: Maybe?

Ty: I want to surprise you.

Indigo: What if I don't want a surprise?

Ty: You do.

Indigo: Okay. I do. But I don't like maybe. It might mean no.

Ty: Do you trust me?

Indigo: Yes.

Ty: So trust me. I'll give you what you need.

Indigo: Do you promise?

Ty: Do I need to?

Indigo: No. Do it anyway.

Ty: I promise.

Chapter Forty-Six

INDIGO

For two days, I think about Ty.

Every time I close my eyes, I see his hand on my thigh, I taste his lips, I feel his nails against my back. All night.

Through a jog with Sienna. Breakfast. A shower. Tea.

As I don cotton panties, a sheer sundress, black sandals.

It's eighty and humid, but the air is nothing compared to the heat inside me. Even when I'm in the sweltering subway station.

Then the overly air-conditioned car.

Even when I'm standing outside of Ty's apartment building, our apartment building.

This time, I don't ask myself what I'm doing. If I'm crazy for how much I want this. If I'm pushing him too far.

I trust him here.

He knows what I want and he's determined to give it to me.

I step into the building. Nod hello to the security guard. Catch my breath in the elevator.

A dozen steps to his door.

It's open.

The lights are off. The room is dark. I don't see him. I don't realize he's here until he pins me to the wall.

"Ty." My breath catches in my throat.

His fingers curl around my wrist. "Do you want me to hurt you?"

He's asking how I want to do the scene.

I can say *yes*. Admit I savor the feel of his teeth on my neck and his hand on my ass.

Or I can say *no*. Play this game. Admit I want him to force me.

"I asked you a question." He wraps some rough fabric around my wrists. Pulls it tight. Binds my arms behind my back. "Do you want me to hurt you?"

"No." I agree to the scene. Because I trust him. I trust him completely.

Enough to ask him to hurt me.

Enough to ask him to force me.

Enough to admit I want this.

"Then do what I say." His voice is all rough edges. There's no tenderness. None of the sweet Ty I know.

This other person.

The brutal man I crave.

"What do you want?" I ask.

He pushes me against the wall. "I want to watch."

Fuck.

My sex clenches. I'm already wet. Already wound so fucking tight.

Without warning, he shoves my dress down my shoulders. Over my chest.

To my waist.

The fabric collects around my wrists, holding them against my back, restraining me further.

He shifts his hips, so his cock is against my ass.

"Can you do that, princess?" He slips his hand under my skirt. Curls his fingers around my thigh. "Can you put on a show for me?"

Fuck.

He pushes my panties off my ass. Lets them fall to my ankles.

He digs his nails into my thigh.

Hard.

Hard enough it hurts.

Maybe hard enough to draw blood.

Too much, but I want more.

I always want more.

"I asked you a question," he growls.

"Please."

"Please?"

"Don't hurt me."

"Then do what I say." He wraps his arms around me. Lifts me—my entire body—and drapes me over his shoulder.

Like before. Only without the tease or the tenderness.

Like he's going to take me somewhere no one can find me.

His fingers dig into my thighs as he moves. Down the hallway.

To the bedroom.

Our bedroom.

He throws me on the bed.

I land on my wrists. On some hard metal. A buckle. His belt or handcuffs, I'm not sure.

It smarts.

But that only winds me tighter.

I look up at him.

He's wearing jeans and a t-shirt.

No suit. No tie. No shoes.

No sign of the buttoned-up man who commands an office.

Only the wild lover I know here.

Handsome. Strong. Brutal.

And, there, in the corner of the room, next to the mirror—

A video camera pointed at the bed.

Holy shit.

"You're recording this?" I barely get the words out.

"I want to watch." He does away with his t-shirt. "Now. Later. Whenever I want to see you take it."

"Just you?"

"Why, princess? Are you shy?" He moves to the bed. Drops to his knees. "You don't want people to know you like being hurt?"

"I—"

He wraps his fingers around my thighs. Pulls me to the edge of the bed.

God yes.

He knows I want to watch, so he's recording this. For us.

I almost break character to congratulate him, tell him how much I need him, how much I appreciate him.

But I don't.

I stay here, in this moment of him threatening me, exposing me.

"You what?" he growls.

"I don't." I need more. It's so fucking good, but, still, I need more. "I don't want anyone to see."

"Then why are you wet?" He slips two fingers inside me.

My eyes close. My body takes over.

He's good at this. Too good.

It terrifies me.

It terrifies me how much it thrills me.

How little I care.

His hand finds my neck. "You like being on display."

My eyes flutter open. Go to the mirror. It's so fucking beautiful, watching Ty standing between my legs, driving his fingers into me.

Fuck.

He drives his fingers into me again and again.

Then he drops between my legs. Brings his lips to my thigh.

He bites me. No teasing, no ramp up.

He bites hard.

I yelp.

Fuck.

He does it again. Only higher. Closer.

Then again.

Again.

Almost.

My thighs shake against his lips.

Then his mouth is on me. He licks me hard and fast. Utterly without tenderness.

It winds me tighter and tighter.

Then his nails scrape my thighs and I come.

He works me through my orgasm, then he brings his teeth to my thigh. To that same spot.

He bites me again.

I let out a groan.

He scrapes his teeth against my thigh. "You like being watched."

"No."

"You want men like me to watch. Men who will hurt you."

I shake my head.

He stands. Flips me onto my stomach. Presses his palm into the space between my shoulder blades, pinning me to the bed. "Admit it."

I do.

I like being watched, I like being hurt, I like everything about this.

"Yes," I breathe.

I expect him to break, to gasp, to show some surprise. But he doesn't.

He lets go, gives in to the scene.

Ty pins me harder. He brings his knee to the back of my thigh. Holds me in place as he unzips his jeans and pulls me in position.

He lifts his knee.

Replaces it with his hands on my hips.

He pulls me onto him.

He slams into me so hard and fast I groan.

I reach for something, but I'm bound.

He presses down, pushing me into the bed and drives into me with steady strokes.

Too hard.

Too fast.

Too deep.

It hurts.

But still, I want more.

I let my eyes close for a second, then I force them open.

I soak up every ounce of sensation.

The camera in the corner.

The sharpness of his nails on my hips.

The earthy scent of his shampoo.

The rough edge to his groan.

The sweet pressure of his cock inside me.

Again and again.

Until I'm there.

Groaning as I come on his cock. Pulsing so hard and fast I can barely breathe.

It pulls him over the edge.

He rakes his nails over my ass as he comes. He works through his orgasm, letting out low deep groans as he spills every drop.

When he's finished, he pulls back. Sits next to me. Undoes the bindings around my wrist.

Helps me out of my dress.

Pulls me into his arms and holds me like he'll never let go.

He is mine.

Here, he's mine.

I'm the only one who gets this part of him.

Whatever else happens, I have that.

Chapter Forty-Seven

INDIGO

For a long time, I lie there in his arms. He helps me wash and dress. Makes dinner. Sits with me on the balcony.

We talk about nothing as we watch the moon bounce off the Hudson.

We stay in this beautiful, perfect place for hours.

Before we go to bed, he takes the tape from the camera, wraps it in a purple gift box, slips it into my purse.

It's mine.

This recording that could destroy him, destroy the reputation he's paying me to fix, is mine.

He trusts me to keep it safe.

He trusts me.

I fall asleep in his arms. Wake to the smell of coffee and tea and a note about meeting me at the engagement party.

It's easier than I expect, stepping into my role.

Listening to Sienna gossip as we dress, sit through hair and makeup, take a car to the party.

Watching her bounce around the room, discussing soccer with anyone who will listen.

I hold Ty's hand. I smile at his co-workers. I laugh as Cam and Ian tease him about my bachelorette party.

They're going to buy me strippers.

And record the whole thing. To make Ty jealous.

They're invited, right?

I laugh. I sip champagne. I circulate.

The blushing bride.

Then the air in the room changes.

I know before I see her.

Rory. In a designer sheath and pearls. Sweet smile, long hair, French-manicured fingers wrapped around Ty's heart.

Chapter Forty-Eight

INDIGO

"**T**hat's a beautiful ring." Ty's coworker goes on about the curving silver adorning my left hand. "Modern."

"I'm a modern man." Ty's voice stays strong, but his eyes wander to her.

It's fast, a second maybe, but I still feel some pull between them.

I'm the only one who gets that side of him.

I repeat the mantra again and again.

It fails to soften my shoulders.

His coworker laughs. "Do you go Dutch on your dates?"

"We trade off," Ty says. "I pay for pizza. She pays for dinner at Le Cirque."

He's teasing. I'm supposed to laugh. But I can't.

His attention is with her. That part of him that wants to be a nice man who likes nice things—

It's with her.

That part of him will always be with her.

Ty presses his palm into my lower back. "Let me get you something to eat."

"I'm fine." I pry my eyes from Rory and her perfect black sheath.

"I remember when I got married," his coworker says. "My wife wouldn't touch carbs. She nearly starved herself to fit into her dress."

That's ridiculous, but it's filling Ty's head with ideas.

I can see it in his eyes. That other part of him. The one that needs to take care of me.

He nods goodbye to his coworker. "If you'll excuse us..."

I open my mouth to protest, but his coworker is already walking away. Ty is already leading me toward the table of appetizers.

He fills a plate with crostini. One is topped with shrimp and mango. Another with goat cheese and raspberry. A third with mozzarella and basil.

"I'm fine," I say.

"When's the last time you ate?" He pushes the plate into my hands.

"Breakfast."

"Indigo..." His eyes flit to her. Rory. She's chatting with Ian. And he's looking at us like he's not looking at us.

"If you don't want this, I'll find something else," he says.

Fine. I take the middle piece. Pop it into my mouth.

Fuck, it's good. Soft bread, tart raspberry, creamy goat cheese.

I stifle a groan.

I'm hungry. No, I'm starving.

He can tell—he can always tell—but he doesn't call me on it. Just fills another plate with goat cheese and raspberry toast and trades me.

He finishes his appetizers.

I finish my second in one bite. The third in two.

"Here." He fills a glass with water from the carafe.

I drink. "Did you know she was coming?"

"No," he says.

"Did Ian?"

"He would have told me."

Unless she swore him to secrecy.

That the two of them hold on to secrets like their lives depend on it.

Rory says goodbye to Ian. Looks to us with a smile. Moves across the room.

I finish my glass. Set it on the table. Wipe my hands on my dress.

He slips his arm around my waist. Holds me like he's waiting for his best friend and not his ex.

Rory stops in front of us. "Hello." She smiles at me. "You must be Indigo."

"I must," I say.

She offers her hand. "I'm Rory."

"I know." I shake. "It's nice to meet you."

"You too." Her smile is soft. Genuine. "I've heard a lot about you."

"You have?" I ask. "From who?"

She laughs. "Friends who keep an eye on Ty for me." Her eyes flit to my left hand. "Your dress is gorgeous."

"Thank you." It's a normal engagement party conversation. And this dress is fantastic. My first choice wasn't available, but this one is better.

A backless silk number that falls mid-thigh. With the high, square neckline, it's sexy, classy, and dramatic at once.

"She looks gorgeous, doesn't she?" Ty turns to me. Looks me up and down. Not like he's assessing me. Not like he's thinking about what he wants to do to me.

Like he loves me so much he loves the sight of me.

Do I have that part of him?

"She does." Rory breaks the moment. "You look stunning, Indigo."

"Not compared to him," I say.

For a moment, his smile is easy, authentic. Then he looks at her and his brow furrows.

"He does wear a suit, doesn't he?" Rory says.

"He does." I move closer reflexively.

"Would you mind if I stole a moment with you, Indigo?" she asks. "Would you mind, Ty?"

"Of course not." He presses his lips to my cheek. Leans closer enough to whisper. "Are you sure?"

I nod.

His hand lingers on my waist.

His lips linger on my neck.

He stays close, like he's going to say more, like he's going to whisper *I love you.*

But he doesn't.

He releases me. "Take care of her."

"I promise." She waits for him to leave.

Ty finds his brother. Tries to laugh at something. Fails to sell casual.

"They're watching, aren't they?" She looks to them.

"What else would they do?" I ask.

She nods *true.* Motions to the rooftop garden outside. "Can I buy you a drink?"

"It's an open bar."

Her laugh is soft. Musical. "Can Ty buy you a drink then?"

"A Manhattan. Thanks. I'll meet you there."

She nods. Moves to the bar.

I step onto the quiet rooftop patio. It's a beautiful night. Warm air. Light breeze. Soft blue sky lit by skyscrapers and paper lanterns.

The city at night.

Paradise.

Rory finds me at the railing. "You look at home."

"I am."

"You are. Aren't you?"

I'm not sure what she's asking, so I don't answer. I accept my drink with a *thank you*. Turn to the Empire State Building.

Its lights are blue today. That bright cobalt. Not our blue. Not any of our blues. But somehow still ours.

Rory brings her wineglass to her lips. "This must be strange for you."

"For you too." I take a long sip. Let the mix of bourbon, vermouth, and bitters warm my lips and throat. It's almost too hot for a Manhattan, but I need the liquid courage.

"I promise my intentions are good." Her fingers curl around the stem. "I'm not here to steal him."

"That's not the most encouraging promise I've ever heard."

"If I was in your shoes, I'd be worried." She takes another sip. "I was worried about you."

"I know."

Her eyes fill with surprise. "He told you?"

"I guessed. When we parted ways, he promised he'd stay in touch. A few months later, he left a message saying he couldn't see me, because he didn't trust himself."

"He didn't?"

"You'd have to ask him."

Her throat quivers as she swallows. "He didn't see you?"

"Not until after you…" My eyes go to my engagement ring. "Months after you ended things."

She nods. "I'm sorry. I know how this must sound. I'm not trying to accuse you of anything, Indigo. You don't strike me as the kind of person who'd sleep with a taken man."

"I haven't." I'd like to think I wouldn't. But if Ty had

come to me, admitted he was with someone else, told me he wanted me anyway—

He wouldn't do it.

But if he did, I'm not sure I'd have denied him.

I'm not sure I would have denied myself.

I need him so fucking badly.

"You must think I'm horrible," I say.

Not in the way she means.

"I'm at your engagement party asking if you slept with your fiancé when he was still with me."

"You asked tactfully," I say. "I barely noticed."

She smiles. "You're lying."

"A little."

"Please, ignore me if you want. Or ask me to leave."

"You don't need the preface." I finish my drink. Set it on the table behind me. "You've already asked if he cheated with me."

"I didn't mean to accuse you."

"I know."

"I'm not here for answers."

She is. But I understand that. And I understand not being able to admit it too.

"I want him to be happy."

"Were you hoping he'd cheated?" The words fall from my lips. It's over the line. But then she did ask if I fucked him. We're not exactly exchanging small talk.

"I was sure he did."

"It's not in his nature."

"No. But people react when they're backed into a corner."

Is that how she saw it? How he saw it? Backed into a corner because he couldn't admit what he wanted.

Either he lost the woman he loved or he denied this part of himself.

Maybe he wasn't in a corner, exactly, but he was stuck.

She continues, "Things were different when he came back from New York. Every time he came back from New York. But especially two years ago. I was sure he'd seen you. I didn't know if he'd slept with you, but I was sure he'd seen you, sure it had changed something."

"Changed what?"

"What he wanted." She finishes her glass. "I know it's none of my business, but I have to ask. What is he like with you?"

"What is he like?"

"You know what I'm asking."

I do. "What do you want me to say?"

"The truth," she says.

"You're right. It's none of your business."

"I know."

As much as I want to tell her to fuck off for asking, I can't. I know how it feels to lose Ty. We lost different parts of him, but we both lost him. "He's rough."

"And he's always—"

"Yes."

"Was it his idea?"

"His. But I... I ask him for more. I push him as much as he pushes me."

She runs her finger over the stem of her glass. "Has he always wanted that?"

"You'd have to ask him."

"Of course." She nods. "I'm sorry. I should go—"

"Is that why you left? Because you didn't want that?"

"No. Ty... he suggested it once. I tried. I wanted to be adventurous. Open. I told myself I was, but I wasn't. My... I didn't take it well."

There's something there, some history, but it's obvious she doesn't want to tell me.

"He acted as if it was a whim," she says. "I knew there was something missing. But... he convinced me it wasn't that."

"And you think it was?"

"I don't know. He was different after. Hiding some part of himself. For a long time, I looked. Eventually, I realized I wouldn't find it. I wouldn't have all of him."

"And you thought, maybe, he got what he wanted somewhere else. And that's why he shut you out."

"Yes, but you're right. He wouldn't. It's not in his nature. It just... what is it they say? Sometimes the simplest explanation is the right one."

And that is the simplest.

He didn't get what he wanted, so he found it somewhere else, then he locked her out.

If it was anyone else, I'd believe that story. I'd be sure he was lying about his fidelity.

But it's not someone else.

It's Ty.

He's loyal to a fault.

He'd stay no matter what.

"I'm sorry for intruding, really." She holds out her hand. "I am here to offer my congratulations."

"You flew across the Atlantic to offer your congratulations?"

"I've always wanted to see New York."

"It's the greatest city in the world."

She looks to the Empire State Building. "I can see the appeal. And I... I really do want you to be happy. Both of you. Are you?"

"We are."

She sighs with her entire body. "He loves you. I want that for him. Really, Indigo. I hope the two of you are together forever."

I shake her hand.

"Be good to him." She releases my hand. Turns to the main room.

To Ty, standing at the bar, watching us talk.

He waits. Says goodbye to her as she passes.

Crosses the room to me.

"Are you okay?" He wraps his arms around me. Pulls me into a tight embrace. Holds me like he'll never let go.

He won't.

This promise we're about to make—

He means it.

Forever.

And I want that so badly. To be his forever.

But I've been lying to myself.

I need all of it.

Not just his body. Not just his loyalty.

His love.

"I have to ask you something," I say.

He presses his lips to my neck. "Can it wait?"

"No."

He turns me around. Brings his hand to my cheek. "What's wrong, baby?"

"Nothing. I just have to say this."

"You're scaring me."

"Let me ask."

He nods.

So I do it. Ask for the thing I'm not allowed to want. For the thing I agreed to live without. "Are you in love with me?"

Chapter Forty-Nine

TY

Are you in love with me?

My thoughts jumble.

My throat dries.

My tongue sticks to the roof of my mouth.

It's a ridiculous question. Unfair. Out of line. "We agreed—"

"I know what we agreed." Her eyes stay glued to mine. "I know what you promised. You don't have to remind me of our arrangement."

"Indigo…" Words well in my throat. *Please, ask for something else. Anything. I'll promise you the fucking moon. Whatever you want. As long as it's not that.* "What did she say?"

"It wasn't anything Rory said." She swallows hard. "Not the way you mean."

"Then what?"

"She just reminded me of something."

"What?"

"Your loyalty."

My loyalty? "My loyalty is a problem?"

"No." Her voice softens. "Yes. It's… please, Ty." Her

fingers brush mine. "Answer the question. Are you in love with me?"

"I don't know."

"You don't know?"

"I don't. I'm sorry. I told you——"

"I know what you told me," she says.

I try to find some words of comfort. Something I can promise her. Some way I can convince her to stay.

"Do you love her?"

"I'll always love her."

"Are you in love with her?"

"No."

"But you still want to be a nice man who likes nice girls?"

A part of me does. A part of me will always fight the darkness in my desires.

"I... I'm sorry, Ty." She blinks and a tear catches on her lashes. "I'm sorry. I can't do this unless you love me."

Her eyes go to her left hand.

Her ring finger.

She runs her index finger over her engagement ring. "I..."

No. Not that. Anything but that.

"I'm sorry." She slides the ring off her finger. Presses it into my palm. "I know we have a deal. I know you can ruin me. But I can't do this. I love you. I'm in love with you. And I can't do this unless you love me too."

"Indigo——"

"I'm sorry, Ty. I love you." She wipes a tear from her eye. Grabs my suit jacket. Pulls me into a fast, hard kiss. "I'm sorry."

Then she releases me.

And she leaves.

And the light drains from my life at once.

Chapter Fifty

INDIGO

C am is standing in front of the elevator like he's guarding it. "Are you all right?"

I'm not having this conversation right now. "I just need some air."

"How about I walk you outside?" He taps the *call* button. "Okay."

The elevator dings. The shiny silver doors part. Cam motions *after you*.

I move into the tiny space.

He moves with me.

I don't want him here. He seems like a good guy, but I don't want him here.

I don't want anyone here.

I want to be home, alone, by myself.

Far away from the pain on Ty's face. Like he wishes he could love me, but he just can't.

Is this how he felt when Rory left? No wonder he fucked half the women in the city.

It's awful.

Finally, the doors close.

Cam leans against the railing. "I'll make sure Sienna gets home okay."

"Don't fuck her. Please."

He lets out a soft laugh. "Not tonight."

I guess that's all the promise I need.

If this is really it, if I'm really walking away, she isn't going to see him again.

He isn't a risk.

He isn't going to break her heart.

If I'm really walking away.

Am I really walking away?

I trace my bare ring finger. Suck a breath through my teeth. Will the elevator to move faster.

It doesn't.

And Cam stands there all tall and broad and imposing, in the way all Hunt men are.

The same posture as Ty.

Younger features, broader shoulders, rounder eyes.

Boyish in places Ty is grown up. But then he is three years Ty's junior. Or was it four? Or two?

It doesn't matter.

If I'm walking away, it doesn't matter.

A sob wells in my throat. I swallow it. Close my eyes. Will my tears to wait.

"Indigo." Cam's voice is soft. "I'm sorry."

I shake my head. Wipe my eyes with the back of my hand. "I'm fine."

"You don't have to convince me."

Okay.

"I won't tell Ty anything."

"You're very secretive."

"I am?"

"You Hunts. You hold on to secrets like it's your job."

"It is our job," he says.

A laugh breaks up my sob. "You work for their company?"

He nods.

"Of course."

"Then you know I mean it."

That's fair. "I, uh…" Finally, the elevator arrives at the ground floor. The doors slide open. Shiny gold fixtures fill my view.

"I never liked her. Rory," he says.

"Me either."

He laughs. "No. I imagine you wouldn't." He offers his hand.

I shake my head.

"Humor me."

Okay. I take his arm. Instantly, I feel steadier.

It's these shoes. They're too tall.

Only three inches, but that's more heel than I can handle.

I wanted to be eye to eye with Ty, but I guess that doesn't matter now.

Even though I'm taller than Cam in my shoes, I feel dwarfed by his presence.

Like Ty's.

Like he knows he can command the room.

He walks me through the lobby. Opens the door. Helps me through.

Warm air greets me. I've only been in the air-conditioning for a minute, two maybe, but it's still a sharp contrast.

Cam pulls out his cell. Taps the screen a few times. "When I saw them together, I didn't get it. I didn't get it until I saw him with you."

"What?" What the fuck does that mean?

"Ty's been alone for a long time. His father on active duty. Then Ian. When he meet Rory, saw her family, her old money stability—he saw a place he could fit in. He wanted to believe he fit into that world so badly he convinced himself he did. He thought that was love. But it wasn't."

"Aren't you supposed to be some player who doesn't care about feelings?"

"Should I offer to fuck you to distract you from your pain?"

"Maybe."

"You wouldn't say yes."

"You could still offer," I say.

He chuckles. "You only have eyes for him."

"I…"

"I read the room better than that."

"You could offer anyway. To make me feel better."

"Do you want to fuck me?"

"No."

"That hurts."

"Sorry." My thumb rubs my bare ring finger. "I… you're right. I only want him."

"He only wants you." His gaze follows. "He will figure it out. If you give him time."

I don't have the same optimism. Ty isn't going to figure it out.

But I can't bring myself to say it aloud.

————

He lets me ride home alone.

I crawl into bed. Put on *Back to Black*. Cry into my cotton sheets.

Around play two, Sienna climbs in with me. "Sorry I took so long. Had to have my way with Cam."

A laugh breaks my sob. "Not funny."

"A little funny."

"Very little," I say.

"But a little?"

I nod into the sheets.

Chapter Fifty-One

TY

Sleep fails me.

Eventually, I give up. Move to the couch. Try to find distraction in a classic movie marathon.

But it only makes me think of her.

Lying here, completely spent, curled into my body.

Laughing at a screwball comedy.

Crying at the end of *Casablanca*.

Bent over the couch, begging me to fuck her.

Then at the party.

Pushing the ring into my palm.

Whispering an apology.

Those same awful words, with one important change.

I'm sorry, Ty.

I can't do this.

I love you.

I'm in love with you.

It hurts worse. Knowing I'm the one failing her.

Knowing I'm the one who can't give her what she needs.

Sometime after dawn, I shower, dress, fix coffee and breakfast.

Play her favorite album.

The ode to misery and self-destruction is perfect. Or it should be.

But it fills my head with memories of Indigo.

Her eyes closed as she loses herself in a song.

Her silky voice falling off her lips.

Her body swaying with the music.

I already miss her so fucking badly.

I can't do this without her.

I can't do anything without her.

———

I LISTEN TO INDIE'S MUSIC ALL DAY.

A few times an hour, I pick up my phone. Consider calling. Begging her to come here. To be mine. To love me.

To stay, even if I'm not sure I love her.

I consider playing the best card I have—

Sending a dirty picture. Ordering her to bend over. Promising to make her come.

But I can't.

I know how it feels, wanting someone to love you. Wanting it more than anything.

I can't ask her to live with it.

I can't call her unless I love her.

Unless I know what the fuck it means to love her.

Chapter Fifty-Two

TY

"**Y**ou look like shit." Ian tosses running shorts onto the bed. "Come on. Get off your arse. I'm not watching this."

"When did I give you a key?"

He chuckles. "You think I need a key?"

"What happened to your reformation?"

"With my girlfriend, not you."

"Fuck off." I roll onto my other side. The one that isn't facing the window. The one facing the side of the bed where she slept.

It's cold without her.

The entire world is cold without her.

"Last time you went to London." He sits at the edge of the bed. "You asked me to water your plants."

"I have plants?"

He chuckles. "On the balcony."

"And you watered them?"

"I did."

"You concocted this story in the last ten seconds."

He shakes his head. "I'll show you the plants."

"No."

"Then get off your arse. We're going on a run."

"I can lap you."

"Talk is cheap." He stands. Taps his running shoes together.

"Where's your girlfriend?"

"Off. Your. Arse." He moves into the hallway. Leaves the door wide open.

Does my brother really expect me to go for a run? Now? Ridiculous.

But he is right. I'm not doing well here.

I rise. Piss. Wash up. Dress.

Ian's in the kitchen. With his offering of mercy.

A touristy thermos with the Empire State Building in dark blue. Filled with too milky, too sweet English Breakfast.

"Is it that bad?" I ask.

He nods. Sips a mug of fresh tea. The leaves Indigo prefers.

The scent is familiar. It makes me think of her.

Everything makes me think of her.

"Ten minutes." He motions to the thermos. "Then we run."

"Do we really have to run?"

"You run every day."

"And?"

He chuckles. "And? You have more discipline than this."

"Did I berate you for drinking yourself stupid after your divorce?"

"Yes."

Arsehole.

"You used your drunken misery quota last year."

It's not that. Last year, after Rory left, I drank myself stupid with Ian. He and Eve had just started seeing each other. He still believed it would end the way all his arrangements did.

He couldn't admit it to himself.

He couldn't admit he was in love with her.

Then he did. And he's spent the last year building in love, trust, devotion.

That's why he's calling me on this now, but I'm not in the mood to argue.

"Run," he says it again. "Or I'm calling Mum."

"No."

He motions to the door *then go*.

"I'll drink the fucking tea first."

He smiles. "It's not a punishment."

"Let's agree to disagree."

Ian shakes his head. It's a look I don't see often. *My brother, so ridiculous.*

I've never been ridiculous.

I've been disciplined. Driven. Practical.

I got things done. Took care of our mother. Took care of myself.

Built this fucking business with him.

Held on to every secret I had.

I pick up the thermos, even though the cheesy tourist logo makes me think of Indigo. She loves the city. Especially the iconic Empire State Building.

"Is it so bad?" Ian asks.

The tea itself is fine. Strong and warm, with enough cream and honey it's more dessert than drink. But the feeling of comfort, of knowing I need comforting—

It's strange.

"Terrible," I say.

He chuckles. "Make coffee then. But you've only got another eight minutes."

"Are you timing me?"

"Maybe."

"Arsehole."

He shrugs *so what if I am*.

I drink with greedy sips. As much as I hate to admit it, I need the comfort.

We sit there in silence for a few minutes.

Then he speaks. "Cam tells me she stormed out."

"You didn't see?"

"No." His voice is soft. "You two have that in common. Quick exits."

"What else did Cam tell you?"

"That you're an idiot who can't see what's in front of his face."

Maybe.

"And that he's going to fuck her sister."

"Is he?"

"Who can tell with Cam?" He chuckles. "Would it really be so bad? You'd have an excuse to see her."

"I can't see her."

"Why not?"

"She's in love with me?"

"It's been a while for me, I admit, but isn't that the idea? You meet someone, fall in love, get married?"

Yes. Of course. "She won't do this unless I'm in love with her."

His eyes fill with surprise. "You're not?"

"No."

"Are you sure?"

"No."

His face screws with confusion. "Why did she agree to marry you?"

"I'm a great fuck."

"I'm sure you are, Ty, but we both know women aren't ruled by the head between their legs."

"Maybe they are," I say. "Maybe they have us fooled."

He considers it. "Maybe."

"That is what you say about Eve."

"I'm teasing. I know it's not true. Do you?"

"Do I what?"

"Do you know why she really agreed to marry you?"

I could lie. Maybe I should. But I don't. "I paid her to."

He fails to hide his surprise.

"My reputation… I was tired of people calling me a whore."

"Tired of me and Mum worrying?"

"Yes."

"But that is her," he says. "She is the girl from the museum?"

I nod.

"The one who fucked with your head."

"She is."

He shakes his head. "You're a fucking idiot, Ty."

Probably.

"You're in love with her. Everyone else sees it. Everyone but you."

"I don't think she's interested in anyone else's opinion."

"You really paid her?"

I nod.

"And you didn't tell me?"

"Why do you think I paid her, Ian?"

"Fuck." He slips out of his chair. Paces to the fridge. And back. "I forget sometimes. I forget how young you were when I left."

"You didn't leave. You enlisted."

"I still left." He looks to me. "I could have stayed closer. Found a job selling shoes."

"You couldn't sell a shoe to save your life."

His laugh is soft. "Maybe. But I know what it was like for

me. Growing up with Dad away all the time. Feeling like I had to keep everything together. I did the same thing. I understood why he enlisted, why he stayed enlisted, but I still hated him for it."

"I don't hate you."

"I still felt like he abandoned me. Abandoned our family."

He did. It might not be a fair accusation. He had to do something to make a living. He had to do something to take care of us.

But did he have to do that?

Did Ian?

"I'm sorry, Ty," he says. "It wasn't fair to you. It felt like something I had to do. Maybe it was. But it wasn't fair to you."

My shoulders soften. My chest eases. Some tension I've been holding for the last two decades fades.

"I should have stayed," he says. "I should have been there. Been your older brother."

"I missed you."

"I know."

"I needed you."

"I know." He looks me in the eyes. "I failed you and I'm sorry. I won't do it again. I promise."

"You moved here." I feel twelve again. A child begging my brother to stay. "I thought you'd stick around, and you flew across an ocean."

"I tried to visit."

"Once a quarter."

His voice stays soft. "I'm sorry. I should have talked to you. I should have sat down and explained. I will now." He sits at the counter. "I'm staying here."

"Because of Eve?"

"Yes. And because I want to be somewhere that feels like home and New York does."

"London is a better city."

"Of course. But try convincing these New Yorkers." He waves his hand *they're ridiculous*.

"Indie is the same. She loves everything about the city."

"She hasn't seen London. She has an excuse."

"But not Eve?"

He nods *it's terrible*. "No one is perfect."

"Is there a single other thing you don't like about her?"

"No." He laughs. "And even that… I love how much she loves it."

"You're disgusting."

"I know." He smiles. "After my divorce, I didn't think I'd ever be happy again. But I am. I'm stupid in love with her. Maybe you're not there yet, Ty. Maybe you're not ready to let your guard down. But you can get there. You have the discipline."

"I have the discipline to fall in love?"

He nods.

"You really are ridiculous."

"Do you ever look at yourself?"

"I know I'm ridiculous."

"No. Do you ever look in the mirror when you're talking about her? Your eyes light up. You smile like you're about to meet the Queen. You're different. Happy."

"I'm happy?"

"She makes you happy. If that's not love, then what the fuck is?"

———

I LET IAN DRAG ME ON A RUN.

I even join him for a brunch with Eve.

She spends the entire time explaining how I can fix things. How I will fix things.

I have two women threatening my life if I don't unfuck this.

And I have absolute faith in both of them. They're equally capable of ruining me.

I leave. Spend the afternoon with my brother's words.

He's right.

She makes me happy.

Is that love?

I don't know.

But I'm ready to try to figure it out.

Chapter Fifty-Three

INDIGO

I'm lying in bed, half-asleep, *Back to Black* on repeat, when a knock on the door rouses me.

Then a familiar voice.

Ty.

He's far away. I can't make out what he's saying, but I recognize his voice.

I drag myself out of bed. Press my ear to the door.

"Is this a booty call?" Sienna asks.

"Doesn't a booty call require a call?"

"Okay. Breakup sex. And don't say you didn't break up. She's been crying for the last thirty-six hours," Sienna says.

"Do you want it to be breakup sex?"

"Hmm… I'd accept it."

"You'd accept it?"

"Yeah." She tries a tough voice. "Do you have a better offer?"

"What would be a better offer?"

"Makeup sex? Or a hot friend with a thing for American soccer players?"

"For Indie?"

"No. For me. Keep up, Ty."

He laughs. "Which is the better offer?"

"Both, obviously."

"You want me to promise makeup sex with your sister and a hot friend for you."

"Is that unreasonable?"

"Aren't you claiming you want to fuck my cousin?"

"I thought I was overselling that," she says.

"You are."

"Then don't argue. Cam can be the hot friend. Or another hot friend. I'm negotiable."

"That is how I'd describe you."

"Thank you," she says. "And you can keep this between me and you. Indie... she's not so much on you introducing me to your friends."

"You're only eighteen."

"You're thirty, Ty. Indie is twenty-two. And you met three years ago."

She has him there.

She has *me* there.

But he just laughs. "I'm not introducing you to any friends from university."

"Hypocrisy!"

"Even so."

"In that case, I'm pretty sure Indie is asleep. And not interested in talking to you." She raises her voice. "Even if you look really good in jeans. I didn't even know you owned jeans." She lowers her voice again. "Is it true you don't wear anything under them?"

"What makes you think that?"

"Well, I asked Indie if you wear boxers or briefs. You know, just to break up the questions about the size of your dick."

"Of course."

"She blushed and said it was none of my business. But the way she said it... it was like the answer was neither."

"What about boxer-briefs?"

"You could tell me. It might help her case."

"Telling you what I wear under my trousers will help me win over your sister?"

She stifles a gasp. "You're here to win her over?"

He doesn't say anything.

"That puts the ball in my court. I have what you want. Now you have to bring hot friends."

He chuckles. "We're back to that already?"

"I think your non-answer speaks for itself," she stage whispers. "Besides, Indie... she tried to play it cool. You know how she is. But I see the way she rubs her wrists. And you know... I might have read her text messages a few times."

"That's an invasion of privacy."

"An innocent mistake," she says. "I thought it was my phone. We have the same model."

"Do you expect me to believe that?"

She laughs. "Yeah. And, uh, well... good for you."

"Good for me?" he asks.

"Swinging for the fences and everything."

Oh god. I pull the door open.

They both look at me.

"Sorry. She's uh... stop reading my text messages." I shoot my sister a *don't*. "You have a different phone case. You know better."

She offers an apologetic shrug. "The case was off. But I'll try..." She looks me in the eyes. "Do you want him here?"

"It's okay," I say.

"Do you want me here?" she asks. "Or do you want to make room for that booty call?"

My eyes flit to Ty's. There's hope in his gorgeous brown eyes. Apology.

Or maybe I'm imagining things.

"Hmm… I don't know," Sienna says. "I'm not hearing a promise sex will be involved. Or a threat it won't be involved if I stay."

"It's okay," I say. "You can go."

"Did I offer to go?" She makes a show of scratching her head. "I don't remember offering to go."

"Scram," I say. "Or no details later."

"So details later?" She fist pumps. "Okay, bye, Ty. Remember what I said."

"Always," he says.

She shoots me one last *are you okay* look. When I nod, she steps into her shoes, grabs her bag, leaves.

The door shuts behind her.

And we're alone.

The two of us. In my space. In my life.

It's not the first time, but it feels different. Charged.

"I brought you something." He takes a step toward me. Pulls the ring box from his jeans. Sets it on the table.

"Is that what I think it is?" I ask.

"Yes. I want you to have it, whatever you decide."

"Whatever I decide?"

He nods.

I wrap my hands around my chest. It's hot in here, but I still need the warmth. The comfort. "Sienna was right. You look good in jeans."

"You've seen them before."

"I can still appreciate them now." I swallow hard. "And I believe the proper response is thank you."

"What about, *how about I take them off and fuck you?*"

My body whines. Yes. Hell yes. Every yes.

It doesn't matter that he broke my heart, that he'll never

love me, that it's entirely possible he spent the night fucking Rory.

It only cares about the feeling of his skin against mine.

"If I said yes?" I ask.

"If it was that or nothing." He nods. "But I'm not here to fuck you."

I swallow hard.

"I'm here to talk." He takes another step toward me. "To tell you something." His eyes meet mine. "I love you."

Fuck. It steals my breath.

"There are so many ways to explain it, but only one makes sense to me. You make me happy."

"I make you happy?"

"If that's not love, what is?"

He's right.

Sometimes it feels complicated, but it's simple. I trust him; I need him; I crave him.

And he makes me happy.

That's love.

"I'm sorry I took so long to see it. I was scared. Scared of opening myself up to loss." He takes my hand. Runs his thumb along the space between my thumb and index finger. "I'm not brave the way you are."

"You have to be scared to be brave. Otherwise, you're just reckless."

"But I'm not. I didn't face my fear. I let it consume me." His voice stays soft. "I told myself that was the only way to stay safe. If I didn't love anyone, no one could leave me. I convinced myself I was incapable. Maybe I was. But that changed. I just didn't realize it."

"When did it change?"

"I don't know. I'm still not sure what it means to love someone. I'm not good at it anymore. Maybe I've never been very good at it."

I shake my head. "You are."

"That's why you've been crying?"

I nod.

"Indie… I'm sorry. I'm sorry I didn't see it. I'm sorry I hurt you. I'd do anything to not hurt you again." He cups my cheek with his palm. "But I will. I'm not good at this. I need you to be patient with me."

I nod into his hand.

"I… I still want to marry you."

"I know."

"But we can wait. If that's what you want, we can wait forever." He runs his thumb over my temple. "I love you. And I want to be what you need. Everything you need."

"I love you too." I kiss him before he can reply.

The kiss he returns is soft and slow.

Love in physical form.

Then it's harder.

Rougher.

Everything else I want. The Ty only I get.

I don't have to ask.

He lifts me into his arms. Carries me to the bed.

Fucks me until I'm groaning his name.

Chapter Fifty-Four

INDIGO

I t's past sunset. It's almost time.

Where's the venue assistant?

Where's Sienna?

I stand. Suck a breath through my teeth. Sink into my heels.

Three inches. So I'm eye to eye with Ty.

Three inches too many today. I need steady. I need my feet on the ground.

The door swings open. Sienna darts through. Runs, really. She's in sensible silver flats and a short purple dress.

A tomboy forced to dress up, compromising with a comfortable fit and flare number. Beautiful in a Sienna way.

She could be my maid of honor. That's what a normal person would do, make her sister her maid of honor.

Instead, I asked her to walk me down the aisle. It felt right. It still does.

"Your shoes?" Sienna asks.

"Huh?"

"You're teetering."

Of course I'm teetering. I'm getting married tonight.

Ty offered to wait until spring. Next summer. After my college graduation.

Not that I'm enrolled yet. I'm applying to universities in the city, but I'm not sure if I want to go back to school.

I know I need music in my life, but I'm not sure school is the way to accomplish that. I'm not sure what I want to accomplish.

After a summer of practice, I'm able to play a set without crying. Sometimes, I even play when Ty or Sienna can overhear.

I'm writing songs again.

But I'm not ready to play for strangers. Not yet.

In another few months, but not yet.

"Are you drunk?" Sienna motions to the champagne flute sitting on the vanity. "You wouldn't be the first bride."

"No. Nervous."

"Why? You look hot."

"Thanks." Between my perfectly straight hair, my expertly applied makeup (dramatic in an *I love you forever* way), and my flowing chiffon gown, I feel hot.

This dress is sexy. Not so sexy I'm embarrassed Ty's mom is here, but close.

She's been here all week. Ty fusses over her the way he fusses over me, even though she can't stand it. She keeps insisting she can take care of herself.

I'm in my fifties, not my eighties, Tyler.

She always calls him Tyler.

He turns into the guy he was at fifteen.

The sweet, shy boy who wants only to take care of his family.

There's so much love in his heart. It's hard to believe he ever felt otherwise.

"Then why are you nervous?" Sienna glances in the mirror. Smooths her hair. It's in a simple braided updo, something she *could* wear on a run, but it's still too fussy for her.

"You look pretty."

"Obviously." She twirls until her skirt spins. "I need to look good for Cam."

"Not now."

"You're nervous. Now is a good time to distract you."

That's a good point, actually.

"Why are you nervous?" She moves closer. "The sex is still good, right?"

"Yeah." My skin flushes at the memory of last night. We slept in separate rooms, so I could sneak out this morning without seeing him, but before that—

Fuck, I can feel his hand around my throat, hear his voice in my ears, taste his lips.

"If you're going to fantasize, do it out loud." Sienna's voice is teasing. "It's that good, and he's rich, and he's hot... why are you nervous?"

"Why am I nervous I'm about to commit to someone for the rest of my life?"

"The sex is good. What else do you need to know?"

A laugh spills from my lips. "You appreciate what matters."

"And he loves you." She smiles. "It's kind of disgusting how much you love each other, actually."

It is.

I try to find something to tease her back, but the door interrupts me. The organizer, a woman in a powder blue pantsuit, motions *come here*.

"You're on." She smiles. "Are you ready, Miss Simms?"

Miss. This is the last time I'm a Miss.

"Am I crazy?" I whisper to Sienna.

"Do I need to go through the logic again?"

"Tell me I'm not."

"Everyone in love is a little crazy." She offers her arm. "But no. You're doing the smart thing, nailing down a rich guy. It's practical."

Practical. That's not a way I'd describe my relationship with Ty, but she's right.

He loves taking care of me.

I love the way he takes care of me.

The sex is fantastic.

And he… he's honest with me. He's himself with me. I can be myself with him. Admit my darkest secrets and my dirtiest desires and know he won't judge me.

Hell, most times, he finds a way to fill those needs.

He won't invite someone to watch. But he will make me come on the balcony of a five-star restaurant. He will demand I watch as I come on his cock.

And he'll take pictures.

Of me. Us.

My cheeks flame.

Sienna laughs. "How many hours until you're alone?"

It's an hour past sunset. I wanted to get married with the glow of the city. Our reception is shorter than most, but we won't be alone until after midnight.

It's too long.

I want it now.

I want everything now.

"Miss Simms?" The organizer asks again. "Do you need a minute?"

"No. I'm ready." I take Sienna's arm and hold her tightly as we follow the organizer.

We move around the corner.

To the long blue carpet.

And he's there, under the altar.

Ty, in a black suit and a purple tie, his smile wide, his eyes on me.

"He's so hot," Sienna whispers. "You're really making the right move."

My laugh floats. Everything floats.

She walks me down the aisle. Then she hugs me. Whispers in my ear. "I love you."

"I love you too."

She kisses me on the cheek, releases me, sits next to Ty's mom.

Then I take Ty's hands and the rest of the world disappears.

Sienna is right. He's painfully handsome.

And the joy on his face—

It is the best thing I've ever seen.

My nerves disappear, but I keep floating.

As the officiant reads a poem and takes us through our vows and pulls out the rings.

I say I do.

He slides the ring onto my finger.

Then it's my ring on his left hand. And his hands on my waist.

He kisses me with everything he has.

And then I'm flying, even though my feet are on the ground.

That's what he does. He helps me fly without the risk of falling.

Epilogue

INDIGO

The warm water pounds my sore shoulders. I tilt my head, let the water work the tension from my neck. The left side. Then the right.

I turn. Adjust the position of the shower head. Usually, I use it for more untoward purposes. Not back massage.

I guess it's not that different.

Sure, I'm using the removable showerhead to work the tension from my muscles. But I'm doing it because I need to be ready for my husband.

I close my eyes. Inhale the warm, wet air, the *tap tap tap* of the shower, the soft music playing in the bedroom.

Our bedroom.

Enough to cover the sound of his footsteps.

He's supposed to surprise me. That's the plan for today.

If it was up to me, he'd have the entire day. The elevator in the building. The desk in his office. The bathroom at lunch.

But I'm not as agile as I used to be.

My hand goes to my stomach. I'm in my third trimester

now. Past the horrible morning sickness. Well into back aches, tired feet, incredible horniness.

I didn't believe my friends. I understood the hormones. I believed mine would surge. But I didn't think it was possible to want Ty more.

To think about his hands, lips, cock more.

But I do.

I'm not sure how I do anything else.

I close my eyes. Let my thoughts flit to last weekend. His hand between my legs. His voice in my ears. His tie around my wrists.

The bright pink one he bought to annoy Ian.

The one he was wearing the night we conceived Amy.

Well. He was wearing it. Then I was wearing it. Exactly the way I was last weekend.

Thankfully, kids don't ask when or how they were conceived.

Ian asks.

Cam asks.

Sienna—

All right, maybe I told her one night, when I was really, really desperate for a sip of her tea.

I'm not totally off caffeine, but the whole *one cup of tea a day* thing is wearing on me. I can't wait until I can inhale a pot of Yunnan Hong Cha.

Spend a night sipping Manhattans on the patio.

Meet my daughter.

Amy is a troublemaker. I can already tell.

It's been a hard pregnancy. Hard enough Ty is incredibly careful with me. Hard enough he's talking about getting a vasectomy.

He can't risk losing me. Amy can't risk losing her mother.

That's a new card he plays.

It works every time.

Of course, I have it too. And it works better on him.

He has two people to protect. I only have the one.

But, god, I can't believe how much I need to protect her. How much I already love her.

I didn't grow up playing with dolls or dreaming of motherhood. I didn't hate kids, but I didn't have a special fondness for them either.

Then Dad died and Mom fell apart, and I stepped up to take care of Sienna. I relished the role—I'd do anything for my sister—but I felt the weight of it too.

It stole my freedom. Stole my chance to be a carefree teenager.

I knew Ty wanted to be a father. I knew he'd be a great father. But I wasn't sure I was ready to step into that role again.

Our first year of marriage, we didn't talk about kids very often. Every so often, I'd see a cute kid in a Prince t-shirt, and I'd broach the topic, ask if he still wanted to be a father.

He always said maybe, one day, after I felt secure in my career, after I finished school, after I knew what I wanted.

When I was accepted to Julliard, we sat down and really talked about it. I knew I wanted four years to consume music without distractions. I knew I needed that time for myself. The time I hadn't had when I was younger.

He wanted that for me too.

He wanted to give me the life I never had. At first, I thought it was about stability. Safety. Comfort.

Living in this gorgeous apartment without worrying about money. Eating at the city's best restaurants.

Spending time with Sienna without the mortgage hanging over my head.

Traveling the world.

Fucking on the dining table, couch, piano, balcony.

He was right. I needed that time. Those years that were mine and mine alone.

My voice came back to me the summer we married, but it took two years of dedicated practice to really feel comfortable.

Then another two to record an album, find my style, figure out where I wanted to fit into the world of music.

Some people say college is the best time in their life. I understand why. I didn't have the transition to adulthood eighteen-year-old students do.

But having nine months to hone my craft, followed by three months traveling the world with my husband, four years in a row—

It was exactly the freedom I needed. The chance to take up space, figure out exactly what I wanted, breathe.

I needed that time to feel like I had a choice. To miss taking care of Sienna. To miss loving someone that way.

Even so, I took a year. I spent a year hustling, promoting my music, recording as a session musician, hanging out with my sister, my friends, my husband.

Then I asked Ty again.

I asked if he was ready to be a father.

He was, but he wasn't ready for me to put someone else first.

I tried to explain it to him. After four years of school, seeing what life was like for full-time musicians, I had a new dream.

I didn't want my life to revolve around the hustle.

I didn't want to live and die by other people's tastes.

I wanted to make music, my music, but I didn't want the demands that came with pursuing A-list status. Or even B-list status.

There were too many strings.

I wanted to be independent. To make music on my terms. To live my life on my terms.

So we negotiated.

Another year.

If I felt the same way after two years pursuing my career, he'd agree.

I insisted we stay here, in Manhattan.

No big house on Long Island.

No gated neighborhood in Jersey.

No career connections in Los Angeles.

He agreed instantly. He wanted to stay in Manhattan too. I should have held out for more. Demanded something else.

But then I didn't mind waiting.

I wanted this. Badly. But I was scared too.

I am scared.

This changes everything. And I don't want to be one of those women who puts herself last.

Most of the women I know are younger. Still pursuing their careers. Not beginning to think about marriage or children.

Some are older. Some have families. A lot of them sacrificed their marriage or their career or their well-being for their kids. They thought they were doing the right thing. Maybe they were.

But I don't want that for my family. I don't want my daughter to grow up thinking women need to be martyrs.

I want her to see how hard I fight for myself. My needs. My desires.

Not the ones Ty is about to fill... well, not yet.

Maybe, one day, when she's older, and I forget to turn down the volume on *You Oughta Know* and she asks what it means to fuck someone...

I'm not going to tell her what her father and I do. But I'm

going to sit her down, explain sex, make sure she's not ashamed of her desires.

No matter how strange they seem.

I want to be a role model for her.

But it's hard. It's scary. I understand how my mother felt now. Why grief drowned her. If something happened to Ty—

I don't know if I could do it. Stay present with Amy.

I hate to think about it.

I love him so much.

We've both lost parents. We both know how terrifying it is. We're both scared.

But that's part of being a parent. The world is as terrifying as it is beautiful.

I try to focus on the latter. So I can show Amy how to live without fear.

It's hard, but I try.

I want her to see that. To see the world as a big, beautiful place she can conquer.

I close my eyes. Run my fingers through my hair. It's short now. A pixie cut.

It needs trimming every six weeks, just like my old hairstyle, but it's wash and go. It was that or a Mom bob, and I'm not going there.

Not yet, at least.

I shampoo. Condition. Rinse.

Towel dry. Don my purple robe. Step into the bedroom.

The lights are off. The door is locked.

And my husband is standing in front of the bed, in his suit, his eyes filled with demand.

He doesn't wait. He moves toward me. Backs me into the wall.

He doesn't slam me the way he usually does. I'll have to

wait another few months for that. Physical roughness is off the table. As are most of our favorite positions.

But Ty is creative. He works around restrictions to keep me satisfied.

He motions to the mirror across from the bed. "Watch."

"Watch?"

He nods as he pushes the robe off my shoulders and slips his hand between my legs. "Watch yourself come."

Fuck, I'm already wound so close. The friction of his index finger is enough to wind me tight.

Then he brings his hand to my throat. He places it there. No pressure. Barely the hint of a threat.

But the sight of his hand on my neck is enough.

I watch him work me.

He winds me tightly, quickly.

A few strokes of his fingers and I'm there. I groan as I come on his hand.

Pleasure overtakes my senses. Makes my legs weak and my breath heavy.

But he keeps me steady as he works me through my orgasm.

Fuck.

I soak in the perfection of the moment.

His hard, safe body. His earthy shampoo. His steady breath mingling with the slow jams.

I love him so much.

Need this so much.

My eyes blink open. Meet his.

He stares back with intense demand. He knows he has me where he wants me. He'll do whatever he wants with me.

"Sit on the bed," he orders.

I do.

He moves next to me. Pulls my hands behind my back.

Then he unhooks his tie. Wraps it around my wrists. Lays me down, on my side, so I'm facing the mirror.

"Don't move." He slips off the bed.

"Or."

"Or I won't fuck you."

Fuck. "Please."

"Don't move," he says it again. "Understand?"

I nod into the pillow.

"Good girl."

It winds me tight. That's all it takes. A little dirty talk and I'm ready to come.

Ty stays still for a minute. Two even. He makes me wait.

Then he strips slowly.

I watch as he does away with his shirt, belt, slacks.

Fuck, my husband is handsome. Tall and broad, his sculpted shoulders covered in tattoos.

His defined torso covered in tattoos.

Those are mine. Ironically enough, Ty is modest. He isn't the kind of guy who runs without a shirt. Even when it's a hundred and humid.

He saves this for me.

The lush rose in deep purple.

The lyrics to his favorite song.

The Latin quote.

et nos cedamus amori

Let us yield to love.

Fuck, it's so romantic.

And so fucking hot.

He moves onto the bed. Lies behind me.

He tugs at the restraints on my wrist. "You're patient today."

I nod into the pillow.

He slips two fingers inside me. "Obedient."

Fuck, that feels good. "Yes, sir."

"Because you want me to fuck you?"

"Yes, sir."

"Good girl." He drives his fingers into me again and again.

He winds me tighter and tighter. Until I'm so, so close.

Then he pulls back. Brings his hands to my hips. Holds me in place as he enters me.

I can't move.

He's not rough or forceful. He's gentle. And he's working with my round belly, but he still has me at his mercy.

Fuck, I love being at his mercy.

Ty brings his hand to my throat as he drives into me. "Come for me, baby."

It pushes me over the edge. I groan his name as I come. My cunt pulses, pulling him closer, deeper.

He keeps his hand on my throat. Slips the other between my legs. Rubs me through another orgasm.

He comes with me this time.

My world goes white, that perfect, soft blinding light. Only bliss. Pure, unadulterated bliss.

He spills every drop. Then he releases me. Undoes the bindings. Cleans me up.

Lies with me.

Ty runs his fingers through my hair. "Too much?"

"Not enough."

He chuckles. "You're insatiable."

"Always."

He presses his lips to my neck as he brings his hand to my stomach.

"Two months now," I say.

He nods.

"Do you think it will change everything?"

"Of course."

"But you'll still fuck me like this after she's born."

"No." He kisses me again. "I'll fuck you the way you like."

"What do you mean?"

"You know what I mean, Indie."

"Say it anyway."

"Harder. Rougher. Hard enough I leave bruises."

Mmm. Yes. "You promise?"

"Always."

————

Want More?

Sign up for my mailing list for the exclusive extended epilogue to *Dirty Wedding* for another taste of Ty and Indigo.

Dirty Secret, Cam and Sienna's book, is coming soon. In the mean time, get to know Ian and Eve in *Dirty Desires*, a virginity sale romance with a twist.

College student Eve is broke and out of options. Tech mogul Ian offers her a lifeline: half a million dollars for every one of her firsts. Turn the page for a sample!

All caught up on the Hunt family? Go back to the beginning of the Dirty-verse with *Dirty Deal*, a fake marriage romance.

Or, if you've already ready every book in the Dirty-verse, check out *Tempting*, a best friend's brother romance with a hero every bit as brooding and bossy as Ty.

Dirty Desires

SPECIAL EXCERPT

Chapter One

EVE

Get *Dirty Desires* Now

"**I**s it really true?" A man with grey hair leans across the bar. Lowers his voice to a stage whisper. "Are you really a virgin?"

I press my lips together. No need to smile. As the owner put it, I'm not here for my charming personality. I'm here because the club is light on girls with a "punk bitch" aesthetic. "What was that? Appletini?" I pretend as if I can't hear the man. "Or was it chocolate martini?"

He looks me up and down. "You."

Is there a drink that sounds like *you?* Something bright pink. With a raunchy name. The kind of drink college girls order on spring break. I don't have a problem with grown men ordering a *blow job* but this guy—

No, that's only going to give him ideas.

Forget it. "Is the well vodka okay?"

He reaches for my hand. Wraps his greedy fingers around my wrist. "Eve, isn't it?"

"The apple martini—"

"Sure. Give me the best you've got."

I guess that answers that question. Is inappropriate question guy embarrassed by a bright green drink? No. He wants the best. The very best vodka. The very best apple liqueur. The very best... shit, what else is in this drink?

The owner didn't hire me for my expertise. He hired me because a) I begged, b) a friend from high school vouched for me, and c) I could start work on my eighteenth birthday.

I guess there's also d) a lack of girls with teal hair and tattoos. I am the only "punk bitch" who works at Devil's Point.

It's a dive and the customers are assholes, but the tips are good. Besides, there's something satisfying about mixing drinks, learning formulas, perfecting recipes.

After six months, I know cocktails pretty well. But this is the first Appletini.

I improvise. Vodka, apple liqueur, lemon.

I shake the drink with ice, strain it into a martini glass, slide it across the bar.

To his credit, Drunk McHandsy offers his credit card without provocation.

I file the card. There's no space for Drunk McHandsy, but it's Tuesday evening. Quiet. Except for the bachelor party by the stage, the club is empty. I need to make this guy feel important if I want to go home with enough tip money to cover rent. "What did you say you do?"

"A doctor. I know the female anatomy well." He winks. Takes a long sip of his apple martini. "Shit, this is good." He turns to the stage for a moment. Watches a lean blond dancer undo the buttons of her blouse one at a time.

Yes, this isn't *just* a dive bar. It's a strip club. That's the other reason why the owner hired me. He was sure I'd "get dollar signs in my eyes as soon as I saw what the dancers were pulling in."

I understand his point.

Between rent, tuition, and Addie's medical expenses, I need money.

On a good night, I go home with a few hundred dollars.

On a good night, the woman working the stage—she goes by Britney—goes home with a few thousand.

Only she has to touch all these strange men. She has to let them touch her.

I see the way men reach for dancers. They think twenty dollars buys them carte blanche.

"Is that why you don't dance?" Drunk McHandsy turns to me with wide eyes. "Because you've never been with a man?"

"I like making drinks." I strain the extra liquor into a martini glass.

"Are you saving yourself for a good man?"

"Why? Do you know one?"

His laugh echoes around the room. "So it is true?"

"That I need a good man?" Let's face it, I need a man like I need another bill to pay. Eighteen years full of disappointing men. My father, my bosses, even the senior year English teacher who refused to let me pick Margaret Atwood for my final project.

"That you're a virgin?"

There's no way I'm getting out of this question with a good tip. Either I lie and say no. Claim an interest in women (if only). Or I tell him the truth.

Well, some of it.

"I am." I finish the green drink. Let it warm my cheeks and throat. Let it sweeten the music and soften the air.

"Really?"

"Really."

"You just..." He glances at Britney as the song shifts to *Hit Me Baby, One More Time*. Dancers work a three-song set.

Clothed, topless, nude. This is number three. Of course, she interprets nude in her way. The panties come off. The schoolgirl skirt stays on.

The frat bros celebrating a friend's wedding go wild.

It's an apt choice. Britney. Apparently, her virginity was *the* gossip of the day. Everyone was obsessed with the pop star maintaining her innocence.

This male obsession with virginity... I don't get it. Yes, I'm a virgin. Yes, I like men. Yes, I've had boyfriends. Two. In high school.

Yes, we did all the normal things.

We kissed, held hands, watched movies. Boyfriend number two even got to second base. His hands were too cold. His touch was too blunt. But I still enjoyed it. I still wanted more.

There was something stopping me. Fear. Nerves. An inability to trust him with my body. I'm not sure. I lost my chance.

Dad left and life got way too complicated for boyfriends.

"You don't look like a virgin." He studies my teal hair. My thick eyeliner. My black mini-dress. "You look like... a sex kitten."

Gross.

"Like you know how to please a strong man."

Even more gross. I reach for the drink, but it's empty. For the best. I need to stay focused. So I make rent. "It's the makeup."

Addie says I look like a punk rock princess.

I prefer to think of my attire as a shield. The eyeliner says *I don't give a fuck what you think.* The dark lipstick says *leave me alone.* The combat boots say *I will kick you in the head if you fuck with me.*

That's probably why this guy is asking. He can't see my

combat boots. He doesn't know I'm at the end of my rope. He doesn't know I'm completely out of patience.

He leans back to finish his Appletini. Then he sets the glass on the bar. Motions for another.

It's hard to keep a poker face with him watching me, but I manage.

There. I tap the order into the machine. Pour. Slide the glass to him.

"Guys must ask all the time." He holds up the drink as if to toast. "If you're a virgin."

"Word gets around."

His eyes fix on my breasts. He watches my chest rise and fall with my exhale. He watches like he's picturing me in his bed. Like he's sure he has me where he wants me. "Do you want them to stop asking?"

Why? Does he have a button that will change the culture. Swap gender roles, so we obsess over male virginity and shrug at the thought of women who sleep around. *Girls will be girls*.

"I have a solution." He holds up his drink. "A proposition, actually."

"Shoot."

"You don't work here for your health."

What gave that away?

"You must need money. I have money. A lot of it. But I don't have you. What do you say, Eve? What do you say we make a trade? Something I want for something you want."

Get *Dirty Desires* Now

427

Author's Note

I'll be honest. I went into *Dirty Wedding* with low expectations. *Dirty Desires* was, by far, my favorite in the Dirty series. It hit so many of my buttons, on so many levels--virgin heroine, sexual lessons, intellectual eighteen year old heroine, online journals, offline journals, secrets, questions of trust. And it was personal in a way the other books in the series are not. When I was a teenager, I kept an online journal. I met a few friends that way. After a few years of dating, my husband (then boyfriend), confessed he'd read one of my online journals when we were dating.

It was a book I wanted to write. I wrote it for me. I wrote the kind of heroine who spoke to me. It was freeing. I adored it.

When I started *Dirty Wedding*, I had more mercenary aims. I liked Ty well enough. He seemed like an interesting enough guy--loyal, with a strict moral code, and incredibly high standards--but nothing about him, or the book, really spoke to me. My thought process was more "I love wedding imagery, so I'm going to write about a wedding." (I really do love wedding imagery though).

I tried to write a little more on trend, some enemies to lovers action, but it didn't work. And I didn't care. I've never really understood the appeal of enemies to lovers as it's often written. A Han and Leia strong personalities who tease each other, yes. Actual hate, not so much. When I hate someone, I hate them. I don't care how hot they are. I don't want to make them come. But I do understand... not hating someone, exactly, but being upset with them because they hurt you. Wanting to hate them for it. Because it's easier to hate someone than accept hurt. That made sense to me. And once I started to dive in, to ask myself why Indigo was so hurt by Ty leaving and embracing a woman so unlike her (and, of course, with her short hair and tattoos, Indigo was quite at Eve's level of "not the kind of girl who appears in billionaire romances, but she was certainly not the type of girl who I saw in these books), why Ty did that...

Of course, I landed on sex. What's more compelling than sex? And what's causes more strife than suppressed desires?

I didn't plan on writing Ty as a guy who couldn't accept his desires. I certainly didn't plan on Indigo as being the bold, brave one--the one who pushes him, who asks him to hurt her, threaten her, play all sorts of dangerous games. I didn't set out to write a book about more dangerous sexual desires, but I'm glad I did.

That's the fun thing about the Dirty series. It's not just the New York City setting, or the handsome men in suits, or the luxury. It's the exploration of sexuality. Darker, kinkier desires. Once I realized their story was about letting go of inhibitions to accept and explore their darker desires, it clicked. I fell in love.

We've all been there. Maybe it wasn't non-consensual role play scenarios or pain or bondage. But we've all had fantasies we tried to ignore. It's part of the culture. Society sends women very mixed messages. We need to be sexy and chaste at the same time.

It's apparent in romance, too. Men are supposed to be the pursuers. They're supposed to be alpha (whatever that means). They're supposed to read the heroine's minds, so the heroines never need to consider what they want, much less ask for it.

There's a certain appeal to that, sure. And, to some degree, that's apparent in some of these books. But the more I write, the more I strive for realism. Some degree of realism. Yes, Ty knows what Indigo wants, but it's not because he reads her mind. It's because they discuss it... and he reads her body language.

She asks herself what she wants. She challenges herself to ask for more. She's the one who pushes him.

I'm not reinventing the wheel, sure, but I like to think I'm challenging norms. I try to challenge readers a little with every book. To push them to explore new ideas, characters, beliefs about themselves and their desire.

I'm not sure *Dirty Wedding* topped *Dirty Desires*. *Dirty Desires* will probably be my favorite for a long time. But I fell in love with Ty and Indigo too. Their journey was new, exciting, fresh... and hot as hell.

I'm not sure what comes next. I'm about to start Cam and Sienna's book. It's more familiar to me, in some ways. I write a lot of brother's best friend (and that's basically what it is). But I've never written such a casual trope in this series. One of the things I love about this series is that the tropes aren't casual. They aren't every day. It's a nice change of pace, from my super, duper grounded tattoo artists.

It's a new challenge, and I'm excited to try. I already love Sienna. Bold, brash, and incredibly curious about sex. A teenage girl, basically.

With every book in the Dirty series, I've written a little

more like me. These last three books (*Dirty Desires, Dirty Wedding, Dirty Secret*) are more like my Inked books. Sure, the guys are kinky and rich, and they're constantly in suits, but they're also friends or family. People who just... hang out and shoot the shit.

And my couples actually hang out now. They drink tea or make dinner or watch TV. Like normal people. Normal, super rich people.

I'd like to write another series with kinky guys in suits. One set in New York City (I need excuses to visit). With plenty of luxury (I like nice things. Okay, I'm a total snob when it comes to tea and chocolate, among other things). But with a more hang out vibe. Kinky guys in suits who are a family, found or biological or adopted. It doesn't matter as long as they're family. I hope I brought that into these last few books.

And I hope I can give you more of it soon. Let me know if you want more of these kinky rich guys. And go ahead and get to know Ian and Eve in *Dirty Desires*. Or go back to the beginning with *Dirty Deal*.

As always, thanks for reading. I hope to see you back for *Dirty Secret*.

Best, Crystal

Acknowledgments

My first thanks goes to my husband, for his support when I'm lost in bookland and for generally being the sun in my sky. Sweetheart, you're better than all the broken bad boys in the world.

The second goes to my father, for insisting I go to the best film school in the country, everything else be damned. I wouldn't love movies, writing, or storytelling half as much if not for all our afternoon trips to the bookstore and weekends at the movies. You've always been supportive of my goals, and that means the world to me.

A big shout out to all my beta readers. You helped give me the confidence to put out a book a little more heartbreaking than usual. And also to my ARC readers for helping spread the word to everyone else in the world.

To all my writer friends who talk me down from the ledge, hold my hand, and tell me when my ideas are terrible and when they're brilliant, thank you.

Thanks so much to my editor Marla, and to Hang Le for the cover design.

As always, my biggest thanks goes to my readers. Thank you for picking up *Dirty Wedding*. I hope you'll be back for Cam's book, *Dirty Secret*.

Also by Crystal Kaswell

Dirty Rich

Dirty Deal - Blake

Dirty Boss - Nick

Dirty Husband - Shep

Dirty Desires - Ian

Dirty Wedding - Ty

Dirty Secret - Cam

Pierce Family

Broken Beast - Adam

Playboy Prince - Liam - coming soon

Ruthless Rival - Simon - coming soon

Inked Hearts

Tempting - Brendon

Hooking Up - Walker

Pretend You're Mine - Ryan

Hating You, Loving You - Dean

Breaking the Rules - Hunter

Losing It - Wes

Accidental Husband - Griffin

The Baby Bargain - Chase

Inked Love

The Best Friend Bargain - Forest

The First Taste - Holden

The Roomie Rulebook - Oliver

Sinful Serenade

Sing Your Heart Out - Miles

Strum Your Heart Out - Drew

Rock Your Heart Out - Tom

Play Your Heart Out - Pete

Sinful Ever After – series sequel

Just a Taste - Miles's POV

Dangerous Noise

Dangerous Kiss - Ethan

Dangerous Crush – Kit

Dangerous Rock – Joel

Dangerous Fling – Mal

Dangerous Encore - series sequel

Standalones

Broken - Trent & Delilah

Come Undone Trilogy

Come Undone

Come Apart

Come To Me

Sign up for the Crystal Kaswell mailing list

Printed in Great Britain
by Amazon

42207286R00249